Henrik Ibsen

Lady Inger of Östrat; The Vikings at Helgeland: The Pretenders

Henrik Ibsen

Lady Inger of Östrat; The Vikings at Helgeland: The Pretenders

ISBN/EAN: 9783337122836

Printed in Europe, USA, Canada, Australia, Japan

Cover: Foto ©Andreas Hilbeck / pixelio.de

More available books at **www.hansebooks.com**

HENRIK IBSEN.

(From a portrait taken about 1858.)

LADY INGER OF ÖSTRÅT: THE VIKINGS AT HELGELAND: THE PRETENDERS: BY HENRIK IBSEN.

AUTHORISED ENGLISH EDITION.

EDITED BY
WILLIAM ARCHER.

SCRIBNER & WELFORD,
743 & 745 BROADWAY,
NEW YORK.

1890.

CONTENTS.

PREFATORY NOTE.

THE three plays contained in this volume are all that Ibsen wrote in prose before he began the series of his social dramas with *The League of Youth.* Two plays in mingled prose and verse, *The Feast at Solhaug* and *Olaf Liliekrans*, intervene between *Lady Inger* and *The Vikings at Helgeland;* one play in verse, *Love's Comedy*, intervenes between *The Vikings* and *The Pretenders.* Of these, *Love's Comedy* at least is certain one day to find a translator ; but, being entirely composed in rhymed decasyllabics, it does not come within the scope of this series.

As *Lady Inger* and *The Pretenders* are founded on Norwegian history, *The Vikings* on Scandinavian legend, it may be well to say something as to Ibsen's treatment of his material. For most of the facts of the case I am indebted to Herr Jæger's painstaking and valuable work, *Henrik Ibsen : et literært Livsbillede.*

In *Lady Inger* Ibsen has chosen a theme from the very darkest hour of Norwegian history. King Sverre's democratic monarchy, dating from the beginning of the thirteenth century, had paralysed the old Norwegian nobility. One by one the great families died out, their possessions being concentrated in the hands of the few survivors, who regarded their wealth as a privilege unhampered by obligations. At the beginning of the sixteenth century, then, patriotism and public spirit were almost dead among the nobles, while the monarchy, before which the old aristocracy had fallen, was itself dead, or rather merged (since 1380) in the crown of Denmark. The peasantry, too, had long ago lost all effective voice in political affairs; so that Norway lay prone and inert at the mercy of her Danish rulers. It is at the moment of deepest national degradation that Ibsen has placed his tragedy; and the degradation was, in fact, even deeper than he represents it, for the longings for freedom, the stirrings of revolt, which form the motive-power of the action, are invented, or at any rate idealised, by the poet. Fru Inger Ottisdatter Gyldenlöve was in fact the greatest personage of her day in Norway. She was the best-born, the wealthiest, and probably the ablest woman in the land. At the time when Ibsen wrote, little more than this seems to have been known of her; so that in making her the victim of a struggle between patriotic duty and maternal love, he was perhaps poetising in the absence of positive evidence rather than in opposition to it. Subsequent research, unfortunately, has shown that Fru Inger was but little troubled with patriotic aspirations. She was a hard and grasping woman, ambitious of social power and predominance, but inaccessible, or nearly so, to national feeling. It was from sheer social ambition, and with no qualms of patriotic conscience, that she married her daughters to Danish noblemen. True, she lent some support to the insurrection of the so-called " Dale-junker," a peasant who gave himself out as the heir of Sten Sture, a former regent of Sweden; but there is not a tittle of ground for making this pretender her son. He might, indeed, have become her son-in-law, for, speculating on his chances of success, she had betrothed one of her daughters to him. Thus the Fru Inger of Ibsen's play is, in her character and circumstances, as much a creation of the poet's as though no historic personage of that name had ever existed. Olaf Skaktavl, Nils Lykke, and Eline Gyldenlöve are also historic names; but with them, too, Ibsen has dealt with the utmost freedom. The real Nils Lykke was married in 1528 to the real Eline Gyldenlöve. She died four years later, leaving him two children; and thereupon Nils Lykke would fain have married her sister Lucia. Such a union, however, was regarded as incestuous, and the lovers failed in their efforts to obtain a special dispensation. Lucia then became her brother-in-law's mistress, and bore him a son. But the ecclesiastical law was, in those days, not to be trifled with. Nils Lykke was thrown into prison for his crime, condemned, and killed in his dungeon, in the year of grace 1535. Thus there was a tragedy ready-made in Ibsen's material, though it was not the one he chose to write.

No one can read *The Vikings at Helgeland* without notic-ing that it stands in a certain relation to the *Völsungasaga*, of which an admirable English version, by Messrs. Magnusson and Morris, is included in the "Camelot Series." Scandinavian critics have been much exercised as to how this relation is to be defined. Can it be called a dramatisation of the saga or even a free adaptation? Henrik Jæger sums up the case, I think, as accurately as need be. "Like Sigurd Fafnir's-bane," he says, "Sigurd Viking has achieved the deed which Hiördis (Brynhild) demands of the man who shall wed her; and, again like his heroic namesake, he has renounced her in favour of his foster-brother, Gunnar, himself taking another to wife. This other woman reveals the secret in the course of an altercation with Hiördis (Brynhild), who, in consequence of this discovery, brings about Sigurd's death and her own. The reader will observe that we must keep to very general terms if they are to fit both the saga and the drama. Are there any further coincidences ? Yes, one. After Gudrun has betrayed the secret, there comes a scene in which **she** seeks to appease Brynhild, and begs her to think no more of it ; then follows a scene in which Sigurd explains to Brynhild how it all happened ; and finally a scene in which Brynhild goads Gunnar to kill Sigurd. All these scenes have their parallels in the third act of *The Vikings ;* but their order is different, and none of their wording has been adopted." Other details in the play are suggested by other sagas. **The** circumstances under which Örnulf sings his "Drapa" over his sons are borrowed from *Egils saga*, and so are Örnulf's questions as to how Thorolf fell ; the feast at Gunnar's house has many analogies **in** Icelandic story ; Hiördis's words **about the** bowstring are suggested by a passage in *Nials saga ;* and Sigurd and Hiördis are perhaps almost as closely related to Kiartan and Gudrun in the *Laxdæla saga*, as to Sigurd Fafnir's-bane and Brynhild. The reader must judge for himself whether the poet's utilisation of hints and suggestions from the sagas impairs, in any valid sense, the originality of his work.

In *The Pretenders* Ibsen stands much nearer to history than in any other play, except, perhaps, *Emperor and Galilean.* All the leading characters and many of the incidents of **the** drama are historical ; but the poet has treated chronology with a very free hand, and has made use of psychological motives which are but faintly indicated, or not at all, in the sources from which he drew. The play deals with the struggle for power between Hakon Hakonsson, **a** grandson of the great King Sverre, and Skule Bårdsson, **a** descendant **of a** collateral branch of the same house. Hakon **was** supported by the Birkebeiner,[1] or Birchlegs, a warlike faction which had been devoted to his grandfather, Sverre. Skule's

<hr>

[1] See Note, p. 215.

adherents were called Varbælgs or Vargbælgs,[1] a nick-name of uncertain origin. In characterising these two factions, the leading Norwegian historian of the day, J. E. Sars, writing thirteen years after the appearance of *The Pretenders*, uses terms which might almost have been suggested by Ibsen's play. "On the one side," he says, " we find strength and certainty, on the other lameness and lack of confidence. The old Birchlegs go to work openly and straightforwardly, like men who are immovably con-vinced of the justice of their cause, and unwaveringly assured of its ultimate victory. Skule's adherents, on the other hand, are ever seeking by intrigues and chicanery to place stumbling-blocks in the way of their opponents' enthusiasm." Hakon represented Sverre's ideal of an independent democratic kingship, no mere tool of an oli-garchy of bishops and barons, but "broad based upon the people's will." " He was," says Sars, " reared in the firm conviction of his right to the throne; he grew up among the veterans of his grandfather's time, men imbued with Sverre's principles, from whom he accepted them as a ready-made system, the realisation of which could only be a question of time. He stood from the first in a clear and straightforward position, to which his whole personality corresponded. . . . He owed his chief strength to the repose and equilibrium of mind which distinguished him, and had its root in his unwavering sense of having right and the people's will upon his side." His "great king's-thought," however, seems to be an invention of the poet's. Skule, on the other hand, represented the old nobility in its struggle against the new monarchy. "He was the centre of a hierarchic aristocratic party; but after its repeated defeats this party must have been lacking alike in numbers and in confidence. . . . It was clear from the first that

[1] See Note, p. 308.

his attempt to reawaken the old wars of succession in Norway was undertaken in the spirit of the desperate gambler, who does not count the chances, but throws at random, in the blind hope that luck may befriend him. . . . Skule's enterprise had thus no support in opinion or in any prevailing interest, and one defeat was sufficient to crush him."

In the character of Bishop Nicholas, too, Ibsen has widened and deepened his historical material rather than poetised with a free hand. "Bishop Nicholas," says Sars, "represented rather the aristocracy . . . than the cloth to which he belonged. He had begun his career as a worldly chieftain, and, as such, taken part in Magnus Erlingsson's struggles with Sverre; and although he must have had some tincture of letters, since he could contrive to be elected a bishop . . . there is no lack of indications that his spiritual lore was not of the deepest. During his long participation in the civil broils, both under Sverre and later, we see in him a man to whose character any sort of religious or ecclesiastical enthusiasm must have been foreign, his leading motives being personal ambition and vengefulness rather than any care for general interests—a cold and calculating nature, shrewd but petty and without any impetus, of whom Hakon Hakonsson, in delivering his funeral speech . . . could find nothing better to say than that he had not his equal in worldly wisdom (*veraldar vit*)." I cannot find that the Bishop played any such prominent part in the struggle between the King and the Earl as Ibsen assigns to him, and the only foundation for the great death-bed scene seems to be the following passage from *Hakon Hakonsson's Saga*, Cap. 138:—"As Bishop Nicholas at that time lay very sick, he sent a messenger to the King praying him to come to him. The King had on this expedition seized certain letters, from which he gathered that the Bishop had

not been true to him. With this he upbraided him, and
the Bishop, confessing it, prayed the King to forgive him.
The King replied that he did so willingly, for God's sake ;
and as he could discern that the Bishop lay near to death,
he abode with him until God called him from the world."

A chronological conspectus of the leading events referred
to in *The Pretenders* (founded on P. A. Munch's *History of
the Norwegian People*) will enable the reader to estimate
for himself the extent of Ibsen's adherence to, and departure
from, history :—

1189. Skule Bårdsson born.

1204. Hakon Hakonsson born.

1206. Hakon is brought by the Birchlegs to King Inge.

1217. Hakon chosen King at the Örething.[1]

1218. Hakon and Skule at Bergen. The Folkmote (Rigs-
     möde). Inga undergoes the ordeal.

1219. Hakon betrothed to Skule's daughter, Margrete.

1219-20. Andres Skialdarband and Vegard Væradal, thanes
     of Halogaland.

1221. Vegard Væradal killed by Andres Skialdarband's
     men (reason unknown).

1225. (January), Hakon's campaign in Vermeland.
     (May 25), Hakon's marriage with Margrete.
     (November 7), Bishop Nicholas's death.

1227. Hakon's eldest son, Olaf, born.

1229. Andres Skialdarband sets forth for Palestine.

1232. Hakon's second son, Hakon, born.

1235. Inga, the King's mother, dies.

1236. The faction of the Vargbælgs arises.

1237. Skule created Duke.
     Dagfinn the Peasant dies.

1239. (November 6), Skule proclaims himself King at the
     Örething.

---

[1] See Note, p. 217.

1240. (March 6), Skule victorious at Låka.
      (April 21), Hakon victorious at Oslo.
      (May 21), Skule's son Peter killed at Elgesæter.
      (May 24), Skule killed at Elgesæter, **and** the convent
            burnt.

The titles of the plays in this volume have cost a good
deal of thought and discussion, and are still far from satis-
factory. My brother, the translator of *Fru Inger til Östråt*,
maintains strenuously **and** very plausibly that *Dame Inger
of Östråt*, not **Lady** *Inger*, is the true rendering of the title.
If words could be divested of mean and trivial associations,
and restored, by an effort of will, to their pristine status,
Dame **would** certainly be preferable **to** *Lady*. But it
seemed to me, and **to** others whom I consulted, that the
word *Dame* must either be taken in its technical sense,
which does not apply, or in its popular sense, which calls
up visions of Dame Schools, Dame Trot, Dame Durden,
and Dames of the Primrose League. *Lady*, on the other
hand, though soiled with **all** ignoble use, possesses an
inalienable distinction. Therefore, taking a base advantage, perhaps, of my brother's absence at the other side of
the world, I stretched my editorial prerogative so far as
to substitute *Lady* for *Dame* throughout the play. If
I have done wrong, I beg the author's, the translator's, and
the reader's **pardon.** *Hærmændene på Helgeland* means
literally *The* **Warriors at** *Helgeland.* I have substituted
Vikings, because *Warriors* seemed pompous, cumbersome,
and un-Teutonic, while Örnulf, Sigurd, and Gunnar all are,
and frequently call themselves, Vikings. *The Pretenders,* as
a rendering of *Kongs-Emnerne,* is peculiarly inadequate
and inconvenient; but no other term seemed available.
The word *Emne* means "material" or "stuff," so that *Kongs-
Emne* might be translated "such stuff as kings are made of."

It is the word habitually used in the *Kings' Sagas* to signify an heir to the throne ; but as the laws of succession were by no means firmly established in Norway, there were frequently, if not always, several *Kongs-Emner* in the field. A *Kongs-Emne* was not necessarily an heir-apparent ; on the contrary, he was often an heir-presumptive in the widest possible sense of the term. Wherever it was possible, I have rendered *Kongs-Emne* by "Pretender" even at the risk of uncouthness. But in several cases I have had to substitute "heir."

As to the vocabulary and style adopted in the following translations, I can only say that where we have erred, either in intention or in details of execution, it has not been for lack of thought and care. It was impossible to render the plays into ordinary, modern English. It would have been absurd, even had we possessed the skill, to adhere rigidly to the style of any particular period—for why should ancient Norwegians talk (say) pure Elizabethan, any more than pure Victorian ? The only possible course, then, seemed to be to suggest archaism by adopting a certain arbitrary convention (or affectation, if you will) and adhering to it as closely as possible, at least within the limits of a single play. The reader will observe that my brother and I have adopted practically the same convention in *Lady Inger* and *The Pretenders*, while in *The Vikings* a different and more archaic convention obtains. The reason for this is that the former plays are historical, their bearings in place and time accurately laid down, while the latter is purely legendary. It is true that Ibsen has placed it in the time of Erik Blood-Axe ; but its theme forms part of the primæval lore of the European peoples, its action is in nowise dependent on any political circumstances, and it belongs in all essentials to "a past that never was present." The style of the original, modelled on that of the sagas, has a peculiar chiselled weightiness, as of marble, quite different from the romantic copiousness of *Lady Inger* and the almost modern flexibility and alertness of *The Pretenders.* Therefore I have used the "thou" form in *The Vikings,* and allowed myself certain archaisms of vocabulary which have been excluded from the other plays. Even in *The Vikings,* however, I have rejected the verb formations in "eth," as they brought with them Biblical associations which seemed undesirable. In some passages of *Lady Inger* and *The Pretenders*—for instance, in the last scene between Nils Lykke and Eline, and the scene between King Skule and Ingeborg—it cost a struggle to adhere to the "you" form; but, on the whole, I am more doubtful of the propriety of the "thou's" in *The Vikings* than of the "you's" in the other plays. The great, incontestable merit of Ibsen's style in these plays (at any rate in *The Vikings* and *The Pretenders*) is its nicely-filed terseness, its transparent simplicity. His language, while clearly distinguishable from everyday Norwegian, is far nearer to it than mine is to everyday English. The use of the "thou" would have made the difference still greater, and involved cumbersome circumlocutions; for our "thou" forms have the disadvantage, for purposes of dialogue, of being often very difficult to pronounce. Even as it is, with the aid of the simpler "you" forms, we have too seldom succeeded in reproducing the Norwegian phrase with anything like its resonant brevity. It would be extravagant to hope that the particular conventions we have adopted will be approved by every reader, or that we shall be found to have adhered to them at all times with perfect consistency. I trust that, before judging our lapses too severely, the reader will try to realise the difficulty of our task.

In the Norwegian of Örnulf's "Drapa" and his other verses, the second and fourth lines of each stanza rhyme. I have ventured to suppress the rhymes, while somewhat emphasising the rude alliteration which is also present in the original. It is doubtful whether a more skilful versifier than I could have reproduced both the rhyme and the alliteration without indulging in paraphrase rather than translation; and I had the less scruple in retaining the alliteration rather than the rhyme, because the rhyme seemed historically out of place in the mouth of an Icelandic skald, and dramatically out of place in an improvisation. Faithfulness to the original is the only merit I can claim for my metrical renderings as a whole. They are line-for-line translations, not loose paraphrases. The Norwegian of Örnulf's death-song, Margrete's lullaby, and Jatgeir's ballad will be found in the Appendix.

W. A.

LADY INGER OF ÖSTRÅT.

(1855.)

Characters.

— ✦ —

LADY INGER OTTISDAUGHTER RÖMER, *widow of High Steward Nils Gyldenlöve.*

ELINA GYLDENLÖVE, *her daughter.*

NILS LYKKE, *Danish knight and councillor.*

OLAF SKAKTAVL, *an outlawed Norwegian noble.*

NILS STENSSON.

JENS BIELKE, *Swedish commander.*

BIÖRN, **major-domo at** *Öströt.*

FINN, *a servant.*

EINAR HUK, *bailiff at Öströt.*

Servants, *peasants, and Swedish men-at-arms.*

The action takes place at Öströt Manor, on the Trondhiem Fiord, in the year 1528.

[PRONUNCIATION OF NAMES.—Öströt = *Östrot;* Inger = *Ingher* (*g* nearly as in "ringer"); Gyldenlöve = *Ghyldenlöve;* Elina (Norwegian, Eline) = *Eleena;* Stensson = *Staynson;* Biörn = *Björn;* Jens Bielke = *Yens Byelke;* Huk = *Hook.* The final *e*'s and the *ö*'s pronounced much as in German.]

LADY INGER OF ÖSTRÅT.

DRAMA IN FIVE ACTS.

Act First.

(*A room at Östråt. Through an open door in the back, the Banquet Hall is seen in faint moonlight, which shines fitfully through a deep bow-window in the opposite wall. To the right, an entrance-door; further forward, a curtained window. On the left, a door leading to the inner rooms; further forward a large open fireplace, which casts a glow over the room. It is a stormy evening.*)

(BIÖRN *and* FINN *are sitting by the fireplace. The latter is occupied in polishing a helmet. Several pieces of armour lie near them, along with a sword and shield.*)

FINN (*after a pause*).   Who was Knut[1] Alfson?

BIÖRN.   My Lady says he was the last of Norway's knighthood.

FINN.   And the Danes killed him at Oslo-fiord?

BIÖRN.   Ask any child of five, if you know not that.

FINN.   So Knut Alfson was the last of our knighthood?   And now he's dead and gone!   (*Holds up the helmet.*)   Well then, hang thou scoured and bright in

---

[1] Pronounce *Knoot.*

the Banquet Hall; for what art thou now but an empty nut-shell?   The kernel—the worms have eaten that many a winter agone.

What say you, Biörn—may not one call Norway's land an empty nut-shell, even like the helmet here; bright without, worm-eaten within?

BIÖRN.   Hold your peace, and mind your work!— Is the helmet ready?

FINN.   It shines like silver in the moonlight.

BIÖRN.   Then put it by.—— —— See here; scrape the rust off the sword.

FINN (*turning the sword over and examining it*).   Is it worth while?

BIÖRN.   What mean you?

FINN.   The edge is gone.

BIÖRN.   What's that to you? Give it me.—— —— Here, take the shield.

FINN (*as before*).   There's no grip to it!

BIÖRN (*mutters*).   If once I got a grip on *you*——

   (FINN *hums to himself for a while.*)

BIÖRN.   What now?

FINN.   An empty helmet, an edgeless sword, a shield without a grip—there's the whole glory for you.   I see not that any can blame Lady Inger for leaving such weapons to hang scoured and polished on the walls, instead of rusting them in Danish blood.

BIÖRN.   Folly!   Is there not peace in the land?

FINN.   Peace? Ay, when the peasant has shot away his last arrow, and the wolf has reft the last lamb from the fold, then is there peace between them. But 'tis a strange friendship.   Well well; let that pass.   It is fitting, as I said, that the harness hang bright in the hall; for you know the old saw: "Call none a man but the knightly man." Now there is no knight left in our land; and where no man is, there must women order things; therefore——

Biörn. Therefore—therefore I order you to hold your foul prate! (*Rises.*)

It grows late. Go hang helm and harness in the hall again.

Finn (*in a low voice*). Nay, best let it be till to-morrow.

Biörn. What, do you fear the dark?

Finn. Not by day. And if so be I fear it at even, I am not the only one. Ah, you may look; I tell you in the housefolk's room there is talk of many things. (*Lower.*) They say that night by night a tall figure, clad in black, walks the Banquet Hall.

Biörn. Old wives' tales!

Finn. Ah, but they all swear 'tis true.

Biörn. That I well believe.

Finn. The strangest of all is that Lady Inger thinks the same——

Biörn (*starting*). Lady Inger? What does she think?

Finn. What Lady Inger thinks no one can tell. But sure it is that she has no rest in her. See you not how day by day she grows thinner and paler? (*Looks keenly at him.*) They say she never sleeps— and that it is because of the dark figure——

> (*While he is speaking*, Elina Gyldenlöve *has appeared in the half-open door on the left. She stops and listens, unobserved.*)

Biörn. And you believe such follies?

FINN. Well, half and half. There be folk, too, that read things another way. But that is pure malice, for sure.—Hearken, Biörn—know you the song that is going round the country?

BIÖRN. A song?

FINN. Ay, 'tis on all folks' lips. 'Tis a shameful scurril thing, for sure; yet it goes prettily. Just listen (*sings in a low voice*):

> *Dame Inger sitteth in Östråt fair,*
> *She wraps her in costly furs—*
> *She decks her in velvet and ermine and vair,*
> *Red gold are the beads that she twines in her hair—*
> *But small peace in that soul of hers.*
>
> ***Dame Inger*** *hath sold her to Denmark's lord.*
> *She bringeth her folk 'neath the stranger's yoke—*
> *In guerdon whereof—— ——*

(BIÖRN *enraged, seizes him by the throat.* ELINA GYLDENLÖVE *withdraws without having been seen.*)

BIÖRN. And I will send you guerdonless to the foul fiend, if you prate of Lady Inger but one unseemly word more.

FINN (*breaking from his grasp*). Why—did *I* make the song?

(*The blast of a horn is heard from the right.*)

BIÖRN. Hush—what is that?

FINN. A horn. So we are to have guests tonight.

BIÖRN (*at the window*). They are opening the gate. I hear the clatter of hoofs in the courtyard. It must be a knight.

Finn.   A knight?   A knight can it scarce be.

Biörn.   Why not?

Finn.   You said it yourself: the last of our knighthood is dead and gone.   (*Goes out to the right.*)

Biörn.   The accursed knave, with his prying and peering!   What avails all my striving to hide and hush things?   They whisper of her even now——; ere long will all men be clamouring for——

Elina (*comes in again through the door on the left; looks round her, and says with suppressed emotion*).   Are you alone, Biörn?

Biörn.   Is it you, Mistress Elina?

Elina.   Come, Biörn, tell me one of your stories; I know you have more to tell than those that——

Biörn.   A story?   Now—so late in the evening ——?

Elina.   If you count from the time when it grew dark at Östråt, it is late indeed.

Biörn.   What ails you?   Has aught crossed you? You seem so restless.

Elina.   May be so.

Biörn.   There is something the matter.   I have hardly known you this half year past.

Elina.   Bethink you: this half year past my dearest sister Lucia has been sleeping in the vault below.

Biörn.   That is not all, Mistress Elina—it is not that alone that makes you now thoughtful and white and silent, now restless and ill at ease, as you are to-night.

Elina.   You think so?   And wherefore not? Was she not gentle and pure and fair as a summer night? Biörn, I tell you, Lucia was dear to me as my life. Have you forgotten how many a time, as children, we sat on your knee in the winter evenings? You sang songs to us, and told us tales——

BIÖRN. Ay, then you were blithe and gay.

ELINA. Ah, then, Biörn! Then I lived a glorious life in the fable-land of my own imaginings. Can it be that the sea-strand was naked then as now? If it were so, I did not know it. It was there I loved to go, weaving all my fair romances; my heroes came from afar and sailed again across the sea; I lived in their midst, and set forth with them when they sailed away. (*Sinks on a chair.*) Now I feel so faint and weary; I can live no longer in my tales. They are only—tales. (*Rises hastily.*) Biörn, do you know what has made me sick? A truth; a hateful, hateful truth, that gnaws me day and night.

BIÖRN. What mean you?

ELINA. Do you remember how sometimes you would give us good counsel and wise saws? Sister Lucia followed them; but I—ah, well-a-day!

BIÖRN (*consoling her*). Well, well——!

ELINA. I know it—I was proud and self-centred! In all our games, I would still be the Queen, because I was the tallest, the fairest, the wisest! I know it!

BIÖRN. That is true.

ELINA. Once you took me by the hand and looked earnestly at me, and said: "Be not proud of your fairness, or your wisdom; but be proud as the mountain eagle as often as you think: I am Inger Gyldenlöve's daughter!"

Biörn.   And was it not matter enough for pride?

Elina.   You told me so often enough, Biörn! Oh, you told me so many tales in those days. (*Presses his hand.*) Thanks for them all! Now, tell me one more; it might make me light of heart again, as of old.

Biörn.   You are a child no longer.

Elina.   Nay, indeed! But let me dream that I am.—Come, tell on!

> (*Throws herself into a chair.* Biörn *sits in the chimney-corner.*)

Biörn.   Once upon a time there was a high-born knight——

Elina (*who has been listening restlessly in the direction of the hall, seizes his arm and breaks out in a vehement whisper*).   Hush! No need to shout so loud; I can hear well!

Biörn (*more softly*).   Once upon a time there was a high-born knight, of whom there went the strange report——

> (Elina *half-rises and listens in anxious suspense in the direction of the hall.*)

Biörn.   Mistress Elina, what ails you?

Elina (*sits down again*).   Me? Nothing. Go on.

Biörn.   Well, as I was saying, when he did but look straight in a woman's eyes, never could she forget it after; her thoughts must follow him wherever he went, and she must waste away with sorrow.

Elina.   I have heard that tale—— —— And, moreover, 'tis no tale you are telling, for the knight you speak of is Nils Lykke, who sits even now in the Council of Denmark——

BIÖRN.   May be so.

ELINA.   Well, let it pass—go on!

BIÖRN.   Now it happened once——

ELINA (*rises suddenly*).   Hush; be still!

BIÖRN.   What now? What is the matter?

ELINA (*listening*).   Do you hear?

BIÖRN.   What?

ELINA.   It *is* there! Yes, by the cross of Christ, it *is* there!

BIÖRN (*rises*).   What is there? Where?

ELINA.   It is she—in the hall. (*Goes hastily towards the hall.*)

BIÖRN (*following*).   How can you think——? Mistress Elina, go to your chamber!

ELINA.   Hush; stand still! Do not move; do not let her see you! Wait—the moon is coming out. Can you not see the black-robed figure——?

BIÖRN.   By all the holy——!

ELINA.   Do you see—she turns Knut Alfson's picture to the wall. Ha-ha; be sure it looks her too straight in the eyes!

BIÖRN.   Mistress Elina, hear me!

ELINA (*going back towards the fireplace*).   Now I know what I know!

BIÖRN (*to himself*).   Then it is true!

ELINA.   Who was it, Biörn? Who was it?

BIÖRN.   You saw as plainly as I.

ELINA.   Well? Whom did I see?

BIÖRN.   You saw your mother.

ELINA (*half to herself*).   Night after night I have heard her steps in there. I have heard her whispering and moaning like a soul in pain. And what says the song——. Ah, now I know! Now I know that——

BIÖRN.   Hush!

(LADY INGER GYLDENLÖVE *enters rapidly from the hall, without noticing the others; she goes to the window, draws the curtain, and gazes out as if watching for some one on the high road; after a while, she turns and goes slowly back into the hall.*)

ELINA (*softly, following her with her eyes*).   White as a corpse——!

(*An uproar of many voices is heard outside the door on the right.*)

BIÖRN.   What can this be?

ELINA.   Go out and see what is amiss.

(EINAR HUK, *the bailiff, appears in the ante-room, with a crowd of Retainers and Peasants.*)

EINAR HUK (*in the doorway*).   Straight in to her! And see you lose not heart!

BIÖRN.   What do you seek?

EINAR HUK.   Lady Inger herself.

BIÖRN.   Lady Inger?   So late?

EINAR HUK.   Late, but time enough, I wot.

THE PEASANTS.   Yes, yes; she must hear us now!

(*The whole rabble crowds into the room.   At the same moment* LADY INGER *appears in the doorway of the hall.   A sudden silence.*)

LADY INGER.   What would you with me?

EINAR HUK.   We sought you, noble lady, to——

LADY INGER.   Well, speak out!

EINAR HUK.   Why, we are not ashamed of our

errand. In one word, we come to pray you for weapons and leave——

LADY INGER. Weapons and leave——? And for what?

EINAR HUK. There has come a rumour from Sweden that the people of the Dales have risen against King Gustav——

LADY INGER. The people of the Dales?

EINAR HUK. Ay, so the tidings run, and they seem sure enough.

LADY INGER. Well, if it were so, what have you to do with the Dale-folk's rising?

THE PEASANTS. We will join them! We will help! We will free ourselves!

LADY INGER (*aside*). Can the time be come?

EINAR HUK. From all our borderlands the peasants are pouring across to the Dales. Even outlaws that have wandered for years in the mountains are venturing down to the homesteads again, and drawing men together, and whetting their rusty swords.

LADY INGER (*after a pause*). Tell me, men, have you thought well of this? Have you counted the cost, if King Gustav's men should win?

BIÖRN (*softly and imploringly to* LADY INGER). Count the cost to the Danes if King Gustav's men should lose.

LADY INGER (*evasively*). That reckoning is not for me to make. (*Turns to the people.*)

You know that King Gustav is sure of help from Denmark. King Frederick is his friend, and will never leave him in the lurch——

Einar Huk. But if the people were now to rise all over Norway's land ?—if we all rose as one man, nobles and peasants together?—ay, Lady Inger Gyldenlöve, the time we have waited for is surely come. We have but to rise now to drive the strangers from the land.

The Peasants. Ay, out with the Danish sheriffs! Out with the foreign masters! Out with the Councillors' lackeys !

Lady Inger (*aside*). Ah, there is metal in them ; and yet, yet——— !

Biörn (*to himself*). She is of two minds. (*To* Elina.) What say you now, Mistress Elina—have you not sinned in misjudging your mother ?

Elina. Biörn, if my eyes have deceived me, I could tear them out of my head !

Einar Huk. See you not, my noble lady, King Gustav must be dealt with first. Once his power is gone, the Danes cannot long hold this land———

Lady Inger. And then ?

Einar Huk. Then we shall be free. We shall have no more foreign masters, and can choose ourselves a king, as the Swedes have done before us.

Lady Inger (*with animation*). A king for ourselves. Are you thinking of the Sture stock ?

Einar Huk. King Christiern and others after him have swept bare our ancient houses. The best of our nobles are outlaws on the hill-paths, if so be they still live ; nevertheless, it might still be possible to find one or other shoot of the old stems———

LADY INGER (*hastily*). Enough, Einar Huk, enough! (*To herself.*) Ah, my dearest hope! (*Turns to the Peasants and Retainers.*)

I have warned you, now, as well as I can. I have told you how great is the risk you run. But if you are fixed in your purpose, it were folly of me to forbid what I have no power to prevent.

EINAR HUK. Then we have your leave to——?

LADY INGER. You have your own firm will; take counsel with **that**. If it be as you say, that you are **daily harassed** and oppressed—— —— I know but **little of these matters**, and would not know more. What **can I, a** lonely woman——? Even if you were to plunder the Banquet Hall—and there's many a good weapon on the walls—you are the masters at Östråt to-night. You must do as seems good to you. Good-night!

> (*Loud cries of joy from the multitude. Candles are lighted; the retainers bring out weapons of different kinds from the hall.*)

BIÖRN (*seizes* LADY INGER'S *hand as she is going*). Thanks, my noble and high-souled mistress! I, that **have known** you from childhood up—I have never doubted **you**.

LADY INGER. Hush, Biörn. It is a dangerous game that I have ventured this night. The others stake only their lives; but I, trust me, a thousandfold more!

BIÖRN. **How mean you?** Do **you** fear for your power and your favour with——?

LADY INGER. **My** power? O God in Heaven!

A RETAINER (*comes from the hall with a large*

sword).   See, here's a real good wolf's-tooth to flay the blood-suckers' lackeys with !

EINAR HUK (*to another*).   What is that you have found ?

THE RETAINER.   The breastplate they call Herlof Hyttefad's.

EINAR HUK.   'Tis too good for such as you. Look, here is the shaft of Sten Sture's[1] lance ; hang the breastplate upon it, and we shall have the noblest standard heart can desire.

FINN (*comes from the door on the left, with a letter in his hand, and goes towards* LADY INGER).   I have sought you through all the house.

LADY INGER.   What do you want ?

FINN (*hands her the letter*).   A messenger is come from Trondhiem with a letter for you.

LADY INGER.   Let me see ! (*opening the letter*). From Trondhiem ?   What can it be ?   (*Runs through the letter.*)   Help, Christ !   From him ! and here in Norway——

(*Reads on with strong emotion, while the men go on bringing out arms from the hall.*)

LADY INGER (*to herself*).   He is coming here.   He is coming here to-night !—Ay, then 'tis with our wits we must fight, not with the sword.

EINAR HUK.   Enough, enough, good fellows ; we are well armed now, and can set forth on our way.

LADY INGER (*with a sudden change of tone*).   No man shall leave my house to-night !

EINAR HUK.   But the wind is fair, noble lady ; we can sail up the fiord, and——

---

[1] Pronounce *Stayn Stoorē*.

LADY INGER.   It shall be as I have said.

EINAR HUK.   Are we to wait till to-morrow, then?

LADY INGER. Till to-morrow, and longer still. No armed man shall go forth from Östråt yet awhile.

(*Signs of displeasure among the crowd.*)

SOME OF THE PEASANTS.   We will go all the same, Lady Inger!

THE CRY SPREADS.   Yes, yes ; we *will* go!

LADY INGER (*advancing a step towards them*). Who dares to move?

(*A silence. After a moment's pause, she adds :*)

I have thought for you.   What do you common folk know of the country's needs?   How dare you judge of such things?   You must even bear your oppressions and burdens yet awhile.   Why murmur at that, when you see that we, your leaders, are as ill bested as you?—— —— Take all the weapons back to the hall.   You shall know my further will hereafter.   Go!

(*The Retainers take back the arms, and the whole crowd then withdraws by the door on the right.*)

ELINA (*softly to* BIÖRN).   Do you still think I have sinned in misjudging—the Lady of Östråt?

LADY INGER (*beckons to* BIÖRN, *and says*).   Have a guest chamber ready.

BIÖRN.   It is well, Lady Inger!

LADY INGER.   And let the gate stand open to all that knock.

BIÖRN.   But—— ?

LADY INGER.   The gate open!

Biörn. The gate open. (*Goes out to the right.*)

Lady Inger (*to* Elina, *who has already reached the door on the left*). Stay here!—— —— Elina—my child—I have something to say to you alone.

Elina. I hear you.

Lady Inger. Elina—— ——you think evil of your mother.

Elina. I think, to my sorrow, what your deeds have forced me to think.

Lady Inger. You answer out of the bitterness of your heart.

Elina. Who has filled my heart with bitterness? From my childhood I have been wont to look up to you as a great and high-souled woman. It was in your likeness I pictured the women we read of in the chronicles and the Book of Heroes. I thought the Lord God himself had set his seal on your brow, and marked you out as the leader of the helpless and the oppressed. Knights and nobles sang your praise in the feast-hall, and the peasants, far and near, called you the country's pillar and its hope. All thought that through you the good times were to come again! All thought that through you a new day was to dawn over the land! The night is still here; and I no longer know if I dare look for any morning to come through you.

Lady Inger. It is easy to see whence you have learnt such venomous words. You have let yourself give ear to what the thoughtless rabble mutters and murmurs about things it can little judge of.

Elina. "Truth is in the people's mouth," was your word when they praised you in speech and song.

LADY INGER. May be so. But if indeed I had chosen to sit here idle, though it was my part to act—do you not think that such a choice were burden enough for me, without your adding to its weight?

ELINA. The weight I add to your burden bears on me as heavily as on you. Lightly and freely I drew the breath of life, so long. as I had you to believe in. For my pride is my life; and well had it become me, if you had remained what once you were.

LADY INGER. And what proves to you I have not? Elina, how can you know so surely that you are not doing your mother wrong?

ELINA (*vehemently*). Oh, that I were!

LADY INGER. Peace! You have no right to call your mother to account—— With a single word I could—— ——; but it would be an ill word for you to hear; you must await what time shall bring; may be that——

ELINA (*turns to go*). Sleep well, my mother!

LADY INGER (*hesitates*). Nay, stay with me; I have still somewhat—Come nearer;—you must hear me, Elina!

(*Sits down by the table in front of the window.*)

ELINA. I am listening.

LADY INGER. For as silent as you are, I know well that you often long to be gone from here. Östråt is too lonely and lifeless for you.

ELINA. Do you wonder at that, my mother?

LADY INGER. It rests with you whether all this shall henceforth be changed.

ELINA. How so?

Lady Inger.   Listen.—I look for a guest to-night.

Elina (*comes nearer*).   A guest?

Lady Inger.   A stranger, who must remain a stranger to all.   None must know whence he comes or whither he goes.

Elina (*throws herself, with a cry of joy, at her mother's feet and seizes her hands*).   My mother! My mother!   Forgive me, if you can, all the wrong I have done you!

Lady Inger.   What do you mean?   Elina, I do not understand you.

Elina.   Then they were all deceived!   You are still true at heart!

Lady Inger.   Rise, rise and tell me——

Elina.   Do you think I do not know who the stranger is?

Lady Inger.   You know?   And yet——?

Elina.   Do you think the gates of Östråt shut so close that never a whisper of evil tidings can slip through?   Do you think I do not know that the heir of many a noble line wanders outlawed, without rest or shelter, while Danish masters lord it in the home of his fathers?

Lady Inger.   And what then?

Elina.   I know well that many a high-born knight is hunted through the woods like a hungry wolf. No hearth has he to rest by, no bread to eat——

Lady Inger (*coldly*).   Enough!   Now I understand you.

Elina (*continuing*).   And that is why the gates of Östråt must stand open by night!   That is why he must remain a stranger to all, this guest of whom none must know whence he comes or whither he goes! You are setting at naught the harsh decree that forbids you to harbour or succour the exiles——

LADY INGER.   Enough, I say!

(*After a short silence, adds with an effort:*)

You mistake, Elina—it is no outlaw that I look for——

ELINA (*rises*).   Then I have understood you ill indeed.

LADY INGER.   Listen to me, my child; but think as you listen; if indeed you can tame that wild spirit of yours.

ELINA.   I am tame, till you have spoken.

LADY INGER.   Then hear what I have to say—I have sought, so far as lay in my power, to keep you in ignorance of all our griefs and miseries. What could it avail to fill your young heart with wrath and care?   It is not weeping and wailing of women that can free us from our evil lot; we need the courage and strength of men.

ELINA.   Who has told you that, when courage and strength are needed, I shall be found wanting?

LADY INGER.   Hush, child;—I might take you at your word.

ELINA.   How mean you, my mother?

LADY INGER.   I might call on you for both; I might——; but let me say my say out first.

Know then that the time seems now to be drawing nigh, towards which the Danish Council have been working for many a year—the time for them to strike a final blow at our rights and our freedom.   Therefore must we now——

Elina (*eagerly*).   Throw off the yoke, my mother?

Lady Inger.   No; we must gain breathing-time. The Council is now sitting in Copenhagen, considering how best to aim the blow. Most of them are said to hold that there can be no end to dissensions till Norway and Denmark are one; for if we should still have our rights as a free land when the time comes to choose the next king, it is most like that the feud will break out openly. Now the Danish Councillors would hinder this——

Elina.   Ay, they would hinder it——! But are we to endure such things? Are we to look on quietly while——?

Lady Inger.   No, we will not endure it. But to take up arms—to begin open warfare—what would come of that, so long as we are not united? And were we ever less united in this land than we are even now?—No, if aught is to be done, it must be done secretly and in silence. Even as I said, we must have time to draw breath. In the South, a good part of the nobles are for the Dane; but here in the North they are still in doubt. Therefore King Frederick has sent hither one of his most trusted councillors, to assure himself with his own eyes how we stand affected.

Elina (*anxiously*).   Well—and then——?

Lady Inger.   He is the guest I look for to-night.

Elina.   He comes here?   And to-night?

Lady Inger.   He reached Trondhiem yesterday by a trading ship. Word has just been brought that he is coming to visit me; he may be here within the hour.

ELINA.   Have you not thought, my mother, how it will endanger your fame thus to receive the Danish envoy? Do not the people already regard you with distrustful eyes? How can you hope that, when the time comes, they will let you rule and guide them, if it be known that——

LADY INGER.   Fear not. All this I have fully weighed; but there is no danger. His errand in Norway is a secret; he has come unknown to Trondhiem, and unknown shall he be our guest at Östråt.

ELINA.   And the name of this Danish lord——?

LADY INGER.   It sounds well, Elina; Denmark has scarce a nobler name.

ELINA.   But what do you purpose then? I cannot yet grasp your meaning.

LADY INGER.   You will soon understand.—Since we cannot trample on the serpent, we must bind him.

ELINA.   Take heed that he burst not your bonds.

LADY INGER.   It rests with you to tighten them as you will.

ELINA.   With me?

LADY INGER.   I have long seen that Östråt is as a cage to you. The young falcon chafes behind the iron bars.

ELINA.   My wings are clipped. Even if you set me free—it would avail me little.

LADY INGER.   Your wings are not clipped, except by your own will.

ELINA.   Will? My will is in your hands. Be what you once were, and I too——

LADY INGER.   Enough, enough. Hear what re-

mains—— It would scarce break your heart to leave
Östråt?

Elina.   Maybe not, my mother!

Lady Inger.   You told me once, that you lived
your happiest life in tales and histories.   What if that
life were to be yours once more?

Elina.   What mean you?

Lady Inger.   Elina—if a mighty noble were now
to come and lead you to his castle, where you should
find damsels and pages, silken robes and lofty halls
awaiting you?

Elina.   A noble, you say?

Lady Inger.   A noble.

Elina (*more softly*).   And the Danish envoy comes
here to-night?

Lady Inger.   To-night.

Elina.   If so be, then I fear to read the meaning
of your words.

Lady Inger.   There is nought to fear if you mis-
read them not.   Be sure it is far from my thought to
put force upon you.   You shall choose for yourself in
this matter, and follow your own counsel.

Elina (*comes a step nearer*).   Have you heard the
story of the mother that drove across the hills by
night with her little children by her in the sledge?
The wolves were on her track; it was life or death
with her;—and one by one she cast out her little
ones, to gain time and save herself.

Lady Inger.   Nursery tales!   A mother would
tear the heart from her breast, before she would cast
her child to the wolves!

Elina.   Were I not my mother's daughter, I would

say you were right. But you are like that mother;
one by one you have cast out your daughters to the
wolves. The eldest went first. Five years ago
Merete[1] went forth from Östråt; now she dwells in
Bergen, and is Vinzents Lunge's[2] wife. But think
you she is happy as the Danish noble's lady? Vinzents Lunge is mighty, well-nigh as a king; Merete
has damsels and pages, silken robes and lofty halls;
but the day has no sunshine for her, and the night no
rest; for she has never loved him. He came hither
and he wooed her; for she was the greatest heiress in
Norway, and he needed to gain a footing in the land.
I know it; I know it well! Merete bowed to your
will; she went with the stranger lord.—But what has
it cost her? More tears than a mother should wish
to answer for at the day of reckoning.

LADY INGER.   I know my reckoning, and I fear it
not.

ELINA.   Your reckoning ends not here.   Where is
Lucia, your second child?

LADY INGER.   Ask God, who took her.

ELINA.   It is you I ask ; it is you that must answer
for her young life. She was glad as a bird in spring
when she sailed from Östråt to be Merete's guest.   A
year passed, and she stood in this room once more ;
but her cheeks were white, and death had gnawed
deep into her breast. Ah, you wonder at me, my
mother ! You thought that the ugly secret was
buried with her ;—but she told me all. A courtly
knight had won her heart. He would have wedded

---

¹ Pronounce *Mayrayte*.   ² Pronounce *Loonghe*.

her. You knew that her honour was at stake; yet your will never bent—and your child had to die. You see, I know all!

LADY INGER. All? Then she told you his name?

ELINA. His name? No; his name she did not tell me. His name was a torturing horror to her;—she never uttered it.

LADY INGER (*relieved, to herself*). Ah, then you do *not* know all—— ——

Elina—it is true that the whole of this matter was well known to me. But there is one thing about it you seem not to have noted. The lord whom Lucia met in Bergen was a Dane——

ELINA. That too I know.

LADY INGER. And his love was a lie. With guile and soft speeches he had ensnared her.

ELINA. I know it; but nevertheless she loved him; and had you had a mother's heart, your daughter's honour had been more to you than all.

LADY INGER. Not more than her happiness. Do you think that, with Merete's lot before my eyes, I could sacrifice my second child to a man that loved her not?

ELINA. Cunning words may befool many, but they befool not me——

Think not I know nothing of all that is passing in our land. I understand your counsels but too well. I know well that our Danish lords have no true friend in you. It may be that you hate them; but you fear them too. When you gave Merete to Vinzents Lunge the Danes held the mastery on all sides throughout our land. Three years later, when you forbade **Lucia** to wed the man she had given her life to, though he had deceived her,—things were far different then.   The King's Danish governors had shamefully misused the common people, and you thought it not wise to link yourself still more closely to the foreign tyrants.

And what have **you** done to avenge her that had to die so young?   **You** have done nothing.   Well then, I will act in your stead ; I will avenge all the shame they have brought upon our people and our house.

LADY INGER.   You?   What will **you** do?

ELINA.   I shall go *my* way, even as you go yours. What I shall **do** I myself know **not** ; but I feel within me the strength to dare all for our righteous **cause.**

LADY INGER.   Then you have a hard fight before you.   I once promised as you do now—and my hair has grown grey under the burden of that promise.

ELINA.   Good-night!   **Your** guest will soon be here, and **at** that meeting I should be out of place.

It may be there is yet time for you———— ; well, God strengthen you and guide your way !   Forget not that the eyes of many thousands are fixed upon you.   Think on Merete, weeping late and early over her wasted **life.**   Think on Lucia, sleeping in her black coffin.

And one thing **more.**   Forget not that in the game you play this night, your stake is your last child.

(Goes out to the left.)

Lady Inger (*looks after her awhile*). My last child? You know not how true was that word——
—— But the stake is not my child only. God help me, I am playing to-night for the whole of Norway's land.

Ah—is not that some one riding through the gateway? (*Listens at the window.*)

No; not yet. Only the wind; it blows cold as the grave—— ——

Has God a right to do this?—To make me a woman—and then to lay a man's duty upon my shoulders?

For I *have* the welfare of the country in my hands. It *is* in my power to make them rise as one man. They look to *me* for the signal; and if I give it not now—— it may never be given.

To delay? To sacrifice the many for the sake of one?—Were it not better if I could—— ——? No, no, no—I *will* not! I *cannot!* (*Steals a glance towards the Banquet Hall, but turns away again as if in dread, and whispers:*)

I can see them in there now. Pale spectres—dead ancestors—fallen kinsfolk.—Ah, those eyes that pierce me from every corner! (*Makes a backward gesture with her hand, and cries:*)

Sten Sture! Knut Alfson! Olaf Skaktavl! Back—back!—I *cannot* do this!

    (*A* Stranger, *strongly built, and with grizzled hair and beard, has entered from the Banquet Hall. He is dressed in a torn lambskin tunic; his weapons are rusty.*)

The Stranger (*stops in the doorway, and*

says in a low voice).   Hail to you, Inger Gylden-löve !

LADY INGER (*turns with a scream*).   Ah, Christ in heaven save me !

> (*Falls back into a chair.   The* STRANGER *stands gazing at her, motionless, leaning on his sword.*)

Act Second.

(*The room at Östråt, as in the first Act.*)
(LADY INGER GYLDENLÖVE *is seated at the table on the right, by the window.* OLAF SKAKTAVL *is standing a little way from her. Their faces show that they have been engaged in an animated discussion.*)

OLAF SKAKTAVL.   For the last time, Inger Gyldenlöve—you are not to be moved from your purpose?

LADY INGER.   I can do nought else.   And my counsel to you is: do as I do.   If it be Heaven's will that Norway perish utterly, perish it must, for all we may do to save it.

OLAF SKAKTAVL.   And think you I can content myself with words like these?   Shall I sit and look quietly on, now that the hour is come?   Do you forget the reckoning I have to pay?   They have robbed me of my lands, and parcelled them out among themselves.   My son, my only child, the last of my race, they have slaughtered like a dog.   Myself they have outlawed and forced to lurk by forest and fell these twenty years.—Once and again have folk whispered of my death; but this I believe, that they shall not lay me beneath the earth before I have seen my vengeance.

LADY INGER.   Then is there a long life before you.   What would you do?

OLAF SKAKTAVL.   Do?   How should I know what I will do?   It has never been my part to plot and plan.   That is where you must help me.   You have the wit for that.   I have but my sword and my two arms.

LADY INGER.   Your sword is rusted, Olaf Skaktavl!   All the swords in Norway are rusted.

OLAF SKAKTAVL.   That is doubtless why some folk fight only with their tongues.—Inger Gyldenlöve—great is the change in you.   Time was when the heart of a man beat in your breast.

LADY INGER.   Put me not in mind of what was.

OLAF SKAKTAVL.   'Tis for that alone I am here. You *shall* hear me, even if——

LADY INGER.   Be it so then ; but be brief ; for— I must say it—this is no place of safety for you.

OLAF SKAKTAVL.   Östråt is no place of safety for an outlaw? That I have long known.   But you forget that an outlaw is unsafe wheresoever he may wander.

LADY INGER.   Speak then ; I will not hinder you.

OLAF SKAKTAVL.   It is nigh on thirty years now since first I saw you.   It was at Akershus[1] in the house of Knut Alfson and his wife.   You were scarce more than a child then ; yet you were bold as the soaring falcon, and wild and headstrong too at times.   Many were the wooers around you.   I too held you dear—dear as no woman before or since. But you cared for nothing, thought of nothing, save your country's evil case and its great need.

LADY INGER.   I counted but fifteen summers then

—

[1] Pronounce *Ahkers-hoos.*

—remember that.   And was it not as though a frenzy had seized us all in those days?

Olaf Skaktavl.   Call it what you will; but one thing I know—even the old and sober men among us doubted not that it was written in the counsels of the Lord that you were she who should break our thraldom and win us all our rights again.   And more: you yourself then thought as we did.

Lady Inger.   It was a sinful thought, Olaf Skaktavl.   It was my proud heart, and not the Lord's call, that spoke in me.

Olaf Skaktavl.   You could have been the chosen one had you but willed it.   You came of the noblest blood in Norway; power and riches were at your feet; and you had an ear for the cries of anguish— then !—— ——

Do you remember that afternoon when Henrik Krummedike and the Danish fleet anchored off Akershus?   The captains of the fleet offered terms of settlement, and, trusting to the safe-conduct, Knut Alfson rowed on board.   Three hours later, we bore him through the castle gate——

Lady Inger.   A corpse; a corpse!

Olaf Skaktavl.   The best heart in Norway burst, when Krummedike's hirelings struck him down. Methinks I still can see the long procession that passed into the banquet-hall, heavily, two by two. There he lay on his bier, white as a spring cloud, with the axe-cleft in his brow.   I may safely say that the boldest men in Norway were gathered there that night.   Lady Margrete stood by her dead husband's head, and we swore as one man to venture lands and life to avenge this last misdeed and all that had gone before.— Inger Gyldenlöve,—who was it that burst through the circle of men? A maiden —then almost a child—with fire in her eyes and her voice half choked with tears.— What was it she swore? Shall I repeat your words?

LADY INGER. I swore what the rest of you swore; neither more nor less.

OLAF SKAKTAVL. You remember your oath— and yet you have forgotten it.

LADY INGER. And how did the others keep their promise? I speak not of you, Olaf Skaktavl, but of your friends, all our Norwegian nobles? Not one of them, in all these years, has had the courage to be a man ; and yet they lay it to my charge that I am a woman.

OLAF SKAKTAVL. I know what you would say. Why have they bent to the yoke, and not defied the tyrants to the last? 'Tis but too true; there is base metal enough in our noble houses nowadays. But had they held together—who knows what might have been? And you could have held them together, for before you all had bowed.

LADY INGER. My answer were easy enough, but it would scarce content you. So let us leave speaking of what cannot be changed. Tell me rather what has brought you to Östråt. Do you need harbour? Well, I will try to hide you. If you would have aught else, speak out ; you shall find me ready——

OLAF SKAKTAVL. For twenty years have I been homeless. In the mountains of Jæmteland my hair has grown grey. My dwelling has been with wolves

and bears.—You see, Lady Inger—*I* need you not ;
but both nobles and people stand in sore need
of you.

Lady Inger.   The old burden.

Olaf Skaktavl.   Ay, it sounds but ill in your
ears, I know ; yet hear it you must for all that.   In
brief, then : I come from Sweden : troubles are at
hand : the Dales are ready to rise.

Lady Inger.   I know it.

Olaf Skaktavl.   Peter Kanzler is with us—
secretly, you understand.

Lady Inger (*starting*).   Peter Kanzler?

Olaf Skaktavl.   It is he that has sent me to
Östråt.

Lady Inger (*rises*).   Peter Kanzler, say you?

Olaf Skaktavl.   He himself ;—but mayhap you
no longer know him ?

Lady Inger (*half to herself*).   Only too well !—
But tell me, I pray you,—what message do you bring?

Olaf Skaktavl.   When the rumour of the rising
reached the border mountains, where I then was, I
set off at once into Sweden.   'Twas not hard to guess
that Peter Kanzler had a finger in the game.   I
sought him out and offered to stand by him ;—he
knew me of old, as you know, and knew that he
could trust me ; so he has sent me hither.

Lady Inger (*impatiently*).   Yes yes,—he sent you
hither to——?

Olaf Skaktavl (*with secrecy*).   Lady Inger—a
stranger comes to Östråt to-night.

Lady Inger (*surprised*).   What ?   Know you
that—— ?

OLAF SKAKTAVL.   Assuredly I know it.   I know all.   'Twas to meet him that Peter Kanzler sent me hither.

LADY INGER.   To meet him?   Impossible, Olaf Skaktavl,—impossible!

OLAF SKAKTAVL.   'Tis as I tell you   If he be not already come, he will soon——

LADY INGER.   Yes, I know; but——

OLAF SKAKTAVL.   Then you know of his coming?

LADY INGER   Ay, surely.   He sent me a message.   That was why they opened to you as soon as you knocked.

OLAF SKAKTAVL (*listens*).   Hush!—some one is riding along the road.   (*Goes to the window.*)   They are opening the gate.

LADY INGER (*looks out*).   It is a knight and his attendant.   They are dismounting in the courtyard.

OLAF SKAKTAVL.   Then it is he.   His name?

LADY INGER.   You know not his name?

OLAF SKAKTAVL.   Peter Kanzler refused to tell it me.   He would only say that I should find him at Östråt the third evening after Martinmas——

LADY INGER.   Ay; even to-night.

OLAF SKAKTAVL.   He was to bring letters with him, and from them, and from you, I was to learn who he is.

LADY INGER.   Then let me lead you to your chamber.   You have need of rest and refreshment. You shall soon have speech with the stranger.

OLAF SKAKTAVL.   Well, be it as you will.   (*Both go out to the left.*)

(*After a short pause,* FINN *enters cautiously*

through the door on the right, looks round the room, and peeps into the Banquet Hall; he then goes back to the door, and makes a sign to some one outside. Immediately after, enter COUNCILLOR NILS LYKKE *and the Swedish Commander,* JENS BIELKE.)

NILS LYKKE (*softly*).   No one?

FINN (*in the same tone*).   No one, master!

NILS LYKKE.   And we may depend on you in all things?

FINN.   The commandant in Trondhiem has ever given me a name for trustiness.

NILS LYKKE.   It is well; he has said as much to me.   First of all, then—has there come any stranger to Östråt to-night, before us?

FINN.   Ay; a stranger came an hour since.

NILS LYKKE (*softly, to* JENS BIELKE).   He is here. (*Turns again to* FINN.)   Would you know him again? Have you seen him?

FINN.   Nay, none have seen him, that I know, but the gatekeeper.   He was brought at once to Lady Inger, and she——

NILS LYKKE.   Well?   What of her?   He is not gone again already?

FINN.   No; but it seems she keeps him hidden in one of her own rooms; for——

NILS LYKKE.   It is well.

JENS BIELKE (*whispers*).   Then the first thing is to put a guard on the gate; then we are sure of him.

NILS LYKKE (*with a smile*).   Hm! (*To* FINN.) Tell me—is there any way of leaving the castle but by the gate?   Gape not at me so!   I mean—can one escape from Östråt unseen, while the castle gate is shut?

FINN. Nay, that I know not. 'Tis true they talk of secret ways in the vaults beneath; but no one knows them save Lady Inger—and mayhap Mistress Elina.

JENS BIELKE. The devil!

NILS LYKKE. It is well. You may go.

FINN. And should you need me in aught again, you have but to open the second door on the right in the Banquet Hall, and I shall presently be at hand.

NILS LYKKE. Good. (*Points to the entrance-door.* FINN *goes out.*)

JENS BIELKE. Now, by my soul, dear friend and brother—this campaign is like to end but scurvily for both of us.

NILS LYKKE (*with a smile*). Oh—not for me, I hope.

JENS BIELKE. Not? First of all, there is small honour to be got in hunting an overgrown whelp like this Nils Sture. Are we to think him mad or in his sober senses after the pranks he has played? First he breeds bad blood among the peasants; promises them help and all their hearts can desire;—and then, when it comes to the pinch, off he runs to hide behind a petticoat!

Moreover, to tell the truth, I repent that I followed your counsel and went not my own way.

NILS LYKKE (*aside*). Your repentance comes somewhat late, my brother.

JENS BIELKE. Look you, I have never loved digging at a badger's earth. I looked for quite other sport. Here have I ridden all the way from the

Jæmteland with my horsemen, and have got me a warrant from the Trondhiem commandant to search for the rebel wheresoever I please. All his tracks point towards Östråt——

Nils Lykke. He *is* here! He *is* here, I tell you!

Jens Bielke. If that were so, should we not have found the gate barred and well guarded? Would that we had; then could I have found use for my men-at-arms——

Nils Lykke. But instead, the gate is opened for us in all hospitality. Mark now—if Inger Gyldenlöve's fame belie her not, I warrant she will not let her guests lack for either meat or drink.

Jens Bielke. Ay, to turn us aside from our errand! And what wild whim was that of yours to persuade me to leave my horsemen a good mile from the castle? Had we come in force——

Nils Lykke. She had made us none the less welcome for that. But mark well that then our coming had made a stir. The peasants round about had held it for an outrage against Lady Inger; she had risen high in their favour once more—and with that, look you, we were ill served.

Jens Bielke. May be so. But what am I to do now? Count Sture is in Östråt, you say. Ay, but how does that profit me? Be sure Lady Inger Gyldenlöve has as many hiding-places as the fox, and more than one outlet to them. We two can go snuffing about here alone as long as we please. I would the devil had the whole affair!

Nils Lykke. Well, then, my friend—if you like

not the turn your errand has taken, you have but to leave the field to me.

JENS BIELKE. To you? What will you do?

NILS LYKKE. Caution and cunning may here do more than could be achieved by force of arms.— And to say truth, Captain Jens Bielke—something of the sort has been in my mind ever since we met in Trondhiem yesterday.

JENS BIELKE. Was that why you persuaded me to leave the men-at-arms?

NILS LYKKE. Both your purpose at Östråt and mine could best be served without them; and so——

JENS BIELKE. The foul fiend seize you—I had almost said! And me to boot! Might I not have known that there is guile in all your dealings?

NILS LYKKE. Be sure I shall need all my guile here, if I am to face my foe with even weapons. And let me tell you 'tis of the utmost moment to me that I acquit me of my mission secretly and well. You must know that when I set forth I was scarce in favour with my lord the King. He held me in suspicion; though I dare swear I have served him as well as any man could, in more than one ticklish charge.

JENS BIELKE. That you may safely boast. God and all men know you for the craftiest devil in all the three kingdoms.

NILS LYKKE. You flatter! But after all, 'tis not much to say. Now this present errand I hold for the crowning proof of my policy; for here I have to outwit a woman——

JENS BIELKE. Ha-ha-ha! In that art you have long since given crowning proofs of your skill, dear brother. Think you we in Sweden know not the song—

Fair maidens a-many they sigh and they pine:
" Ah God, that Nils Lykke were mine, mine, mine !"

NILS LYKKE. Alas, it is women of twenty and thereabouts that ditty speaks of. Lady Inger Gyldenlöve is nigh on fifty, and wily to boot beyond all women. It will be no light matter to overcome her. But it must be done—at any cost. If I succeed in winning certain advantages over her that the King has long desired, I can reckon on the embassy to France next spring. You know that I spent three years at the University in Paris? My whole soul is bent on coming thither again, most of all if I can appear in lofty place, a king's ambassador.—Well, then—is it agreed?—do you leave Lady Inger to me? Remember—when you were last at Court in Copenhagen, I made way for you with more than one fair lady——

JENS BIELKE. Nay, truly now—that generosity cost you little; one and all of them were at your beck and call. But let that pass; now that I have begun amiss in this matter, I had as lief that you should take it on your shoulders. One thing, though, you must promise—if the young Count Sture be in Östråt, you will deliver him into my hands, dead or alive!

NILS LYKKE. You shall have him all alive. I, at any rate, mean not to kill him. But now you must ride back and join your people. Keep guard on the road. Should I mark aught that mislikes me, you shall know it forthwith.

JENS BIELKE. Good, good. But how am I to get out?

NILS LYKKE. The fellow that brought us in will show the way. But go quietly——

JENS BIELKE. Of course, of course. Well—good fortune to you!

NILS LYKKE. Fortune has never failed me in a war with women. Haste you now!

(JENS BIELKE *goes out to the right.*)

NILS LYKKE (*stands still for a while; then walks about the room, looking round him; at last he says softly*). So I am at Östråt at last—the ancient seat that a child, two years ago, told me so much of.

Lucia. Ay, two years ago she was still a child. And now—now she is dead. (*Hums with a half-smile.*) "Blossoms plucked are blossoms withered —— ——" (*Looks round him again.*)

Östråt. 'Tis as though I had seen it all before; as though I were at home here.—In there is the Banquet Hall. And underneath is—the grave-vault. It must be there that Lucia lies.

(*In a lower voice, half seriously, half with forced gaiety.*)

Were I timorous, I might well find myself fancying that when I set foot within Östråt gate she turned about in her coffin; as I walked across the courtyard she lifted the lid; and when I named her name but now, 'twas as though a voice summoned her forth from the grave-vault.—Maybe she is even now groping her way up the stairs. The face-cloth blinds her, but she gropes on and on in spite of it.

Now she has reached the Banquet Hall; she stands watching me from behind the door!

(*Turns his head backwards over one shoulder, nods,
  and says aloud:*)

Come nearer, Lucia! Talk to me a little! Your
mother keeps me waiting. 'Tis tedious waiting—
and you have helped me to while away many a
tedious hour—— ——

(*Passes his hand over his forehead, and takes one
  or two turns up and down.*)

Ah, there!—Right, right ; there is the deep curtained window. It is there that Inger Gyldenlöve is
wont to stand gazing out over the road, as though
looking for one that never comes. In there—(*looks
towards the door on the left*)—somewhere in there is
Sister Elina's chamber. Elina? Ay, Elina is her
name. Can it be that she is so rare a being—so wise
and so brave as Lucia drew her? Fair, too, they
say. But for a wedded wife——? I should not have
written so plainly—— ——

(*Lost in thought, he is on the point of sitting down
  by the table, but stands up again.*)

How will Lady Inger receive me? She will
scarce burn the castle over our heads, or slip me
through a trap-door. A stab from behind——? No,
not that way either——

(*Listens towards the hall.*)

Aha!

(LADY INGER GYLDENLÖVE *enters from the hall.*)

LADY INGER (*coldly*). My greeting to you, Sir
Councillor——

NILS LYKKE (*bows deeply*). Ah—the Lady of
Östråt !

LADY INGER. And my thanks that you have forewarned me of your visit.

NILS LYKKE. I could do no less. I had reason to think that my coming might surprise you——

LADY INGER. In truth, Sir Councillor, you thought right there. Nils Lykke was certainly the last guest I looked to see at Östråt.

NILS LYKKE. And still less, mayhap, did you think to see him come as a friend?

LADY INGER. As a friend? You add insult to all the shame and sorrow you have heaped upon my house? After bringing my child to the grave, you still dare——

NILS LYKKE. With your leave, Lady Inger Gyldenlöve—on that matter we should scarce agree; for you count as nothing what *I* lost by that same unhappy chance. I purposed nought but in honour. I was tired of my unbridled life; my thirtieth year was already past; I longed to mate me with a good and gentle wife. Add to all this the hope of becoming *your* son-in-law——

LADY INGER. Beware, Sir Councillor! I have done all in my power to hide my child's unhappy fate. But because it is out of sight, think not it is out of mind. It may yet happen——

NILS LYKKE. You threaten me, Lady Inger? I have offered you my hand in amity; you refuse to take it. Henceforth, then, it is to be open war between us?

LADY INGER. Was there ever aught else?

NILS LYKKE. Not on *your* side, mayhap. *I* have

never been your enemy,—though as a subject of the King of Denmark I lacked not good cause.

LADY INGER. I understand you. I have not been pliant enough. It has not proved so easy as some of you hoped to lure me over into your camp.— Yet methinks you have nought to complain of. My daughter Merete's husband is your countryman— further I cannot go. My position is no easy one, Nils Lykke!

NILS LYKKE. That I can well believe. Both nobles and people here in Norway think they have an ancient claim on you—a claim, 'tis said, you have but half fulfilled.

LADY INGER. Your pardon, Sir Councillor,—I account for my doings to none but God and myself. If it please you, then, let me understand what brings you hither.

NILS LYKKE. Gladly, Lady Inger! The purport of my mission to this country can scarce be unknown to you——?

LADY INGER. I know the mission that report assigns you. Our King would fain know how the Norwegian nobles stand affected towards him.

NILS LYKKE. Assuredly.

LADY INGER. Then that is why you visit Östråt?

NILS LYKKE. In part. But it is far from my purpose to demand any profession of loyalty from you——

LADY INGER. What then?

NILS LYKKE. Hearken to me, Lady Inger! You said yourself but now that your position is no easy one. You stand half way between two hostile camps,

neither of which dares trust you fully. Your own
interest must needs bind you to *us*. On the other
hand, you are bound to the disaffected by the bond of
nationality, and—who knows?—mayhap by some
secret tie as well.

LADY INGER (*aside*). A secret tie! Christ, does
he——?

NILS LYKKE (*notices her emotion, but makes no sign,
and continues without change of manner*). You cannot but see that such a position must ere long become
impossible.—Suppose, now, it lay in my power to
free you from these embarrassments which——

LADY INGER. In your power, you say?

NILS LYKKE. First of all, Lady Inger, I would
beg you to lay no stress on any careless words I may
have used concerning that which lies between us two.
Think not that I have forgotten for a moment the
wrong I have done you. Suppose, now, I had long
purposed to make atonement, as far as might be,
where I had sinned. Suppose that were my reason
for undertaking this mission.

LADY INGER. Speak your meaning more clearly,
Sir Councillor;—I cannot follow you.

NILS LYKKE. I can scarce be mistaken in thinking that you, as well as I, know of the threatened
troubles in Sweden. You know, or at least you can
guess, that this rising is of far wider aim than is commonly supposed, and you understand therefore that
our King cannot look on quietly and let things take
their course. Am I not right?

LADY INGER. Go on.

NILS LYKKE (*searchingly, after a short pause*).

There is one possible chance that might endanger
Gustav Vasa's throne——

Lady Inger (*aside*).   Whither is he tending?

Nils Lykke.   ——the chance, namely, that there
should exist in Sweden a man entitled by his birth
to claim election to the kingship.

Lady Inger (*evasively*).   The Swedish nobles have
been even as bloodily hewn down as our own, Sir
Councillor.   Where would you seek for——?

Nils Lykke (*with a smile*).   Seek?   The man is
found already——

Lady Inger (*starts violently*).   Ah!   He is
found?

Nils Lykke.   ——And he is too closely akin to
you, Lady Inger, to be far from your thoughts at this
moment.

   (*Looks at her.*)

The last Count Sture left a son——

Lady Inger (*with a cry*).   Holy Saviour, how
know you——?

Nils Lykke (*surprised*).   Be calm, Madam, and
let me finish.—This young man has lived quietly
till now with his mother, Sten Sture's widow.

Lady Inger (*breathes more freely*).   With——?
Ah, yes—true, true!

Nils Lykke.   But now he has come forward
openly.   He has shown himself in the Dales as
leader of the peasants; their numbers are growing
day by day; and—as perhaps you know—they are
finding friends among the peasants on this side of
the border-hills.

Lady Inger (*who has in the meantime regained*

her composure). Sir Councillor,—you speak of all these things as though they must of necessity be known to me. What ground have I given you to believe so? I know, and wish to know, nothing. All my care is to live quietly within my own domain; I give no helping hand to the rebels; but neither must you count on me if it be your purpose to put them down.

NILS LYKKE (*in a low voice*). Would you still be inactive, if it were my purpose to stand by them?

LADY INGER. How am I to understand you?

NILS LYKKE. Have you not seen whither I have been aiming all this time?—Well, I will tell you all, honestly and straightforwardly. Know, then, that the King and his Council see clearly that we can have no sure footing in Norway so long as the nobles and the people continue, as now, to think themselves wronged and oppressed. We understand to the full that willing allies are better than sullen subjects; and we have therefore no heartier wish than to loosen the bonds that hamper *us*, in effect, quite as straitly as you. But you will scarce deny that the temper of Norway towards us makes such a step too dangerous—so long as we have no sure support behind us.

LADY INGER. And this support—— ?

NILS LYKKE. Should naturally come from Sweden. But, mark well, not so long as Gustav Vasa holds the helm; *his* reckoning with Denmark is not settled yet, and mayhap never will be. But a new king of Sweden, who had the people with him, and who owed his throne to the help of Denmark—— —— Well, you begin to understand me? *Then* we could safely say to you Norwegians: "Take back your old ancestral rights; choose you a ruler after your own mind; be our friends in need, as we will be yours!"—Maik you well, Lady Inger, herein is our generosity less than it may seem; for you must see that, far from weakening, 'twill rather strengthen us.

And now that I have opened my heart to you so fully, do you too cast away all mistrust. And therefore (*confidently*)—the knight from Sweden, who came hither an hour before me——

LADY INGER. Then you already know of his coming?

NILS LYKKE. Most certainly. It is him I seek.

LADY INGER (*to herself*). Strange! It must be as Olaf Skaktavl said. (*To* NILS LYKKE.) I pray you wait here, Sir Councillor! I go to bring him to you.

(*Goes out through the Banquet Hall.*)

NILS LYKKE (*looks after her a while in exultant astonishment*). She is bringing him! Ay, truly— she is bringing him! The battle is half won. I little thought it would go so smoothly——

She is deep in the counsels of the rebels; she started in terror when I named Sten Sture's son——

And now? Hm! Since Lady Inger has been simple enough to walk into the snare, Nils Sture will not make many difficulties. A hot-blooded boy, thoughtless and rash—— —— With my promise of help he will set forth at once—unhappily Jens Bielke will snap him up by the way—and the whole rising will be nipped in the bud.

And then? Then one step more in our own

behalf. It is spread abroad that the young Count Sture has been at Östråt,—that a Danish envoy has had audience of Lady Inger—that thereupon the young Count Nils has been snapped up by King Gustav's men-at-arms a mile from the castle—— —— Let Inger Gyldenlöve's name among the people stand never so high—it will scarce recover from such a blow.

(*Starts up in sudden uneasiness.*)

By all the devils——! What if she has scented mischief! It may be he is slipping through our fingers even now—— (*Listens towards the hall, and says with relief.*) Ah, there is no fear. Here they come.

(LADY INGER GYLDENLÖVE *enters from the hall along with* OLAF SKAKTAVL.)

LADY INGER (*to* NILS LYKKE). Here is the man you seek.

NILS LYKKE (*aside*). In the name of hell—what means this?

LADY INGER. I have told this knight your name and all that you have imparted to me——

NILS LYKKE (*irresolutely*). Ay? Have you so? Well——

LADY INGER—— And I will not hide from you that his faith in your help is none of the strongest.

NILS LYKKE. Is it not?

LADY INGER. Can you marvel at that? You know, surely, both the cause he fights for and his bitter fate——

NILS LYKKE. This man's——? Ah—yes, truly——

OLAF SKAKTAVL (*to* NILS LYKKE). But seeing

'tis Peter Kanzler himself that has appointed us this meeting——

NILS LYKKE. Peter Kanzler——? (*Recovers himself quickly.*) Ay, right,—I have a mission from Peter Kanzler——

OLAF SKAKTAVL. He must know best whom he can trust. So why should I trouble my head with thinking how——

NILS LYKKE. Ay, you are right, noble Sir; that were folly indeed.

OLAF SKAKTAVL. Rather let us come straight to the matter.

NILS LYKKE. Straight to the point; no beating about the bush—'tis ever my fashion.

OLAF SKAKTAVL. Then will you tell me your errand here?

NILS LYKKE. Methinks you can partly guess my errand——

OLAF SKAKTAVL. Peter Kanzler said something of papers that——

NILS LYKKE. Papers? Ay, true, the papers!

OLAF SKAKTAVL. Doubtless you have them with you?

NILS LYKKE. Of course; safely bestowed; so safely that I cannot at once——

(*Appears to search the inner pockets of his doublet; says to himself:*)

Who the devil is he? What pretext shall I make? I may be on the brink of great discoveries——

(*Notices that the Servants are laying the table and lighting the lamps in the Banquet Hall, and says to* OLAF SKAKTAVL:)

Ah, I see Lady Inger has taken order for the evening meal. We could perhaps better talk of our affairs at table.

OLAF SKAKTAVL. Good; as you will.

NILS LYKKE (*aside*). Time gained—all gained!
    (*To* LADY INGER *with a show of great friendliness.*)

And meanwhile we might learn what part Lady Inger Gyldenlöve purposes to take in our design?

LADY INGER. I?—None.

NILS LYKKE AND OLAF SKAKTAVL. None!

LADY INGER. Can ye marvel, noble Sirs, that I venture not on a game, wherein all is staked on one cast? And that, too, when none of my allies dare trust me fully.

NILS LYKKE. That reproach touches not me. I trust you blindly; I pray you be assured of that.

OLAF SKAKTAVL. Who should believe in you, if not your countrymen?

LADY INGER. Truly,—this confidence rejoices me.
    (*Goes to a cupboard in the back wall and fills two goblets with wine.*)

NILS LYKKE (*aside*). Curse her, will she slip out of the noose?

LADY INGER (*hands a goblet to each*). And since so it is, I offer you a cup of welcome to Östrât. Drink, noble knights! Pledge me to the last drop!
    (*Looks from one to the other after they have drunk, and says gravely :*)

But now I must tell you—one goblet held a welcome for my friend; the other—death for my enemy!

Nils Lykke (*throws down the goblet*).   Ah, I am poisoned!

Olaf Skaktavl (*at the same time, clutches his sword*).   Death and hell, have you murdered me?

Lady Inger (*to* Olaf Skaktavl, *pointing to* Nils Lykke).   You see the Danes' trust in Inger Gyldenlöve——

> (*To* Nils Lykke, *pointing to* Olaf Skaktavl.)

——and likewise my countrymen's faith in me!

> (*To both of them.*)

And I am to place myself in your power?   Gently, noble Sirs—gently!   The Lady of Östråt is not yet in her dotage.

> (Elina Gyldenlöve *enters by the door on the left.*)

Elina.   I heard loud voices!   What is amiss?

Lady Inger (*to* Nils Lykke).   My daughter Elina.

Nils Lykke (*softly*).   Elina!   I had not pictured her thus.

> (Elina *catches sight of* Nils Lykke, *and stands still, as in surprise, gazing at him.*)

Lady Inger (*touches her arm*).   My child—this knight is——

Elina (*motions her mother back with her hand, still looking intently at him, and says :*)   There is no need!   I see who he is.   He is Nils Lykke.

Nils Lykke (*aside, to* Lady Inger).   How?   Does she know me?   Can Lucia have——?   Can she know——?

Lady Inger.   Hush!   She knows nothing.

Elina (*to herself*).   I knew it ;—even so must Nils Lykke appear.

NILS LYKKE (*approaches her*). Yes, Elina Gyldenlöve,—you have guessed rightly. And as it seems
that, in some sense, you know me,—and, moreover, as
I am your mother's guest,—you will not deny me the
flower-spray you wear in your bosom. So long as it is
fresh and fragrant I shall have in it an image of yourself.

ELINA (*proudly, but still gazing at him*). Pardon
me, Sir Knight—it was plucked in my own chamber,
and *there* can grow no flower for you.

NILS LYKKE (*loosening a spray of flowers that he
wears in the front of his doublet*). At least you will
not disdain this humble gift. 'Twas a farewell
token from a courtly lady when I set forth from
Trondhiem this morning. — But mark me, noble
maiden,—were I to offer you a gift that were fully
worthy of you, it could be naught less than a
princely crown.

ELINA (*who has taken the flowers passively*). And
were it the royal crown of Denmark you held forth to
me—before I shared it with *you*, I would crush it to
pieces between my hands, and cast the fragments at
your feet !

    (*Throws down the flowers at his feet, and goes
        into the Banquet Hall.*)

OLAF SKAKTAVL (*mutters to himself*). Bold—as
Inger Ottisdaughter by Knut Alfson's bier !

LADY INGER (*softly, after looking alternately at
ELINA and NILS LYKKE*). The wolf *can* be tamed.
Now to forge the fetters.

NILS LYKKE (*picks up the flowers and gazes in
rapture after ELINA*). God's holy blood, but she is
proud and fair !

Act Third.

*(The Banquet Hall.   A high bow-window in the background;
a smaller window in front on the left.   Several doors on each
side.   The roof is supported by massive wooden pillars, on
which, as well as on the walls, are hung all sorts of weapons.
Pictures of saints, knights, and ladies hang in long rows.
Pendent from the roof, a large many-branched lamp, alight.
In front, on the right, an ancient carven high-seat.   In the
middle of the hall, a table with the remnants of the evening
meal.)*

*(*ELINA GYLDENLÖVE *enters from the left, slowly and in deep
thought.   Her expression shows that she is going over again
in her mind the scene with* NILS LYKKE.   *At last she repeats
the motion with which she flung away the flowers, and says in
a low voice :)*

ELINA. —— ——And then he gathered up the
fragments of the crown of Denmark—no, 'twas the
flowers—and : " God's holy blood, but she is proud
and fair ! "

Had he whispered the words in the remotest corner,
long leagues from Östråt,—still had I heard them !

How I hate him !   How I have always hated him,
—this Nils Lykke!—There lives not another man
like him, 'tis said.   He plays with women—and treads
them under his feet.

And it was to him my mother thought to offer me !
—How I hate him !

They say Nils Lykke is unlike all other men.   It

is not true! There is nothing strange in him. There are many, many like him! When Biörn used to tell me his tales, all the princes looked as Nils Lykke looks. When I sat lonely here in the hall and dreamed my histories, and my knights came and went,—they were one and all even as he.

How strange and how good it is to hate! Never have I known how sweet it can be—till to-night. Ah—not to live a thousand years would I sell the moments I have lived since I saw him!—

"God's holy blood, but she is proud—— ——"

> (*Goes slowly towards the background, opens the window and looks out.* NILS LYKKE *comes in by the first door on the right.*)

NILS LYKKE (*to himself*). "Sleep well at Östråt, Sir Knight," said Inger Gyldenlöve as she left me. Sleep well? Ay, it is easily said, but—— —— Out there, sky and sea in tumult; below, in the grave-vault, a young girl on her bier; the fate of two kingdoms in my hand; and in my breast a withered flower that a woman has flung at my feet. Truly, I fear me sleep will be slow of coming.

> (*Notices* ELINA, *who has left the window, and is going out on the left.*)

There she is. Her haughty eyes seem veiled with thought.—Ah, if I but dared—(*aloud*). Mistress Elina!

ELINA (*stops at the door*). What will you? Why do you pursue me?

NILS LYKKE. You err; I pursue you not. I am myself pursued.

ELINA. You?

Nils Lykke.   By a multitude of thoughts.   Therefore 'tis with sleep as with you :—it flees me.

Elina.   Go to the window, and there you will find pastime ;—a storm-tossed sea——

Nils Lykke (*smiles*).   A storm-tossed sea?   That I may find in you as well.

Elina.   In me ?

Nils Lykke.   Ay, of that our first meeting has assured me.

Elina.   And that offends you ?

Nils Lykke.   Nay, in nowise ; yet I could wish to see you of milder mood.

Elina (*proudly*).   Think you that you will ever have your wish ?

Nils Lykke.   I am sure of it.   I have a welcome word to say to you.

Elina.   What is it ?

Nils Lykke.   Farewell.

Elina (*comes a step nearer him*).   Farewell?   You are leaving Östråt—so soon ?

Nils Lykke.   This very night.

Elina (*seems to hesitate for a moment ; then says coldly :*)   Then take my greeting, Sir Knight !   (*Bows and is about to go.*)

Nils Lykke.   Elina Gyldenlöve,—I have no right to keep you here ; but 'twill be unlike your nobleness if you refuse to hear what I have to say to you.

Elina.   I hear you, Sir Knight.

Nils Lykke.   I know you hate me.

Elina.   You are keen-sighted, I perceive.

Nils Lykke.   But I know, too, that I have fully merited your hate.   Unseemly and insolent were the words I wrote of you in my letter to Lady Inger.

ELINA.   It may be; I have not read them.

NILS LYKKE.   But at least their purport is not unknown to you; I know your mother has not left you in ignorance of the matter; at the least she has told you how I praised the lot of the man who——; surely you know the hope I nursed——

ELINA.   Sir Knight—if it is of that you would speak——

NILS LYKKE.   I speak of it, only to excuse what I have done; for no other reason, I swear to you. If my fame has reached you—as I have too much cause to fear—before I myself set foot in Östråt, you must needs know enough of my life not to wonder that in such things I should go to work something boldly. I have met many women, Elina Gyldenlöve; but not one have I found unyielding.   Such lessons, look you, teach a man to be secure.   He loses the habit of roundabout ways——

ELINA.   May be so.   I know not of what metal those women can have been.

For the rest, you err in thinking 'twas your letter to my mother that aroused my soul's hatred and bitterness against you.   It is of older date.

NILS LYKKE (uneasily).   Of older date?   What mean you?

ELINA.   'Tis as you guessed :—your fame has gone before you, to Östråt, even as over all the land. Nils Lykke's name is never spoken save with the name of some woman whom he has beguiled and cast off.   Some speak it in wrath, others with laughter and wanton jeering at those weak-souled creatures. But through the wrath and the laughter and the jeers rings the song they have made of you, masterful and insolent as an enemy's song of triumph.

'Tis all this that has begotten my hate for you. You were ever in my thoughts, and I longed to meet you face to face, that you might learn that there are women on whom your soft speeches are lost—if you should think to use them.

NILS LYKKE.   You judge me unjustly, if you judge from what rumour has told of me. Even if there be truth in all you have heard,— you know not the causes that have made me what I am.—As a boy of seventeen I began my course of pleasure. I have lived full fifteen years since then.   Light women granted me all that I would —even before the wish had shaped itself into a prayer ; and what I offered them they seized with eager hands. You are the first woman that has flung back a gift of mine with scorn at my feet.

Think not I reproach you. Rather I honour you for it, as never before have I honoured woman. But for this I reproach my fate—and the thought is a gnawing pain to me—that I did not meet you sooner—— ——

Elina Gyldenlöve! Your mother has told me of you. While far from Östråt life ran its restless course, you went your lonely way in silence, living in your dreams and histories. Therefore you will understand what I have to tell you.—Know, then, that once I too lived even such a life as yours. Methought that when I stepped forth into the great

world, a noble and stately woman would come to
meet me, and would beckon me to her and point me
the path towards a lofty goal.—I was deceived, Elina
Gyldenlöve! Women came to meet me; but *she*
was not among them. Ere yet I had come to full
manhood, I had learnt to despise them all.

Was it my fault? Why were not the others even
as you?—I know the fate of your fatherland lies
heavy on your soul, and you know the part I have
in these affairs—— —— 'Tis said of me that I am
false as the sea-foam. Mayhap I am; but if I be, it
is women who have made me so. Had I sooner
found what I sought,—had I met a woman proud
and noble and high-souled even as you, then had my
path been different indeed. At this moment, maybe,
I had been standing at your side as the champion of
all that suffer wrong in Norway's land. For *this* I
believe: a woman is the mightiest power in the world,
and in her hand it lies to guide a man whither God
Almighty would have him go.

ELINA (*to herself*). Can it be as he says? Nay
nay; there is falsehood in his eyes and deceit
on his lips. And yet—no song is sweeter than his
words.

NILS LYKKE (*coming closer, speaks low and more
intimately*). How often, when you have been sitting
here at Östråt, alone with your changeful thoughts,
have you felt your bosom stifling; how often have the
roof and walls seemed to shrink together till they
crushed your very soul. Then have your longings
taken wing with you; then have you yearned to fly
far from here, you knew not whither.—How often

have you not wandered alone by the fiord ; far out
a ship has sailed by in fair array, with knights and
ladies on her deck, with song and music of stringed
instruments ;—a faint, far-off rumour of great events
has reached your ears ;—and you have felt a longing
in your breast, an unconquerable craving to know all
that lies beyond the sea. But you have not understood what ailed you. At times you have thought it
was the fate of your fatherland that filled you with all
these restless broodings. You deceived yourself ;—a
maiden so young as you has other food for musing
—— —— Elina Gyldenlöve! Have you never had
visions of an unknown power—a strong mysterious
might, that binds together the destinies of mortals?
When you dreamed of the many-coloured life far out
in the wide world—when you dreamed of knightly
jousts and joyous festivals—saw you never in your
dreams a knight, who stood in the midst of the
gayest rout, with a smile on his lips and with bitterness in his heart,—a knight that had once dreamed
a dream as fair as yours, of a woman noble
and stately, for whom he went ever seeking, and
in vain?

ELINA. Who are you, that have power to clothe
my most secret thoughts in words? How can you
tell me what I have borne in my inmost soul—and
knew it not myself? How know you——?

NILS LYKKE. All that I have told you, I have
read in your eyes.

ELINA. Never has any man spoken to me as you
have. I have understood you but dimly; and yet—
all, all seems changed since——

(*To herself.*) Now I understand why they said that Nils Lykke was unlike all others.

NILS LYKKE. There is one thing in the world that might drive a man to madness, but to think of it; and that is the thought of what might have been if things had fallen out in this way or that. Had I met you on my path while the tree of my life was yet green and budding, at this hour, mayhap, you had been—— ——

But forgive me, noble lady! Our speech of these past few moments has made me forget how we stand one to another. 'Twas as though a secret voice had told me from the first that to you I could speak openly, without flattery or dissimulation.

ELINA. That can you.

NILS LYKKE. 'Tis well;—and it may be that this openness has already in part reconciled us. Ay—my hope is yet bolder. The time may yet come when you will think of the stranger knight without hate or bitterness in your soul. Nay,—mistake me not! I mean not now—but some time, in the days to come. And that this may be the less hard for you—and as I have begun once for all to speak to you plainly and openly—let me tell you——

ELINA. Sir Knight——!

NILS LYKKE (*smiling*). Ah, I see the thought of my letter still affrights you. Fear nought on that score. I would from my heart it were unwritten, for —I know 'twill concern you little enough, so I may even say it right out—for I love you not, and shall never come to love you. Fear nothing, therefore, as I said before ; I shall in no wise seek to—— ——

But what ails you——?

ELINA.   Me?   Nothing, nothing.—Tell me but one thing.   Why do you still wear those flowers? What would you with them?

NILS LYKKE.   These?   Are they not a gage of battle you have thrown down to the wicked Nils Lykke on behalf of all womankind?   What could I do but take it up?

You asked what I would with them.   (*Softly.*) When I stand again amidst the fair ladies of Denmark— when the music of the strings is hushed and there is silence in the hall—then will I bring forth these flowers and tell a tale of a young maiden sitting alone in a gloomy black-beamed hall, far to the north in Norway——

(*Breaks off and bows respectfully.*)
But I fear I keep the noble daughter of the house too long.   We shall meet no more ; for before day-break I shall be gone.   So now I bid you farewell.

ELINA.   Fare you well, Sir Knight!

(*A short silence.*)

NILS LYKKE.   Again you are deep in thought, Elina Gyldenlöve!   Is it the fate of your fatherland that weighs upon you still?

ELINA (*shakes her head, absently gazing straight in front of her*).   My fatherland?—I think not of my fatherland.

NILS LYKKE.   Then 'tis the strife and misery of the time that cause you dread.

ELINA.   The time?   I have forgotten time——
—— You go to Denmark?   Said you not so?

NILS LYKKE.   I go to Denmark.

ELINA.   Can I see towards Denmark from this hall?

NILS LYKKE (*points to the window on the left*). Ay, from this window.   Denmark lies there, to the south.

ELINA.   And is it far from here?   More than a hundred miles?

NILS LYKKE.   **Much more.**   The sea lies between you and Denmark.

ELINA (*to herself*).   The sea?   Thought has seagull's wings.   The sea cannot stay it.

(*Goes out to the left.*)

NILS LYKKE (*looks after her awhile; then says:*) If I could but spare two days now—or even one—I would have her in my power, even as the others. And yet is there rare stuff in this maiden.   She is proud.   Might I not after all——?   No; rather humble her—— ——

(*Paces the room.*)

Verily, I believe she has set my blood on fire.   Who would have thought it possible after all these years? —Enough of this!   I must **get** out of the tangle I am entwined in here.

(*Sits in a chair on the right.*)

What is the meaning of it?   Both Olaf Skaktavl and Inger Gyldenlöve seem blind to the mistrust 'twill waken, when 'tis rumoured that I am in their league. —Or can Lady Inger have seen through my purpose?   Can she have seen that all **my** promises were but designed to lure Nils Sture forth from his hiding-place?

(*Springs up.*)

Damnation! Is it I that have been fooled? 'Tis like enough that Count Sture is not at Östråt at all? It may be the rumour of his flight was but a feint. He may be safe and sound among his friends in Sweden, while I——

(*Walks restlessly up and down.*)

And to think I was so sure of success! If I should effect nothing? If Lady Inger should penetrate all my designs—and publish my discomfiture—— To be a laughing-stock both here and in Denmark! To have sought to lure Lady Inger into a trap—and given her cause the help it most needed—strengthened her in the people's favour——! Ah, I could well-nigh sell myself to the Evil One, would he but help me to lay hands on Count Sture.

(*The window in the background is pushed open.* NILS STENSSON *is seen outside.*)

NILS LYKKE (*clutches at his sword*). What now?

NILS STENSSON (*jumps down on to the floor*). Ah; here I am at last then!

NILS LYKKE (*aside*). What means this?

NILS STENSSON. God's peace, master!

NILS LYKKE. Thanks, good Sir! Methinks you have chosen a strange mode of entrance.

NILS STENSSON. Ay, what the devil was I to do? The gate was shut. Folk must sleep in this house like bears at Yuletide.

NILS LYKKE. God be thanked! Know you not that a good conscience is the best pillow?

NILS STENSSON. Ay, it must be even so; for all my rattling and thundering, I——

NILS LYKKE. ——You won not in?

NILS STENSSON. You have hit it. So I said to myself: As you are bidden to be in Östrât to-night, if you have to go through fire and water, you may surely make free to creep through a window.

NILS LYKKE (*aside*). Ah, if it should be——!

(*Moves a step or two nearer.*)
Was it, then, of the last necessity that you should reach Östrât to-night?

NILS STENSSON. Was it? Ay, faith but it was. I love not to keep folk waiting, I can tell you.

NILS LYKKE. Aha,—then Lady Inger Gyldenlöve looks for your coming?

NILS STENSSON. Lady Inger Gyldenlöve? Nay, that I can scarce say for certain; (*with a sly smile*) but there might be some one else——

NILS LYKKE (*smiles in answer*). Ah, so there might be some one else?

NILS STENSSON. Tell me—are you of the house?

NILS LYKKE. I? Well, in so far that I am Lady Inger's guest this evening.

NILS STENSSON. A guest?—Is not to-night the third night after Martinmas?

NILS LYKKE. The third night after——? Ay, right enough.—Would you seek the lady of the house at once? I think she is not yet gone to rest. But might you not sit down and rest awhile, dear young Sir? See, here is yet a flagon of wine remaining, and doubtless you will find some food. Come, fall to; you will do wisely to refresh your strength.

NILS STENSSON. You are right, Sir; 'twere not amiss.

(*Sits down by the table and eats and drinks.*)
Both roast meat and sweet cakes! Why, you live like lords here! When one has slept, as I have, on the naked ground, and lived on bread and water for four or five days——

Nils Lykke (*looks at him with a smile*). Ay, such a life must be hard for one that is wont to sit at the high-table in noble halls——

Nils Stensson. Noble halls——?

Nils Lykke. But now can you take your rest at Östråt, as long as it likes you.

Nils Stensson (*pleased*). Ay? Can I truly? Then I am not to begone again so soon?

Nils Lykke. Nay, that I know not. Sure you yourself can best say that.

Nils Stensson (*softly*). Oh, the devil! (*Stretches himself in the chair.*) Well, you see—'tis not yet certain. I, for my part, were nothing loath to stay quiet here awhile ; but——

Nils Lykke. ——But you are not in all points your own master? There be other duties and other circumstances——?

Nils Stensson. Ay, that is just the rub. Were I to choose, I would rest me at Östråt at least the winter through; I have seldom led aught but a soldier's life——

> (*Interrupts himself suddenly, fills a goblet, and drinks.*)

Your health, Sir !

Nils Lykke. A soldier's life? Hm !

Nils Stensson. Nay, what I would have said is this: I have long been eager to see Lady Inger

Gyldenlöve, whose fame has spread so wide. She must be a queenly woman,—is't not so?—The one thing I like not in her, is that she shrinks so cursedly from open action.

NILS LYKKE. From open action?

NILS STENSSON. Ay ay, you understand me; I mean she is so loath to take a hand in driving the foreign rulers out of the land.

NILS LYKKE. Ay, you are right. But if you do your best now, you will doubtless work her to your will.

NILS STENSSON. I? God knows it would but little serve if *I*——

NILS LYKKE. Yet 'tis strange you should seek her here if you have so little hope.

NILS STENSSON. What mean you?—Tell me, know you Lady Inger?

NILS LYKKE. Surely; I am her guest, and——

NILS STENSSON. Ay, but it does not at all follow that you know her. I too am her guest, yet have I never seen so much as her shadow.

NILS LYKKE. Yet did you speak of her——

NILS STENSSON. ——As all folk speak. Why should I not? And besides, I have often enough heard from Peter Kanzler——

(*Stops in confusion, and begins eating again.*)

NILS LYKKE. You would have said——?

NILS STENSSON (*eating*). I? Nay, 'tis all one.

(NILS LYKKE *laughs.*)

NILS STENSSON. Why laugh you, Sir?

NILS LYKKE. 'Tis nought, Sir!

Nils Stensson (*drinks*). A pretty vintage ye have in this house.

Nils Lykke (*approaches him confidentially.*) Listen — were it not time now to throw off the mask?

Nils Stensson (*smiling*). The mask? Why, do as seems best to you.

Nils Lykke. Then off with all disguise. You are known, Count Sture!

Nils Stensson (*with a laugh*). Count Sture? Do you too take me for Count Sture?

(*Rises from the table.*)
You mistake, Sir; I am not Count Sture.

Nils Lykke. You are not? Then who are you?

Nils Stensson. My name is Nils Stensson.

Nils Lykke (*looks at him with a smile*). Hm! Nils Stensson? But you are not Sten Sture's son Nils? The name chimes at least.

Nils Stensson. True enough; but God knows what right I have to bear it. My father I never knew; my mother was a poor peasant-woman, that was robbed and murdered in one of the old feuds. Peter Kanzler chanced to be on the spot; he took me into his care, brought me up, and taught me the trade of arms. As you know, King Gustav has been hunting him this many a year; and I have followed him faithfully, wherever he went.

Nils Lykke. Peter Kanzler has taught you more than the trade of arms, meseems—— —— Well, well; then you are not Nils Sture. But at least you come from Sweden. Peter Kanzler has sent you here to find a stranger, who——

NILS STENSSON (*nods cunningly*). ——Who is found already.

NILS LYKKE (*somewhat uncertain*). And whom you do not know?

NILS STENSSON. As little as you know me; for I swear **to you by** God himself: I am not Count Sture!

NILS LYKKE. In sober earnest, Sir?

NILS STENSSON. **As** truly as I live! Wherefore should I deny it, if I were?

NILS LYKKE. Then where is Count Sture?

NILS **STENSSON** (*in a low voice*). Ay, *that* is just **the** secret.

NILS LYKKE (*whispers*). Which is known **to you, is it not**?

NILS STENSSON (*nods*). **And** which I have **to tell to you.**

NILS **LYKKE.** To me? Well then,—where is he?
    (NILS STENSSON *points upwards.*)

NILS LYKKE. Up there? Lady Inger holds him hidden in the loft-room?

NILS STENSSON. **Nay, nay;** you mistake me.
    (*Looks round cautiously.*)
Nils Sture is in Heaven!

NILS LYKKE. Dead? **And** where?

NILS STENSSON. **In his** mother's castle,—three weeks since.

NILS LYKKE. **Ah,** you are deceiving me! 'Tis but five or **six** days since he crossed the frontier into Norway.

NILS STENSSON. Oh, that was I.

NILS LYKKE. But just before that the Count had

appeared in the Dales. The people were restless already, and on his coming they broke out openly and would have chosen him for king.

NILS STENSSON.   Ha-ha-ha ; that was me too !

NILS LYKKE.   You ?

NILS STENSSON.   I will tell you how it came about.   One day Peter Kanzler called me to him and gave me to know that great things were preparing. He bade me set out for Norway and go to Östråt, where I must be on a certain fixed day——

NILS LYKKE (*nods*).   The third night after Martinmas.

NILS STENSSON.   I was to meet a stranger there——

NILS LYKKE.   Ay, right; I am he.

NILS STENSSON.   He was to tell me what more I had to do.   Moreover, I was to let him know that the Count was dead of a sudden, but that as yet 'twas known to no one save to his mother the Countess, together with Peter Kanzler and a few old servants of the Stures.

NILS LYKKE.   I understand.   The Count was the peasants' rallying-point.   Were the tidings of his death to spread, they would fall asunder,—and the whole project would come to nought.

NILS STENSSON.   Ay, maybe so ;   I know little of such matters.

NILS LYKKE.   But how came you to give yourself out for the Count ?

NILS STENSSON.   How came I to——?   Nay, what know I ?   Many's the mad prank I've hit on in my day.   And yet 'twas not I hit on it neither ;

wherever I appeared in the Dales, the people crowded round me and greeted me as Count Sture. Deny it as I pleased, 'twas wasted breath. **The** Count had been there two years before, they said—and the veriest child knew me again. Well, be it so, thought I ; **never** again will you be a Count in this life ; why not try what 'tis like for once ?

NILS LYKKE. Well,—and what did you more ?

NILS STENSSON. I ? I ate and drank and took my ease. Pity 'twas that I must away again so soon. But when I **set** forth across the frontier—ha-ha-ha—I promised them I would soon be **back** with three or four thousand men—I know not **how many** I said— and then we would lay on in earnest.

NILS LYKKE. And you did **not** bethink you that you were acting rashly ?

NILS STENSSON. Ay, afterwards ; but then, to **be** sure, 'twas too late.

NILS LYKKE. It grieves me for you, my young friend ; but you will soon **come to** feel the effects of your folly. Let **me tell** you that you are pursued. A troop of Swedish men-at-arms is out after you.

NILS STENSSON. **After me ?** Ha-ha-ha. Nay, that is rare ! And when they come and think they have Count Sture in their clutches—ha-ha-ha !

NILS LYKKE (*gravely*). ——Then farewell to your life.

NILS STENSSON. My——? But I am not Count Sture.

NILS LYKKE. You have called the people to arms. You have given seditious promises, and raised troubles in the land.

Nils Stensson.   Ay, but 'twas only in jest!

Nils Lykke.   King Gustav will scarce look on the matter in that light.

Nils Stensson.   Truly, there is something in what you say. To think I could be such a mad-man—— —— Well well, I'm not a dead man yet! You will protect me ; and besides—the men-at-arms can scarce be at my heels.

Nils Lykke.   But what else have you to tell me?

Nils Stensson.   I?   Nothing.   When once I have given you the packet——

Nils Lykke (*unguardedly*).   The packet?

Nils Stensson.   Ay, sure you know——

Nils Lykke.   Ah, right, right ; the papers from Peter Kanzler——

Nils Stensson.   See, here they all are.

> (*Takes out a packet from inside his doublet, and
> hands it to* Nils Lykke.)

Nils Lykke (*aside*).   Letters and papers for Olaf Skaktavl.

> (*To* Nils Stensson.)

The packet is open, I see. 'Tis like you know what it contains?

Nils Stensson.   No, good sir ; I am ill at read-ing writing ; and for reason good.

Nils Lykke.   I understand ; you have given most care to the trade of arms.

> (*Sits down by the table on the right, and runs
> through the papers.*)

Aha !   Here is light enough and to spare on what is brewing.

This small letter tied with a silken thread——

(*Examines the address.*) **This too** for Olaf Skaktavl.
(*Opens the letter, and glances through its contents.*)
From Peter Kanzler. I thought as much. (*Reads
under his breath.*) "I am hard bested, for——"; ay,
sure enough; here it stands,—"Young Count Sture
has been gathered to his fathers, even at the time
fixed for the revolt to break forth"— "—but all may
yet be made good——" What now? (*Reads on in
astonishment.*) "You must know, then, Olaf Skaktavl,
that the young man who brings you this letter is a
son of——" Heaven and earth—can it be so?—Ay,
by Christ's blood, even so 'tis written! (*Glances at
NILS STENSSON.*) Can he be——? Ah, if it were
so! (*Reads on.*) "I have nurtured him since he was
a year old; but up to this day I have ever refused to
give him back, trusting to have in him a sure hostage
for Inger Gyldenlöve's faithfulness to us and to our
friends. Yet in that respect he has been of but little
service to us. You may marvel that I told you not
this secret when you were with me here of late;
therefore will I confess freely that I feared you might
seize upon him, even as I had done. But now,
when you have seen Lady Inger, and have doubtless
assured yourself how loath she is to have a hand in our
undertaking, you will see that 'tis wisest to give her
back her own as soon as may be. Well might it
come to pass that in her joy and security and thank-
fulness—" —— "—that is now our last hope."

(*Sits for awhile as though struck dumb with sur-
prise; then exclaims in a low voice:*)
Aha,—what a letter! Gold would not buy it!
NILS STENSSON. 'Tis plain I have brought you

weighty tidings.   Ay, ay,—Peter Kanzler has many
irons in the fire, folk say.

NILS LYKKE (*to himself*).   What to do with all
this?   A thousand paths are open to me—— Suppose I——?   No, 'twere to risk too much.   But if—
ah, if I——?   I will venture it!

> (*Tears the letter across, crumples up the pieces, and
> hides them inside his doublet; puts back the
> other papers into the packet, which he sticks
> inside his belt; rises and says:*)

A word, my young friend!

NILS STENSSON.   Well—your looks say that the
game goes bravely.

NILS LYKKE.   Ay, by my soul it does.   You
have given me a hand of nought but court cards,—
queens and knaves and——

NILS STENSSON.   But what of me, that have
brought all these good tidings?   Have I nought
more to do?

NILS LYKKE.   You?   Ay, that have you.   You
belong to the game.   You are a king—and king of
trumps too.

NILS STENSSON.   I a king?   Oh, now I understand;
you are thinking of my exaltation——

NILS LYKKE.   Your exaltation?

NILS STENSSON.   Ay; that which you foretold for
me, if King Gustav's men got me in their clutches——

> (*Makes a motion to indicate hanging.*)

NILS LYKKE.   True enough;—but let that trouble
you no more.   It now lies with yourself alone whether
within a month you shall have the hempen noose or a
chain of gold about your neck.

NILS STENSSON. A chain of gold? And it lies with me?

(NILS LYKKE *nods.*)

NILS STENSSON. Why then, the devil take musing! Do you tell me what I am to do.

NILS LYKKE I will. But first you must swear me a solemn oath that no living creature in the wide world shall know what I am to tell you.

NILS STENSSON. Is that all? You shall have ten oaths, if you will.

NILS LYKKE. Not so lightly, young Sir! It is no jesting matter.

NILS STENSSON. Well well ; I am grave enough.

NILS LYKKE. In the Dales you called yourself a Count's son ;—is't not so?

NILS STENSSON. Nay—begin you now on that again? Have I not made free confession——

NILS LYKKE. You mistake me. What you said in the Dales was the truth.

NILS STENSSON. The truth? What mean you by that? Tell me but——!

NILS LYKKE. First your oath! The holiest, the most inviolable you can swear.

NILS STENSSON. That you shall have. Yonder on the wall hangs the picture of the Holy Virgin——

NILS LYKKE. The Holy Virgin has grown impotent of late. Know you not what the monk of Wittenberg maintains?

NILS STENSSON. Fie! how can you heed the monk of Wittenberg? Peter Kanzler says he is a heretic.

NILS LYKKE. Nay, let us not wrangle concerning

him.   Here can I show you a saint will serve full well to make oath to.

(Points to a picture hanging on one of the panels.) Come hither,—swear that you will be silent till I myself release your tongue—silent, as you hope for Heaven's salvation for yourself and for the man whose picture hangs there.

NILS STENSSON *(approaching the picture).*   I swear it—so help me God's holy word!

(Falls back a step in amazement.) But—Christ save me——!

NILS LYKKE.   What now?

NILS STENSSON.   The picture——!   Sure 'tis myself!

NILS LYKKE.   'Tis old Sten Sture, even as he lived and moved in his youthful years.

NILS STENSSON.   Sten Sture!—And the like-ness——?   And—said you not I spoke the truth, when I called myself a Count's son?   Was't not so?

NILS LYKKE.   So it was.

NILS STENSSON.   Ah, I have it, I have it!   I am——

NILS LYKKE.   You are Sten Sture's son, good Sir.

NILS STENSSON *(with the quiet of amazement).*   *I* Sten Sture's son!

NILS LYKKE.   On the mother's side too your blood is noble.   Peter Kanzler spoke not the truth, if he said that a poor peasant woman was your mother.

NILS STENSSON.   Oh strange, oh marvellous!— But can I believe——?

NILS LYKKE. You may believe all I tell you. But remember, all this will be merely your ruin, if you should forget what you swore to me by your father's salvation.

NILS STENSSON.   Forget it?   Nay, that you may be sure I never shall.—But you to whom I have given my word,—tell me—who are you?

NILS LYKKE.   My name is Nils Lykke.

NILS STENSSON (*surprised*).   Nils Lykke?   Surely not the Danish Councillor?

NILS LYKKE.   Even so.

NILS STENSSON.   And it was you——?   'Tis strange.   How come you——?

NILS LYKKE.   ——To be receiving missives from Peter Kanzler?   You marvel at that?

NILS STENSSON.   I cannot deny it.   He has ever named you as our bitterest foe——

NILS LYKKE.   And therefore you mistrust me?

NILS STENSSON.   Nay, not wholly that; but—well, the devil take musing!

NILS LYKKE.   Well said.   Go but your own way, and you are as sure of the halter as you are of a Count's title and a chain of gold if you trust to me.

NILS STENSSON.   That will I.   My hand upon it, dear Sir!   Do you but help me with good counsel as long as there is need; when counsel gives place to blows I shall look to myself.

NILS LYKKE.   It is well.   Come with me now into yonder chamber, and I will tell you how all these matters stand, and what you have still to do.

(*Goes out to the right.*)

NILS STENSSON (*with a glance at the picture*).   I Sten Sture's son!   Oh, marvellous as a dream—!

(*Goes out after* NILS LYKKE.)

Act Fourth.

(The Banquet Hall, as before, but without the supper-table.)
*(*BIÖRN, *the major-domo, enters carrying a lighted branch-
candlestick, and lighting in* LADY INGER *and* OLAF SKAKTAVL
by the second door on the left. LADY INGER *has a bundle of
papers in her hand.)*

LADY INGER (*to* BIÖRN). And you are sure my
daughter spoke with the knight, here in the hall?

BIÖRN (*putting down the branch-candlestick on the
table on the left*). Sure as may be. I met her even
as she stepped into the passage.

LADY INGER. And she seemed greatly moved?
Said you not so?

BIÖRN. She looked all pale and disturbed. I
asked if she were sick; she answered not, but said:
" Go to my mother and tell her the knight sets forth
from here ere daybreak; if she have letters or mes-
sages for him, beg her not to delay him needlessly."
And then she added somewhat that I heard not
rightly.

LADY INGER. Did you not hear it at all?

BIÖRN. It sounded to me as though she said:—
" I almost fear he has already stayed too long at
Östrât."

LADY INGER. And the knight? Where is he?

BIÖRN. In his chamber belike, in the gate-wing.

LADY INGER. It is well. What I have to send by him is ready. Go to him and say I await him here in the hall.

(BIÖRN *goes out to the right.*)

OLAF SKAKTAVL. Know you, Lady Inger,—'tis true that in such things I am blind as a mole; yet seems it to me as though—hm!

LADY INGER. Well?

OLAF SKAKTAVL. ——As though Nils Lykke loved your daughter.

LADY INGER. Then it seems you are not so blind after all; I am the more deceived if you be not right. Marked you not at supper how eagerly he listened to the least word I let fall concerning Elina?

OLAF SKAKTAVL. He forgot both food and drink.

LADY INGER. And our secret business as well.

OLAF SKAKTAVL. Ay, and what is more—the papers from Peter Kanzler.

LADY INGER. And from all this you conclude ——?

OLAF SKAKTAVL. From all this I chiefly conclude that, as you know Nils Lykke and the name he bears, especially as concerns women——

LADY INGER. ——I should be right glad to know him outside my gates?

OLAF SKAKTAVL. Ay; and that as soon as may be.

LADY INGER (*smiling*). Nay—the case is just the contrary, Olaf Skaktavl!

OLAF SKAKTAVL. How mean you?

LADY INGER. If things be as we both think, Nils Lykke must in nowise depart from Östrät yet awhile.

OLAF SKAKTAVL (*looks at her with disapproval*). Are you beginning on crooked courses again, Lady Inger? What scheme have you now in your mind? Something that may increase your own power at the cost of our——

LADY INGER. Oh this blindness, that makes you all unjust to me! I see well you think I purpose to make Nils Lykke my daughter's husband. Were such a thought in my mind, why had I refused to take part in what is afoot in Sweden, when Nils Lykke and all the Danish crew seem willing to support it?

OLAF SKAKTAVL. Then if it be not your wish to win him and bind him to you—what would you with him?

LADY INGER. I will tell you in few words. In a letter to me, Nils Lykke has spoken of the high fortune it were to be allied to our house; and I do not say but, for a moment, I let myself think of the matter.

OLAF SKAKTAVL. Ay, see you!

LADY INGER. To wed Nils Lykke to one of my house were doubtless a great step toward reconciling many jarring forces in our land.

OLAF SKAKTAVL. Meseems your daughter Merete's marriage with Vinzents Lunge might have taught you the cost of such a step as this. Scarce had my lord gained a firm footing in our midst, when he began to make free with both our goods and our rights——

LADY INGER. I know it even too well, Olaf Skaktavl! But times there be when my thoughts are manifold and strange. I cannot impart them fully either to you or to any one else. Often I know not what were best for me. And yet—a second time to choose a Danish lord for a son-in-law,—nought but the uttermost need could drive me to that resource; and heaven be praised—things have not yet come to that !

OLAF SKAKTAVL. I am no wiser than before, Lady Inger;—why would you keep Nils Lykke at Östråt ?

LADY INGER (*softly*). Because I owe him an undying hate. Nils Lykke has done me deadlier wrong than any other man. I cannot tell you where-in it lies; but I shall never rest till I am avenged on him. See you not now ? Say that Nils Lykke were to love my daughter—as meseems were like enough. I will persuade him to remain here; he shall learn to know Elina well. She is both fair and wise.—Ah, if he should one day come before me, with hot love in his heart, to beg for her hand ! Then—to chase him away like a hound; to drive him off with jibes and scorn; to make it known over all the land that Nils Lykke had come a-wooing to Östråt in vain ! I tell you I would give ten years of my life but to see that day !

OLAF SKAKTAVL. In faith and truth, Inger Gyldenlöve—is this your purpose towards him ?

LADY INGER. This and nought else, as sure as God lives ! Trust me, Olaf Skaktavl, I mean honestly by my countrymen; but I am in no way my own master. Things there be that must be kept hidden, or 'twere my death-blow. But let me once be safe on *that* side, and you shall see if I have forgotten the oath I swore by Knut Alfson's corpse.

Olaf Skaktavl (*shakes her by the hand*). Thanks for those words! I am loath indeed to think evil of you.—Yet, touching your design towards this knight, methinks 'tis a dangerous game you would play. What if you had misreckoned? What if your daughter——? 'Tis said no woman can stand against this subtle devil.

Lady Inger. My daughter? Think you that she——? Nay, have no fear of that; I know Elina better. All she has heard of his renown has but made her hate him the more. You saw with your own eyes——

Olaf Skaktavl. Ay, but—a woman's mind is shifting ground to build on. 'Twere best you looked well before you.

Lady Inger. That will I, be sure; I will watch them narrowly. But even were he to succeed in luring her into his toils, I have but to whisper two words in her ear, and——

Olaf Skaktavl. What then?

Lady Inger. ——She will shrink from him as though he were sent by the foul Tempter himself. Hist, Olaf Skaktavl! Here he comes. Now be cautious.

(Nils Lykke *enters by the foremost door on the right.*)

Nils Lykke (*approaches* Lady Inger *courteously*). My noble hostess has summoned me.

Lady Inger. I have learned through my daughter that you are minded to leave us to-night.

NILS LYKKE.   Even so, to my sorrow;—since my business at Östråt is over.

OLAF SKAKTAVL.   Not before I have the papers.

NILS LYKKE.   True, true.   I had well-nigh forgotten the weightiest part of my errand.   'Twas the fault of our noble hostess.   With such pleasant skill did she keep her guests in talk at table——

LADY INGER.   That you no longer remembered what had brought you hither?   I rejoice to hear it; for that was my design.   Methought that if my guest, Nils Lykke, were to feel at ease in Östråt, he must forget——

NILS LYKKE.   What, lady?

LADY INGER.   ——First of all his errand—and then all that had gone before it.

NILS LYKKE (*to* OLAF SKAKTAVL, *while he takes out the packet and hands it to him*).   The papers from Peter Kanzler.   You will find in them a full account of our partizans in Sweden.

OLAF SKAKTAVL.   It is well.

(*Sits down by the table on the left, where he opens the packet and examines its contents.*)

NILS LYKKE.   And now, Lady Inger Gyldenlöve, —I know not that aught remains to keep me here.

LADY INGER.   Were it things of state alone that had brought us together, you might be right.   But I should be loath to think so.

NILS LYKKE.   You would say——?

LADY INGER.   I would say that 'twas not alone as a Danish Councillor or as the ally of Peter Kanzler that Nils Lykke came to be my guest.—Do I err in fancying that somewhat you may have heard down in

Denmark may have made you desirous of closer acquaintance with the Lady of Östråt.

Nils Lykke.   Far be it from me to deny——

Olaf   Skaktavl   (*turning over the papers*). Strange.   No letter.

Nils Lykke.   ——Lady Inger Gyldenlöve's fame is all too widely spread that I should not long have been eager to see her face to face.

Lady Inger.   So I thought.   But what, then, is an hour's jesting talk at the supper-table?   Let us try to sweep away all that has separated us till now; it may well happen that the Nils Lykke I know may wipe out the grudge I bore the one I knew not. Prolong your stay here but a few days, Sir Councillor! I dare not persuade Olaf Skaktavl thereto, since his secret charge in Sweden calls him hence.   But as for you, doubtless your sagacity has placed all things beforehand in such train, that your presence can scarce be needed.   Trust me, your time shall not pass tediously with us ; at least you will find me and my daughter heartily desirous to do all we may to pleasure you.

Nils Lykke.   I doubt neither your goodwill toward me nor your daughter's ; of that I have had full proof.   And you will doubtless allow that the necessity which calls for my presence elsewhere must be most vital, since, despite your kindness, I must declare my longer stay at Östråt impossible.

Lady Inger.   Is it even so!—Know you, Sir Councillor, were I evilly disposed, I might fancy you had come to Östråt to try a fall with me, and that, having lost, you like not to linger on the battlefield among the witnesses of your defeat.

NILS LYKKE (*smiling*).   There might be some show of reason for such a reading of the case ; but sure it is that as yet *I* hold not the battle lost.

LADY INGER.   Be that as it may, it might at any rate be retrieved, if you would tarry some days with us. You see yourself, I am still doubting and wavering at the parting of the ways,—persuading my redoubtable assailant not to quit the field.—Well, to speak plainly, the thing is this : your alliance with the disaffected in Sweden still seems to me somewhat —ay, what shall I call it ?—somewhat miraculous, Sir Councillor !   I tell you this frankly, dear Sir !   The thought that has moved the King's Council to this secret step is in truth most politic ; but it is strangely at variance with the deeds of certain of your countrymen in bygone years.   Be not offended, then, if my trust in your fair promises needs to be some- what strengthened ere I can place my whole welfare in your hands.

NILS LYKKE.   A longer stay at Östråt would scarce help towards that end ; since I purpose not to make any further effort to shake your resolution.

LADY INGER.   Then must I pity you from my heart.   Ay, Sir Councillor—'tis true I stand here an unfriended widow ; yet may you trust my word when I prophesy that this visit to Östråt will strew your future path with thorns.

NILS LYKKE (*with a smile*).   Is that your prophecy, Lady Inger ?

LADY INGER.   Truly it is !   What can one say

dear Sir? 'Tis a calumnious age. Many a scurril knave will make scornful rhymes concerning you. Ere half a year is out, you will be all men's fable; people will stop and gaze after you on the high roads; 'twill be: "Look, look; there rides Sir Nils Lykke, that fared north to Östråt to trap Inger Gyldenlöve, and was caught in his own nets."—Nay nay, why so impatient, Sir Knight! 'Tis not that *I* think so; I do but forecast the thoughts of the malicious and evil-minded; and of them, alas! there are many.—Ay, 'tis shame; but so it is—you will reap nought but mockery—mockery, because a woman was craftier than you. "Like a cunning fox," men will say, "he crept into Östråt; like a beaten hound he slunk away."—And one thing more: think you not that Peter Kanzler and his friends will forswear your alliance, when 'tis known that I venture not to fight under a standard borne by you?

NILS LYKKE. You speak wisely, lady! And so, to save myself from mockery—and further, to avoid breaking with all our dear friends in Sweden—I must needs——

LADY INGER (*hastily*). ——prolong your stay at Östråt?

OLAF SKAKTAVL (*who has been listening*). He is in the trap!

NILS LYKKE. No, my noble lady;—I must needs bring you to terms within this hour.

LADY INGER. But what if you should fail?

NILS LYKKE. I shall *not* fail.

LADY INGER. You lack not confidence, it seems.

NILS LYKKE. What shall we wager that you

make not common cause with myself **and** Peter Kanzler?

LADY INGER.   Östråt Castle against your knee-buckles!

NILS LYKKE (*points to himself and cries:*) Olaf Skaktavl—here stands the master of Östråt!

LADY INGER.   **Sir** Councillor——!

OLAF **SKAKTAVL** (**rises** *from the table*).   What now?

NILS LYKKE (*to* LADY INGER).   I accept not the wager; for **in a** moment **you** will gladly give Östråt **Castle, and more to boot, to** be freed from the snare wherein **not I** but you are tangled.

LADY INGER.   Your jest, Sir, grows a vastly merry one.

NILS LYKKE.   'Twill be merrier yet—at least for me.   **You** boast that you have overreached me.   You threaten to heap on **me** all men's scorn and mockery. Ah, beware that you stir **not** up my vengefulness; **for** with two words I can bring you to your knees at my feet.

LADY INGER.   Ha-ha—— ——!
    (*Stops suddenly, as if struck by a foreboding.*)
And the two words, Nils Lykke?—the two words——?

NILS LYKKE.   ——The secret of Sten Sture's son and yours.

LADY INGER (*with a shriek*).   Oh, Jesus Christ——!

OLAF SKAKTAVL.   Inger Gyldenlöve's son!   What say you?

LADY INGER (*half **kneeling** to* NILS LYKKE). Mercy! oh, be merciful——!

Nils Lykke (*raises her up*).   Collect yourself, and let us talk calmly.

Lady Inger (*in a low voice, as though bewildered*). Did your hear it, Olaf Skaktavl? or was it but a dream?   Heard you what he said?

Nils Lykke.   It was no dream, Lady Inger!

Lady Inger.   And you know it!   You,—you!— Where is he then?   Where have you got him?   What would you do with him?   (*Screams.*)   Do not kill him, Nils Lykke!   Give him back to me!   Do not kill my child!

Olaf Skaktavl.   Ah, I begin to understand—— .

Lady Inger.   And this fear——this torturing dread!   Through all these years it has been ever with me—— ——and then all fails at last, and I must bear this agony!—Oh Lord my God, is it right of thee? Was it for this thou gavest him to me?

(*Controls herself and says with forced composure:*) Nils Lykke—tell me *one* thing.   Where have you got him?   Where is he?

Nils Lykke.   With his foster-father.

Lady Inger.   Stiii with his foster-father.   Oh, that merciless man——!   For ever to deny my prayers.—But it *must* not go on thus!   Help me, Olaf Skaktavl!

Olaf Skaktavl.   I?

Nils Lykke.   There will be no need, if only you——

Lady Inger.   Hearken, Sir Councillor!   What you know you shall know thoroughly.   And you too, my old and faithful friend——!

Listen then.   To-night you bade me call to mind

that fatal day when Knut Alfson was slain at Oslo. You bade me remember the promise I made as I stood by his corpse amid the bravest men in Norway. I was scarce full-grown then; but I felt God's strength in me, and methought, as many have thought since, that the Lord himself had set his mark on me and chosen me to fight in the forefront for my country's cause.

Was it vanity? Or was it a calling from on high? That I have never clearly known. But woe to him that has a great mission laid upon him.

For seven years I fear not to say that I kept my promise faithfully. I stood by my countrymen in all their miseries. All my playmates were now wives and mothers. I alone could give ear to no wooer— not to one. That you know best, Olaf Skaktavl!

Then I saw Sten Sture for the first time. Fairer man had never met my sight.

NILS LYKKE. Ah, now it grows clear to me! Sten Sture was then in Norway on a secret errand. We Danes were not to know that he wished your friends well.

LADY INGER. Disguised as a mean serving-man he lived a whole winter under one roof with me.

That winter I thought less and less of the country's weal—— ——. So fair a man had I never seen, and I had lived well-nigh five-and-twenty years.

Next autumn Sten Sture came once more; and when he departed again he took with him, in all secrecy, a little child. 'Twas not folk's evil tongues I feared; but our cause would have suffered had it got about that Sten Sture stood so near to me.

The child was given to Peter Kanzler to rear. I waited for better times, that were soon to come. They never came. Sten Sture took a wife two years later in Sweden, and, dying, left a widow——

OLAF SKAKTAVL. ——And with her a lawful heir to his name and rights.

LADY INGER. Time after time I wrote to Peter Kanzler and besought him to give me back my child. But he was ever deaf to my prayers. "Cast in your lot with us once for all," he said, "and I send your son back to Norway ; not before." But 'twas even that I dared not do. We of the dis-affected party were then ill regarded by many timorous folk. If these had got tidings of how things stood—oh, I know it !—to cripple the mother they had gladly meted to the child the fate that would have been King Christiern's had he not saved himself by flight.[1]

But, besides that, the Danes were active. They spared neither threats nor promises to force me to join them.

OLAF SKAKTAVL. 'Twas but reason. The eyes of all men were fixed on you as the vane that should show them how to shape their course.

LADY INGER. Then came Herlof Hyttefad's revolt. Do you remember that time, Olaf Skaktavl?

---

[1] King Christian II. of Denmark (the perpetrator of the massacre at Stockholm known as the Blood-Bath) fled to Holland in 1523, five years before the date assigned to this play, in order to escape death or imprisonment at the hands of his rebellious nobles, who summoned his uncle, Frederick I., to the throne. Returning to Denmark in 1532, Christian was thrown into prison, where he spent the last twenty-seven years of his life.

Was it not as though the whole land was filled with the sunlight of a new spring.   Mighty voices summoned me to come forth ;—yet I dared not.   I stood doubting—far from the strife—in my lonely castle. At times it seemed as though the Lord God himself were calling me ; but then would come the killing dread again to paralyse my will.   " Who will win ? " that was the question that was ever ringing in my ears.

'Twas but a short spring that had come to Norway. Herlof Hyttefad, and many more with him, were broken on the wheel during the months that followed. None could call me to account ; yet there lacked not covert threats from Denmark.   What if they knew the secret?   At last methought they must know ; I knew not how else to understand their words.

'Twas even in that time of agony that Gyldenlöve, the High Steward, came hither and sought me in marriage.   Let any mother that has feared for her child think herself in my place !—A month after, I was the High Steward's wife—and homeless in the hearts of my countrymen.

Then came the quiet years.   There was now no whisper of revolt.   Our masters might grind us down even as heavily as they listed.   There were times when I loathed myself.   What had I to do? Nought but to endure terror and scorn and bring forth daughters into the world.   My daughters !   God forgive me if I have had no mother's heart towards them.   My wifely duties were as serfdom to me ; how then could I love my daughters ?   Oh, how different with my son !   *He* was the child of my very soul. He was the one thing that brought to mind the time when I was a woman and nought but a woman. —And him they had taken from me! He was growing up among strangers, who might sow in him the seed of destruction! Olaf Skaktavl—had I wandered like you on the lonely hills, hunted and forsaken, in winter and storm—if I had but held my child in my arms,—trust me, I had not sorrowed and wept so sore as I have sorrowed and wept for him from his birth even to this hour.

OLAF SKAKTAVL. There is my hand. I have judged you too hardly, Lady Inger! Command me even as before ; I will obey.—Ay, by all the saints, I know what it is to sorrow for a child.

LADY INGER. Yours was slain by bloody men. But what is death to the restless terror of all these long years?

NILS LYKKE. Mark, then—'tis in your power to end this terror. You have but to reconcile the opposing parties, and neither will think of seizing on your child as a pledge of your faith.

LADY INGER (*to herself*). This is the vengeance of Heaven. (*Looks at him.*) In one word, what do you demand ?

NILS LYKKE. I demand first that you shall call the people of the northern districts to arms, in support of the disaffected in Sweden.

LADY INGER. And next——?

NILS LYKKE. ——that you do your best to advance young Count Sture's ancestral claim to the throne of Sweden.

LADY INGER. His ? You demand that I——?

OLAF SKAKTAVL (*softly*).   It is the wish of many Swedes, and 'twould serve our turn too.

NILS LYKKE.   You hesitate, lady?   You tremble for your son's safety.   What better can you wish than to see his half-brother on the throne?

LADY INGER (*in thought*).   True—true——

NILS LYKKE (*looks at her sharply*).   Unless there be other plans afoot——

LADY INGER.   What mean you?

NILS LYKKE.   Inger Gyldenlöve might have a mind to be—a king's mother.

LADY INGER.   No, no!   Give me back my child, and let who will have the crowns.

But know you so surely that Count Sture is willing——?

NILS LYKKE.   Of that he will himself assure you.

LADY INGER.   Himself?

NILS LYKKE.   Even now.

OLAF SKAKTAVL.   How now?

LADY INGER.   What say you?

NILS LYKKE.   In one word, Count Sture is in Östråt.

OLAF SKAKTAVL.   Here?

NILS LYKKE (*to* LADY INGER).   You have doubtless been told that another rode through the gate along with me?   The Count was my attendant.

LADY INGER (*softly*).   I am in his power.   I have no longer any choice.

(*Looks at him and says :*)

'Tis well, Sir Councillor—I will assure you of my support.

NILS LYKKE.   In writing?

Lady Inger.   As you will.
   (*Goes to the table on the left, sits down, and takes
      writing materials from the drawer.*)
Nils Lykke (*aside, standing by the table on the
right*).   At last, then, I win!
   Lady Inger (*after a moment's thought, turns
suddenly in her chair to* Olaf Skaktavl *and
whispers*).   Olaf Skaktavl—I am certain of it now—
Nils Lykke is a traitor!
   Olaf Skaktavl (*softly*).   What?   You think
——?
   Lady Inger.   He has treachery in his heart.
   (*Lays the paper before her and dips the pen in the
      ink.*)
   Olaf Skaktavl.   And yet you would give him a
written promise that may be your ruin?
   Lady Inger.   Hush; leave me to act.   Nay, wait
and listen first——
   (*Talks with him in a whisper.*)
   Nils Lykke (*softly, watching them*).   Ah, take
counsel together as much as ye list!   All danger is
over now.   With her written consent in my pocket, I
can denounce her when I please.   A secret message
to Jens Bielke this very night.—I tell him but the
truth—that the young Count Sture is not at Östrât.
And then to-morrow, when the road is open—to
Trondhiem with my young friend, and thence by ship
to Copenhagen with him as my prisoner.   Once we
have him safe in the castle-tower, we can dictate to
Lady Inger what terms we will.   And I——?   Methinks after this the King will scarce place the French
mission in other hands than mine.

LADY INGER (*still whispering* **to** OLAF SKAK-TAVL). Well, you understand me?

OLAF SKAKTAVL. Ay, fully. **Let** us risk it.

> (*Goes out by the back, to the right.* NILS STENS-SON *comes in by the first door on the right, unseen by* LADY INGER, *who has begun to write.*)

NILS STENSSON (*in a low voice*). Sir Knight,—Sir Knight!

NILS LYKKE (*moves towards him*). Rash boy! What would you here? Said I not you **were to** wait within until I called you?

NILS **STENSSON.** How could I? Now you have told me that Inger Gyldenlöve **is** my mother, I thirst more than ever to see her face to face——

Oh, it is she! How proud and lofty she seems! Even thus did I ever picture her. Fear not, dear Sir, I shall do nought rashly. Since I have learnt this secret, I feel, **as it** were, **older** and wiser. I will no longer **be wild and heedless;** I will be even as other well-born youths.—Tell me,—knows she that I am here? Surely **you** have prepared her?

NILS LYKKE. Ay, sure enough; **but**——

NILS STENSSON. Well?

NILS **LYKKE.** ——She will **not** own you for her son.

NILS STENSSON. **Will not** own me? But she *is* my mother.—Oh, if there **be** no other way—(*takes out a ring which he wears on a cord round his neck*)—show her **this** ring. I have worn it since my earliest childhood; she must surely know its history.

NILS LYKKE. Hide the ring, man! Hide it, I **say**!

You mistake me. Lady Inger doubts not at all that you are her child; but—ay, look about you; look at all this wealth; look at these mighty ancestors and kinsmen whose pictures deck the walls both high and low; look lastly at herself, the haughty dame, used to bear sway as the first noblewoman in the kingdom. Think you it can be to her mind to take a poor ignorant youth by the hand before all men's eyes and say: Behold my son!

NILS STENSSON. Ay, you are right, I am poor and ignorant. I have nought to offer her in return for what I crave. Oh, never have I felt my poverty weigh on me till this hour! But tell me—what think you I should do to win her love? Tell me, dear Sir; sure you must know!

NILS LYKKE. You must win your father's kingdom. But until that may be, look well that you wound not her ears by hinting at kinship or the like. She will bear her as though she believed you to be the real Count Sture, until you have made yourself worthy to be called her son.

NILS STENSSON. Oh, but tell me——!

NILS LYKKE. Hush; hush!

LADY INGER (*rises and hands him a paper*). Sir Knight—here is my promise.

NILS LYKKE. I thank you.

LADY INGER (*notices* NILS STENSSON). Ah,—this young man is——?

NILS LYKKE. Ay, Lady Inger, he is Count Sture.

LADY INGER (*aside, looks at him stealthily*). Feature for feature;—ay, by God,—it is Öten Sture's son!

(*Approaches him and says with cold courtesy.*)

I bid you welcome under my roof, Count! It rests with you whether or not we shall bless this meeting a year hence.

NILS STENSSON. With me? Oh, do but tell me what I must do! Trust me, I have courage and good-will enough——

NILS LYKKE (*listens uneasily*). What is this noise and uproar, Lady Inger? There are people pressing hitherward. What does this mean?

LADY INGER (*in a loud voice*). 'Tis the spirits awaking!

> (OLAF SKAKTAVL, EINAR HUK, BIÖRN, FINN, *and a number of Peasants and Retainers come in from the back, on the right.*)

THE PEASANTS AND RETAINERS. Hail to Lady Inger Gyldenlöve!

LADY INGER (*to* OLAF SKAKTAVL). Have you told them what is in hand?

OLAF SKAKTAVL. I have told them all they need to know.

LADY INGER (*to the Crowd*). Ay, now, my faithful house-folk and peasants, now must ye arm you as best you can and will. What I forbade you to-night you have now my fullest leave to do. And here I present to you the young Count Sture, the coming ruler of Sweden—and Norway too, if God will it so.

THE WHOLE CROWD. Hail to him! Hail to Count Sture!

> (*General excitement. The Peasants and Retainers choose out weapons and put on breastplates and helmets, amid great noise.*)

NILS LYKKE (*softly and uneasily*). The spirits

awaking, she said?   I but feigned to conjure up the
devil of revolt—'twere a cursed spite if he got the
upper hand of us.

LADY INGER (*to* NILS STENSSON).   Here I give
you the first earnest of our service—thirty mounted
men, to follow you as a bodyguard.   Trust me—ere you
reach the frontier many hundreds will have ranged
themselves under my banner and yours.   Go, then,
and God be with you!

NILS STENSSON.   Thanks,—Inger Gyldenlöve!
Thanks—and be sure that you shall never have cause
to shame you for—for Count Sture!   If you see me
again I shall have won my father's kingdom.

NILS LYKKE (*to himself*).   Ay, *if* she see you
again!

OLAF SKAKTAVL.   The horses wait, good fellows!
Are ye ready?

THE PEASANTS.   Ay, ay, ay!

NILS LYKKE (*uneasily, to* LADY INGER).   What?
You mean not to-night, even now——?

LADY INGER.   This very moment, Sir Knight!

NILS LYKKE.   Nay, nay, impossible!

LADY INGER.   I have said it.

NILS LYKKE (*softly, to* NILS STENSSON).   Obey
her not!

NILS STENSSON.   How can I otherwise?   I *will;*
I *must!*

NILS LYKKE.   But 'tis your certain ruin——

NILS STENSSON.   What then!   *Her* must I obey
in all things——

NILS LYKKE (*with authority*).   And *me!*

NILS STENSSON.   I shall keep my word; be sure

of that. The secret shall not **pass** my lips **till** you yourself release me. But she is my mother!

NILS LYKKE (*aside*). And Jens Bielke in wait on the road! Damnation! He will snatch the **prize** out of my fingers——

(*To* LADY INGER.)
Wait till to-morrow!

LADY INGER (*to* NILS STENSSON). Count Sture—do you obey me or not?

NILS STENSSON. **To** horse! (*Goes up towards the background*).

NILS LYKKE (*aside*). Unhappy boy! He knows not what he does.

(*To* LADY INGER.)
Well, since so it must be,—farewell!

(*Bows hastily, and begins to move away.*)

LADY INGER (*detains him*). **Nay, stay!** Not so, Sir Knight,—not so!

NILS LYKKE. What mean you?

LADY INGER (*in a low voice*). Nils Lykke—you are a traitor! Hush! **Let no** one see there is dissension in the camp of the leaders. **You** have won **Peter** Kanzler's trust by some devilish cunning that as yet I see not through. You have forced me to rebellious acts—not to help our cause, but to further your own plots, whatever they may be. I can draw back no more. But think not therefore that you have conquered! I shall contrive to make you harmless——

NILS LYKKE (*lays his hand involuntarily on his sword*). Lady Inger!

LADY INGER. Be calm, Sir Councillor! Your

life is safe.   But you come not outside the gates of Östrât before victory is ours.

Nils Lykke.   Death and destruction!

Lady Inger.   It boots not to resist.   You come not from this place.   So rest you quiet; 'tis your wisest course.

Nils Lykke (*to himself*).   Ah,—I am overreached. She has been craftier than I.   (*A thought strikes him.*) But if I yet—— ?

Lady Inger (*to* Olaf Skaktavl).   Ride with Count Sture's troops to the frontier ; then without pause to Peter Kanzler, and bring me back my child.   Now has he no longer any plea for keeping from me what is my own.

(*Adds, as* Olaf Skaktavl *is going:*)

Wait ; a token.—He that wears Sten Sture's ring is my son.

Olaf Skaktavl.   By all the saints, you shall have him!

Lady Inger.   Thanks, — thanks, my faithful friend !

Nils Lykke (*to* Finn, *whom he has beckoned to him unobserved, and with whom he has been whispering*).   Good—now manage to slip out.   Let none see you.   The Swedes are in ambush two miles hence.   Tell the commander that Count Sture is dead.   The young man you see there must not be touched.   Tell the commander so.   Tell him the boy's life is worth thousands to me.

Finn.   It shall be done.

Lady Inger (*who has meanwhile been watching* Nils Lykke).   And now go, all of you ; go with

God! (*Points to* NILS LYKKE.) This noble knight cannot find it in his heart to leave his friends at Östråt so hastily. He will abide here with me till the tidings of your victory arrive.

NILS LYKKE (*to himself*). Devil!

NILS STENSSON (*seizes his hand*). Trust me—you shall not have long to wait!

NILS LYKKE. It is well; it is well! (*Aside.*) All may yet be saved. If only my message reach Jens Bielke in time——

LADY INGER (*to* EINAR HUK, *the bailiff, pointing to* FINN). And let that man be placed under close guard in the castle dungeon.

FINN. Me?

THE BAILIFF AND THE SERVANTS. Finn!

NILS LYKKE (*aside*). My last anchor gone!

LADY INGER (*imperatively*). To the dungeon with him!

    (EINAR HUK, BIÖRN, *and a couple of the house-servants lead* FINN *out to the left.*)

ALL THE REST (*except* NILS LYKKE, *rushing out to the right*). Away! To horse,—to horse! Hail to Lady Inger Gyldenlöve!

LADY INGER (*passes close to* NILS LYKKE *as she follows the others*). Who wins?

NILS LYKKE (*remains alone*). Who? Ay, woe to you;—your victory will cost you dear. *I* wash my hands of it. 'Tis not *I* that am murdering him.

But my prey is escaping me none the less; and the revolt will grow and spread!—Ah, 'tis a foolhardy, a frantic game I have been playing here!

    (*Listens at the window.*)

There they go clattering out through the gateway.—
Now 'tis closed after them—and I am left here a
prisoner.

No way of escape! Within half-an-hour the
Swedes will be upon him. He has thirty well-armed
horsemen with him. 'Twill be life or death.

But if they should take him alive after all?—Were
I but free, I could overtake the Swedes ere they
reach the frontier, and make them deliver him up.
(*Goes towards the window in the background and looks
out.*) Damnation! Guards outside on every hand.
Can there be no way out of this? (*Comes quickly
forward again ; suddenly stops and listens.*)

What is that? Music and singing. It seems to
come from Elina's chamber. Ay, it is she that is
singing. Then she is still awake——

(*A thought seems to strike him.*)

Elina!—Ah, if *that* could be! If it could but——
And why should I not? Am I not still myself?
Says not the song :—

> *Fair maidens a-many they sigh and they pine :*
> " *Ah God, that Nils Lykke were mine, mine, mine.*"

And she——? —— ——Elina Gyldenlöve shall set
me free!

(*Goes quickly but stealthily towards the first door
on the left.*)

Act Fifth.

(*The Banquet Hall. It is still night. The hall is but dimly
   lighted by a branch-candlestick on the table, in front, on the
   right.*)
(LADY INGER *is sitting by the table, deep in thought.*)

LADY INGER (*after a pause*).   They call me keen-
witted beyond all others in the land.   I believe they
are right.   The keenest-witted——   No one knows
how I became so.   For more than twenty years I
have fought to save my child.   *That* is the key to the
riddle.   Ay, that sharpens the wits!

My wits?   Where have they flown to-night?   What
has become of my forethought?   There is a ringing
and rushing in my ears.   I see shapes before me,
so life-like that methinks I could lay hold on them.
   (*Springs up.*)
Lord Jesus—what is this?   Am I no longer mistress
of my reason?   Is it to come to that——?
   (*Presses her clasped hands over her head; sits
      down again, and says more calmly:*)
Nay, 'tis nought.   It will pass.   There is no fear;—
it will pass.

How peaceful it is in the hall to-night!   No
threatening looks from forefathers or kinsfolk.   No
need to turn their faces to the wall.
   (*Rises again.*)

Ay, 'twas well that I took heart at last. We shall conquer ;—and then I am at the end of my longings. I shall have my child again.

> (*Takes up the light as if to go, but stops and says musingly:*)

At the end ? The end ? To get him back ? Is that all ?—is there nought further ?

> (*Sets the light down on the table.*)

That heedless word that Nils Lykke threw forth at random—— How could he see my unborn thought ?

> (*More softly.*)

A king's mother ? A king's mother, he said—— Why not ? Have not my forefathers ruled as kings, even though they bore not the kingly name ? Has not *my* son as good a title as the other to the rights of the house of Sture ? In the sight of God he has— if so be there is justice in Heaven.

And in an hour of terror I have signed away his rights. I have recklessly squandered them, as a ransom for his freedom.

If they could be recovered ?—Would Heaven be angered, if I——? Would it call down fresh troubles on my head if I were to—— ? Who knows ;—who knows ! It may be safest to refrain. (*Takes up the light again.*) I shall have my child again. *That* must suffice me. I will try to rest. All these desperate thoughts,—I will sleep them away.

> (*Goes towards the back, but stops in the middle of the hall, and says broodingly :*)

A king's mother !

> (*Goes slowly out at the back, to the left.*)
> (*After a short pause,* Nils Lykke *and* Elina

GYLDENLÖVE *enter noiselessly by the first door
on the left.* NILS LYKKE *has a small lantern
in his hand.*)

NILS LYKKE (*throws the light from his lantern
around, so as to search the room*). All is still. I must
begone.

ELINA. Oh, let me look but once more into your
eyes, before you leave me.

NILS LYKKE (*embraces her*). Elina!

ELINA (*after a short pause*). Will you come nevermore to Östråt?

NILS LYKKE. How can you doubt that I will
come? Are you not henceforth my betrothed?—
But will *you* be true to *me*, Elina? Will you not
forget me ere we meet again?

ELINA. Do you ask if I *will* be true? Have I
any will left then? Have I power to be untrue to
you, even if I would?—You came by night; you
knocked upon my door;—and I opened to you.
You spoke to me. What was it you said? You
gazed in my eyes. What was the mystic might that
turned my brain and lured me, as it were, within a
magic net? (*Hides her face on his shoulder.*) Oh,
look not on me, Nils Lykke! You must not look upon
me after this—— True, say you? Do you not own
me? I am yours;—I must be yours—to all eternity.

NILS LYKKE. Now, by my knightly honour, ere
the year be past, you shall sit as my wife in the hall
of my fathers.

ELINA. No vows, Nils Lykke! No oaths to me.

NILS LYKKE. What mean you? Why do you
shake your head so mournfully?

Elina.   Because I know that the same soft words wherewith you turned my brain, you have whispered to so many a one before.   Nay nay, be not angry, my beloved!   In nought do I reproach you, as I did while yet I knew you not.   Now I understand how high above all others is your goal.   How can love be aught to you but a pastime, or woman but a toy?

Nils Lykke.   Elina,—hear me!

Elina.   As I grew up, your name was ever in my ears.   I hated the name, for meseemed that all women were dishonoured by your life.   And yet,—how strange!—when I built up in my dreams the life that should be mine, you were ever my hero, though I knew it not.   Now I understand it all—now know I what it was I felt.   It was a foreboding, a mysterious longing for you, you only one—for you that were one day to come and glorify my life.

Nils Lykke (*aside, putting down the lantern on the table*).   How is it with me?   This dizzy fascination—— If this it be to love, then have I never known it till this hour.—Is there not yet time——? Oh horror—Lucia!

(*Sinks into the chair.*)

Elina.   What ails you?   So heavy a sigh——

Nils Lykke.   O, 'tis nought,—nought!   Elina,— now will I confess all to you.   I have beguiled many with both words and glances; I have said to many a one what I whispered to you this night.   But trust me——

Elina.   Hush!   No more of that.   My love is no exchange for that you give me.   No, no; I love you because your every glance commands it like a king's decree.

(*Lies down at his feet.*)
Oh, let me once more stamp that kingly message deep into my soul, though well I know it stands imprinted there for all time and eternity.

Dear God—how little I have known myself! 'Twas but to-night I said to my mother: " My pride is my life." And what is my pride? Is it to know that my countrymen are free, or that my house is held in honour throughout many lands? Oh, no, no! My love is my pride. The little dog is proud when he may sit by his master's feet and eat bread-crumbs from his hand. Even so am I proud, so long as I may sit at your feet, while your looks and your words nourish me with the bread of life. See, therefore, I say to you, even as I said but now to my mother: " My love is my life ;" for therein lies all my pride, now and evermore.

NILS LYKKE (*raises her up on his lap*). Nay, nay— not at my feet, but at my side is your place,—should fate set me never so high. Ay, Elina—you have led me into a better path ; and if it be granted me some day to atone by a deed of fame for the sins of my reckless youth, the honour shall be yours as well as mine.

ELINA. Ah, you speak as though I were still the Elina that but this evening flung down the flowers at your feet.

I have read in my books of the many-coloured life in far-off lands. To the winding of horns the knight rides forth into the greenwood, with his falcon on his

wrist. Even so do you go your way through life ;—
your name rings out before you whithersoever you
fare.—All that I desire of your glory, is to rest like
the falcon on your arm. I too was blind as he to light
and life, till you loosed the hood from my eyes and
set me soaring high over the leafy tree-tops.—But,
trust me—bold as my flight may be, yet shall I ever
turn back to my cage.

NILS LYKKE (*rises*). Then I bid defiance to the
past ! See now ;—take this ring, and be *mine* before
God and men—*mine*,—ay, though it should trouble
the dreams of the dead.

ELINA. You make me afraid. What is it that——?

NILS LYKKE. It is nought. Come, let me place
the ring on your finger.—Even so—now are you my
betrothed !

ELINA. *I* Nils Lykke's bride ! It seems but a
dream, all that has befallen this night. Oh, but so
fair a dream ! My breast is so light. No longer is
there bitterness and hatred in my soul. I will atone
to all whom I have wronged. I have been unloving
to my mother. To-morrow will I go to her; she
must forgive me my offence.

NILS LYKKE. And give her consent to our bond.

ELINA. That will she. Oh, I am sure she will.
My mother is kind; all the world is kind;—I can feel
hatred no more for any living soul—save *one*.

NILS LYKKE. Save *one*?

ELINA. Ah, it is a mournful history. I had a
sister——

NILS LYKKE. Lucia?

ELINA. Have you known Lucia ?

NILS LYKKE.   No, no; I have but heard her name.

ELINA.   She too gave her heart to a knight.   He betrayed her;—and now she is in Heaven.

NILS LYKKE.   And you——?

ELINA.   I hate him.

NILS LYKKE.   Hate him not!   If there be mercy in your heart, forgive him his sin.   Trust me, he bears his punishment in his own breast.

ELINA.   Him I will never forgive!   I *cannot*, even if I would; for I have sworn so dear an oath——

(*Listening.*)

Hush!   Can you hear——?

NILS LYKKE.   What?   Where?

ELINA.   Without; far off.   The noise of many horsemen on the high-road.

NILS LYKKE.   Ah, it is they!   And I had forgotten——!   They are coming hither.   Then is the danger great;—I must begone!

ELINA.   But whither?   Oh, Nils Lykke, what are you hiding——?

NILS LYKKE.   To-morrow, Elina——; for as God lives, I will return then.—Quickly now—where is the secret passage you told me of?

ELINA.   Through the grave-vault.   See,—here is the trap-door.

NILS LYKKE.   The grave-vault!   (*To himself.*)   No matter, he *must* be saved!

ELINA (*by the window*).   The horsemen have reached the gate——

(*Hands him the lantern.*)

NILS LYKKE.   Well, now I go— —

(*Begins to descend.*)

Elina.   Go forward along the passage till you reach the coffin with the death's-head and the black cross ; it is Lucia's——

Nils Lykke (*climbs back hastily and shuts the trap-door to*).   Lucia's !   Pah——!

Elina.   What said you ?

Nils Lykke.   Nay, nought.   It was the scent of the grave that made me dizzy.

Elina.   Hark ; they are hammering at the gate !

Nils Lykke (*lets the lantern fall*).   Ah ! too late——!

   (Biörn *enters hurriedly from the right, carrying a light.*)

Elina (*goes towards him*).   What is amiss, Biörn ? What is it ?

Biörn.   An ambuscade !   Count Sture——

Elina.   Count Sture ?   What of him ?

Nils Lykke.   Have they killed him ?

Biörn (*to* Elina).   Where is your mother ?

Two House-Servants (*rushing in from the right*).   Lady Inger !   Lady Inger !

   (Lady Inger Gyldenlöve *enters by the first door on the left, with a branch-candlestick, lighted, in her hand, and says quickly:*)

Lady Inger.   I know all.   Down with you to the courtyard !   Keep the gate open for our friends, but closed against all others !

   (*Puts down the candlestick on the table to the left.* Biörn *and the two House-Servants go out again to the right.*)

Lady Inger (*to* Nils Lykke).   So *that* was the trap, Sir Councillor !

NILS LYKKE.   Inger Gyldenlöve, trust me——!

LADY INGER.   An ambuscade that was to snap him up, as soon as you had got the promise that should destroy me!

NILS LYKKE (*takes out the paper and tears it to pieces*).   There is your promise.   I keep nothing that can bear witness against you.

LADY INGER.   What will you do?

NILS LYKKE.   From this hour I am your champion. If I have sinned against you,—by Heaven I will strive to repair my crime.   But now I *must* out, if I have to hew my way through the gate!—Elina—tell your mother all!—And you, Lady Inger, let our reckoning be forgotten!   Be generous—and silent! Trust me, ere the day dawns you shall owe me a life's gratitude.

(*Goes out quickly to the right.*)

LADY INGER (*looks after him with exultation*).   It is well!   I understand him!

(*Turns to* ELINA.)

Nils Lykke——?   Well——?

ELINA.   He knocked upon my door, and set this ring upon my finger.

LADY INGER.   And he loves you with all his heart?

ELINA.   He has said so, and I believe him.

LADY INGER.   Bravely done, Elina!   Ha-ha, Sir Knight, now is it *my* turn!

ELINA.   My mother—you are so strange.   Oh, ay —I know—it is my unloving ways that have angered you.

LADY INGER.   Not so, dear Elina!   You are an

obedient child. You have opened your door to him; you have hearkened to his soft words. I know full well what it must have cost you; for I know your hatred——

ELINA. But, my mother——

LADY INGER. Hush! We have played into each other's hands. What wiles did you use, my subtle daughter? I saw the love shine out of his eyes. Hold him fast now! Draw the net closer and closer about him, and then—— Ah, Elina, if we could but rend his perjured heart within his breast!

ELINA. Woe is me—what is it you say?

LADY INGER. Let not your courage fail you. Hearken to me. I know a word that will keep you firm. Know then—— (*Listening.*) They are fighting outside the gate. Courage! Now comes the pinch! (*Turns again to* ELINA.) Know then, Nils Lykke was the man that brought your sister to her grave.

ELINA (*with a shriek*). Lucia!

LADY INGER. He it was, as truly as there is an Avenger above us!

ELINA. Then Heaven be with me!

LADY INGER (*appalled*). Elina——?!

ELINA. I am his bride in the sight of God.

LADY INGER. Unhappy child,—what have you done?

ELINA (*in a toneless voice*). Made shipwreck of my soul.—Good-night, my mother!

   (*She goes out to the left.*)

LADY INGER. Ha-ha-ha! It goes down-hill now with Inger Gyldenlöve's house. There went the last of my daughters.

Why could I not keep silence? Had she known nought, it may be she had been happy—after a kind.

It *was* to be so. It is written up there in the stars that I am to break off one green branch after another, till the trunk stand leafless at last.

'Tis well, 'tis well! I am to have my son again. Of the others, of my daughters, I will not think.

My reckoning? To face my reckoning?—It falls not due till the last great day of wrath.— *That* comes not yet awhile.

NILS STENSSON (*calling from outside on the right*). Ho—shut the gate!

LADY INGER.   Count Sture's voice——!

NILS STENSSON (*rushes in, unarmed, and with his clothes torn, and shouts with a desperate laugh*).   Well met again, Inger Gyldenlöve!

LADY INGER.   What have you lost?

NILS STENSSON.   My kingdom and my life!

LADY INGER.   And the peasants? My servants? —where are they?

NILS STENSSON.   You will find the carcasses along the highway.   Who has the rest, I know not.

OLAF SKAKTAVL (*outside on the right*).   Count Sture! Where are you?

NILS STENSSON.   Here, here!

(OLAF SKAKTAVL *comes in with his right hand wrapped in a cloth*).

LADY INGER.   Alas, Olaf Skaktavl, you too——!

OLAF SKAKTAVL.   It was impossible to break through.

LADY INGER.   You are wounded, I see!

Olaf Skaktavl.   A finger the less ; that is all.

Nils Stensson.   Where are the Swedes ?

Olaf Skaktavl.   At our heels.   They are breaking open the gate——

Nils Stensson.   Oh, Jesus ! No, no ! I *cannot*—I *will* not die.

Olaf Skaktavl.   A hiding-place, Lady Inger ! Is there no corner where we can hide him ?

Lady Inger.   But if they search the castle——?

Nils Stensson.   Ay, ay ; they will find me ! And then to be dragged away to prison, or be strung up——! Oh no, Inger Gyldenlöve,—I know full well,—you will never suffer that to be !

Olaf Skaktavl (*listening*).   There burst the lock.

Lady Inger (*at the window*).   Many men rush in at the gateway.

Nils Stensson.   And to lose my life *now !* Now, when my true life was but beginning ! Now, when I have so lately learnt that I have aught to live for. No, no, no !—Think not I am a coward. Might I but have time to show——

Lady Inger.   I hear them now in the hall below.
  (*Firmly to* Olaf Skaktavl.)
He *must* be saved—cost what it will !

Nils Stensson (*seizes her hand*).   Oh, I knew it ;—you are noble and good !

Olaf Skaktavl.   But how ? Since we cannot hide him——

Nils Stensson.   Ah, I have it ! I have it ! The secret——!

Lady Inger.   The secret ?

NILS STENSSON.   Even so ; yours and mine!

LADY INGER.   Christ in Heaven—you know it ?

NILS STENSSON.   From first to last.   And now when 'tis life or death——   Where is Nils Lykke ?

LADY INGER.   Fled.

NILS STENSSON.   Fled ?   Then God help me ; for he only can unseal my lips.—But what is a promise against a life !   When the Swedish captain comes——

LADY INGER.   What then ?   What will you do ?

NILS STENSSON.   Purchase life and freedom ;— tell him all.

LADY INGER.   Oh no, no ;—be merciful !

NILS.STENSSON.   Nought else can save me.   When I have told him what I know——

LADY INGER (*looks at him with suppressed excitement*).   You will be safe ?

NILS STENSSON.   Ay, safe !   Nils Lykke will speak for me.   You see, 'tis the last resource.

LADY INGER (*composedly, with emphasis*).   The last resource ?   Right, right—the last resource stands open to all.   (*Points to the left.*)   See, meanwhile you can hide in there.

NILS STENSSON (*softly*).   Trust me—you will never repent of this.

LADY INGER (*half to herself*).   God grant that you speak the truth !

> (NILS STENSSON *goes out hastily by the furthest door on the left.*   OLAF SKAKTAVL *is following; but* LADY INGER *detains him.*)

LADY INGER.   Did you understand his meaning ?

OLAF SKAKTAVL.   The dastard !   He would betray your secret. He would sacrifice your son to save himself.

LADY INGER. When life is at stake, he said, we must try the last resource.—It is well, Olaf Skaktavl, —let it be as he has said !

OLAF SKAKTAVL. What mean you ?

LADY INGER. Life for life! One of them must perish.

OLAF SKAKTAVL. Ah—you would——?

LADY INGER. If we close not the lips of him that is within ere he come to speech with the Swedish captain, then is my son lost to me. But if he be swept from my path, when the time comes I can claim all his rights for my own child. Then shall you see that Inger Ottisdaughter has metal in her yet. And be assured you shall not have long to wait for the vengeance you have thirsted after for twenty years.—Hark ! They are coming up the stairs ! Olaf Skaktavl,—it lies with you whether to-morrow I shall be a childless woman, or——

OLAF SKAKTAVL. So be it ! I have one sound hand left yet. (*Gives her his hand.*) Inger Gyldenlöve—your name shall not die out through me.

(*Follows* NILS STENSSON *into the inner room.*)

LADY INGER (*pale and trembling*). But dare I——?
(*A noise is heard in the room; she rushes with a scream towards the door.*)
No, no,—it must not be !
(*A heavy fall is heard within; she covers her ears with her hands and hurries back across the hall with a wild look. After a pause she takes*

*her hands cautiously away, listens again and
    says softly :)*

Now it is over.   All is still within——

Thou **sawest** it, God—I repented **me**!   But Olaf
Skaktavl **was too** swift of hand.

    (OLAF SKAKTAVL *comes silently into the hall.*)

LADY INGER (*after a pause, without looking at him*).
Is it done?

OLAF SKAKTAVL.   You need fear him no more;
he will betray no one.

LADY INGER (*as before*).   Then he is dumb?

OLAF SKAKTAVL.   Six inches of steel in his
breast.   I felled him with **my** left hand.

LADY INGER.   Ay—the right was too good for
such work.

OLAF SKAKTAVL.   That is your affair ;—the
thought was yours.—And now to Sweden!   Peace
be with you meanwhile!   When next we meet at
Östrât, I shall bring another with me.

    (*Goes **out** by the furthest door on the right.*)

LADY INGER.   Blood on my hands.   Then it was
to come to that!—He begins to be dear-bought now.

    (BIÖRN *comes in, with a number of Swedish men-
        at-arms, by the first door on the right.*)

ONE OF THE MEN-AT-ARMS.   Pardon me, if you
are the lady of the house——

LADY INGER.   Is it Count Sture you seek?

THE MAN-AT-ARMS.   The same.

LADY INGER.   Then you are on the right scent.
The Count has sought refuge with me.

THE MAN-AT-ARMS.   Refuge?   Pardon, my noble
lady,—you have no power to harbour him ; for——

LADY INGER.   That the Count himself has doubtless understood ; and therefore he has—ay, look for yourselves—therefore he has taken his own life.

THE MAN-AT-ARMS.   His own life !

LADY INGER.   Look for yourselves.   You will find the corpse within there.   And since he already stands before another judge, it is my prayer that he may be borne hence with all the honour that beseems his noble birth.—Biörn, you know my own coffin has stood ready this many a year in the secret chamber. (*To the Men-at-Arms.*)   I pray that in it you will bear Count Sture's body to Sweden.

THE MAN-AT-ARMS.   It shall be as you command. (*To one of the others.*)   Haste with these tidings to Jens Bielke.   He holds the road with the rest of the troop.   We others must in and——

> (*One of the Men-at-Arms goes out to the right ; the others go with* BIÖRN *into the room on the left.*)

LADY INGER (*moves about for a time in uneasy silence*).   If Count Sture had not said farewell to the world so hurriedly, within a month he had hung on a gallows, or had sat for all his days in a dungeon. Had he been better served with such a lot ?

Or else he had bought his life by betraying my child into the hands of my foes.   Is it *I*, then, that have slain him ?   Does not even the wolf defend her cubs ?   Who dare condemn me for striking my claws into him that would have reft me of my flesh and blood ?—It had to be.   No mother but would have done even as I.

But 'tis no time for idle musings now.   I must to work.

(*Sits down by the table on the left.*)

I will write to all my friends throughout the land. They must rise as one man to support the great cause. A new king,—regent first, and then king——

(*Begins to write, but falls into thought, and says softly :*)

Whom will they choose in the dead man's place?—A king's mother——? 'Tis a fair word. It has but one blemish—the hateful likeness to another word. —King's *mother* and—king's *murderer*.[1] — King's murderer—one that takes a king's life. King's mother—one that gives a king life.

(*She rises.*)

Well, then ; I will make good what I have taken.— My son shall be king!

(*She sits down again and begins writing, but pushes the paper away again, and leans back in her chair.*)

There is no comfort in a house where lies a corpse. 'Tis therefore I feel so strangely. (*Turns her head to one side as if speaking to some one.*) Not therefore? Why else should it be?

(*Broodingly.*)

Is there such a great gulf, then, between openly striking down a foe and slaying one—thus? Knut Alfson had cleft many a brain with his sword ; yet was his own as peaceful as a child's. Why then do I ever see this—(*makes a motion as though striking with a knife*)—this stab in the heart—and the gush of red blood after?

---

[1] The words in the original are "Kongemoder" and "Konge-morder," a difference of one letter only.

(*Rings, and goes on speaking while shifting about her papers.*)

Hereafter I will have none of these ugly sights. I will work both day and night. And in a month—in a month my son will be here—— ——

Biörn (*entering*). Did you strike the bell, my lady?

Lady Inger (*writing*). Bring more lights. See to it in future that there are many lights in the room.

(Biörn *goes out again to the left.*)

Lady Inger (*after a pause, rises impetuously*). No, no, no;—I cannot guide the pen to-night! My head is burning and throbbing——

(*Startled, listens.*)

What is *that?* Ah, they are screwing the lid on the coffin in there.

When I was a child they told me the story of Sir Åge,[1] who rose up and walked with his coffin on his back.—If he in there were one night to think of coming with the coffin on his back, to thank me for the loan? (*Laughs quietly.*) Hm—what have we grown people to do with childish fancies? (*Vehemently.*) But such stories are hurtful none the less! They give uneasy dreams. When my son is king, they shall be forbidden.

(*Goes up and down once or twice; then opens the window.*)

How long is it, commonly, ere a body begins to rot? All the rooms must be aired. 'Tis not wholesome here till that be done.

[1] Pronounce *Oaghë.*

> (BIÖRN *comes in with two lighted branch-candle-*
> *sticks, which he places on the tables.*)

LADY INGER (*who has begun on the papers again*).
It is well. See you forget not what I have said.
Many lights on the table!

What are they about now in there?

BIÖRN. They are busy screwing down the coffin-lid.

LADY INGER (*writing*). Are they screwing it down
tight?

BIÖRN. As tight as need be.

LADY INGER. Ay, ay—who can tell how tight it
needs to be? Do you see that 'tis well done.

> (*Goes up to him with her hand full of papers, and*
> *says mysteriously :*)

Biörn, you are an old man; but *one* counsel I will
give you. Be on your guard against all men—both
those that *are* dead and those that are still to die.—
Now go in—go in and see to it that they screw the
lid down tightly.

BIÖRN (*softly, shaking his head*). I cannot make
her out.

> (*Goes back again into the room on the left.*)

LADY INGER (*begins to seal a letter, but throws it*
down half-closed; walks up and down awhile, and
then says vehemently :)

Were I a coward I had never done it—never to all
eternity! Were I a coward, I had shrieked to myself:
Refrain, ere yet thy soul is utterly lost!

> (*Her eye falls on Sten Sture's picture ; she*
> *turns to avoid seeing it, and says softly :*)

He is laughing down at me as though he were
alive! Pah!

(*Turns the picture to the wall without looking
    at it.*)

Wherefore did you laugh? Was it because I did
evil to your son? But the other,—is not he your son
too? And he is *mine* as well; mark that!

(*Glances stealthily along the row of pictures.*)

So wild as they are to-night, I have never seen
them yet. Their eyes follow me wherever I may
go. (*Stamps on the floor.*) I will not have it! I
will have peace in my house! (*Begins to turn all
the pictures to the wall.*) Ay, if it were the Holy
Virgin herself—— —— Thinkest thou *now* is the
time——? Why didst thou never hear my prayers,
my burning prayers, that I might get back my
child? Why? Because the monk of Wittenberg is
right. There is no mediator between God and man!

(*She draws her breath heavily and continues in
    ever-increasing distraction.*)

It is well that I know what to think in such things.
There was no one to see what was done in there.
There is none to bear witness against me.

(*Suddenly stretches out her hands and whispers:*)

My son! My beloved child! Come to me! Here
I am! Hush! I will tell you something: They hate
me up there—beyond the stars—because I bore you
into the world. It was meant that I should bear the
Lord God's standard over all the land. But I went
my own way. It is therefore I have had to suffer so
much and so long.

BIÖRN (*comes from the room on the left*). My lady,
I have to tell you—— Christ save me—what is
this?

LADY INGER (*has climbed up into the high-seat by the right-hand wall*). Hush! Hush! I am the King's mother. They have chosen my son king. The struggle was hard ere it came to this—for 'twas with the Almighty One himself I had to strive.

NILS LYKKE (*comes in breathless from the right*). He is **saved**! I **have** Jens Bielke's promise. Lady Inger,—know that——

LADY INGER. **Peace, I** say! look how the people swarm.

(*A funeral hymn is heard from the room within.*)
There comes the procession. What **a** throng! All men bow themselves before the King's mother. Ay, ay; has **she** not fought **for her** son—even till her hands grew red withal?—Where are my daughters? I see them **not**.

NILS LYKKE. God's blood!—what has befallen here?

LADY INGER. **My** daughters—my fair daughters! I have none any more. I had *one* left, and her I lost even as she was mounting her bridal bed. (*Whispers.*) Lucia's corpse lay in it. There was **no** room for two.

NILS LYKKE. Ah—it has come to this! The Lord's vengeance is upon me.

LADY INGER. Can you **see** him? Look, look! It is **the** King. **It is** Inger Gyldenlöve's son! I know him by the crown and by Sten Sture's ring that he wears round his **neck**. Hark, what a joyful sound! **He** is coming! Soon will he be in my arms! Ha-ha!—who conquers, God or I?

(*The Men-at-Arms come out with the coffin.*)

Lady Inger (*clutches at her head and shrieks*). The corpse! (*Whispers.*) Pah! It is a hideous dream.

    (*Sinks back into the high-seat.*)

Jens Bielke (*who has come in from the right, stops and cries in astonishment*). Dead! Then after all——

One of the Men-at-Arms. It was himself——

Jens Bielke (*with a look at* Nils Lykke). He himself——?

Nils Lykke. Hush!

Lady Inger (*faintly, coming to herself*). Ay, right;—now I remember it all.

Jens Bielke (*to the Men-at-Arms*). Set down the corpse. It is not Count Sture.

One of the Men-at-Arms. Your pardon, Captain;—this ring that he wore round his neck——

Nils Lykke (*seizes his arm*). Be still!

Lady Inger (*starts up*). The ring? The ring!

    (*Rushes up and snatches the ring from him.*)

Sten Sture's ring! (*With a shriek.*) Oh, Jesus Christ—my son!

    (*Throws herself down on the coffin.*)

The Men-at-Arms. Her son?

Jens Bielke (*at the same time*). Inger Gyldenlöve's son?

Nils Lykke. So it is.

Jens Bielke. But why did you not tell me——?

Biörn (*trying to raise her up*). Help! help! My lady—what ails you?

Lady Inger (*in a faint voice, half raising herself*).

What ails me? I lack but another coffin, and a
grave beside my child.

> (*Sinks again, senseless, on the coffin.* Nils Lykke
> *goes hastily out to the right.   General consterna-*
> *tion among* **the rest.**)

THE VIKINGS AT HELGELAND.

(1858.)

Characters.

——◆◆——

ÖRNULF OF THE FIORDS, *an Icelandic Chieftain.*
SIGURD THE STRONG, *a Sea-King.*
GUNNAR HEADMAN,[1] *a rich yeoman of Helgeland.*
THOROLF, *Örnulf's youngest son.*
DAGNY, *Örnulf's daughter.*
HIÖRDIS, *his foster-daughter.*
KÅRE THE PEASANT, *a Helgeland-man.*
EGIL, *Gunnar's son, four years old.*
ÖRNULF'S SIX OLDER SONS.
ÖRNULF'S AND SIGURD'S MEN.
Guests, house-carls, serving-maids, outlaws, etc.

The action takes place in the time of Erik Blood-axe (about A.D. 933) *at, and in the neighbourhood of, Gunnar's house, on the island of Helgeland, in the north of Norway.*

[PRONUNCIATION OF NAMES. — Helgeland = *Helgheland;* Ornulf = *Örnoolf;* Sigurd = *Sigoord;* Gunnar = *Goonnar;* Thorolf = *Toorolf;* Hiördis = *Yördeess;* Kåre = *Koarë;* Egil = *Ayghil.* The letter ö as in German.]

[1] Failing to find a better equivalent for the Norwegian "Herse," I have used the word "Headman" wherever it seemed necessary to give Gunnar a title or designation. He is generally spoken of as "Gunnar Herse" in the Norwegian text; but where it could be done without inconvenience, the designation has here been omitted.

THE VIKINGS AT HELGELAND.

PLAY IN FOUR ACTS.

——◆——

Act First.

(*A rocky coast, running precipitously down to the sea at the back. To the left, a boat-house; to the right, rocks and pine-woods. The masts of two war-ships can be seen down in the cove. Far out to the right, the ocean, dotted with reefs and rocky islands; the sea is running high; it is a stormy snow-grey winter day.*)

(SIGURD *comes up from the ships; he is clad in a white tunic with a silver belt, a blue cloak, cross-gartered hose, untanned shoes, and a steel cap; at his side hangs a short sword.* ÖRNULF *comes in sight immediately afterwards, up among the rocks, clad in a dark lamb-skin tunic with a breastplate and greaves, woollen stockings, and untanned shoes; over his shoulders he has a cloak of brown frieze, with the hood drawn over his steel cap, so that his face is partly hidden. He is very tall and massively built, with a long white beard, but somewhat bowed by age; his weapons are a round shield, sword, and spear.*)

SIGURD (*enters first, looks around, sees the boat-shed, goes quickly up to it, and tries to burst open the door.*)

ÖRNULF (*appears among the rocks, starts on seeing* SIGURD, *seems to recognise him, descends and cries :*) Give place, Viking!

SIGURD (*turns, lays his hand on his sword, and answers :*) 'Twere the first time if I did !

ÖRNULF. Thou shalt and must! I have need of the shelter for my stiff-frozen men.

SIGURD. And I for a weary woman !

ÖRNULF. My men are worth more than thy women !

SIGURD. Then must outlaws be highly prized in Helgeland !

ÖRNULF. Dearly shalt thou aby that word !

SIGURD. Now will it go ill with thee, old man !

 (ÖRNULF *rushes upon him;* SIGURD *defends himself.*)

 (DAGNY *and some of* SIGURD'S *men come up from the strand;* ÖRNULF'S *six sons appear on the rocks to the right.*)

DAGNY (*who is a little in front, clad in a red kirtle, blue cloak, and fur hood, calls down to the ships :*) Up, all Sigurd's men ! My husband is fighting with a stranger !

ÖRNULF'S SONS. Help for Örnulf ! (*They descend.*)

SIGURD (*to his men*). Hold ! I can master him alone !

ÖRNULF (*to his sons*). Let me fight in peace ! (*Rushes in upon* SIGURD.) I will see thy blood !

SIGURD. First see thine own ! (*Wounds him in the arm so that his spear falls.*)

ÖRNULF. A stout stroke, Viking !

   Swift the sword thou swingest,
   keen thy blows and biting ;
   Sigurd's self, the Stalwart,
   stood before thee shame-struck.

SIGURD (*smiling*). Then were his shame his glory!

ÖRNULF'S SONS (*with a cry of wonder*). Sigurd himself! Sigurd the Strong!

ÖRNULF. But sharper was thy stroke that night thou didst bear away Dagny, my daughter. (*Casts his hood back.*)

SIGURD AND HIS MEN. Örnulf of the Fiords!

DAGNY (*glad, yet uneasy*). My father and my brothers!

SIGURD. Stand thou behind me.

ÖRNULF. Nay, no need. (*Approaching* SIGURD). I knew thy face as soon as I was ware of thee, and therefore I stirred the strife; I was fain to prove the fame that tells of thee as the stoutest man of his hands in Norway. Henceforth let peace be between us.

SIGURD. Best if so it could be.

ÖRNULF. Here is my hand. Thou art a warrior indeed; stouter strokes than these has old Örnulf never given or taken.

SIGURD (*seizes his outstretched hand*). Let them be the last strokes given and taken between us two; and do thou thyself adjudge the matter between us. Art thou willing?

ÖRNULF. That am I, and straightway shall the quarrel be healed. (*To the others.*) Be the matter, then, known to all. Five winters ago came Sigurd and Gunnar Headman as vikings to Iceland; they lay in harbour close under my homestead. Then Gunnar, by force and craft, carried away my foster-daughter, Hiördis; but thou, Sigurd, didst take

Dagny, my own child, and sailed with her over the sea. For that thou art now doomed to pay three hundred pieces of silver, and thereby shall thy misdeed be atoned.

SIGURD. Fair is thy judgment, Örnulf; the three hundred pieces will I pay, and add thereto a silken cloak fringed with gold. It is a gift from King Æthelstan of England, and better has no Icelander yet borne.

DAGNY. So be it, my brave husband; and my father, I thank thee. Now at last is my mind at ease.

> (*She presses her father's and brothers' hands, and talks low to them.*)

ÖRNULF. Then thus stands the treaty between us; and from this day shall Dagny be to the full as honourably regarded as though she had been lawfully betrothed to thee, with the good will of her kin.

SIGURD. And in me canst thou trust, as in one of thine own blood.

ÖRNULF. That doubt I not; and see! I will forthwith prove thy friendship.

SIGURD. Ready shalt thou find me; say, what dost thou crave?

ÖRNULF. Thy help in rede and deed. I have sailed hither to Helgeland to seek out Gunnar Headman and draw him to reckoning for the carrying away of Hiördis.

SIGURD (*surprised*). Gunnar!

DAGNY (*in the same tone*). And Hiördis—where are they?

ÖRNULF. In Gunnar's homestead, I ween.

SIGURD. And it is—— ?

ÖRNULF.   Not many bow-shots hence; did ye not know?

SIGURD (*with suppressed emotion*).   No, truly. Small tidings have I had of Gunnar since we sailed from Iceland together.   I have wandered far and wide and served many outland kings, while Gunnar sat at home.   Hither we drove at day-dawn, before the storm; I knew, indeed, that Gunnar's homestead lay here in the north, but——

DAGNY (*to* ÖRNULF).   So *that* errand has brought thee hither?

ÖRNULF.   That and no other.   (*To* SIGURD.) Our meeting is the work of the Mighty Ones above; they willed it so.   Had I wished to find thee, little knew I where to seek.

SIGURD (*thoughtfully*).   True, true!—But concerning Gunnar—tell me, Örnulf, art thou minded to go sharply to work, with all thy might, be it for good or ill?

ÖRNULF.   That must I.   Listen, Sigurd, for thus it stands: Last summer I rode to the Council where many honourable men were met.   When the Council-days were over, I sat in the hall and drank with the men of my hundred, and the talk fell upon the carry-ing-away of the women; scornful words they gave me, because I had let that wrong rest unavenged.   Then, in my wrath, I swore to sail to Norway, seek out Gunnar, and crave reckoning or revenge, and never again to set foot in Iceland till my claim was made good.

SIGURD.   Ay, ay, since so it stands, I see well that if need be the matter must be pressed home.

ÖRNULF. It must; but I shall not crave over much, and Gunnar has the fame of an honourable man. Glad am I, too, that I set about this quest; the time lay heavy on me in Iceland ; out upon the blue waters had I grown old and grey, and I longed to fare forth once again before I——; well well—Bergthora, my good wife, was dead these many years; my eldest sons sailed on viking-ventures summer by summer ; and since Thorolf was growing up——

DAGNY (*gladly*). Thorolf is with thee? Where is he?

ÖRNULF. On board the ship. (*Points towards the background, to the right.*) Scarce shalt thou know the boy again, so stout and strong and fair has he grown. He will be a mighty warrior, Sigurd ; one day he will equal thee.

DAGNY (*smiling*). I see it is now as ever ; Thorolf stands nearest thy heart.

ÖRNULF. He is the youngest, and like his mother; therefore it is.

SIGURD. But tell me—thy errand to Gunnar— thinkest thou to-day—— ?

ÖRNULF. Rather to-day than to-morrow. Fair amends will content me ; if Gunnar says me nay, then must he take what comes.

(KÅRE THE PEASANT *enters hastily from the right; he is clad in a grey frieze cloak and low-brimmed felt hat; he carries in his hand a broken fence-rail.*)

KÅRE. Well met, Vikings !

ÖRNULF. Vikings are seldom well met.

Kåre.   If ye be honourable men, ye will grant me refuge among you; Gunnar Headman's house-carls are hunting me to slay me.

Örnulf.   Gunnar's?

Sigurd.   Then hast thou done him some wrong!

Kåre.   I have done myself right.   Our cattle fed together upon an island, hard by the coast; Gunnar's men carried off my best oxen, and one of them flouted me for a thrall.   Then bare I arms against him and slew him.

Örnulf.   That was a lawful deed.

Kåre.   But this morning his men came in wrath against me.   By good hap I heard of their coming, and fled; but my foemen are on my tracks, and short shrift can I look for at their hands.

Sigurd. Ill can I believe thee, peasant!   In bygone days I knew Gunnar as I know myself, and this I wot, that never did he wrong a peaceful man.

Kåre.   Gunnar has no part in this wrong-doing; he is in the south-land; nay, it is Hiördis his wife——

Dagny.   Hiördis!

Örnulf (*to himself*).   Ay, ay, 'tis like her!

Kåre.   I offered Gunnar amends for the thrall, and he was willing; but then came Hiördis, and egged her husband on with scornful words, and hindered the peace. Since then has Gunnar gone to the south, and to-day——

Sigurd (*looking out to the left*). Here come wayfarers northward.   Is it not——?

Kåre.   It is Gunnar himself!

Örnulf.   Be of good heart; methinks I can make peace between you.

(GUNNAR HEADMAN, *with several men, enters from the left. He is in peaceful attire, wearing a brown tunic, cross-gartered hose, a blue mantle, and a broad hat; he has no weapon but a small axe.*)

GUNNAR (*stops in surprise and uncertainty on seeing the knot of men*). Örnulf of the Fiords! Yes, it is——!

ÖRNULF.   **Thou** seest aright.

GUNNAR (*approaching*). Then peace and welcome to thee in my land, if **thou come in peace.**

ÖRNULF.   If thy will be **as mine, there shall be no** strife between us.

SIGURD (*standing forward*).   Well met, Gunnar!

GUNNAR (*gladly*). Sigurd—foster-brother! (*Shakes his hand.*) Now **truly,** since thou art here, **I** know that Örnulf comes in peace. (*To* ÖRNULF.) **Give me thy hand,** greybeard! Thy errand here in the north is lightly **guessed: it has** to do with Hiördis, thy foster-daughter.

ÖRNULF.   As thou sayest; great wrong was done me when thou didst bear her away from Iceland without **my will.**

GUNNAR.   Thy claim is just; what the youth has marred, the **man must mend.** Long have I looked for thee, Örnulf, for this cause; and if amends content thee, **we** shall soon be at one.

SIGURD.   So deem I too. Örnulf will not press thee hard.

GUNNAR (*warmly*). Nay, Örnulf, didst thou crave her full worth, all my goods would not suffice.

ÖRNULF.   I shall go by law and usage, be sure of

that. But now another matter. (*Pointing to* Kåre.)
Seest thou yonder man?

Gunnar. Kåre! (*To* Örnulf.) Thou knowest,
then, that there is a strife between us?

Örnulf. Thy men have stolen his cattle, and
theft must be atoned.

Gunnar. Murder no less; he has slain my
thrall.

Kåre. Because he flouted me.

Gunnar. I have offered thee terms of peace.

Kåre. But that had Hiördis no mind to, and this
morning, whilst thou wert gone, she fell upon me and
hunts me now to my death.

Gunnar (*angrily*). Is it true what thou sayest?
Has she—— ?

Kåre. True, every word.

Örnulf. Therefore the peasant besought me to
stand by him, and that will I do.

Gunnar (*after a moment's thought*). Honourably
hast thou dealt with me, Örnulf ; therefore is it fit that
I should yield to thy will. Hear then, Kåre : I am
willing to let the slaying of the thrall and the wrongs
done toward thee quit each other.

Kåre (*gives* Gunnar *his hand*). It is a good
offer ; I am content.

Örnulf. And he shall have peace for thee and
thine?

Gunnar. Peace shall he have, here and overall.

Sigurd (*pointing to the right*). See yonder!

Gunnar (*disturbed*). It is Hiördis!

Örnulf. With armed men!

Kåre. She is seeking me!

(HIÖRDIS *enters, **with a troop** of house-carls.   She is clad in black, wearing **a kirtle, cloak, and hood;** the men are armed with swords and axes; she herself carries a light spear.*)

HIÖRDIS (*stops on entering*).   A meeting of many, meseems.

DAGNY (*rushes to **meet** her*).   Peace and joy to thee, Hiördis!

HIÖRDIS (*coldly*).   Thanks.   It was told me that thou wast not far off.

(*Comes forward, looking sharply at those assembled.*)

Gunnar, and—Kåre, **my** foeman—Örnulf and his sons, and——

(***As** she catches sight of* SIGURD, *she starts almost imperceptibly, is silent a moment, but collects herself and **says** :*)

Many I see here who are known to me—but little I know who is best minded towards me.

ÖRNULF.   We are all well-minded towards thee.

HIÖRDIS.   **If so be, thou wilt not** deny to give Kåre into my husband's hands.

ÖRNULF.   **There is** no need.

GUNNAR.   **There is** peace and friendship between us.

HIÖRDIS (*with suppressed scorn*).   Friendship? Well well, I **know** thou art a wise man, Gunnar!   Kåre has met mighty friends, and well I wot thou deem'st it safest——

GUNNAR.   Thy taunts avail not!   (*With dignity.*) Kåre is at peace for us!

HIÖRDIS (*restraining herself*).   Well and good ; if thou hast sworn him peace, the vow must be held.

Gunnar (*forcibly, **but without anger***). It must and it shall.

Örnulf (*to* Hiördis). Another pact had been well-nigh made ere thy coming.

Hiördis (*sharply*). Between thee and Gunnar.

Örnulf (*nods*). It had to do with thee.

Hiördis. Well can I guess what it had to do with; but this I tell thee, foster-father, never shall it be said that Gunnar let himself be cowed because thou camest in arms to the isle. Hadst thou come alone, a single wayfarer, to our hall, the quarrel had more easily been healed.

Gunnar. Örnulf and his sons come in peace.

Hiördis. Mayhap; but otherwise will it sound in the mouths of men; and thou thyself, Gunnar, didst show scant trust in the peace yesterday, in sending our son Egil to the southland so soon as it was known that Örnulf's warship lay in the fiord.

Sigurd (*to* Gunnar). Didst thou send thy son to the south?

Hiördis. Ay, that he might be in safety should Örnulf fall upon us.

Örnulf. Scoff not at that, Hiördis; what Gunnar has done may prove wise in the end, if so be thou hinderest the pact.

Hiördis. Life must take its chance; come what will, I had liever die than save my life by a shameful pact.

Dagny. Sigurd makes atonement, and will not be deemed the lesser man for that.

Hiördis. Sigurd best knows what his own honour can bear.

SIGURD. On that score shall I never need reminding.

HIÖRDIS. Sigurd has done famous deeds, but the boldest deed of all was Gunnar's, when he slew the white bear that guarded my bower.

GUNNAR (*with an embarrassed glance at Sigurd*). Nay nay, no more of that!

ÖRNULF. In truth it was the boldest deed that e'er was seen in Iceland; and therefore——

SIGURD. The more easily can Gunnar yield, and not be deemed a coward.

HIÖRDIS. If amends are to be made, amends shall also be craved. Bethink thee, Gunnar, of thy vow!

GUNNAR. That vow was ill bethought; wilt thou hold me to it?

HIÖRDIS. That will I, if we two are to dwell under one roof after this day. Know then, Örnulf, that if atonement is to be made for the carrying away of thy foster-daughter, thou, too, must atone for the slaying of Jökul my father, and the seizure of his goods and gear.

ÖRNULF. Jökul was slain in fair fight;[1] thy kinsmen did me a worse wrong when they sent thee to Iceland and entrapped me into adopting[2] thee, unwitting who thou wast.

HIÖRDIS. Honour, and no wrong, befell thee in adopting Jökul's daughter.

---

[1] "I ærlig holmgang." The established form of duel in the viking times was to land the combatants on one of the rocky islets or "holms" that stud the Norwegian coast, and there let them fight it out. Hence "holmgang" = duel.

[2] "At knæsætte" = to knee set a child, to take it on one's knee, an irrevocable form of adoption.

Örnulf.   Nought but strife hast thou brought me, that I know.

Hiördis.   Sterner strife may be at hand, if——

Örnulf.   I came not hither to bandy words with women!—Gunnar, hear my last word : art willing to make atonement ?

Hiördis (*to* Gunnar).   Think of thy vow!

Gunnar (*to* Örnulf).   Thou hearest, I have sworn a vow, and that must I——

Örnulf (*irritated*).   Enough, enough!   Never shall it be said that I made atonement for slaying in fair fight.

Hiördis (*forcibly*).   Then we bid defiance to thee and thine.

Örnulf (*in rising wrath*).   And who has the right to crave atonement for Jökul ?   Where are his kinsmen ?   There is none alive !   Where is his lawful avenger ?

Hiördis.   That is Gunnar, on my behalf.

Örnulf.   Gunnar!   Ay, hadst thou been betrothed to him with thy foster-father's good-will, or had he made atonement for carrying thee away, then were he thy father's lawful avenger ; but——

Dagny (*apprehensive and imploring*).   Father, father!

Sigurd (*quickly*).   Do not speak it !

Örnulf (*raising his voice*).   Nay, loudly shall it be spoken !   A woman wedded by force has no lawful husband !

Gunnar (*vehemently*).   Örnulf!

Hiördis (*in a wild outburst*).   Flouted and shamed !   (*In a quivering voice*) This—this shalt thou come to rue !

ÖRNULF (*continuing*).   **A woman** wedded by force is lawfully no more than a leman! Wilt thou regain thine honour, then must thou——

HIÖRDIS (*controlling herself*).   Nay, Örnulf, I know better what is fitting. If I am to be held as Gunnar's leman—well and good, then must he **win** me honour by his deeds—by deeds so mighty **that my** shame shall be shame no more! And thou, Örnulf, beware! Here our ways part, and from this day I shall make **war upon** thee and thine whensoever and wheresoever **it** may be ; thou shalt **know** no safety, thou, or any whom thou—— (*Looking fiercely at* KÅRE.) Kåre! Örnulf has stood **thy** friend, forsooth, and there is peace between **us ; but** I counsel **thee not to** seek thy home yet awhile ; the man thou slewest has **many** avengers, and it well might befall—— See, I have shown thee the danger ; thou must e'en take what follows.   Come, Gunnar, we must gird ourselves for the fight.   A famous deed didst thou achieve in Iceland, but greater deeds must here **be done, if** thou wouldst not have thy —thy leman shrink with shame from thee and from herself !

GUNNAR.   Curb thyself, Hiördis ; it is unseemly **to bear thee** thus.

DAGNY (*imploringly*).   Stay, foster-sister—stay ; I will appease my father.

HIÖRDIS (*without listening to her*).   Homewards, homewards ! Who could have foretold me that I should wear out my life as a worthless leman ? But if I am to bear this life of shame, ay, even a single day longer, then must my **husband** do such a deed—

such a deed as shall make his name more famous than all other names of men.

(*Goes out to the right.*)

GUNNAR (*softly*). Sigurd, this thou must promise me, that we shall have speech together ere thou leave the land.

(*Goes out with his men to the right.*)

(*The storm has meanwhile ceased ; the mid-day sun is now visible, like a red disc, low upon the rim of the sea.*)

ÖRNULF (*threateningly*). Dearly shalt thou aby this day's work, foster-daughter !

DAGNY. Father, father ! Surely thou wilt not harm her !

ÖRNULF. Let me be ! Now, Sigurd, now can no amends avail between Gunnar and me.

SIGURD. What thinkest thou to do?

ÖRNULF. That I know not; but far and wide shall the tale be told how Örnulf of the Fiords came to Gunnar's hall.

SIGURD (*with quiet determination*). That may be ; but this I tell thee, Örnulf, that thou shalt never bear arms against him so long as I am alive.

ÖRNULF. So, so ! And what if it be my will to ?

SIGURD. It shall not be—let thy will be never so strong.

ÖRNULF (*angrily*). Go then ; join thou with my foes ; I can match the twain of you !

SIGURD. Hear me out, Örnulf ; the day shall never dawn that shall see thee and me at strife. There is honourable peace between us, Dagny is dearer to me than weapons or gold, and never shall I forget that thou art her nearest kinsman.

ÖRNULF.   There I know thee again, brave Sigurd!

SIGURD.   But Gunnar is my foster-brother; faith and friendship have we sworn each other.   Both in war and peace have we faced fortune together, and of all men he is dearest to me.   Stout though he be, he loves not war;—but as for me, ye know, all of you, that I shrink not from strife; yet here I stand forth, Örnulf, and pray for peace on Gunnar's behalf.   Let me have my will!

ÖRNULF.   I cannot; I should be a scoff to all brave men, were I to fare empty-handed back to Iceland.

SIGURD.   Empty-handed shalt thou not fare. Here in the cove my two long-ships are lying, with all the wealth I have won in my viking-ventures. There are many costly gifts from outland kings, good weapons by the chestful, and other priceless chattels. Take thou one of the ships; choose which thou wilt, and it shall be thine with all it contains—be that the atonement for Hiördis, and let Gunnar be at peace.

ÖRNULF.   Brave Sigurd, wilt thou do this for Gunnar?

SIGURD.   For a faithful friend, no man can do too much.

ÖRNULF.   Give half thy goods and gear!

SIGURD (*urgently*).   Take the whole, take both my ships, take all that is mine, and let me fare with thee to Iceland as the poorest man in thy train.   What I give, I can win once more; but if thou and Gunnar come to strife, I shall never see a glad day again. Now, Örnulf, thy answer?

Örnulf (*reflecting*). Two good long - ships, weapons and other chattels—too much gear can no man have; but—— (*vehemently*) no no!—Hiördis has threatened me; I will not! It were shameful for me to take thy goods!

Sigurd. Yet listen——

Örnulf. No, I say! I must fight my own battle, be my fortune what it may.

Kåre (*approaching*). Right friendly is Sigurd's rede, but if thou wilt indeed fight thine own battle with all thy might, I can counsel thee better. Dream not of atonement so long as Hiördis has aught to say; but revenge can be thine if thou wilt hearken to me.

Örnulf. Revenge? What dost thou counsel?

Sigurd. Evil, I can well see.

Dagny (*to* Örnulf). Oh, do not hear him!

Kåre. Hiördis has declared me an outlaw; with cunning will she seek to take my life; do thou swear to see me scatheless, and this night will I burn Gunnar's hall and all within it. Is that to thy mind?

Sigurd. Dastard!

Örnulf (*quietly*). To my mind? Knowest thou, Kåre, what were more to my mind? (*In a voice of thunder.*) To hew off thy nose and ears, thou vile thrall. Little dost thou know old Örnulf if thou thinkest to have his help in such a deed of shame!

Kåre (*who has shrunk backwards*). If thou fall not upon Gunnar he will surely fall upon thee.

ÖRNULF.   Have I not weapons, and strength to wield them ?

SIGURD (*to* KÅRE).   And now away with thee! Thy presence is a shame to honourable men !

KÅRE (*going off*).   Well well, I must shield myself as best I can.   But this I tell you : if ye think to deal gently with Hiördis, ye will come to rue it ; I know her—and I know where to strike her sorest !

(*Goes down towards the shore.*)

DAGNY.   He is plotting revenge.   Sigurd, it must be hindered !

ÖRNULF (*with annoyance*).   Nay, let him do as he will ; she is worth no better !

DAGNY.   That meanest thou not ; bethink thee, she is thy foster-child.

ÖRNULF.   Woe worth the day when I took her under my roof !   Jökul's words are coming true.

SIGURD.   Jökul's ?

ÖRNULF.   Ay, her father's.   When I gave him his death-wound he fell back upon the sward, and fixed his eyes on me and sang :—

> Jökul's kin for Jökul's slayer
> many a woe shall still be weaving;
> Jökul's hoard whoe'er shall harry
> heartily shall rue his rashness.

When he had sung that, he was silent a while, and laughed; and thereupon he died.

SIGURD.   Why should'st thou heed his words ?

ÖRNULF.   Who knows ?   The story goes, and many believe it, that Jökul gave his children a wolf's heart to eat, that they might be fierce and fell ; and Hiördis has surely had her share, that one can well

see. (*Breaks off, on looking out towards the right.*)
Gunnar!—Are we two to meet again !

GUNNAR (*enters*).   Ay, Örnulf, think of me what
thou wilt, but I cannot part from thee as thy foe.

ÖRNULF.   What is thy purpose ?

GUNNAR.   To hold out the hand of fellowship to
thee ere thou depart.   Hear me all of you : go with
me to my homestead, and be my guests as long as ye
will.   We lack not meat or drink or sleeping-room,
and there shall be no talk of our quarrel either to-day
or to-morrow.

SIGURD.   But Hiördis—— ?

GUNNAR.   Yields to my will; she changed her
thought on the homeward way, and deemed, as I did,
that we would soon be at one if ye would but be
our guests.

DAGNY.   Yes, yes ; let it be so.

SIGURD (*doubtfully*).   But I know not whether——

DAGNY.   Gunnar is thy foster-brother; little I
know thee if thou say him nay.

GUNNAR (*to* SIGURD).   Thou hast been my friend
where’er we fared; thou wilt not stand against me now.

DAGNY.   And to depart from the land, leaving
Hiördis with hate in her heart—no, no, that must we
not !

GUNNAR.   I have done Örnulf a great wrong;
until it is made good, I cannot be at peace with
myself.

SIGURD (*vehemently*).   All else will I do for thee,
Gunnar, but not stay here ! (*Mastering himself.*)
I am in King Æthelstan’s service, and I must be
with him in England ere the winter is out.

DAGNY. But that thou canst be, nevertheless.

GUNNAR. No man can know what lot awaits him ; mayhap this is our last meeting, Sigurd, and thou wilt repent that thou didst not stand by me to the end.

DAGNY. And long will it be ere thou see me glad again, if thou set sail to-day.

SIGURD (*determined*). Well, be it so ! It shall be as ye will, although—— But no more of that ; here is my hand ; I will stay to feast with thee and Hiördis.

GUNNAR (*shakes his hand*). Thanks, Sigurd, I never doubted thee.—And thou, Örnulf, dost thou say likewise ?

ÖRNULF (*unappeased*). I shall think upon it. Bitterly has Hiördis wounded me ;—I will not answer to-day.

GUNNAR. It is well, old warrior ; Sigurd and Dagny will know how to smooth thy brow. Now must I prepare the feast ; peace be with you the while, and well met in my hall ! (*Goes out by the right.*)

SIGURD (*to himself*). Hiördis has changed her thought, said he ? Little he knows her ; I rather deem that she is plotting—— (*interrupting himself and turning to his men*). Come, follow me all to the ships ; good gifts will I choose for Gunnar and his household.

DAGNY Gifts of the best we have. And thou, father—thou shalt have no peace for me until thou yield thee. (*She goes with* SIGURD *and his men down towards the shore at the back.*)

Örnulf. Yield me? Ay, if there were no women-folk in Gunnar's house, then—— Oh, if I but knew how to pierce her armour!—Thorolf, thou here!

Thorolf (*who has entered hastily*). As thou seest. Is it true that thou hast met with Gunnar?

Örnulf. Yes.

Thorolf. And art at enmity with him?

Örnulf. Hm—at least with Hiördis.

Thorolf. Then be of good cheer; soon shalt thou be avenged!

Örnulf. Avenged? Who shall avenge me?

Thorolf. Listen: as I stood on board the ship, there came a man running, with a staff in his hand, and called to me: "If thou be of Örnulf's shipfolk, then greet him from Kåre the Peasant, and say that now am I avenging the twain of us." Thereupon he took a boat and rowed away, saying as he passed: "Twenty outlaws are at haven in the fiord; with them I fare southward, and ere eventide shall Hiördis be childless."

Örnulf. He said that! Ha, now I understand; Gunnar has sent his son away; Kåre is at feud with him——

Thorolf. And now he is rowing southward to slay the boy!

Örnulf (*with sudden resolution*). Up all! That booty will we fight for!

Thorolf. What wilt thou do?

Örnulf. Ask me not; it shall be I, and not Kåre, that will take revenge!

Thorolf. I will go with thee!

ÖRNULF.   Nay, do thou follow with Sigurd **and** thy sister to Gunnar's hall.

THOROLF.   Sigurd?   Is he in the isle?

ÖRNULF.   There may'st thou see his warships; we are at one—do thou go with him.

THOROLF.   Among thy foes?

ÖRNULF.   Go thou **to** the feast. Now shall Hiördis **learn to** know old Örnulf! But hark thee, Thorolf, **to** no one must thou **speak** of what I purpose; dost hear? to no one!

THOROLF.   I **promise.**

ÖRNULF (*takes his hand and looks at him affectionately*).   Farewell then, **my fair** boy; bear thee in courtly wise at the feast-house, that I may have honour of **thee.**   Beware **of** idle babbling; but what **thou sayest, let it** be keen as **a** sword.   Be friendly **to** those **that** deal with thee in friendly wise; but if thou be taunted, hold not **thy peace.**   Drink not more than thou canst bear; but put not the horn aside when it is offered thee in measure, lest thou be deemed womanish.

THOROLF.   Nay, **be at** ease!

ÖRNULF.   Then away to the feast at Gunnar's hall. I too will come to the feast, and that in the guise they least think of. (*Blithely to the rest.*) Come, my wolf-cubs; **be** your fangs keen;—now shall ye have blood **to** drink.

> (*He goes off with his elder sons to the right, at the back.*)

> (SIGURD *and* DAGNY *come up from the ships, richly dressed for the banquet. They are followed by two men, carrying a chest, who lay it down and return as they came.*)

THOROLF (*looking out after his father*).   Now fare they all forth to fight, and I must stay behind; it is hard to be the youngest of the house.—Dagny! all hail and greetings to thee, sister mine!

DAGNY.   Thorolf!   All good powers!—thou art a man, grown!

THOROLF.   That may I well be, forsooth, in five years——

DAGNY.   Ay, true, true.

SIGURD (*giving him his hand*).   In thee will Örnulf find a stout carl, or I mistake me.

THOROLF.   Would he but prove me——!

DAGNY (*smiling*).   He spares thee more than thou hast a mind to?   Thou wast ever well-nigh too dear to him.

SIGURD.   Whither has he gone?

THOROLF.   Down to his ships;—he will return ere long.

SIGURD.   I await my men; they are mooring my ships and bringing ashore wares.

THOROLF.   There must I lend a hand!

(*Goes down towards the shore.*)

SIGURD (*after a moment's reflection*).   Dagny, my wife, we are alone; I have that to tell thee which must no longer be hidden.

DAGNY (*surprised*).   What meanest thou?

SIGURD.   There may be danger in this faring to Gunnar's hall.

DAGNY.   Danger?   Thinkest thou that Gunnar——?

SIGURD.   Nay, Gunnar is brave and true—yet better had it been that I had sailed from the isle without crossing his threshold.

DAGNY.   Thou makest me fear!   Sigurd, what is amiss?

SIGURD.   First answer me this: the golden ring that I gave thee, where hast thou it?

DAGNY (*showing it*).   Here, on my arm; thou badest me wear it.

SIGURD.   Cast it to the bottom of the sea, so deep that none may ever set eyes on it again; else may it be the bane of many men!

DAGNY.   The ring!

SIGURD (*in a low voice*).   That evening when we carried away thy father's daughters—dost remember it?

DAGNY.   Do I remember it!

SIGURD.   It is of that I would speak.

DAGNY (*in suspense*).   What is it?   Say on!

SIGURD.   Thou knowest there had been a feast; thou didst seek thy chamber betimes; but Hiördis still sat among the men in the feast-hall.   The horn went busily round, and many a great vow was sworn. I swore to bear away a fair maid with me from Iceland; Gunnar swore the same as I, and passed the cup to Hiördis.   She grasped it and stood up, and vowed this vow, that no warrior should have her to wife, save he who should go to her bower, slay the white bear that stood bound at the door, and carry her away in his arms.

DAGNY.   Yes, yes; all this I know!

SIGURD.   All men deemed that it might not be, for the bear was the fiercest of beasts; none but Hiördis might come near it, and it had the strength of twenty men.

Dagny. But Gunnar slew it, and by that deed won fame throughout all lands.

Sigurd (*in a low voice*). He won the fame—but—*I* did the deed!

Dagny (*with a cry*). Thou!

Sigurd. When the men left the feast-hall, Gunnar prayed me to come with him alone to our sleeping-place. Then said he : " Hiördis is dearer to me than all women ; without her I cannot live." I answered him : " Then go to her bower ; thou knowest the vow she hath sworn." But he said : " Life is dear to him that loves ; if I should assail the bear, the end were doubtful, and I am loath to lose my life, for then should I lose Hiördis too." Long did we talk, and the end was that Gunnar made ready his ship, while I drew my sword, donned Gunnar's harness, and went to the bower.

Dagny (*with pride and joy*). And thou—thou didst slay the bear !

Sigurd. I slew him. In the bower it was dark as under a raven's wing ; Hiördis deemed it was Gunnar that sat by her—she was heated with the mead—she drew a ring from her arm and gave it to me—it is that thou wearest now.

Dagny (*hesitating*). And thou didst pass the night with Hiördis in her bower ?

Sigurd. My sword lay drawn between us. (*A short pause*). Ere the dawn, I bore Hiördis to Gunnar's ship ; she dreamed not of our wiles, and he sailed away with her. Then went I to thy sleeping-place and found thee there among thy women ;—what followed, thou knowest ; I sailed from Iceland with a fair maid, as I had sworn, and from that day hast thou stood faithfully at my side whithersoever I might wander.

DAGNY (*much moved*).   My brave husband ! And that great deed was thine !—Oh, I should have known it ; none but thou would have dared ! Hiördis, that proud and stately woman, couldst thou have won, yet didst choose me ! Now wouldst thou be tenfold dearer to me, wert thou not already dearer than all the world.

SIGURD.   Dagny, my sweet wife, now thou knowest all—that is needful. I could not but warn thee ; for that ring—Hiördis must never set eyes on it ! Wouldst thou do my will, then cast it from thee—into the depths of the sea.

DAGNY.   Nay, Sigurd, it is too dear to me ; is it not thy gift ? But be thou at ease, I shall hide it from every eye, and never shall I breathe a word of what thou hast told me.

(THOROLF *comes up from the ships, with* SIGURD'S *men.*)

THOROLF.   All is ready for the feast.

DAGNY.   Come then, Sigurd—my brave, my noble warrior !

SIGURD.   Beware, Dagny—beware ! It rests with thee now whether this meeting shall end peacefully or in bloodshed. (*Cheerfully to the others.*)   Away then, to the feast in Gunnar's hall !

(*Goes* out *with* DAGNY *to the right ; the others follow.*)

Act Second.

(The feast-room in GUNNAR'S house. The entrance-door is in the back; smaller doors in the side-walls. In front, on the left, the greater high-seat; opposite it, on the right, the lesser. In the middle of the floor, a wood fire is burning on a built-up hearth. In the background, on both sides of the door, are daïses for the women of the household. From each of the high-seats, a long table, with benches, stretches backwards, parallel with the wall. It is dark outside; the fire lights the room.)

(HIÖRDIS *and* DAGNY *enter from the right.*)

DAGNY. Nay, Hiördis, I cannot understand thee. Thou hast shown me all the house; I know not what thing thou lackest, and all thou hast is fair and goodly;—then why bemoan thy lot?

HIÖRDIS. Cage an eagle and it will bite at the wires, be they of iron or of gold.

DAGNY. In one thing at least thou art richer than I; thou hast Egil, thy little son.

HIÖRDIS. Better no child, than one born in shame.

DAGNY. In shame?

HIÖRDIS. Dost thou forgot thy father's saying? Egil is the son of a leman; that was his word.

DAGNY. A word spoken in wrath—why wilt thou heed it?

HIÖRDIS. Nay, nay, Örnulf was right; Egil is weak; one can see he is no freeborn child.

DAGNY. Hiördis, how canst thou——?

HIÖRDIS (*unheeding*). Thus is shame sucked into

the blood, like the venom of a snake-bite. Of another mettle are the freeborn sons of mighty men. I have heard of a queen that took her son and sewed his kirtle fast to his flesh, yet he never blinked an eye. (*With a look of cruelty.*) Dagny, that will I try with Egil!

DAGNY (*horrified*). Hiördis, Hiördis!

HIÖRDIS (*laughing*). Ha-ha-ha! Dost thou think I meant my words? (*Changing her tone.*) But, believe me or not as thou wilt, there are times when such deeds seem to lure me; it must run in the blood,—for I am of the race of the Jotuns,[1] they say. —Come, sit thou here, Dagny. Far hast thou wandered in these five long years; tell me, thou hast ofttimes been a guest in the halls of kings?

DAGNY. Many a time—and chiefly with Æthelstan of England.

HIÖRDIS. And everywhere thou hast been held in honour, and hast sat in the highest seats at the board?

DAGNY. Doubtless. As Sigurd's wife——

HIÖRDIS. Ay, ay—a famous man is Sigurd—though Gunnar stands above him.

DAGNY. Gunnar?

HIÖRDIS. One deed did Gunnar do that Sigurd shrank from. But let that be! Tell me, when thou didst go a-viking with Sigurd, when thou didst hear the sword-blades sing in the fierce war-game, when the blood streamed red on the deck—came there not over thee an untameable longing to plunge into the strife? Didst thou not don harness and take up arms?

---

[1] The giants or Titans of Scandinavian mythology.

Dagny. Never! How canst thou think it? I, a woman!

Hiördis. A woman, a woman,—who knows what a woman may do!—But one thing thou canst tell me, Dagny, for that thou surely knowest: when a man clasps to his breast the woman he loves—is it true that her blood burns, that her bosom throbs—that she swoons in a shuddering ecstasy?

Dagny (*blushing*). Hiördis, how canst thou——!

Hiördis. Come, tell me——!

Dagny. Surely thou thyself hast known it.

Hiördis. Ay once, and only once; it was that night when Gunnar sat with me in my bower; he crushed me in his arms till his byrnie burst, and then, then——!

Dagny (*exclaiming*). What! Sigurd——!

Hiördis. Sigurd? What of Sigurd? I spoke of Gunnar—that night when he bore me away——

Dagny (*collecting herself*). Yes, yes, I remember —I know well——

Hiördis. That was the only time; never, never again! I deemed I was bewitched; for that Gunnar could so clasp a woman—— (*Stops and looks at* Dagny.) What ails thee? Methinks thou turnest pale and red!

Dagny. Nay, nay!

Hiördis (*without noticing her*). The merry viking-raid should have been *my* lot; it had been better for me, and—mayhap for all of us. That were life, full and rich life! Dost thou not wonder, Dagny, to find me here alive? Art not afraid to be alone with me in the hall, thus in the dark? Deem'st thou not that

I must have died in all these years, and that it is my ghost that stands at thy side?

DAGNY (*painfully affected*).   Come—let us go—to the others.

HIÖRDIS (*seizing her by the arm*).   No, stay! Seems it not strange to thee, Dagny, that any woman can yet live after five such nights?

DAGNY.   Five nights?

HIÖRDIS.   Here in the north each night is a whole winter long.   (*Quickly and with an altered expression.*) Yet the place is fair enough, doubt it not!   Thou shalt see sights here such as thou hast not seen in the halls of the English king.   We shall be together as sisters whilst thou bidest with me; we shall go down to the sea when the storm begins once more; thou shalt see the billows rushing upon the land like wild, white-maned horses—and then the whales far out in the offing!   They dash one against another like steel-clad knights!   Ha, what joy to be a witch-wife and ride on a whale's back—to speed before the skiff, and wake the storm, and lure men to the deeps with lovely songs of sorcery!

DAGNY.   Fie, Hiördis, how canst thou talk so!

HIÖRDIS.   Canst thou sing sorceries, Dagny?

DAGNY (*with horror*).   I!

HIÖRDIS.   I trow thou canst; how else didst thou lure Sigurd to thee?

DAGNY.   Thou speakest shameful things; let me go!

HIÖRDIS (*holding her back*).   Because I jest!   Nay, hear me to the end!   Think, Dagny, what it is to sit by the window in the eventide and hear the kelpie[1]

---

[1] "Draugen," a vague and horrible sea-monster.

wailing in the boat-house; to sit waiting and listening for the dead men's ride to Valhal; for their way lies past us here in the north. They are the brave men that fell in fight, the strong women that did not drag out their lives tamely, like thee and me; they sweep through the storm-night on their black horses, with jangling bells! (*Embraces* Dagny, *and presses her wildly in her arms.*) Ha, Dagny! think of riding the last ride on so rare a steed!

Dagny (*struggling to escape*). Hiördis, Hiördis! Let me go! I will not hear thee!

Hiördis (*laughing*). Weak art thou of heart, and easily affrighted.

(Gunnar *enters from the back, with* Sigurd *and* Thorolf.)

Gunnar. Now, truly, are all things to my very mind! I have found thee again, Sigurd, my brave brother, as kind and true as of old. I have Örnulf's son under my roof, and the old man himself follows speedily after; is it not so?

Thorolf. So he promised.

Gunnar. Then all I lack is that Egil should be here.

Thorolf. 'Tis plain thou lovest the boy, thou namest him so oft.

Gunnar. Truly I love him; he is my only child; and he is like to grow up fair and kindly.

Hiördis. But no warrior.

Gunnar. Nay—that thou must not say.

Sigurd. I marvel thou didst send him from thee——

Gunnar. Would that I had not! (*Half aside.*) But thou knowest, Sigurd, he who loves overmuch, takes not always the manliest part. (*Aloud.*) I had few men in my house, and none could be sure of his life when it was known that Örnulf lay in the cove with a ship of war.

HIÖRDIS. One thing I know that ought first to be made safe, life afterwards.

THOROLF. And that is——?

HIÖRDIS. Honour and fame among men.

GUNNAR. Hiördis!

SIGURD. It shall not be said of Gunnar that he has risked his honour by doing this.

GUNNAR (*sternly*). None shall make strife between me and Örnulf's kinsfolk!

HIÖRDIS (*smiling*). Hm; tell me, Sigurd—can thy ship sail with any wind?

SIGURD. Ay, when it is cunningly steered.

HIÖRDIS. Good! I too will steer my ship cunningly, and make my way whither I will.

(*Retires towards the back.*)

DAGNY (*whispers, uneasily*). Sigurd, let us hence—this very night!

SIGURD. It is too late now; it was thou that——

DAGNY. Then I held Hiördis dear; but now——; I have heard her speak words I shudder to think of.

(SIGURD'S *men, with other guests, men and women, house-carls and handmaidens, enter from the back.*)

GUNNAR (*after a short pause for the exchange of greetings and so forth*). Now to the board! My chief guest, Örnulf of the Fiords, comes later; so Thorolf promises.

HIÖRDIS (*to the house-folk*). Pass ale and mead

around, that hearts may wax merry and tongues may be loosed.

> (GUNNAR *leads* SIGURD *to the high-seat on the right.* DAGNY *seats herself on* SIGURD'S *right,* HIÖRDIS *opposite him, at the other side of the same table.* THOROLF *is in like manner ushered to a place at the other table, and thus sits opposite* GUNNAR, *who occupies the greater high-seat. The others take their seats further back.*)

HIÖRDIS (*after a pause in which they drink with each other and converse quietly across the tables*). It seldom chances that so many brave men are seated together, as I see to-night in our hall. It were fitting, then, that we should essay the old pastime: Let each man name his chief exploit, that all may judge which is the mightiest.

GUNNAR. That is an ill custom at a drinking-feast; it will oft breed strife.

HIÖRDIS. Little did I deem that Gunnar was afraid.

SIGURD. That no one deems; but it were long ere we came to an end, were we all to tell of our exploits, so many as we be. Do thou rather tell us, Gunnar, of thy journey to Biarmeland; 'tis no small exploit to fare so far to the north, and gladly would we hear of it.

HIÖRDIS. The journey to Biarmeland is chapman's work, and little worthy to be named among warriors. Nay, do thou begin, Sigurd, if thou would'st not have me deem that thou shrinkest from hearing my husband's praise! Say on; name that one of thy deeds which thou dost prize the highest.

SIGURD.   Well, since thou will have it so, so must it be.   Let it be told, then, that I lay a-viking among the Orkneys; there came foemen against us, but we swept them from their ships, and I fought alone against eight men.

HIÖRDIS.   Good was that deed; but wast thou fully armed?

SIGURD.   Fully armed, with axe, spear, and sword.

HIÖRDIS.   Still the deed was good.   Now must thou, my husband, name that which thou deemest the greatest among thy exploits.

GUNNAR (*unwillingly*).   I slew two berserkers who had seized a merchant-ship; and thereupon I sent the captive chapmen home, giving them their ship freely, without ransom.   The King of England deemed well of that deed; he said that I had done honourably, and gave me thanks and good gifts.

HIÖRDIS.   Nay truly, Gunnar, a better deed than that couldst thou name.

GUNNAR (*vehemently*).   I will boast of no other deed!   Since last I fared from Iceland I have lived at peace and traded in merchandise.   No word more on this matter!

HIÖRDIS.   If thou thyself wilt hide thy renown, thy wife shall speak.

GUNNAR.   Peace, Hiördis—I command thee!

HIÖRDIS.   Sigurd fought with eight men, being fully armed; Gunnar came to my bower in the black night, slew the bear that had twenty men's strength, and yet had but a short sword in his hand.

GUNNAR (*violently agitated*).   Woman, not a word more!

DAGNY (*softly*). Sigurd, wilt thou bear——?

SIGURD (*likewise*). Be still!

HIÖRDIS (*to the company*). And now, ye brave men—which is the mightier, Sigurd or Gunnar?

GUNNAR. Silence!

HIÖRDIS (*loudly*). Speak out; I have the right to crave your judgment.

AN OLD MAN (*among the guests*). If the truth be told, then is Gunnar's deed greater than all other deeds of men; Gunnar is the mightiest warrior, and Sigurd is second to him.

GUNNAR (*with a glance across the table*). Ah, Sigurd, Sigurd, didst thou but know——!

DAGNY (*softly*). This is too much—even for a friend!

SIGURD. Peace, wife! (*Aloud, to the others.*) Ay truly, Gunnar is the most honourable of all men; so would I esteem him to my dying day, even had he never done that deed; for that I hold more lightly than ye.

HIÖRDIS. There speaks thy envy, Sigurd Viking!

SIGURD (*smiling*). Mightily art thou mistaken. (*Kindly, to* GUNNAR, *drinking to him across the table.*) Hail, noble Gunnar; our friendship shall stand fast, whosoever may seek to break it.

HIÖRDIS. No one, that I wot of, has such a thought.

SIGURD. Say not that; I could almost find it in me to think that thou hadst bidden us hither to stir up strife.

HIÖRDIS. That is like thee, Sigurd; now art thou

wroth that thou may'st not be held the mightiest man at the feast-board.

SIGURD. I have ever esteemed Gunnar more highly than myself.

HIÖRDIS. Well, well—second to Gunnar is still a good place, and—— (*with a side-glance at* THOROLF) had Örnulf been here, he could have had the third seat.

THOROLF. Then would Jökul, thy father, find a low place indeed; for he fell before Örnulf.

 (*The following dispute is carried on, by both parties,*
  with rising and yet repressed irritation.)

HIÖRDIS. That shalt thou never say! Örnulf is a skald, and men whisper that he has praised himself for greater deeds than he has done.

THOROLF. Then woe to him who whispers so loudly that it comes to my ear!

HIÖRDIS (*with a smile of provocation*). Wouldst thou avenge it?

THOROLF. Ay, so that my vengeance should be told of far and wide.

HIÖRDIS. Then here I pledge a cup to this, that thou may'st first have a beard on thy chin.

THOROLF. Even a beardless lad is too good to wrangle with women.

HIÖRDIS. But too weak to fight with men; therefore thy father let thee lie by the hearth at home in Iceland, whilst thy brothers went a-viking.

THOROLF. It had been well had he kept as good an eye on thee; for then hadst thou not left Iceland a dishonoured woman.

GUNNAR AND SIGURD. Thorolf!

DAGNY (*simultaneously*). Brother!

HIÖRDIS (*softly, and quivering with rage*). Ha! wait—wait!

THOROLF (*gives* GUNNAR *his hand*). Be not wroth, Gunnar; evil words came to my tongue; but thy wife egged me!

DAGNY (*softly and imploringly*). Foster-sister, by any love thou hast ever borne me, stir not up strife!

HIÖRDIS (*laughing*). Jests must pass at the feast-board, if the merriment is to thrive.

GUNNAR (*who has been talking softly to* THOROLF). Thou art a brave lad! (*Hands him a sword which hangs beside the high-seat.*) Here, Thorolf, here is a good gift for thee. Wield it well, and let us be friends.

HIÖRDIS. Beware how thou givest away thy weapons, Gunnar; for men may say thou dost part with things thou canst not use!

THOROLF (*who has meanwhile examined the sword*). Thanks for the gift, Gunnar; it shall never be drawn in an unworthy cause.

HIÖRDIS. If thou wilt keep that promise, then do thou never lend the sword to thy brothers.

GUNNAR. Hiördis!

HIÖRDIS (*continuing*). Neither let it hang on thy father's wall; for there it would hang with base men's weapons.

THOROLF. True enough, Hiördis—for there thy father's axe and shield have hung this many a year.

HIÖRDIS (*mastering herself*). That Örnulf slew my father,—that deed is ever on thy tongue; but if report speak true, it was scarce so honourable a deed as thou deemest.

THOROLF.   Of what report dost thou speak?

HIÖRDIS.   I dare not name it, for it would make thee wroth.

THOROLF.   Then hold thy peace—I ask no better.

(*Turns from her.*)

HIÖRDIS.   Nay, why should I not tell it?   Is it true, Thorolf, that for three nights thy father sat in woman's weed, doing sorceries with the witch of Smalserhorn, ere he dared face Jökul in fight.

(*All rise; violent excitement among the guests.*)

GUNNAR, SIGURD, AND DAGNY.   Hiördis!

THOROLF (*bitterly exasperated*).   So base a lie has no man spoken of Örnulf of the Fiords!   Thou thyself hast made it, for no one less venomous than thou could dream of such a thing.   The blackest crime a man can do hast thou laid at my father's door. (*Throwing the sword away.*)   There, Gunnar, take thy gift again; I can take nought from that house wherein my father is reviled.

GUNNAR.   Thorolf, hear me——!

THOROLF.   Let me go! But beware both thou and Hiördis; for my father has now in his power one whom ye hold dearest of all!

HIÖRDIS (*starting*).   Thy father has——!

GUNNAR (*with a cry*).   What sayst thou!

SIGURD (*vehemently*).   Where is Örnulf?

THOROLF (*with mocking laughter*).   Gone southward—with my brothers.

GUNNAR.   Southward!

Hiördis (*shrieking*). Gunnar! Örnulf has slain Egil, our son.

Gunnar. Slain!—Egil slain! Then woe to Örnulf and all his race! Thorolf, speak out;—is this true?

Sigurd. Gunnar, Gunnar—hear me!

Gunnar. Speak out, if thou care for thy life!

Thorolf. Thou canst not fright me! Wait till my father comes; he shall plant a mark of shame over against Gunnar's house! And meanwhile, Hiördis, do thou cheer thee with these words I heard to-day: "Ere eventide shall Gunnar and his wife be childless."

(*Goes out by the back.*)

Gunnar (*in the deepest pain*). Slain—slain! My little Egil slain!

Hiördis (*wildly*). And thou—dost thou let him go? Let Egil, thy child, lie unavenged! Then wert thou the dastard of dastards——!

Gunnar (*as if beside himself*). A sword—an axe! It is the last message he shall bring!

(*Seizes an axe from one of the bystanders and rushes out.*)

Sigurd (*about to follow*). Gunnar, hold thy hand!

Hiördis (*holding him back*). Stay, stay! The men will part them; I know Gunnar!

(*A cry from the crowd, which has flocked together at the main door.*)

Sigurd and Dagny. What is it?

A Voice among the Crowd. Thorolf has fallen.

SIGURD. Thorolf! **Ha, let me go!**

DAGNY. My brother! Oh, my brother!

(SIGURD *is on the point of rushing out. At the same moment, the crowd parts,* GUNNAR *enters, and throws down the axe at the door.*)

GUNNAR. Now it is done. Egil is avenged!

SIGURD. Well for thee if thy hand has not been too hasty.

GUNNAR. Mayhap, mayhap; but Egil, Egil, my sweet boy!

HIÖRDIS. Now must we arm us, and seek help among our friends; for Thorolf has many avengers.

GUNNAR (*gloomily*). He will be his own worst avenger; he will haunt me night and day.

HIÖRDIS. Thorolf got his reward. Kinsmen must suffer for kinsmen's deeds.

GUNNAR. True, true; but this I know, my mind was lighter ere this befell.

HIÖRDIS. The first night[1] is ever the worst;— when that is over, thou wilt heed it no more. Örnulf has sought his revenge by shameful wiles; he would not come against us in open strife; he feigned to be peacefully-minded; and then he falls upon our defenceless child! Ha, I saw more clearly than ye; well I deemed that Örnulf was evil-minded and false; I had good cause to egg thee on against him and all his faithless tribe!

GUNNAR (*fiercely*). That hadst thou! My vengeance is poor beside Örnulf's crime. He has lost Thorolf, but he has six sons left—and I have none— none!

---

[1] Literally the "blood-night."

A HOUSE-CARL (*enters hastily from the back*). Örnulf of the Fiords is at hand!

GUNNAR. Örnulf!

HIÖRDIS AND SEVERAL MEN. To arms! to arms!

DAGNY (*simultaneously*). My father!

SIGURD (*as if seized by a foreboding*). Örnulf——! Ah, Gunnar, Gunnar!

GUNNAR (*draws his sword*). Up all my men! Vengeance for Egil's death!

(ÖRNULF *enters, with* EGIL *in his arms.*)

GUNNAR (*with a shriek*). Egil!

ÖRNULF. Here I bring you little Egil.

ALL (*one to another*). Egil! Egil alive!

GUNNAR (*letting his sword fall*). Woe is me! what have I done?

DAGNY. Oh, Thorolf, my brother!

SIGURD. I knew it! I knew it!

ÖRNULF (*setting* EGIL *down*). There, Gunnar, hast thou thy pretty boy again.

EGIL. Father! Old Örnulf would not do me ill, as thou saidst when I went away.

ÖRNULF (*to* HIÖRDIS). Now have I atoned for thy father; now surely there may be peace between us.

HIÖRDIS (*with repressed emotion*). Mayhap!

GUNNAR (*as if waking up*). Is it a ghastly dream that maddens me! Thou—thou bringest Egil home!

ÖRNULF. As thou seest; but in truth he has been near his death.

GUNNAR. That I know.

ÖRNULF. And hast no more joy in his return?

GUNNAR. Had he **come sooner, I had** been glad indeed. But tell me all that has befallen!

ÖRNULF. That is soon done. **Kåre** the Peasant was plotting evil against **you ; with other** caitiffs he fared southward after Egil.

GUNNAR. Kåre! (*To himself.*) **Ha,** now I understand Thorolf's words!

ÖRNULF. His purpose came **to my ears ; I** needs must **thwart so** black a deed. I would **not** give atonement **for** Jökul, **and, had** things so befallen, I had willingly slain thee, Gunnar, in single combat— yet I could not but protect thy child. With my sons, I hasted after Kåre.

SIGURD (*softly*). An accursed deed **has** here been done.

ÖRNULF. **When I came** up with him, Egil's **guards lay bound ;** thy son was already in thy foe- men's hand, **and they** would not long have spared him. Hot was the fight! Seldom have I given and taken keener strokes ; Kåre and two men fled inland ; the rest sleep safely, and will be hard to waken.

GUNNAR (*in eager suspense*). But thou—thou, Örnulf——?

ÖRNULF (*gloomily*). Six **sons** followed me into the fight.

GUNNAR (*breathlessly*). But homewards——?

ÖRNULF. None.

GUNNAR (*appalled*). None! (*Softly.*) And Tho- rolf, Thorolf!

   (*Deep emotion among the bystanders.* HIÖRDIS
      shows signs of a violent mental struggle ;
      DAGNY *weeps silently by the high-seat on the*

right. SIGURD *stands beside her, painfully agitated.*)

ÖRNULF (*after a short pause*). It is hard for a many-branching pine to be stripped in a single storm. But men die and men live ;—I will drink to my sons' memory. (*One of* SIGURD'S *men hands him a horn.*) Hail to you where now ye ride, my bold sons! Close upon your heels shall the copper-gates not clang, for ye come to the hall with a great following. (*Drinks, and hands back the horn.*) And now home to Iceland! Örnulf has fought his last fight ; the old tree has but one green branch left, and it must be shielded warily. Where is Thorolf?

EGIL (*to his father*). Ay, show me Thorolf! Örnulf told me he would carve me a ship with many, many warriors aboard.

ÖRNULF. I praise all good wights that Thorolf came not with us; for if he too—nay, strong though I be, that had been too heavy for me to bear. But why comes he not? He was ever the first to meet his father ; for to both of us it seemed we could not live without each other a single day.

GUNNAR. Örnulf, Örnulf!

ÖRNULF (*with growing uneasiness*). Ye stand all silent, I mark it now. What ails you? Where is Thorolf?

DAGNY. Sigurd, Sigurd—this will be the direst blow to him!

GUNNAR (*struggling with himself*). Old man!— No—— —— and yet, it cannot be hid——

ÖRNULF (*vehemently*). My son! Where is he!

GUNNAR. Thorolf is slain!

ÖRNULF. Slain! **Thorolf?** Thorolf? Ha, thou liest!

GUNNAR. I would give my warmest heart-blood to know him alive!

HIÖRDIS (*to* ÖRNULF). Thorolf **was** himself to blame for what befell; with dark sayings he gave us to **wit that thou** hadst fallen upon Egil and slain him; —we had parted half in wrath, and thou hast ere now brought death among my kindred. And moreover— Thorolf bore himself **at the feast** like a wanton boy; he brooked **not our** jesting, and spoke many evil things. Not till then did **Gunnar wax wroth;** not till then did he raise his **hand** upon thy **son;** and well I wot that **he** had good and lawful ground for that deed.

ÖRNULF (*calmly*). Well may we see that thou art a woman, for thou usest many words. To what end? If Thorolf is slain, then is his saga over.

EGIL. If Thorolf is slain, I shall have no warriors.

ÖRNULF. Nay, Egil—we **have** lost our warriors, both thou and I. (*To* HIÖRDIS.) Thy father sang:

> Jökul's kin **for** Jökul's slayer
>
> **many a** woe shall still be weaving.

Well **hast** thou wrought that his words should come true. (*Pauses a moment, then turns **to** one of the men.*) Where got he his death-wound?

THE MAN. Right **across his brow.**

ÖRNULF (*pleased*). Hm; **that is an** honourable spot; he did not turn his back. But fell he sideways, or in towards Gunnar's feet?

THE MAN. Half sideways and half towards Gunnar

ÖRNULF. That bodes but half vengeance; well well,—we shall see!

GUNNAR (*approaching*). Örnulf, I know well that all my goods were naught against thy loss; but crave of me what thou wilt——

ÖRNULF (*sternly interrupting him*). Give me Thorolf's body, and let me go! Where lies he?

(GUNNAR *points silently to the back.*)

ÖRNULF (*takes a step or two, but turns and says in a voice of thunder to* SIGURD, DAGNY, *and others who are preparing to follow him, sorrowing*). Stay! Think ye Örnulf will be followed by a train of mourners, like a whimpering woman? Stay, I say! —I can bear my Thorolf alone. (*With calm strength.*) Sonless I go; but none shall say that he saw me bowed. (*He goes slowly out.*)

HIÖRDIS (*with forced laughter*). Ay, let him go as he will; we shall scarce need many men to face him should he come with strife again! Now, Dagny—I wot it is the last time thy father shall sail from Iceland on such a quest!

SIGURD (*indignant*). Oh, shame!

DAGNY (*likewise*). And thou canst scoff at him— scoff at him, after all that has befallen?

HIÖRDIS. A deed once done, 'tis wise to praise it. This morning I swore hate and vengeance against Örnulf;—the slaying of Jökul I might have forgotten —all, save that he cast shame upon my lot. He called me a leman; if it *be* so, it shames me not; for Gunnar is mightier now than thy father; he is greater and more famous than Sigurd, thine own husband!

DAGNY (*in wild indignation*). There thou errest,

Hiördis—and even **now** shall all men know that thou dwellest under **a** weakling's roof!

SIGURD (*vehemently*).   Dagny, beware!

GUNNAR.   A weakling!

HIÖRDIS (*with scornful laughter*).   Thou pratest senselessly.

DAGNY.   It shall no longer be hidden; I held my peace **till** thou didst **scoff** at my father and my dead brothers; I held my **peace** while Örnulf was here, lest **he should learn** that Thorolf fell by a dastard's hand.   But now—praise Gunnar nevermore for that deed in Iceland; for **Gunnar is** a weakling!   The sword that **lay drawn between** thee and the bear-slayer hangs **at** my husband's side—and the **ring** thou didst **take** from thy arm thou gavest to Sigurd. (*Takes it off and holds it aloft.*)   Behold it!

HIÖRDIS (*wildly*).   Sigurd!

THE CROWD.   Sigurd!   Sigurd did the deed!

HIÖRDIS (*quivering with agitation*).   He! he!— Gunnar, is this true?

GUNNAR (*with lofty calm*).   It is all true, save only that I am a weakling; I am neither a weakling nor a coward.

SIGURD (*moved*).   That **art** thou not, Gunnar! That hast thou never been!   (*To the rest.*)   Away, my men!   Away from here!

DAGNY (*at the door, to* HIÖRDIS).   Who is now the mightiest man at the board—my husband, or thine?

      (*She goes out with* SIGURD *and his men.*)

HIÖRDIS (*to herself*).   Now **have** I but one thing left to do—but one deed to brood upon: Sigurd or I must die!

Act Third.

(*The hall in* GUNNAR'S *house.   It is day.*)
(HIÖRDIS *sits on the bench in front of the smaller high-seat, busy weaving a bow-string; on the table lie a bow and some arrows.*)

HIÖRDIS (*pulling at the bow-string*).   It is tough and strong ; (*with a glance at the arrows*) the shaft is both keen and well-weighted—(*lets her hands fall in her lap*) but where is the hand that——! (*Vehemently.*) Befooled, befooled by him—by Sigurd !   I must hate him more than others, that can I well mark ; but ere many days have passed I will—— (*Meditating.*) Ay, but the arm, the arm that shall do the deed——?
   (GUNNAR *enters, silent and thoughtful, from the back.*)
HIÖRDIS (*after a short pause*).   How goes it with thee, my husband ?
GUNNAR.   Ill, Hiördis ; I cannot away with that deed of yesterday ; it lies heavy on my heart.
HIÖRDIS.   Do as I do ; get thee some work to busy thee.
GUNNAR.   Doubtless I must.
   (*A pause ;* GUNNAR *paces up and down the hall, notices what* HIÖRDIS *is doing, and approaches her.*)
GUNNAR.   What dost thou there ?

HIÖRDIS (*without looking up*). I am weaving a bow-string ; canst thou not see ?

GUNNAR. A bow-string—of thine own hair ?

HIÖRDIS (*smiling*). Great deeds are born with every hour in these times ; yesterday thou didst slay my foster-brother, and I have woven this since day-break.

GUNNAR. Hiördis, Hiördis !

HIÖRDIS (*looking up*). What is amiss ?

GUNNAR. Where wast thou last night ?

HIÖRDIS. Last night ?

GUNNAR. Thou wast not in the sleeping-room.

HIÖRDIS. Know'st thou that ?

GUNNAR. I could not sleep ; I tossed in restless dreams of that—that which befell Thorolf. I dreamt that he came—— No matter ; I wakened. Then meseemed I heard a strange, fair song through all the house ; I arose ; I stole hither to the door ; here I saw thee sitting by the log-fire—it burned blue and red—fixing arrow-heads, and singing sorceries over them.

HIÖRDIS. The work was not wasted ; for strong is the breast that must be pierced this day.

GUNNAR. I understand thee well ; thou wouldst have Sigurd slain.

HIÖRDIS. Hm, mayhap.

GUNNAR. Thou shalt never have thy will. I shall keep peace with Sigurd, howe'er thou goad me.

HIÖRDIS (*smiling*). Dost think so ?

GUNNAR. I know it !

HIÖRDIS (*hands him the bow-string*). Tell me, Gunnar—canst loose this knot ?

GUNNAR (*tries it*). Nay, it is too cunningly and firmly woven.

HIÖRDIS (*rising*). The Norns[1] weave yet more cunningly ; their web is still harder to unravel.

GUNNAR. Dark are the ways of the Mighty Ones ;—neither thou nor I know aught of them.

HIÖRDIS. Yet one thing I know surely : that to both of us must Sigurd's life be baleful.

(*A pause;* GUNNAR *stands lost in thought.*)

HIÖRDIS (*who has been silently watching him*). Of what thinkest thou ?

GUNNAR. Of a dream I had of late. Methought I had done the deed thou cravest ; Sigurd lay slain on the earth ; thou didst stand beside him, and thy face was wondrous pale. Then said I : " Art thou glad, now that I have done thy will?" But thou didst laugh and answer : "Blither were I didst thou, Gunnar, lie there in Sigurd's stead."

HIÖRDIS (*with forced laughter*). Ill must thou know me if such a senseless dream can make thee hold thy hand.

GUNNAR. Hm !—Tell me, Hiördis, what thinkest thou of this hall ?

HIÖRDIS. To speak truly, Gunnar,—it sometimes seems to me but straitened.

GUNNAR. Ay, ay, so I have thought ; we are one too many.

HIÖRDIS. Two, mayhap.

GUNNAR (*who has not heard her last words*). But that shall be remedied.

---

[1] The " Nornir " were the Fates of northern mythology.

HIÖRDIS (*looks at him interrogatively*).   Remedied?
Then thou art minded to——?

GUNNAR.   To fit out my warships and put to sea;
I will win back the honour I have lost because thou
wast dearer to me than all beside.

HIÖRDIS (*thoughtfully*).   Thou wilt put to sea?
Ay, so it may be best for us both.

GUNNAR.   Even from the day we sailed from
Iceland, I saw that it would go ill with us.   Thy soul
is strong and proud; there are times when I well
nigh fear thee; yet, it is strange—chiefly for that do
I hold thee so dear.   Dread enwraps thee like a
spell; methinks thou could'st lure me to the blackest
deeds, and all would seem good to me that thou didst
crave.   (*Shaking his head reflectively.*)   Unfathomable
is the Norn's rede; Sigurd should have been thy
husband.

HIÖRDIS (*vehemently*).   Sigurd!

GUNNAR.   Yes, Sigurd.   Vengefulness and hatred
blind thee, else would'st thou prize him better.   Had
I been like Sigurd, I could have made life bright for
thee.

HIÖRDIS (*with strong but suppressed emotion*).   That
—that deemest thou Sigurd could have done?

GUNNAR.   He is strong of soul, and proud as thou
to boot.

HIÖRDIS (*violently*).   If that be so—(*Collecting herself*).   No matter, no matter!   (*With a wild outburst.*)
Gunnar, take Sigurd's life!

GUNNAR.   Never!

HIÖRDIS.   By fraud and falsehood thou mad'st me
thy wife—that shall be forgotten!   Five joyless

years have I spent in this house—all shall be forgotten from the day when Sigurd lives no more!

GUNNAR. From my hand he need fear no harm. (*Shrinks back involuntarily*). Hiördis, Hiördis, tempt me not!

HIÖRDIS. Then must I find another avenger; Sigurd shall not live long to flout at me and thee! (*Clenching her hands in convulsive rage.*) With her —that simpleton—with her mayhap he is even now sitting alone, dallying, and laughing at us; speaking of the bitter wrong that was done me when in thy stead he bore me away; telling how he laughed over his guile as he stood in my dark bower, and I knew him not!

GUNNAR. Nay, nay, he does not so!

HIÖRDIS (*firmly*). Sigurd and Dagny must die! I cannot breathe till they are gone! (*Comes close up to him, with sparkling eyes, and speaks passionately, but in a whisper.*) Would'st thou help me with *that*, Gunnar, then should I live in love with thee; then should I clasp thee in such warm and wild embraces as thou hast never dreamt of!

GUNNAR (*wavering*). Hiördis! Would'st thou——

HIÖRDIS. Do the deed, Gunnar—and the heavy days shall be past. I will no longer quit the hall when thou comest, no longer speak harsh things and quench thy smile when thou art glad. I will clothe me in furs and costly silken robes. When thou goest to war, I will go with thee; when thou ridest forth in peace, I will ride by thy side. At the feast I will sit by thee and fill thy horn, and drink to thee and sing fair songs to make glad thy heart!

GUNNAR (*almost overcome*).   Is it true?   Thou wouldst—— !

HIÖRDIS.   More than that, trust me, ten times more!   Give me revenge!   Revenge on Sigurd and Dagny, and I will—— (*Stops as she sees the door open.*) Dagny—comest thou here!

DAGNY (*from the back*).   Haste thee, Gunnar! Call thy men to arms!

GUNNAR.   To arms!   Against whom?

DAGNY.   Kåre the Peasant is coming, and many outlaws with him ; he means **thee** no good ; Sigurd has barred **his** way **for the** time ; but who **can** tell——

GUNNAR (*moved*).   Sigurd has done this for me!

DAGNY.   Sigurd is **ever** thy faithful friend.

GUNNAR.   And we, Hiördis—we, who thought to——!   It is as I say—there is a spell in all thy speech ; no deed but seemeth fair to me, when thou dost name it.

DAGNY (*astonished*).   What meanest thou ?

GUNNAR.   Nothing, nothing!   **Thanks** for thy tidings, Dagny ; **I go to gather** my **men** together. (*Turns towards the door, but stops and comes forward again.*)   Tell me—how goes it with Örnulf?

DAGNY (*bowing her head*).   Ask me not.   Yesterday he bore Thorolf's body to the ships ; now he is raising a grave-mound on the shore ;—there shall his son be laid.

(GUNNAR *says nothing and goes out by the back.*)

DAGNY.   Until evening there is no danger. (*Coming nearer.*)   Hiördis, I have another errand in thy house ; it is to thee I come.

HIÖRDIS. To me? After all that befell yesterday?

DAGNY. Just because of that. Hiördis, foster-sister, do not hate me ; forget the words that sorrow and evil spirits placed in my mouth ; forgive me all the wrong I have done thee ; for, trust me, I am tenfold more hapless than thou !

HIÖRDIS. Hapless—thou ! Sigurd's wife !

DAGNY. It was *my* doing, all that befell—the stirring up of strife, and Thorolf's death, and all the scorn that fell upon Gunnar and thee. Mine is all the guilt ! Woe upon me !—I have lived so happily ; but after this day I shall never know joy again.

HIÖRDIS (*as if seized by a sudden thought*). But before—in these five long years—all that time hast thou been happy ?

DAGNY. Canst thou doubt it ?

HIÖRDIS. Hm ; yesterday I doubted it not ; but——

DAGNY. What meanest thou ?

HIÖRDIS. Nay, 'tis nought ; let us speak of other matters.

DAGNY. No truly. Hiördis, tell me——!

HIÖRDIS. It will profit thee little ; but since thou wilt have it so—— (*With a malignant expression.*) Canst thou remember once, over in Iceland—we had followed with Örnulf thy father to the Council, and we sat with our playmates in the Council Hall, as is the manner of women. Then came two strangers into the hall.

DAGNY. Sigurd and Gunnar.

HIÖRDIS. They greeted us in courteous fashion, and sat on the bench beside us ; and there passed between us much merry **talk**. There were some who must needs know why these two vikings came thither, and if they were not minded to take them wives there in the island. Then said Sigurd: " It will be hard for me to find the woman that shall be to my mind." Örnulf laughed, and said there was **no** lack of high-born and well-dowered women in Iceland ; but Sigurd answered : " The warrior needs a high-souled **wife**. She whom I choose must not rest content with **a** humble lot ; **no honour** must seem too high for her to strive for ; she must **go with me** gladly a-viking ; war-weed must she wear ; **she** must egg me on to strife, and never wink **her eyes where** sword-blades lighten ; for if she be faint-hearted, **scant** honour will befall me."   Is it not true, so Sigurd spake ?

DAGNY (*hesitatingly*).   True, he did—but——

HIÖRDIS.   *Such* was she to be, the woman who could make life fair to him; and then—(*with a scorn-ful smile*) then he chose thee !

DAGNY (*starting, as in pain*).   Ha, thou wouldst say that——?

HIÖRDIS.   Doubtless thou has proved thyself proud **and** high-souled; hast claimed honour of all, that Sigurd might be honoured in thee—is it not so ?

DAGNY.   Nay, Hiördis, but——

HIÖRDIS.   Thou hast egged him on to great deeds, followed him in war-weed, and joyed to be where the strife raged hottest—hast thou not ?

DAGNY (*deeply moved*).   **No**, no !

HIÖRDIS.   Hast thou, then, been faint of heart, so that Sigurd has been put to shame ?

DAGNY (*overpowered*).   Hiördis, Hiördis !

HIÖRDIS (*smiling scornfully*).   Yet thy lot has been a happy one all these years;—think'st thou that Sigurd can say the same?

DAGNY.   Torture me not.   Woe is me! thou hast made me see myself too clearly.

HIÖRDIS.   A jesting word, and at once thou art in tears!   Think no more of it.   Look what I have done to-day. (*Takes some arrows from the table.*)   Are they not keen and biting—feel!   I know well how to sharpen arrows, do I not?

DAGNY.   And to use them too; thou strikest surely, Hiördis!   All that thou hast said to me—I had never thought of before. (*More vehemently.*)   But that Sigurd——!   That for all these years I should have made his life heavy and unhonoured;—no, no, it cannot be true!

HIÖRDIS.   Nay now, comfort thee, Dagny; indeed it is not true.   Were Sigurd of the same mind as in former days, it might be true enough; for then was his whole soul bent on being the foremost man in the land;—now he is content with a lowlier lot.

DAGNY.   No, Hiördis; Sigurd is high-minded now as ever; I see it well, I am not the right mate for him.   He has hidden it from me; but it shall be so no longer.

HIÖRDIS.   What wilt thou do?

DAGNY.   I will no longer hang like a clog upon his feet; I will be a hindrance to him no longer.

HIÖRDIS.   Then thou wilt——?

DAGNY.   Peace; some one comes!

(*A House-carl enters from the back.*)

THE CARL.   Sigurd Viking is coming to the hall.

HIÖRDIS. Sigurd! Then call Gunnar hither.

THE CARL. Gunnar has ridden forth to gather his neighbours together; for Kåre the Peasant would——

HIÖRDIS. Good, good, I know it; go! (*The Carl goes. To* DAGNY, *who is also going.*) Whither wilt thou?

DAGNY. I will not meet Sigurd. Too well I feel that we must part; but to meet him now—no, no, I cannot!

(*Goes out to the left.*)

HIÖRDIS (*looks after her in silence for a moment*). And it was she I would have——(*completes her thought by a glance at the bow-string*). That had been a poor revenge;—nay, I have cut deeper now! Hm; it is hard to die, but sometimes it is harder still to live!

(SIGURD *enters from the back.*)

HIÖRDIS. Doubtless thou seekest Gunnar; be seated, he will be here even now.

(*Is going.*)

SIGURD. Nay, stay; it is thee I seek, rather than him.

HIÖRDIS. Me?

SIGURD. And 'tis well I find thee alone.

HIÖRDIS. If thou comest to mock me, it would sure be no hindrance to thee though the hall were full of men and women.

SIGURD. Ay, ay, well I know what thoughts thou hast of me.

HIÖRDIS (*bitterly*). I do thee wrong mayhap! Nay, nay, Sigurd, thou hast been as a poison to all my days. Bethink thee who it was that wrought that shameful guile; who it was that sat by my side in the bower, feigning love with the laugh of cunning in his heart; who it was that flung me forth to Gunnar, since for him I was good enough, forsooth—and then sailed away with the woman he held dear!

SIGURD. Man's will can do this and that; but fate rules in the deeds that shape our lives—so has it gone with us twain.

HIÖRDIS. True enough; evil Norns hold sway over the world; but their might is little if they find not helpers in our own heart. Happy is he who has strength to battle with the Norn—and it is that I have now in hand.

SIGURD. What mean'st thou?

HIÖRDIS. I will essay a trial of strength against those—those who are over me. But let us not talk more of this; I have much to do to-day. (*She seats herself at the table.*)

SIGURD (*after a short pause*). Thou makest good weapons for Gunnar.

HIÖRDIS (*with a quiet smile*). Not for Gunnar, but against thee.

SIGURD. Most like it is the same thing.

HIÖRDIS. Ay, most like it is; for if I be a match for the Norn, then sooner or later shalt thou and Gunnar—— (*breaks off, leans backwards against the table, and says with an altered ring in her voice:*) Hm; knowest thou what I sometimes dream? I have often made it my pastime to limn pleasant pictures in my mind; I sit and close my eyes and think: Now comes Sigurd the Strong to the isle;—he will burn us in our house, me and my husband. All Gunnar's men have fallen; only he and I are left; they set light to the roof from without:—"A bow-shot," cries Gunnar, "one bow-shot may save us;"—then the bow-string breaks—"Hiördis, cut a tress of thy hair and make a bow-string of it,—our life is at stake." But then I laugh—"Let it burn, let it burn—to me, life is not worth a handful of hair!"

SIGURD.   There is a strange might in all thy speech. (*Approaches her.*)

HIÖRDIS (*looks coldly at him*).   Wouldst sit beside me?

SIGURD.   Thou deemest my heart is bitter towards thee. Hiördis, this is the last time we shall have speech together; there is something that gnaws me like a sore sickness, and thus I cannot part from thee; thou must know me better.

HIÖRDIS.   What wouldst thou?

SIGURD.   Tell thee a saga.

HIÖRDIS.   Is it sad?

SIGURD.   Sad, as life itself.

HIÖRDIS (*bitterly*).   What knowest thou of the sadness of life?

SIGURD.   Judge when my saga is over.

HIÖRDIS.   Then tell it me; I shall work the while.
    (*He sits on a low stool to her right.*)

SIGURD.   Once upon a time there were two young vikings, who set forth from Norway to win wealth and honour; they had sworn each other friendship, and held truly together, how far soever they might fare.

HIÖRDIS.   And the two young vikings hight Sigurd and Gunnar?

SIGURD. Ay, we may call them so. At last they came to Iceland ; and there dwelt an old chieftain, who had come forth from Norway in King Harald's days. He had two fair women in his house ; but one, his foster-daughter, was the noblest, for she was wise and strong of soul ; and the vikings spoke of her between themselves, and never had they seen a fairer woman, so deemed they both.

HIÖRDIS (*in suspense*). Both ? Wilt thou mock me ?

SIGURD. Gunnar thought of her night and day, and that did Sigurd no less ; but both held their peace, and no man could say from her bearing whether Gunnar found favour in her eyes ; but that Sigurd misliked her, that was easy to discern.

HIÖRDIS (*breathlessly*). Go on, go on—— !

SIGURD. Yet ever the more must Sigurd dream of her ; but of that wist no man. Now it befell one evening that there was a drinking-feast ; and then swore that proud woman that no man should possess her save he who wrought a mighty deed, which she named. High beat Sigurd's heart for joy ; for he felt within him the strength to do that deed ; but Gunnar took him apart and told him of his love ;— Sigurd said naught of his, but went to the——

HIÖRDIS (*vehemently*). Sigurd, Sigurd ! (*Controlling herself.*) And this saga—is it true?

SIGURD. True it is. One of us had to yield ; Gunnar was my friend ; I could do nought else. So thou becamest Gunnar's wife, and I wedded another woman.

HIÖRDIS. And came to love her !

SIGURD.   I learned to prize her ; but one woman only has Sigurd loved, and that is she who frowned upon him from the first day they met.   Here ends my saga ; and now let us part.—Farewell, Gunnar's wife ; never shall we meet again.

HIÖRDIS (*springing up*).   Stay, stay !   Woe to us both ; Sigurd, what hast thou done ?

SIGURD (*starting*).   I, done ?   What ails thee ?

HIÖRDIS.   And all this dost thou tell me now ! But no—it cannot be true !

SIGURD.   These are my last words to thee, and every word is true.   I would not thou shouldst think hardly of me, therefore I needs must speak.

HIÖRDIS (*involuntarily clasps her hands together and gazes at him in voiceless astonishment*).   Loved—loved me—thou ! (*Vehemently, coming close up to him.*)   I will not believe thee ! (*Looks hard at him, and bursts forth in wild grief.*)   Yes, it is true, and—baleful for us both !

    (*Hides her face in her hands, and turns away from him.*)

SIGURD (*terror-stricken*).   Hiördis !

HIÖRDIS (*softly, struggling with tears and laughter.*) Nay, heed me not !   This was all I meant, that—— (*Lays her hand on his arm.*)   Sigurd, thou hast not told thy saga to the end ; that proud woman thou didst tell of—she returned thy love !

SIGURD (*starts backwards*).   Thou ?

HIÖRDIS (*with composure*).   Yes, Sigurd, I have loved thee, at last I understand it.   Thou sayest I was ungentle and short of speech towards thee ; what wouldst thou have a woman do ?   I could not offer thee my love, for then had I been little worthy of thee. I deemed thee ever the noblest man of men; and then to know thee another's husband—'twas that caused me the bitter pain, that myself I could not understand!

SIGURD (*much moved*). A baleful web has the Norn woven around us twain.

HIÖRDIS. The blame is thine own; bravely and firmly it becomes a man to act. When I set that hard proof for him who should win me, my thought was all of thee;—yet couldst thou——!

SIGURD. I knew Gunnar's soul-sickness; I alone could heal it;—was there aught for me to choose? And yet, had I known what I now know, I scarce dare answer for myself; for great is the might of love.

HIÖRDIS (*with animation*). But now, Sigurd!— A baleful hap has held us apart all these years; now the knot is loosed; the days to come shall make good the past to us.

SIGURD (*shaking his head*). It cannot be; we must part again.

HIÖRDIS. Nay, we must not. I love thee, that may I now say unashamed; for my love is no mere dalliance, like a weak woman's; were I a man—by all the Mighty Ones, I could still love thee, even as now I do! Up then, Sigurd! Happiness is worth a daring deed; we are both free if we but will it, and then the game is won.

SIGURD. Free? What meanest thou?

HIÖRDIS. What is Dagny to thee? What can she be to thee? No more than I count Gunnar in

my secret heart. What matters it though two worthless lives be wrecked ?

SIGURD. Hiördis, Hiördis !

HIÖRDIS. Let Gunnar stay where he is ; let
Dagny fare with her father to Iceland ; I will follow
thee in harness of steel, whithersoever thou wendest.
(SIGURD *makes a movement.*) Not as thy wife will
I follow thee ; for I have belonged to another, and
the woman lives that has lain by thy side. No,
Sigurd, not as thy wife, but like those mighty women,
like Hilde's sisters,[1] will I follow thee, and fire thee to
strife and to manly deeds, so that thy name shall be
heard over every land. In the sword-game will I
stand by thy side ; I will fare forth among thy
warriors on the stormy viking-raids ; and when thy
death-song is sung, it shall tell of Sigurd and Hiördis
in one !

SIGURD. Once was that my fairest dream ; now,
it is too late. Gunnar and Dagny stand between us,
and that by right. I crushed my love for Gunnar's
sake ;—how great soever my suffering, I cannot undo
my deed. And Dagny—full of faith and trust she
left her home and kindred ; never must she dream
that I longed for Hiördis as often as she took me to
her breast.

HIÖRDIS. And for such a cause wilt thou lay a
burden on thy life ! To what end hast thou strength
and might, and therewith all noble gifts of the mind ?
And deemest thou it can now beseem me to dwell
beneath Gunnar's roof ? Nay, Sigurd, trust me, there
are many tasks awaiting such a man as thou. Erik

---

[1] The Valkyries.

is king of Norway—do thou rise against him!   Many
goodly warriors will join thee and swear thee fealty;
with unconquerable might will we press onward, and
fight and toil unresting until thou art seated on the
throne of Hårfager!

SIGURD.   Hiördis, Hiördis, so have I dreamt in my
wild youth; let it be forgotten—tempt me not!

HIÖRDIS (*impressively*).   It is the Norn's will that
we two shall hold together; it cannot be altered.
Plainly now I see my task in life: to make thee
famous over all the world.   Thou hast stood before
me every day, every hour of my life; I sought to tear
thee out of my mind, but I lacked the might; now it
is needless, now that I know thou lovest me.

SIGURD (*with forced coldness*).   If that be so—then
know—I *have* loved thee; it is past now;—I have
forgot those days.

HIÖRDIS.   Sigurd, in that thou liest! So much at
least am I worth, that if thou hast loved me once,
thou canst never forget it.

SIGURD (*vehemently*).   I must; and now I will.

HIÖRDIS.   So be it; but thou *canst* not. Thou
wilt seek to hinder me, but in vain; ere evening falls,
Gunnar and Dagny shall know all.

SIGURD.   Ha, that wilt thou never do!

HIÖRDIS.   That will I do!

SIGURD.   Then must I know thee ill; high-souled
have I ever deemed thee.

HIÖRDIS.   Evil days breed evil thoughts; too great
has been thy trust in me.   I will, I must, go forth by
thy side—forth to face life and strife; Gunnar's roof-
tree is too low for me.

SIGURD (*with emphasis*).   But honour between man and man hast thou highly prized.   There lack not grounds for strife between me and Gunnar; say, now, that he fell by my hand, wouldst thou still make all known and follow me?

HIÖRDIS (*starting*).   Wherefore askest thou?

SIGURD.   Answer me first: what wouldst thou do, were I to give thy husband his bane.

HIÖRDIS (*looks hard at him*).   Then must I keep silence and never rest until I had seen thee slain.

SIGURD (*with a smile*).   It is well, Hiördis—I knew it.

HIÖRDIS (*hastily*).   But it can never come to pass!

SIGURD.   It must come to pass; thou thyself hast cast the die for Gunnar's life and mine.

(GUNNAR, *with some House-carls, enters from the back*.)

GUNNAR (*gloomily, to* HIÖRDIS).   See now; the seed thou hast sown is shooting bravely!

SIGURD (*approaching*).   What is amiss with thee?

GUNNAR.   Sigurd, is it thou?   What is amiss? Nought but what I might well have foreseen.   As soon as Dagny, thy wife, had brought tidings of Kåre the Peasant, I took horse and rode to my neighbours to crave help against him.

HIÖRDIS (*eagerly*).   Well?

GUNNAR.   I was answered awry where'er I came: my dealings with Kåre had been little to my honour, it was said;—hm, other things were said to boot, that I will not utter.—I am spurned at by all; I am thought to have done a dastard deed; men hold it a shame to make common cause with me.

SIGURD.   It shall not long be held a shame; ere evening comes, thou shalt have men enough to face Kåre.

GUNNAR.   Sigurd!

HIÖRDIS (*in a low voice, triumphantly*).   Ha, I knew it well!

SIGURD (*with forced resolution*).   But then is there an end to the peace between us; for hearken to my words, Gunnar—thou hast slain Thorolf, my wife's kinsman, and therefore do I challenge thee to single combat[1] to-morrow at break of day.

> (HIÖRDIS, *in violent inward emotion, makes a stride towards* SIGURD, *but collects herself and remains standing motionless during the following.*)

GUNNAR (*in extreme astonishment*).   To single combat——!   Me!—Thou art jesting, Sigurd!

SIGURD.   Thou art lawfully challenged to single combat; 'twill be a game for life or death; one of us must fall!

GUNNAR (*bitterly*).   Ha, I understand it well. When I came, thou didst talk with Hiördis alone; she has goaded thee afresh!

SIGURD.   Mayhap. (*Half towards* HIÖRDIS.)   A high-souled woman must ever guard her husband's honour. (*To the men in the background.*)   And do ye, house-carls, now go to Gunnar's neighbours, and say to them that to-morrow he is to ply sword-strokes with me; none dare call that man a dastard who bears arms against Sigurd Viking!

> (*The House-carls go out by the back.*)

----

[1] *Holmgang*—see note, p. 138.

GUNNAR (*goes quickly up to* SIGURD *and presses his hands, in strong emotion*). Sigurd, my brave brother, now I understand thee! Thou venturest thy life for my honour, as of old for my happiness!

SIGURD. Thank thy wife; she has the largest part in what I do. To-morrow at break of day——

GUNNAR. I will meet thee. (*Tenderly.*) Foster-brother, wilt thou have a good blade of me? It is a gift of price.

SIGURD. I thank thee; but let it hang.—Who knows if next evening I may have any use for it.

GUNNAR (*shakes his hand*). Farewell, Sigurd!

SIGURD. Again farewell, and fortune befriend thee this night!

  (*They* **part.** GUNNAR *goes out to the right.* SIGURD *casts a glance at* HIÖRDIS, *and goes out by the back.*)

HIÖRDIS (**after a pause,** *softly and thoughtfully*). To-morrow they fight! Which will fall? (*After a moment's silence,* **she bursts forth as if seized by a strong** *resolution.*) Let fall who will—Sigurd and I shall still be together!

Act Fourth.

(*By the coast. It is evening; the moon breaks forth now and again, from among dark and ragged storm-clouds. At the back, a black grave-mound, newly heaped-up.*)
(ÖRNULF *sits on a stone, in front on the right, his head bare, his elbows resting on his knees, and his face buried in his hands. His men are digging at the mound; some give light with pine-knot torches. After a short pause,* SIGURD *and* DAGNY *enter from the boat-house, where a wood fire is burning.*)

DAGNY (*in a low voice*). There sits he still. (*Holding* SIGURD *back.*) Nay, speak not to him !

SIGURD. Thou say'st well ; it is too soon ; best leave him to himself.

DAGNY (*goes over to the right, and gazes at her father in quiet sorrow*). So strong was he yesterday when he bore Thorolf's body on his back ; strong was he as he helped to heap the grave-mound ; but when they were all laid to rest, and earth and stones piled over them—then the sorrow seized him ; then seemed it of a sudden as though his fire were quenched. (*Dries her tears.*) Tell me, Sigurd, when thinkest thou to fare homeward to Iceland ?

SIGURD. So soon as the storm abates, and my quarrel with Gunnar is ended.

DAGNY. And then wilt thou buy land and build thee a homestead, and go a-viking no more ?

SIGURD.   Yes, yes,—that have I promised.

DAGNY.   And I **may** believe without doubt that Hiördis spoke falsely **when** she said that I was unworthy to be thy wife?

SIGURD.   **Yes** yes, Dagny, trust thou to my word.

DAGNY.   **Then am I** glad again, **and** will try to forget all **the** evil **that** here has been wrought.   In the long winter evenings we will talk together of Gunnar and Hiördis, and——

SIGURD.   **Nay, Dagny,** wouldst thou have **things** go well with us, **do thou never** speak Hiördis' name when we sit together in Iceland.

DAGNY (*mildly upbraiding him*).   Unjust is thy hatred towards her.   Sigurd, **Sigurd, it is** unlike **thee.**

ONE OF THE **MEN** (*approaching*).   There now, **the mound is** finished.

ÖRNULF (*as if awaking*).   The mound?   Is it— ay, ay——

SIGURD.   **Now** speak **to him,** Dagny.

DAGNY (*approaching*).   Father, it is cold out here; a storm is gathering to-night.

ÖRNULF.   Hm; heed it not; **the** mound is close-heaped and crannyless; they lie warm in there.

DAGNY.   Ay, but thou——

ÖRNULF.   I?   I am **not** cold.

DAGNY. Nought **hast thou** eaten to-day; wilt thou not **go in?** The supper-board stands ready.

ÖRNULF.   Let the supper-board stand; I have **no** hunger.

DAGNY   **But to** sit here so still—trust me, thou wilt take hurt of it; thou art ever wont to be stirring.

Örnulf. True, true; there is somewhat that crushes my breast; I cannot draw breath.

(*He again hides his face in his hands. A pause. Dagny seats herself beside him.*)

Dagny. To-morrow wilt thou make ready thy ship and set forth for Iceland?

Örnulf (*without looking up*). What should I do there? Nay, I will to my sons.

Dagny (*with pain*). Father!

Örnulf (*raises his head*). Go in and let me sit here; when the storm has played with me for a night or two, the game will be over, I ween.

Sigurd. Thou canst not think to deal thus with thyself.

Örnulf. Dost marvel that I fain would rest? My day's work is done; I have laid my sons in their grave. (*Vehemently.*) Go from me!—Go, go!

(*He hides his face.*)

Sigurd (*softly, to* Dagny, *who rises*). Let him sit yet a while.

Dagny. Nay, I have one rede yet untried;—I know him. (*To* Örnulf.) Thy day's work done, say'st thou? Nay, that it is not. Thou hast laid thy sons in the grave;—but art thou not a skald? It is meet that thou should'st sing their memory.

Örnulf (*shaking his head*). Sing? Nay, nay; yesterday I could sing; I am too old to-day.

Dagny. But needs must thou; honourable men were thy sons, one and all; a song must be made of them, and that can none of our kin but thou.

Örnulf (*looks inquiringly at* Sigurd). To sing? What thinkest *thou*, Sigurd?

SIGURD.   Meseems it is but meet ; thou must e'en do as she says.

DAGNY.   Thy neighbours in Iceland will deem it ill done when the grave-ale is drunk over Örnulf's children, and there is no song to sing with it.   Thou hast ever time enough to follow thy sons.

ÖRNULF.   Well well, I will try it ; and thou, Dagny, give heed, that afterwards thou mayst carve the song on staves.

(The men approach with the torches, forming a group around him ; he is silent for a time, reflecting ; then he says :)

Bragi's[1] gift is bitter
when the heart is broken ;
sorrow-laden singer,
singing, suffers sorely.

Natheless, since the Skald-god
gave me skill in song-craft,
in a lay loud-ringing
be my loss lamented!

(Rises.)

Ruthless Norn[2] and wrathful
wrecked my life and ravaged,
wiled away my welfare,
wasted Örnulf's treasure.

Sons had Örnulf seven,
by the great gods granted ;- -

---

[1] Bragi, the god of poetry and eloquence.   [2] See note, p. 175.

lonely now and life-sick
goes the greybeard, sonless.

Seven sons so stately,
bred among the sword-blades,
made a mighty bulwark
round the snow-locked sea-king.

Levelled lies the bulwark,
dead my swordsmen seven ;
gone the greybeard's gladness,
desolate his dwelling.

Thorolf,—thou my last-born !
Of the bold the boldest !
Soon were spent my sorrow
so but thou wert left me !

Fair thou wast as springtide,
fond towards thy father,
waxing straight and stalwart
to so wight a warrior.

Dark and drear his death-wound
leaves my life's lone evening ;
grief hath gripped my bosom
as 'twixt hurtling targes.

Nought the Norn denied me
of her rueful riches,
showering woes unstinted
over Örnulf's world-way.

Weak are now my weapons.
But, were god-might given me,
then, oh Norn, I swear it,
scarce should'st thou go scatheless!

Dire were then my vengeance;
then had dawned thy doomsday,
Norn, that now hast left me
nought but yonder grave-mound.

Nought, I said?   Nay, truly,
somewhat still is Örnulf's,
since of Suttung's[1] mead-horn
he betimes drank deeply.

(*With rising enthusiasm.*)

Though she stripped me sonless,
one great gift she gave me—
songcraft's mighty secret,
skill to sing my sorrows.

On my lips she laid it,
goodly gift of songcraft ;
loud, then, let my lay sound,
e'en where they are lying !

Hail, my stout sons seven !
Hail, as homeward ride ye !
Songcraft's glorious god-gift
stauncheth woe and wailing.

---

[1] Suttung was a giant who kept guard over the magic mead of
poetical inspiration.

(*He draws a deep breath, throws back the hair from his brow, and says calmly :*)

So—so ; now is Örnulf sound and strong again. (*To the men.*) Follow me to the supper-board, lads ; we have had a heavy day's work !

(*Goes with the men into the boat-house.*)

DAGNY. Praised be the Mighty Ones on high that gave me so good a rede. (*To* SIGURD.) Wilt thou not go in ?

SIGURD. Nay, I list not to. Tell me, are all things ready for to-morrow ?

DAGNY. They are ; a silk-sewn shroud lies on the bench ; but I know full surely that thou wilt hold thee against Gunnar, so I have not wept over it.

SIGURD. Grant all good powers, that thou mayst never weep for my sake. (*He stops and looks out.*)

DAGNY. What art thou listening to ?

SIGURD. Hear'st thou nought—*there ?*

(*Points towards the left.*)

DAGNY. Ay, there goes a fearsome storm over the sea !

SIGURD (*going up a little towards the background*). Hm, there will fall hard hailstones in that storm. (*Shouts.*) Who comes ?

KÅRE THE PEASANT (*without on the left*). Folk thou wot'st of, Sigurd Viking !

(*KÅRE THE PEASANT, with a band of armed men, enters from the left.*)

SIGURD. Whither would ye ?

KÅRE. To Gunnar's hall.

SIGURD. As foemen ?

KÅRE.   Ay, trust me for that! Thou didst hinder me before; but now I ween thou wilt scarce do the like.

SIGURD.   Maybe not.

KÅRE.   I have heard of thy challenge to Gunnar; but if things go to my mind, weak will be his weapons when the time comes for your meeting.

SIGURD.   'Tis venturesome work thou goest about; take heed for thyself, Peasant!

KÅRE (*with defiant laughter*). **Leave** that to me; if thou wilt tackle thy ship to-night, **we** will give thee light for the task!—Come, all **my** men; here goes the way.

(*They go off to the right, at the back.*)

DAGNY.   Sigurd, Sigurd, this misdeed must thou hinder.

SIGURD (*goes quickly to the door of the hut, and calls in*). Up from the board, Örnulf; take vengeance on Kåre the Peasant.

ÖRNULF (*comes out, with the rest*). Kåre the Peasant—where is he?

SIGURD.   He is **making** for Gunnar's hall to burn it over their heads.

ÖRNULF.   Ha-ha—let him do as he will; so shall I be avenged on Gunnar and Hiördis, and afterwards I can deal with Kåre.

SIGURD.   Nay, that rede avails not; wouldst thou strike at **Kåre,** thou must seek him out to-night; for **when** his misdeed is done, he will take to the mountains.   I have challenged Gunnar to single combat; him thou hast safely enough, unless I myself—but no matter —To-night he must be shielded from his foes;

it would ill befit thee to let such a dastard as Kåre rob thee of thy revenge.

ÖRNULF. Thou say'st truly. To-night will I shield the slayer of Thorolf; but to-morrow he must die.

SIGURD. He or I—doubt not of that!

ÖRNULF. Come then, to take vengeance for Örnulf's sons.

(*He goes out with his men by the back, to the right.*)

SIGURD. Dagny, do thou follow them;—I must bide here; for the rumour of the combat is already abroad, and I may not meet Gunnar ere the time comes. But thou—do thou keep rein on thy father; he must go honourably to work; in Gunnar's hall there are many women; no harm must befall Hiördis or the rest.

DAGNY. Yes, I will follow them. Thou hast a kind thought even for Hiördis; I thank thee.

SIGURD. Go, go, Dagny!

DAGNY. I go; but be thou at ease as to Hiördis; she has gilded armour in her bower, and will know how to shield herself.

SIGURD. That deem I too; but go thou nevertheless; guide thy father's course; watch over all—and over Gunnar's wife!

DAGNY. Trust to me. Farewell, till we meet again!

(*She follows the others.*)

SIGURD. 'Tis the first time, foster-brother, that I stand weaponless whilst thou art in danger. (*Listens.*) I hear shouts and sword-strokes;—they are already at the hall. (*Goes towards the right, but stops and recoils in astonishment.*) Hiördis! Comes she hither!

(HIÖRDIS *enters, clad in a short scarlet kirtle, with gilded armour: helmet, hauberk, arm-plates, and greaves. Her hair is flying loose; at her back hangs a quiver, and at her belt a small shield. She has in her hand the bow strung with her hair.*)

HIÖRDIS (*hastily looking behind her, as though in dread of something pursuing her, goes close up to* SIGURD, *seizes him by the arm, and whispers :*) Sigurd, Sigurd, canst thou see it ?

SIGURD.   What ?   Where ?

HIÖRDIS.   The wolf there—close behind me; it does not move; it glares at me with its two red eyes. It is my wraith,[1] Sigurd! Three times has it appeared to me; that bodes that I shall surely die to-night !

SIGURD.   Hiördis, Hiördis !

HIÖRDIS.   It has sunk into the earth! Yes, yes, now it has warned me.

SIGURD.   Thou art sick ; come, go in with me.

HIÖRDIS.   Nay, here will I bide ; I have but little time left.

SIGURD.   What has befallen thee ?

HIÖRDIS.   What has befallen ? That know I not; but true was it what thou said'st to-day, that Gunnar and Dagny stand between us ; we must away from them and from life : then can we be together !

SIGURD.   We ?   Ha, thou meanest—— !

---

[1] The word "wraith" is here used in an obviously inexact sense; but the wraith seemed to be the nearest equivalent in English mythology to the Scandinavian "fylgie," an attendant spirit, often regarded as a sort of emanation from the person it accompanied, and sometimes (as in this case) typifying that person's moral attributes.

HIÖRDIS (*with dignity*).   I have been homeless in this world from that day thou didst take another to wife.   That was ill done of thee!   All good gifts may a man give his faithful friend—all, save the woman he loves; for if he do that, he rends the Norn's secret web, and two lives are wrecked.   An unerring voice within me tells me I came into the world that my strong soul might cheer and sustain thee through heavy days, and that thou wast born to the end I might find in *one* man all that seemed to me great and noble; for this I know, Sigurd — had we two held together, thou hadst become more famous than all others, and I happier.

SIGURD.   It avails not now to mourn.   Thinkest thou it is a merry life that awaits me?   To be by Dagny's side day by day, and feign a love my heart shrinks from?   Yet so it must be ; it cannot be altered.

HIÖRDIS (*in a growing frenzy*).   It *shall* be altered! We must out of this life, both of us!   Seest thou this bow-string?   With it can I surely hit my mark; for I have crooned fair sorceries over it!   (*Places an arrow in the bow, which is strung.*)   Hark! hearest thou that rushing in the air?   It is the dead men's ride to Valhal : I have bewitched them hither ;—we two will join them in their ride!

SIGURD (*shrinking back*).   Hiördis, Hiördis—I fear thee !

HIÖRDIS (*not heeding him*).   Our fate no power can alter now!   Oh, 'tis better so than if thou hadst wedded me here in this life—if I had sat in thy homestead weaving linen and wool for thee and bearing thee children—pah!

SIGURD.   Hold, hold!   Thy sorcery has been too strong for thee; thou art soul-sick, Hiördis!   (*Horror-struck.*)   Ha, see—see!   Gunnar's hall—it is burning!

HIÖRDIS.   Let it burn, let it burn!   The cloud-hall up yonder is loftier than Gunnar's rafter-roof!

SIGURD.   But Egil, thy son—they are slaying him!

HIÖRDIS.   Let him die—my shame dies with him!

SIGURD.   And Gunnar—they are taking thy husband's life!

HIÖRDIS.   What care I!   A better husband shall I follow home this night!   Ay, Sigurd, so must it be; here on this earth is no happiness for me.   The White God is coming northward; him will I not meet; the old gods are strong no longer;—they sleep, they sit half shadow-like on high;—with them will we strive! Out of this life, Sigurd; I will enthrone thee king in heaven, and I will sit at thy side.   (*The storm bursts wildly.*)   Hark, hark, here comes our company! Canst see the black steeds galloping?—one is for me and one for thee.   (*Draws the arrow to her ear and shoots.*)   Away, then, on thy last ride home!

SIGURD.   Well aimed, Hiördis!

    (*He falls.*)

HIÖRDIS (*jubilant, rushes up to him*).   Sigurd, my brother,—now art thou mine at last!

SIGURD.   Now less than ever.   Here our ways part; for I am a Christian man.

HIÖRDIS (*appalled*).   Thou——!   Ha, no, no!

SIGURD.   The White God is mine; King Æthelstan taught me to know him; it is to him I go.

HIÖRDIS (*in despair*). And I——! (*Drops her bow.*) Woe! woe!

SIGURD. Heavy has my life been from the hour I tore thee out of my own heart and gave thee to Gunnar. Thanks, Hiördis;—now am I so light and free.

(*Dies.*)

HIÖRDIS (*quietly*). Dead! Then truly have I brought my soul to wreck! (*The storm increases; she breaks forth wildly.*) They come! I have bewitched them hither! No, no! I will not go with you! I will not ride without Sigurd! It avails not —they see me; they laugh and beckon to me; they spur their horses! (*Rushes out to the edge of the cliff at the back.*) They are upon me;—and no shelter no hiding-place! Ay, mayhap at the bottom oi the sea!

(*She casts herself over.*)

(ÖRNULF, DAGNY, GUNNAR, *with* EGIL, *followed by* SIGURD'S *and* ÖRNULF'S *men, gradually enter from the right.*)

ÖRNULF (*turning towards the grave-mound*). Now may ye sleep in peace; for ye lie not unavenged.

DAGNY (*entering*). Father, father—I die of fear—all that bloody strife—and the storm;—hark, hark!

GUNNAR (*carrying* EGIL). Peace, and shelter for my child!

ÖRNULF. Gunnar!

GUNNAR. Ay, Örnulf, my homestead is burnt and my men are slain; I am in thy power; do with me what thou wilt!

ÖRNULF.   That Sigurd must look to.   But in, under roof!   It is not safe out here.

DAGNY.   Ay, in, in!   (*Goes towards the boat-house, catches sight of* SIGURD'S *body, and shrieks.*)   Sigurd, my husband!—They have slain him!   (*Throwing herself upon him.*)

ÖRNULF (*rushes up*).   Sigurd!

GUNNAR (*sets* EGIL *down*).   Sigurd dead!

DAGNY (*looks despairingly at the men, who surround the* body).   No, no, it is not so;—he must be alive!   (*Catches sight of the bow.*)   Ha, what is that?   (*Rises.*)

ÖRNULF.   Daughter, it is as first thou saidst—Sigurd is slain.

GUNNAR (*as if seized by a sudden thought*).   And Hiördis!—Has Hiördis been here?

DAGNY (*softly and with self-control*).   I know not; but this I know, that her bow has been here.

GUNNAR.   Ay, I thought as much!

DAGNY.   Hush, hush!   (*To herself.*)   So bitterly did she hate him!

GUNNAR (*aside*).   She has slain him—the night before the combat; then she loved me after all.

(*A thrill of dread runs through the whole group;*
    ASGÅRDSREIEN—*the ride of the fallen heroes
    to Valhal—hurtles through the air.*)

EGIL (*in terror*).   Father!   See, see!

GUNNAR.   What is it?

EGIL.   Up there—all the black horses——!

GUNNAR.   It is the clouds that——

ÖRNULF.   Nay, it is the dead men's home-faring.

EGIL (*with a shriek*).   Mother is with them!

DAGNY.   All good spirits!

GUNNAR.   Child, what say'st thou?

EGIL.   There—in front—on the black horse!
Father, father!

> (EGIL *clings in terror to his father; a short*
> *pause; the storm passes over, the clouds part,*
> *the moon shines peacefully on the scene.*)

GUNNAR (*in quiet sorrow*).   Now is Hiördis surely
dead!

ÖRNULF.   So it must be, Gunnar;—and my vengeance was rather against her than thee.   Dear has this
meeting been to both of us;—— —— there is my
hand; be there peace between us!

GUNNAR.   Thanks, Örnulf!   And now aboard;
I sail with thee to Iceland.

ÖRNULF.   Ay, to Iceland!   Long will it be ere
our forth-faring is forgotten.

> Weapon-wielding warriors' meeting,
> woful, by the northern seaboard,
> still shall live in song and saga
> while our stem endures in Iceland.

THE PRETENDERS.

(1864.)

Characters.

----◆----

HAKON HAKONSSON, *the King elected by the Birchlegs.*
INGA OF VARTEIG, *his mother.*
EARL SKULE.
LADY RAGNHILD, *his wife.*
SIGRID, *his sister.*
MARGRETE, *his daughter.*
GUTHORM INGESSON.
SIGURD RIBBUNG.
NICHOLAS ARNESSON, *Bishop of Oslo.*
DAGFINN THE PEASANT, *Hakon's marshal.*
IVAR BODDE.
VEGARD VÆRADAL, *one of his guard.*
GREGORIUS JONSSON, *a nobleman.*
PAUL FLIDA, *a nobleman.*
INGEBORG, *Andres Skialdarband's wife.*
PETER, *her son, a young priest.*
SIRA VILIAM, *Bishop Nicholas's chaplain.*
MASTER SIGARD OF BRABANT, *a physician.*
JATGEIR SKALD, *an Icelander.*
BÅRD BRATTE, *a chieftain from the Trondhiem district.*
Populace and Citizens of Bergen, Oslo, and Nidaros.
Priests, Monks, and Nuns.
Guests, Guards, and Ladies.
Men-at-Arms, etc., etc.

The action passes in the first half of the Thirteenth Century.

[PRONUNCIATION OF NAMES.—Skule = *Skoolë*; Margrete = *Margraytë*; Guthorm = *Gootorm*; Sigurd Ribbung = *Sigoord Ribboong*; Dagfinn = *Daagfin* (*a* as in "hard"); Ivar Bodde = *Eevar Boddë*; Vegard = *Vaygard*; Jonsson = *Yoonson*; Flida = *Fleeda*; Ingeborg = *Ingheborg*; Jatgeir = *Yatgheir*; Bård Bratte = *Board Brattë*. The names "Hakon" and "Ingeborg" appear as "Håkon" and "Ingebjörg" in Ibsen's text. The forms I have substituted are equally current in Norway, and less troublesome to English readers.]

THE PRETENDERS.

HISTORIC PLAY IN FIVE ACTS.

Act First.

(The Churchyard of Christ Church, Bergen. At the back rises the church, the main portal of which faces the spectators. In front, on the left, stands HAKON HAKONSSON, *with* DAGFINN THE PEASANT, VEGARD OF VÆRADAL, IVAR BODDE, *and several other nobles and chieftains. Opposite to him stand* EARL SKULE, GREGORIUS JONSSON, PAUL FLIDA, *and others of the Earl's men. Further back on the same side are seen* SIGURD RIBBUNG *and his followers, and a little way from him* GUTHORM INGESSON, *with several chiefs. Men-at-arms line the approaches to the church; the common people fill the churchyard; many are perched in the trees and seated on the walls; all seem to await, in suspense, the occurrence of some event. Bells are ringing in all the church-towers far and near.)*

EARL SKULE (*softly and impatiently, to* GREGORIUS JONSSON). Why tarry they so long in there?

GREGORIUS JONSSON. Hush! Now begins the psalm.

(From inside the closed church doors, to the accompaniment of trumpets, is heard a CHOIR OF

MONKS AND NUNS *singing* Domine coeli, *etc.,
etc.   While the singing is going on, the church
door is opened from inside ; in the vestibule*
BISHOP NICHOLAS *is seen, surrounded by Priests
and Monks.*)

BISHOP NICHOLAS (*steps forward to the doorway
and proclaims with uplifted crozier*).   Inga of Varteig
is undergoing the ordeal on behalf of Hakon the
Pretender !

(*The church door is closed again : the singing
inside continues.*)

GREGORIUS JONSSON (*in a low voice, to the* EARL).
Call upon holy King Olaf to protect the right.

EARL SKULE (*hurriedly, with a deprecating gesture*).
Not now.   Best not remind him of me.

IVAR BODDE (*seizing* HAKON *by the arm*).   Pray
to the Lord thy God, Hakon Hakonsson.

HAKON.   No need ; I am sure of him.

(*The singing in the church grows louder ; all
uncover ; many fall upon their knees and pray.*)

GREGORIUS JONSSON (*to the* EARL).   A solemn
hour for you and for many !

EARL SKULE (*looking anxiously towards the church*).
A solemn hour for Norway.

PAUL FLIDA (*near the* EARL).   Now is the glowing
iron in her hands.

DAGFINN (*beside* HAKON).   They are coming down
the nave.

IVAR BODDE.   Christ protect thy tender hands,
Inga, mother of the King !

HAKON.   My whole life shall surely reward her for
this hour.

EARL SKULE (*who has been listening anxiously, breaks out suddenly*).   Did she cry out ?   Has she let the iron fall ?

PAUL FLIDA (*goes up*).   I know not what it was.

GREGORIUS JONSSON.   The women are weeping loudly in the outer hall.

THE CHOIR IN THE CHURCH (*breaks forth in jubilation*).   *Gloria in excelsis deo !*

(*The doors are thrown open.* INGA *comes forth, followed by Nuns, Priests, and Monks.*)

INGA (*on the church steps*).   God has given judgment !   Behold these hands ; with them I bore the iron !

VOICES AMONGST THE MULTITUDE.   They are tender and white as before !

OTHER VOICES.   Fairer still !

THE WHOLE MULTITUDE.   He is Hakon's son ! He is Sverre's grandson !

HAKON (*embraces her*).   Have thanks, have thanks, thou blessed among women !

BISHOP NICHOLAS (*in passing, to the* EARL).   We did wrong to accept the ordeal.

EARL SKULE.   Nay, my lord Bishop, we could not but pray for God's voice in this matter.

HAKON (*deeply moved, holding* INGA *by the hand*). It is done, then, that which my every fibre cried out against—that which has made my heart shrivel and writhe within me——

DAGFINN (*turning towards the multitude*).   Ay, look upon this woman and bethink you, all that are gathered here !   Who ever doubted her word, until certain people required that it should be doubted.

PAUL FLIDA. Doubt has whispered in every corner from the hour when Hakon the Pretender was borne, a little child, into King Inge's hall.

GREGORIUS JONSSON. And last winter it swelled to a roar, and sounded forth over the land, both north and south; I trow every man can bear witness to that.

HAKON. I myself can best bear witness to it. Even therefore have I yielded to the counsel of many faithful friends, and humbled myself as no other chosen king has done for many a day. I have proved my birth by the ordeal, proved my right, as the son of Hakon Sverresson, to succeed to the throne of Norway. I will not now question who fostered the doubt, and made it, as the Earl's kinsman says, swell into a roar; but this I know, that I have suffered bitterly under it. I have been chosen king from boyhood, but little kingly honour has been shown me, even where it seemed I might look for it most securely. I will but remind you of last Palm Sunday in Nidaros,[1] when I went up to the altar to make my offering, and the Archbishop turned away and made as though he saw me not, to escape greeting me as kings are wont to be greeted. Yet such slights I could easily have borne, had not open war been like to break out in the land; that I must needs hinder.

DAGFINN. It may be well for kings to hearken to counsels of prudence; but had *my* counsel been heard in this matter, it had not been with hot iron, but with

---

[1] The old name for Trondhiem.

cold steel that Hakon Hakonsson should have called for judgment between himself and his foes.

HAKON. Curb yourself, Dagfinn ; think what beseems the man who is to be foremost in the state.

EARL SKULE (*with a slight smile*). 'Tis easy to call every one the King's foe who chimes not with the King's will. Methinks he is the King's worst foe who would dissuade him from making good his right to the kingship.

HAKON. Who knows ? Were my right alone in question, mayhap I had not paid so dear to prove it ; but there are higher things at stake : my calling and my duty. I feel deeply and warmly within me—and I shrink not from saying it—that I alone am he who can guide the land for the best in these times ; kingly birth begets kingly duty——

EARL SKULE. There are others here who bear themselves the like fair witness.

SIGURD RIBBUNG. That do I, and with even as good ground. My grandfather was King Magnus Erlingsson——

HAKON. Ay, if your father, Erling Steinvæg, was indeed King Magnus's son ; but most people deny it, and the matter has not yet been put to the ordeal.

SIGURD RIBBUNG. The Ribbungs[1] received me as king of their own free will, whilst Dagfinn the Peasant and other Birchlegs[1] must needs use threats to gain for you the kingly title.

---

[1] The " Birkebeiner " or Birchlegs were at this period a political faction. They were so called because, at the time of their first appearance, when they seem to have been little more than bandits,

HAKON. Ay, so ill had you dealt with Norway that the stock of Sverre had to claim its right with threats.

GUTHORM INGESSON. I am of the stock of Sverre as much as you——

DAGFINN. But not in the direct male line.

BISHOP NICHOLAS. You are on the female side, Guthorm.

GUTHORM INGESSON. Yet this I know, that my father, Inge Bårdsson, was lawfully chosen king of Norway.

HAKON. Because none knew that Sverre's grandson was alive. From the day that became known, he held the kingdom in trust for me—not otherwise.

EARL SKULE. That cannot truly be said ; Inge was king all his days, with all lawful power and without reserve. It may be true enough that Guthorm has but little claim, for he was born out of wedlock ; but I am King Inge's lawfully-begotten brother, and the law is with me if I claim, and take, his full inheritance.

DAGFINN. Ah, Sir Earl, of a truth you have contrived to inherit in full, not only your father's family possessions, but all the wealth Hakon Sverresson left behind him.

---

they eked out their scanty attire by making themselves leggings of birch bark.   Norway at this time swarmed with factions, such as the "Bagler" or Croziers (Latin, *baculus*), so called because Bishop Nicholas was their chief, the Ribbungs, the Slittungs, etc., devoted, for the most part, to one or other of the many pretenders to the crown.

Bishop Nicholas.   Not all, good Dagfinn.   Respect the truth ;—King Hakon has kept a brooch and the golden ring he wears on his arm.

Hakon.   Be that as it will; with God's help I shall win myself wealth again.   And now, ye barons and thanes, ye churchmen and chieftains and men-at-arms, now it is time to form the folkmote, as has been agreed.   I have sat with bound hands until this day ; methinks no man will blame me for longing to get them loosed.

Earl Skule.   There are many in like case, Hakon Hakonsson.

Hakon (*on the alert*).   What mean you, Sir Earl ?

Earl Skule.   I mean that all we Pretenders have the same cause for longing.   We have all alike been straitly bound, for none of us has known how far his right held good.

Bishop Nicholas.   The church has been even as unsettled as the kingdom ; but now must we abide by the sainted King Olaf's law.

Dagfinn (*half aloud*).   Fresh stratagems !

(Hakon's *men gather more closely together.*)

Hakon (*with forced calmness, advances a couple of paces towards the* Earl).   I trust I have not rightly taken your meaning.   The ordeal has made good my hereditary right to the kingdom, and therefore, as I deem, the folkmote has nought to do but to ratify my election, which took place at the Örething[1] six years ago.

---

[1] A "thing," or assembly, held from time to time on the "öre" or foreshore at the mouth of the river Nid, at Trondhiem.

SEVERAL OF THE EARL'S AND SIGURD'S MEN. No, no! That we deny!

EARL SKULE. Not to that end did we agree to hold the folkmote here. The ordeal has not given you the kingdom; it has but proved your title to come forward to-day, along with us other Pretenders, and assert the right you hold to be yours——

HAKON (*constraining himself to be calm*). That means, in brief, that for six years I have unlawfully borne the name of King, and for six years, you, Sir Earl, have unlawfully ruled the land as regent for me.

EARL SKULE. In no wise. Some one must needs bear the kingly title, since my brother was dead. The Birchlegs, and most of all Dagfinn the Peasant, were active in your cause, and hastened your election through before we others could set forth our claims.

BISHOP NICHOLAS (*to* HAKON). The Earl would say that that election gave you but the usufruct of the kingly power, not its rightful ownership.

EARL SKULE. You have enjoyed all the privileges; but Sigurd Ribbung and Guthorm Ingesson and I hold ourselves to the full as near inheritors as you; and now shall the law adjudge between us, and say whose shall be the inheritance for all time.

BISHOP NICHOLAS. In truth, the Earl's reasoning is good.

EARL SKULE. Both ordeal and folkmote have more than once been talked of in these years, but something has ever come between. And, Sir Hakon, if you deemed your right immovably established by the first election, how came you to accept the ordeal?

DAGFINN (*bitterly*). To your swords, King's-men, let *them* decide!

MANY OF THE KING'S MEN (*rushing forward*). Down with the King's enemies!

EARL SKULE (*calls to his men*). Slay none! Wound none! Only keep them off.

HAKON (*restraining his men*). Up with your blades, all who have drawn them!—Up with your blades, I say! (*Calmly.*) In doing thus you make things tenfold worse for me.

EARL SKULE. So goes it wherever men meet men, all the country over. You see now, Hakon Hakonsson; does not this show you what you have to do if you have any care for the country's peace and the lives of men?

HAKON (*after some reflection*). Yes—I see it. (*Takes* INGA *by the hand and turns to one of those standing by him.*) Torkell, you were a trusty man in my father's guard; take this woman to your own abode and see you tend her well; she was very dear to Hakon Sverresson.—God bless you, my mother,— now I must gird me for the folkmote. (INGA *presses his hand, and goes with* TORKELL. HAKON *is silent awhile, then steps forward and says with emphasis :*) The law shall decide, and it alone. Ye Birchlegs who, at the Örething, took me for your King, I free you from the oath ye sware to me. You, Dagfinn, are no longer my marshal; I will not appear with marshal or with guard,[1] with vassals or with hirelings. I am a poor man; all my inheritance is a brooch and this gold ring;—these are scant goods wherewith to reward so many good men's service. Now, ye other Pretenders, now we stand equal; I will have no advantage of you, save the right which I have from above,—*that* I neither can nor will share with any one.—Let the assembly-call be sounded, and then let God and the sainted King Olaf's law decide.

(*Goes out with his men to the left; blasts of trumpets and horns are heard far away.*)

GREGORIUS JONSSON (*to the* EARL, *as the crowd prepare to depart*). Methought you seemed afraid during the ordeal, and now you look so glad and hopeful.

EARL SKULE (*with an expression of contentment*). Marked you that he had Sverre's eyes as he spoke? Whether he or I be chosen, the choice will be a good one.

GREGORIUS JONSSON (*uneasily*). But do not you give way. Think of all who stand or fall with your cause.

EARL SKULE. I stand now upon justice; I no longer fear to call upon Saint Olaf.

(*Goes out to the left with his followers.*)

---

[1] The word *hird* is very difficult to render. It meant something between "court," "household," and "guard." I have never translated it "court," as that word seemed to convey an idea of peaceful civilisation foreign to the country and period ; but I have used either "guard" or "household" as the context seemed to demand. *Hird-mand* I have generally rendered "man-at-arms." *Lendermand* I have represented by "baron," *lagmand* and *sysselmand* by "thane," and *stallare* by "marshal"—all mere rough approximations.

BISHOP NICHOLAS (*hastening after* DAGFINN THE PEASANT). 'Twill go well, good Dagfinn, 'twill go well ;—but keep the Earl far from the King when he is chosen ;—see you keep them far apart !
(*All go out to the left, behind the church.*)

(*A hall in the Palace.   On the left, in the foreground, is a low window ; on the right the entrance-door ; in the background a larger door which leads into the King's Hall.   By the window, a table ; chairs and benches stand about.*)

(LADY RAGNHILD *and* MARGRETE *enter by the smaller door ;* SIGRID *follows immediately.*)

LADY RAGNHILD.   In here?

MARGRETE.   Ay, here it is darkest.

LADY RAGNHILD (*goes to the window*).   And here we can look down upon the mote-stead.

MARGRETE (*looks out cautiously*).   Ay, there they are all gathered behind the church.   (*Turns, in tears.*) Yonder must now betide what will bring so much in its train.

LADY RAGNHILD.   Who will be master in this hall to-morrow?

MARGRETE.   Oh, hush ! So heavy a day I had never thought to see.

LADY RAGNHILD.   It had to be ; the regency was no full work for *him.*

MARGRETE.   Ay, it had to be ; *he* could never rest content with the mere name of king.

LADY RAGNHILD.   Of whom speak you ?

MARGRETE.   Of Hakon.

LADY RAGNHILD.   I spoke of the Earl.

MARGRETE.   There breathe not nobler men than they two.

LADY RAGNHILD.   See you Sigurd Ribbung? With what a look of evil cunning he sits there—like a wolf in chains.

MARGRETE.   Yes, see!—He folds his hands before him upon his sword-hilt and rests his chin upon them.

LADY RAGNHILD.   He bites his beard and laughs——

MARGRETE.   'Tis an evil laugh.

LADY RAGNHILD.   He knows that none will take his part;—it is that which makes him wroth.   Who is yonder thane that speaks now?

MARGRETE.   That is Gunnar Grionbak.

LADY RAGNHILD.   Is he for the Earl?

MARGRETE.   No, he is for the King——

LADY RAGNHILD (looking at her).   For whom say you?

MARGRETE.   For Hakon Hakonsson.

LADY RAGNHILD (looks out; after a short pause). Where sits Guthorm Ingesson?—I see him not.

MARGRETE.   Behind his men, lowest of all there— in a long mantle.

LADY RAGNHILD.   Ay, there.

MARGRETE.   He looks as though he were ashamed——

LADY RAGNHILD.   That is for his mother's sake.

MARGRETE.   So did not Hakon.

LADY RAGNHILD.   Who speaks now?

MARGRETE (*looking out*).   Tord Skolle, the thane of Ranafylke.

LADY RAGNHILD.   Is he for the Earl?

MARGRETE.   No—for Hakon.

LADY RAGNHILD.   How motionless the Earl sits listening!

MARGRETE.   Hakon seems thoughtful—but strong none the less. (*With animation.*) Were a stranger here, he could pick out those two amongst all the thousand others.

LADY RAGNHILD.   See, Margrete! Dagfinn the Peasant drags forth a gilded chair for Hakon——

MARGRETE.   Paul Flida places one like it behind the Earl——

LADY RAGNHILD.   Hakon's men seek to hinder it!

MARGRETE.   The Earl holds the chair fast——!

LADY RAGNHILD.   Hakon speaks angrily to him. (*Starts back, with a cry, from the window.*) Oh Christ! Saw you his eyes—and his smile——! No, that was not the Earl!

MARGRETE (*who has followed her in terror*). Nor Hakon either! Neither one nor the other!

SIGRID (*at the window*). Oh pitiful! Oh pitiful!

MARGRETE.   Sigrid!

LADY RAGNHILD.   You here!

SIGRID.   Goes the path so low that leads up to the throne!

MARGRETE.   Oh, pray with us, that all be guided for the best.

LADY RAGNHILD (*white and horror-stricken, to* SIGRID). Saw you him? Saw you my husband?

His eyes and his smile—I should not have known him!

SIGRID. Looked he like Sigurd Ribbung?

LADY RAGNHILD (*softly*). Ay, he looked like Sigurd Ribbung.

SIGRID. Laughed he like Sigurd?

LADY RAGNHILD. Ay, ay!

SIGRID. Then must we all pray.

LADY RAGNHILD (*with despairing strength*). The Earl *must* be chosen King! 'Twill work ruin in his soul if he become not the first man in the land!

SIGRID (*more loudly*). Then must we all pray!

LADY RAGNHILD. Hist! What is that? (*At the window.*) What shouts! All the men have risen; all the banners and standards wave in the wind.

SIGRID (*seizes her by the arm*). Pray, woman! Pray for your husband!

LADY RAGNHILD. Ay, holy King Olaf, give him all the power in this land!

SIGRID (*wildly*). None—none! Else is he lost!

LADY RAGNHILD. He *must* have the power. All the good in him will grow and blossom if he gets it.— Look forth, Margrete! Listen! (*Starts back a step.*) All hands are lifted for an oath!

(MARGRETE *listens at the window.*)

LADY RAGNHILD. God and Saint Olaf, who wins?

SIGRID. Pray!

(MARGRETE *listens, and with uplifted hand motions for silence.*)

LADY RAGNHILD (*after a little while*). Speak!

(*From the mote-stead is heard a loud blast of trumpets and horns.*)

Lady Ragnhild. God and Saint Olaf!   Who has won?

(*A short pause.*)

Margrete (*turns her head and says:*) 'Tis Hakon Hakonsson they choose for king.

> (*The music of the royal procession is heard, first in the distance and then nearer and nearer. Lady Ragnhild clings weeping to Sigrid, who leads her quietly out on the right; Margrete remains immovable, leaning against the window-frame. The King's attendants open the great doors, disclosing the interior of the Hall, which is gradually filled by the procession from the mote-stead.*)

Hakon (*in the doorway, turning to Ivar Bodde*). Bring me a pen and wax and silk—I have parchment here. (*Advances exultantly to the table and lays some rolls of parchment upon it.*) Margrete, now am I King!

Margrete.   Hail to my lord and King!

Hakon. I thank you! (*Looks at her and takes her hand.*) Forgive me; I forgot that it must wound you.

Margrete (*drawing her hand away*). It did not wound me;—of a surety you are born to be king.

Hakon (*with animation*). Ay, must not all men own it, who remember how marvellously God and the saints have shielded me from all harm? I was but a year old when the Birchlegs bore me over the mountains, through frost and storm, and through the very midst of those who sought my life. At Nidaros I

15

came scatheless from the Baglers[1] when they burnt the town with so great a slaughter, while King Inge himself barely saved his life by climbing on shipboard up the anchor-cable.

MARGRETE.   Your youth has been a hard one.

HAKON (*looking steadily at her*).   Methinks you might have made it easier.

MARGRETE.   I ?

HAKON.   You might have been so good a foster-sister to me, through all the years when we were growing up together.

MARGRETE.   But it **fell out** otherwise.

HAKON.   Ay, it fell out otherwise;—we looked at each other, I from my corner, you from yours, but we seldom spoke—— (*Impatiently.*)   What is keeping him?   (IVAR BODDE *comes with the writing materials.*)   Are you there?   Give me the things!

> (HAKON *seats himself at the table and writes.   A little while after,* EARL SKULE *comes in; then* DAGFINN THE PEASANT, BISHOP NICHOLAS, *and* VEGARD VÆRADAL.)

HAKON (*looks up and lays down his pen*).   Know you, Sir Earl, what I am writing here?   (*The* EARL *approaches.*)   This is to my mother; I thank her for all her love, and kiss her a thousand times—here in the letter you understand.   She is to be sent eastward to Borgasyssel, and to live there with all kingly honours.

EARL SKULE.   You will not keep her in the palace?

HAKON.   She is too dear to me, Earl;—a king

<hr>

must have none about him whom he loves too well. A king must act with free hands; he must stand alone; he must neither be led nor lured. There is so much to be mended in Norway.

(*Goes on writing.*)

VEGARD VÆRADAL (*softly to* BISHOP NICHOLAS). 'Tis by my counsel he deals thus with Inga, his mother.

BISHOP NICHOLAS. I knew your hand in it at once.

VEGARD VÆRADAL. But now one good turn deserves another.

BISHOP NICHOLAS. Wait. I will keep that I promised.

HAKON (*gives the parchment to* IVAR BODDE). Fold it together and take it to her yourself, with many loving greetings——

IVAR BODDE (*who has glanced at the parchment*). My Lord—will you not delay a day——!

HAKON.   The wind is fair for a southward course.

DAGFINN (*slowly*). Bethink you, my lord King, that she has lain all night on the altar-steps in prayer and fasting.

IVAR BODDE.   And she may well be weary after the ordeal.

HAKON.   True, true;—my good kind mother——! (*Collects himself.*) Well, if she be too weary, let her wait until to-morrow.

IVAR BODDE.   It shall be as you will. (*Puts another parchment forward.*) But this other, my lord.

HAKON.   That other ?—Ivar Bodde, I cannot.

DAGFINN (*points to the letter for* INGA). Yet you could do that.

IVAR BODDE.   There must be an end to sin.

BISHOP NICHOLAS (*who has drawn near in the meantime*).   Now is the time to bind the Earl's hands, King Hakon.

HAKON.   Think you that is needful?

BISHOP NICHOLAS.   You cannot buy the peace in the land at a cheaper rate.

HAKON.   Then must I do it.   Give me the pen!   (*Writes.*)

EARL SKULE (*to the* BISHOP, *who crosses to the right*).   You have the King's ear, it would seem.

BISHOP NICHOLAS.   For your behoof.

EARL SKULE.   Say you so?

BISHOP NICHOLAS.   Before nightfall you will thank me.   (*He moves away.*)

HAKON (*hands the* EARL *the parchment*).   Read that, Earl.

EARL SKULE (*reads, looks in surprise at the* KING, *and says in a low voice*).   You break with Kanga the Young?

HAKON.   With Kanga whom I have loved more than all the world.   From this day forth she must never more cross the King's path.

EARL SKULE.   In this do you show yourself great, Hakon—I know well by mine own self what it must cost.

HAKON.   Whoever is too dear to the King must away.—Tie up the letter.   (*Gives it to* IVAR BODDE.)

BISHOP NICHOLAS (*bending over the chair*).   You have made a great stride towards the Earl's friendship, my lord King.

HAKON (*holds out his hand to him*). Thanks, Bishop Nicholas; you counselled me for the best. Ask a grace of me, and I will grant it.

BISHOP NICHOLAS.   Will you?

HAKON.   I promise it on my kingly faith.

BISHOP NICHOLAS.   Then make Vegard Væradal thane of Halogaland.

HAKON.   Vegard?   He is well-nigh the trustiest friend I have; I am loath to send him so far from me.

BISHOP NICHOLAS.   The King's friend must be royally rewarded.   Bind the Earl's hands as I have counselled you, and you will be secure for ever and a day.

HAKON (*takes a sheet of parchment*).   Vegard shall have the thane-ship of Halogaland.   (*Writing.*) I hereby grant it to him under my royal hand.

(*The* BISHOP *retires.*)

EARL SKULE (*approaches the table*).   What write you now?

HAKON (*hands him the sheet*).   Read.

EARL SKULE (*reads, and looks steadily at the* KING). Vegard Væradal?   In Halogaland?

HAKON.   The northern part stands vacant.

EARL SKULE.   Bethink you that Andres Skialdarband[1] has also a charge in the north.   They two are bitter foes;—Andres Skialdarband is of my following——

HAKON (*smiling and rising*).   And Vegard Væradal of mine.   Therefore they must e'en make friends again, the sooner the better.   Henceforth there must be no enmity between the King's men and the Earl's.

---

[1] Pronounce *Shaldarband.*

BISHOP NICHOLAS. Hm. This may go too far. (*Approaches, uneasy.*)

EARL SKULE. Your thoughts are wise and deep, Hakon.

HAKON (*warmly*). Earl Skule, to-day have I taken the kingdom from you—let your daughter share it with me!

EARL SKULE. My daughter!

MARGRETE. Oh God!

HAKON. Margrete—will you be my Queen? (MARGRETE *is silent.*)

HAKON (*takes her hand*). Answer me.

MARGRETE (*softly*). I will gladly be your wife.

EARL SKULE (*pressing* HAKON'S *hand*). Peace and friendship from my heart!

HAKON. I thank you!

IVAR BODDE (*to* DAGFINN). Heaven be praised; here is the dawn.

DAGFINN. I almost believe it. Never before have I seen so much good in the Earl.

BISHOP NICHOLAS (*behind him*). Ever on your guard, good Dagfinn, ever on your guard.

IVAR BODDE (*to* VEGARD). Now are you thane of Halogaland; here you have it under the King's hand.

(*Gives him the letter.*)

VEGARD VÆRADAL. I will thank the King for his favour another time. (*About to go.*)

BISHOP NICHOLAS (*stops him*). Andres Skialdar-band is an ugly adversary; be not cowed by him.

VEGARD VÆRADAL. No one has yet cowed Vegard Væradal. (*Goes.*)

Bishop Nicholas (*following*).   Be as rock and flint to Andres Skialdarband,—and take my blessing with you, if you will.

Ivar Bodde (*who has been waiting behind the* King *with the parchments in his hand*).   Here are the letters, my lord.

Hakon.   Good; give them to the Earl.

Ivar Bodde.   To the Earl?   Will not you seal them?

Hakon.   The Earl is wont to do that;—he holds the seal.

Ivar Bodde (*softly*).   Ay, hitherto—while he was regent—but now!

Hakon.   Now as before;—the Earl holds the seal. (*Retires.*)

Earl Skule.   Give me the letters, Ivar Bodde.
 (*Goes to the table with them, takes out the Great Seal which he wears under his girdle, and seals the letters during the following.*)

Bishop Nicholas (*muttering*).   Hakon Hakonsson is King and the Earl holds the royal seal;—I like that—I like that.

Hakon.   What says my lord Bishop?

Bishop Nicholas.   I say that God and Saint Olaf watch over their holy church.
 (*Goes into the King's Hall.*)

Hakon (*approaching* Margrete).   A wise queen can do great things in the land: I have chosen you fearlessly, for I know you are wise.

Margrete.   That only!

Hakon.   What mean you?

Margrete.   Nothing, my lord, nothing.

HAKON.   And you will bear me no grudge if for my sake you have had to let slip fair hopes.

MARGRETE.   I have let slip no fair hopes for your sake.

HAKON.   And you will stand ever near me, and give me good counsel?

MARGRETE.   I would fain stand near to you.

HAKON.   And give me good counsel.   Thanks for that; a woman's counsel profits every man, and henceforth I have none but you—my mother I have sent away——

MARGRETE.   Ay, she was too dear to you——

HAKON.   And I am King.   Farewell then, Margrete!   You are so young yet; but next summer shall our bridal be, and from that hour I swear to keep you by my side in all seemly faith and honour.

MARGRETE (*smiles sadly*).   Ay, I know 'twill be long ere you send me away.

HAKON (*brightly*).   Send you away?   That will I never do!

MARGRETE (*with tears in her eyes*).   No, that Hakon does only to those who are too dear to him.

(*She goes towards the entrance door.* HAKON *gazes thoughtfully after her.*)

LADY RAGNHILD (*from the right*).   The King and the Earl so long in here!   My fears are killing me; —Margrete, what has the King said and done?

MARGRETE.   Oh, much, much!   Last of all, he chose a thane and a Queen.

LADY RAGNHILD.   You, Margrete!

MARGRETE (*throws her arms round her mother's neck*).   Yes!

Lady Ragnhild.   You are to be Queen!

Margrete.   Queen only;—but I think I am glad even of that.

(*She and her mother go out to the right.*)

Earl Skule (*to* Ivar Bodde).   Here are our letters; bear them to the King's mother and to Kanga.

(Ivar Bodde *bows and goes.*)

Dagfinn (*in the doorway of the hall*).   The Archbishop of Nidaros craves leave to offer King Hakon Hakonsson his homage.

Hakon (*draws a deep breath*).   At last I am King of Norway.

(*Goes into the hall.*) ˙

Earl Skule (*places the Great Seal in his girdle*). But *I* rule the realm.

THE CURTAIN FALLS.

Act Second.

(*Banquet Hall in the Palace at Bergen. A large bay-window in the middle of the back wall, along which there is a daïs with seats for the ladies. Against the left wall stands the throne, raised some steps above the floor; in the centre of the opposite wall is the great entrance door. Banners, standards, shields and weapons, with many-coloured draperies, hang from the wall-timbers and from the carven rafters. Around the hall stand drinking-tables, with flagons, horns, and beakers.*)

(KING HAKON *sits upon the daïs, with* MARGRETE, SIGRID, LADY RAGNHILD, *and many noble ladies.* IVAR BODDE *stands behind the King's chair. Round the drinking-tables are seated the King's and the Earl's men, with guests. At the foremost table on the right sit, amongst others,* DAGFINN THE PEASANT, GREGORIUS JONSSON, *and* PAUL FLIDA. EARL SKULE *and* BISHOP NICHOLAS *are playing chess at a table on the left. The Earl's house-folk go to and fro, bearing cans of liquor. From an adjoining room, music is heard during the following scene.*)

DAGFINN. 'Tis now wearing on for the fifth day, yet the henchmen are none the less nimble at setting forth the brimming flagons.

PAUL FLIDA. It was never the Earl's wont to stint his guests.

DAGFINN. No, so it would seem. So royal a bridal-feast was never seen in Norway before.

PAUL FLIDA. Earl Skule has never before given a daughter in marriage.

Dagfinn.   True, true; the Earl is a mighty man.

A Man-at-Arms.   He holds a third part of the kingdom.   That is more than any Earl has held heretofore.

Paul Flida.   But the King's part is larger.

Dagfinn.   We talk not of that here; we are friends now, and fully at one.   (*Drinks to* Paul.)   So let King be King and Earl be Earl.

Paul Flida (*laughs*).   'Tis easy to hear that you are a King's man.

Dagfinn.   That should the Earl's men also be.

Paul Flida.   Never.   We have sworn fealty to the Earl, not to the King.

Dagfinn.   That may still be done.

Bishop Nicholas (*to the* Earl, *under cover of the game*).   Hear you what Dagfinn the Peasant says?

Earl Skule (*without looking up*).   I hear.

Gregorius Jonsson (*looking steadily at* Dagfinn).   Has the King thoughts of that?

Dagfinn.   Nay, nay,—let be;—no wrangling to-day.

Bishop Nicholas.   The King would force your men to swear him fealty, Earl.

Gregorius Jonsson (*louder*).   Has the King thoughts of that, I ask?

Dagfinn.   I will not answer.   Let us drink to peace and friendship between the King and the Earl.   The ale is good.

Paul Flida.   It has had time enough to mellow.

Gregorius Jonsson.   Three times has the Earl prepared the bridal—three times the King promised to come—three times he came not.

DAGFINN.   Blame the Earl for that : he gave us plenty to do in Viken.

PAUL FLIDA.   They say Sigurd Ribbung gave you still more to do in Vermeland.

DAGFINN (*flaring up*).   Ay, who was it that let Sigurd Ribbung slip through their fingers ?

GREGORIUS JONSSON.   Sigurd Ribbung fled from us at Nidaros, that is well known.

DAGFINN.   But it is not well known that you did aught to hinder him.

BISHOP NICHOLAS (*to the* EARL, *who is pondering on a move*).   Hear you, Earl ?   It was you who let Sigurd Ribbung escape.

EARL SKULE (*makes a move*).   That is an old story.

GREGORIUS JONSSON.   Have you not heard, then, of the Icelander Andres Torsteinsson, Sigurd Ribbung's friend——

DAGFINN.   Ay ; when Sigurd had escaped, you hanged the Icelander—that I know.

BISHOP NICHOLAS (*makes a move and says laughingly to the* EARL).   I take the pawn, Sir Earl.[1]

EARL SKULE (*aloud*).   Take him ; a pawn is not worth much.

DAGFINN.   No; that the Icelander found to his cost, when Sigurd Ribbung escaped to Vermeland.

(*Suppressed laughter amongst the King's-men ; the*

---

[1] Bishop Nicholas's speech, "Nu slår jeg bonden, herre jarl," means literally, "Now I strike (or slay) the peasant;" the pawn being called in Norwegian "bonde," peasant, as in German "Bauer." Thus in this speech and the next the Bishop and the Earl are girding at Dagfinn the Peasant. [Our own word "pawn" comes from the Spanish *peon* = a foot-soldier or day-labourer.]

conversation is continued in a low tone ; presently a man comes in and whispers to GREGORIUS JONSSON.)

BISHOP NICHOLAS.   Then I move here, and you have lost.

EARL SKULE.   So it seems.

BISHOP NICHOLAS (*leaning back in his chair*). You did not guard the king well at the last.

EARL SKULE (*strews the pieces topsy-turvy and rises*).   I have long wearied of being the King's guardian.

GREGORIUS JONSSON (*approaches and says in a low tone*).   Sir Earl, Jostein[1] Tamb sends word that the ship now lies ready for sea.

EARL SKULE (*softly*).   Good.   (*Takes out a sealed parchment.*)   Here is the letter.

GREGORIUS JONSSON (*shaking his head*).   Earl, Earl, is this prudent ?

EARL SKULE.   What ?

GREGORIUS JONSSON.   It bears the King's seal.

EARL SKULE.   I am acting for the King's good.

GREGORIUS JONSSON.   Then let the King himself reject the offer.

EARL SKULE.   That he will not, if he has his own way.   His whole heart is bent on cowing the Ribbungs, therefore he is fain to secure himself on other sides.

GREGORIUS JONSSON.   Your way may be wise, but it is bold.

EARL SKULE.   Leave that to me.   Take the letter, and bid Jostein sail forthwith.

<hr>

[1] Pronounce " Yostein.'

GREGORIUS JONSSON. It shall be as you command. (*Goes out to the right, and comes in again presently.*)

BISHOP NICHOLAS (*to the* EARL). You have much to see to, it would seem.

EARL SKULE. But small thanks for it.

BISHOP NICHOLAS. The King has risen. (HAKON *comes down ; all the men rise from the tables.*)

HAKON (*to the* BISHOP). We are rejoiced to see you bear up so bravely and well through all these days of merriment.

BISHOP NICHOLAS. There comes a flicker now and then, my lord King ; but 'twill scarce last long. I have lain sick all the winter through.

HAKON. Ay, ay,—you have lived a strong life, rich in deeds of fame.

BISHOP NICHOLAS (*shakes his head*). Ah, 'tis little enough I have done, and I have much still left to do. If I but knew whether I should have time for it all !

HAKON. The living must take up the tasks of those who are gone, honoured lord ; we have all the welfare of the land at heart. (*Turns to the* EARL.) I marvel much at one thing : that neither of our thanes from Halogaland has come to the bridal.

EARL SKULE. True ; I doubted not that Andres Skialdarband would be here.

HAKON (*smiling*). And Vegard Væradal too.

EARL SKULE. Ay, Vegard too.

HAKON (*in jest*). And I trust you would now have received my old friend better than you did seven years ago on Oslo wharf, when you stabbed him in the cheek so that the blade cut its way out.

EARL SKULE (*with a forced laugh*). Ay, the time that Gunnulf, your mother's brother, cut off the right hand of Sira Eiliv, my best friend and counsellor.

BISHOP NICHOLAS (*merrily*). And when Dagfinn the Peasant and the men-at-arms set a strong night-watch on the King's ship, saying that the King was unsafe in the Earl's ward!

HAKON (*seriously*). Those days are old and forgotten.

DAGFINN (*approaching*). Now may we sound the summons to the weapon-sports on the green, if so please you, my lord.

HAKON. Good. To-day will we give up to nought but merriment; to-morrow we must turn our thoughts again to the Ribbungs and the Earl of Orkney.

BISHOP NICHOLAS. Ay, he refuses to pay tribute, does he not?

HAKON. Were I once rid of the Ribbungs, I would myself fare westward.

> (HAKON *goes towards the daïs, gives his hand to* MARGRETE, *and leads her out to the right; the others gradually follow.*)

BISHOP NICHOLAS (*to* IVAR BODDE). Hearken here—who is the man called Jostein Tamb?

IVAR BODDE. He is a trader from Orkney.

BISHOP NICHOLAS. From Orkney? So, so! And now he sails home again?

IVAR BODDE. So I think.

BISHOP NICHOLAS (*softly*). With a precious freight, Ivar Bodde !

IVAR BODDE. Corn and clothing, most like.

BISHOP NICHOLAS. And a letter from Earl Skule.

IVAR BODDE (*starting*). To whom ?

BISHOP NICHOLAS. I know not ; it bore the King's seal——

IVAR BODDE (*seizes him by the arm*). Lord Bishop, —is it as you say ?

BISHOP NICHOLAS. Hist ! Do not mix me up in the matter. (*Retires.*)

IVAR BODDE. Then must I forthwith—— Dagfinn the Peasant ! Dagfinn ! Dagfinn——! (*Pushes through the crowd towards the door.*)

BISHOP NICHOLAS (*in a tone of commiseration, to* GREGORIUS JONSSON). Not a day but one or another must suffer in goods or freedom.

GREGORIUS JONSSON. Who is it now ?

BISHOP NICHOLAS. A poor trader,—Jostein Tamb methinks they called him.

GREGORIUS JONSSON. Jostein—— ?

BISHOP NICHOLAS. Dagfinn the Peasant would forbid him to set sail.

GREGORIUS JONSSON. Dagfinn would forbid him, say you ?

BISHOP NICHOLAS. He went even now.

GREGORIUS JONSSON. I crave your pardon, my lord ; I must make speed——

BISHOP NICHOLAS. Ay, do even so, my dear lord ; —Dagfinn the Peasant is so hasty.

(GREGORIUS JONSSON *hastens out to the right*

along with the remainder of the company ; only EARL SKULE *and* BISHOP NICHOLAS *are left behind in the hall.*)

EARL SKULE (*walks up and down in deep thought ; he seems suddenly to awaken ; looks round him, and says :*) How still it has become here all at once !

BISHOP NICHOLAS. The King has gone.

EARL SKULE. And every one has followed him.

BISHOP NICHOLAS. All, save us.

EARL SKULE. It is a great thing to be King.

BISHOP NICHOLAS (*tentatively*). Are you fain to try it, Earl ?

EARL SKULE (*with a serious smile*). I *have* tried it ; every night that brings me sleep makes me King of Norway.

BISHOP NICHOLAS. Dreams forebode.

EARL SKULE. Ay, and tempt.

BISHOP NICHOLAS. Not you, surely. Formerly, that I could understand—but now, when you hold a third part of the kingdom, rule as the first man in the land, and are the Queen's father——

EARL SKULE. Now most of all—now most of all.

BISHOP NICHOLAS. Hide nothing ! Confess ; for I see a great pain is gnawing you.

EARL SKULE. Now most of all, I say. This is the great curse that lies upon my whole life : to stand so near to the highest, but with an abyss between. One leap, and on the other side are the kingly title, the purple robes, the throne, the might, and all ! I have it daily before my eyes—but can never reach it.

BISHOP NICHOLAS. True, Earl, true.

EARL SKULE. When they made Guthorm Sigurdsson king, I was in the full strength of my youth ; it was as though a voice cried aloud within me : Away with the child,—I am the man, the strong man !—But Guthorm was the king's-son ; there yawned an abyss between me and the throne.

BISHOP NICHOLAS.   And you dared not——

EARL SKULE.   Then Erling Steinvæg was chosen by the Slittungs.   The voice cried within me again : Skule is a greater chieftain than Erling Steinvæg ! But I must needs have broken with the Birchlegs,— that was the abyss that time.

BISHOP NICHOLAS.   And Erling became king of the Slittungs, and afterwards of the Ribbungs, and still you waited !

EARL SKULE.   I waited for Guthorm to die.

BISHOP NICHOLAS.   And Guthorm died, and Inge Bårdsson, your brother, became king.

EARL SKULE.   Then I waited for my brother's death.   He was sickly from the first ; every morning, when we met at holy mass, I would cast stolen glances to see whether his sickness increased.   Every twitch of pain that crossed his face was as a puff of wind in my sails, and bore me nearer to the throne.   Every sigh he breathed in his agony sounded to me like a trumpet-blast echoed from distant leas, heralding a messenger from afar to tell me that the throne should soon be mine.   Thus I tore up by the roots every thought of brotherly kindness ; and Inge died, and Hakon came—and the Birchlegs made *him* king.

BISHOP NICHOLAS.   And you waited——

EARL SKULE.   Methought help must come from above.   I felt the kingly strength within me, and I was growing old; every day that passed was a day taken from my life-work. Each evening I thought: To-morrow will come the miracle that shall strike him down and set me in the empty seat.

BISHOP NICHOLAS. At that time Hakon's power was small; he was no more than a child; it wanted but a single step from you—yet you took it not.

EARL SKULE. That step was hard to take; it would have parted me from my kindred and from all my friends.

BISHOP NICHOLAS. Ay, *there* is the rub, Earl Skule,—*that* is the curse which has lain upon your life. You would fain know every way open at need, —you dare not break all your bridges and keep only one, defend it alone, and conquer or fall upon it. You lay snares for your foe, you set traps for his feet, and hang sharp swords over his head; you strew poison in every dish, and you spread a hundred nets for him; but when he walks into your toils you dare not draw the string; if he stretches out his hand for the poison, you think it safer that he should fall by the sword; if he is like to be caught in the morning, you think it wiser to wait till eventide.

EARL SKULE (*looking seriously at him*). And what would *you* do, my lord Bishop?

BISHOP NICHOLAS. Speak not of me; my work is to build up thrones in this land, not to sit on them and rule.

EARL SKULE (*after a short pause*). Answer me one thing, my honoured lord, and answer me truly. How comes it that Hakon can follow the straight path so unflinchingly? He is no wiser, no bolder than I.

BISHOP NICHOLAS.   Who does the greatest deeds in this world?

EARL SKULE.   The greatest man.

BISHOP NICHOLAS.   But who is the greatest man?

EARL SKULE.   The bravest.

BISHOP NICHOLAS.   So says the warrior. A priest would say: the man of greatest faith,—a philosopher: the most learned. But it is none of these, Earl. The most fortunate man[1] is the greatest man. It is the most fortunate man that does the greatest deeds—he whom the cravings of his time seize like a passion, begetting thoughts he himself cannot fathom, and pointing to paths which lead he knows not whither, but which he follows and must follow till he hears the people shout for joy, and, looking around him with wondering eyes, finds himself the hero of a great achievement.

EARL SKULE.   Ay, there is that unflinching confidence in Hakon.

BISHOP NICHOLAS.   It is that which the Romans called *ingenium.*—Truly I am not strong in Latin; but 'twas called *ingenium.*

EARL SKULE (*thoughtfully at first, afterwards in increasing excitement*). Is Hakon made of other clay than mine? The fortunate man?—Ay, does not everything thrive with him? Does not everything shape itself for the best, when he is concerned? Even the peasants note it; they say the trees bear

---

[1] *Den lykkeligste mand.* The word *lykke* means not only luck or fortune, but happiness. To render *lykkeligste* completely, we should require a word in which the ideas "fortunate" and "happy" should be blent.

fruit twice, and the fowls hatch out two broods every summer, whilst Hakon is king. Vermeland, where he burned and harried, stands smiling with its houses built afresh, and its cornlands bending heavy-eared before the breeze. 'Tis as though blood and ashes fertilised the land where Hakon's armies pass; 'tis as though the Lord clothed with double verdure what Hakon had trampled down; 'tis as though the holy powers made haste to blot out all evil in his track. And how easy has been his path to the throne! He needed that Inge should die early, and Inge died: his youth needed to be watched and warded, and his men kept watch and ward around him; he needed the ordeal, and his mother bore the iron for him.

BISHOP NICHOLAS (*with an involuntary outburst*). But we—we two——!

EARL SKULE. We?

BISHOP NICHOLAS. You, I would say—what of you?

EARL SKULE. The right is Hakon's, Bishop.

BISHOP NICHOLAS. The right is his, for he is the fortunate one; 'tis even the summit of fortune, to have the right. But by what right has Hakon the right, and not you?

EARL SKULE (*after a short pause*). There are things I pray God to save me from thinking upon.

BISHOP NICHOLAS. Saw you never an old picture in Christ's Church at Nidaros? It shows the Deluge rising and rising over all the hills, so that there is but one single peak left above the waters. Up it clambers a whole household, father and mother and son and son's wife and children;—and the son is hurling the father back into the flood to gain better footing ; and he will cast his mother down and his wife and all his children, to win to the top himself;—for up there he sees a handsbreadth of ground, where he may keep life in him for an hour.—That, Earl, that is the saga of wisdom, and the saga of every wise man.

EARL SKULE. But the right !

BISHOP NICHOLAS. The son *had* the right. He had strength, and the craving for life ;—fulfil your cravings and use your strength: so much right has every man.

EARL SKULE. Ay, for that which is good.

BISHOP NICHOLAS. Words, words! There is neither good nor evil, up nor down, high nor low. You must forget such words, else will you never take the last stride, never leap the abyss. (*In a subdued voice and insistently.*) You must not hate a party or a cause because the party or the cause would have this and not that; but you must hate every man of a party because he is against you, and you must hate all who gather round a cause, because the cause clashes with your will. Whatever is helpful to you, is good—whatever lays stumbling-blocks in your path, is evil.

EARL SKULE (*gazing thoughtfully before him*). What has that throne not cost me, which yet I have not reached ! And what has it cost Hakon, who now sits in it so securely ! I was young, and I renounced my sweet secret love to ally myself with a powerful house. I prayed to the saints that I might be blessed with a son—I got only daughters.

BISHOP NICHOLAS. Hakon will have sons, Earl —mark that !

EARL SKULE (*crossing to the window on the right*). Ay—all things fall out to Hakon's wish.

BISHOP NICHOLAS. And you—will you suffer yourself to be outlawed from happiness all your life through? Are you blind? See you not that it is a stronger might than the Birchlegs that stands at Hakon's back, and furthers all his life-work? He has help from above, from—from those that are against you—from those that have been your enemies, even from your birth! Rouse you, man; straighten your back! To what end got you your masterful soul? Bethink you that the first great deed the world knows of was done by one who rose against a mighty realm!

EARL SKULE. Who?

BISHOP NICHOLAS. The angel who rose against the light!

EARL SKULE. And was hurled into the bottomless pit——

BISHOP NICHOLAS (*wildly*). And there founded a kingdom, and made himself a king, a mighty king— mightier than any of the ten thousand—earls up yonder! (*Sinks down upon a bench beside the table.*)

EARL SKULE (*looks long at him*). Bishop Nicholas, are you something more or something less than a man?

BISHOP NICHOLAS (*smiling*). I am in the state of innocence: I know not good from evil.

EARL SKULE (*half to himself*). Why did they send me into the world, if they meant not to order it better for me? Hakon has so firm and unswerving a faith in himself—all his men have so firm and unswerving a faith in him——

BISHOP NICHOLAS. Let no man see that *you* have not so firm a faith in yourself! Speak as though you had it, swear great oaths that you have it—and all will believe you.

EARL SKULE. Had I a son! Had I but a son, to receive the inheritance at my hands!

BISHOP NICHOLAS (*eagerly*). And if you *had* a son, Earl?

EARL SKULE. I have none.

BISHOP NICHOLAS. Hakon will have sons.

EARL SKULE (*clasping his hands together*). And is king-born!

BISHOP NICHOLAS. Earl—if he were not so?

EARL SKULE. Has he not proved it? The ordeal——

BISHOP NICHOLAS. And if he were not—in spite of the ordeal?

EARL SKULE. Would you say that God lied in the issue of the ordeal?

BISHOP NICHOLAS. What was it Inga of Varteig called upon God to witness?

EARL SKULE. That the child she bore in the eastland, in Borgasyssel, was the son of Hakon Sverresson.

BISHOP NICHOLAS (*nods, looks round, and says softly*). And if King Hakon were not that child?

EARL SKULE (*starts a step backwards*). Great God! (*Controls himself.*) It is beyond belief.

BISHOP NICHOLAS. Hearken to me, Earl. I have lived seventy years and six; it begins to go sharply downhill with me now, and I dare not take this secret with me over to the other side——

EARL SKULE. Speak, speak! Is he not the son of Hakon Sverresson?

BISHOP NICHOLAS. Hear me. It was known to none that Inga was with child. Hakon Sverresson was lately dead, and doubtless she feared Inge Bårdsson, who was then king, and you, and—well, and the Baglers[1] too mayhap. She was brought to bed secretly in the house of Trond the Priest, east in Heggen parish, and nine days afterwards she departed homewards; but the child remained a whole year with the priest, she not daring to look to it, and none knowing that it breathed save Trond and his two sons.

EARL SKULE. Ay, ay—and then?

BISHOP NICHOLAS. When the child was a year old, it could scarce be kept hidden longer. So Inga made the matter known to Erlend of Huseby—an old Birchleg of Sverre's days, as you know.

EARL SKULE. Well?

BISHOP NICHOLAS. He and other chiefs from the Uplands took the child, bore it over the mountains in midwinter, and brought it to the King, who was then at Nidaros.

EARL SKULE. And yet you can say that——?

BISHOP NICHOLAS. You can well believe that it was a dangerous matter for a humble priest to rear a king's-child. So soon as the child was born, then, he laid the matter before one of his superiors in the church, and prayed for his counsel. This his superior

[1] See note, p. 215.

bade Trond send the **true** king's-son with secrecy to a place of safety, **and give Inga** another, if she or the Birchlegs should afterwards ask for her child.

EARL SKULE (*indignantly*). And who was **the** hound that gave that counsel ?

BISHOP NICHOLAS. It was I.

EARL SKULE. **You ?** Ay, you have **ever** hated the race of Sverre.

BISHOP NICHOLAS. I deemed it unsafe for the king's-son to fall into **your** hands.

EARL SKULE. **But the priest——?**

BISHOP NICHOLAS. Promised to do as I bade.

EARL SKULE (*seizing him by the arm*). **And is** Hakon the other ?

BISHOP NICHOLAS. **Ay,** if the priest kept his **promise.**

EARL SKULE. *If* he kept it ?

BISHOP NICHOLAS. Trond the Priest departed **the** land the same **winter** that **the** child was brought to King Inge. He journeyed to Thomas Beckett's grave, and afterwards abode **in** England till his death.

EARL SKULE. He departed the land, say you ? Then must he have changed the children and dreaded the vengeance of the Birchlegs.

BISHOP NICHOLAS. **Or he** did *not* change the children, and dreaded *my* vengeance.

EARL SKULE. Which surmise hold you for the truth ?

BISHOP NICHOLAS. Either may well be true.

EARL SKULE. But the sons you spoke of ?

BISHOP NICHOLAS. They went with the crusaders to the **Holy Land.**

EARL SKULE. And you have had no tidings of them?

BISHOP NICHOLAS. Ay, tidings I have had.

EARL SKULE. Where are they?

BISHOP NICHOLAS. They were drowned in the Greek Sea on the journey forth.

EARL SKULE. And Inga——?

BISHOP NICHOLAS. Knows nought, either of priest's confession or of my counsel.

EARL SKULE. Her child was but nine days old when she left it, you said?

BISHOP NICHOLAS. Ay, and the child she next saw was over a year——

EARL SKULE. Then no living creature can throw light on this matter! (*Paces rapidly to and fro.*) Almighty God, can this be true? Hakon—the King —he who holds sway over all this land, is he not king-born!—And why should it not be like enough? Has not all fortune miraculously followed him?— Why not this also, to be taken as a child from a poor cottar's hut and laid in a king's cradle——?

BISHOP NICHOLAS. Whilst the whole people believes that he is the king's son——

EARL SKULE. Whilst *he himself* believes it, Bishop—*that* is the heart of his fortune, *that* is the girdle of strength! (*Goes to the window.*) See how bravely he sits his horse! None sits like him. His eyes are filled with laughing, dancing sunshine; he looks forth into the day as though he knew himself created to go forward, ever forward. (*Turns towards the* BISHOP.) I am a king's arm, mayhap a king's brain as well; but he is the whole King.

BISHOP NICHOLAS. Yet no king after all, may-hap.

EARL SKULE. Mayhap no king after all.

BISHOP NICHOLAS (*lays his hand on the* EARL'S *shoulder*). Hearken to me, Earl Skule——

EARL SKULE (*still looking out*). There sits the Queen. Hakon speaks gently to her; she turns red and white with joy. He took her to wife because it was wise to choose the daughter of the mightiest man in the land. There was then no thought of love for her in his heart;—but that will come; Hakon has fortune with him. She will shed light over his life—— (*Stops, and cries in astonishment.*) What is that?

BISHOP NICHOLAS. What?

EARL SKULE. Dagfinn the Peasant bursts violently through the crowd. Now he is giving the King some tidings.

BISHOP NICHOLAS (*looking out from behind the* EARL). Hakon seems angered—does he not? He clenches his fist——

EARL SKULE. He looks hitherward—what can it be? (*Going.*)

BISHOP NICHOLAS (*holding him back*). Hearken to me, Earl Skule—there may yet be one means of winning assurance as to Hakon's right.

EARL SKULE. One means, you say?

BISHOP NICHOLAS. Trond the Priest, ere he died, wrote a letter telling his whole tale, and took the sacrament in witness of its truth.

EARL SKULE. And that letter—for God's pity's sake—where is it?

BISHOP NICHOLAS. You must know that——

(*Looks towards the door.*)   Hist!—here comes the King.

EARL SKULE.   The letter, Bishop—the letter!

BISHOP NICHOLAS.   Here is the King.

    (HAKON *enters, followed by his Guard and many guests. Immediately afterwards,* MARGRETE *appears; she seems anxious and alarmed, and is about to rush up to the King, when she is restrained by* LADY RAGNHILD, *who, with other ladies, has followed her.* SIGRID *stands somewhat apart, towards the back. The* EARL'S *men appear uneasy and gather in a group on the right, where* SKULE *is standing, but some way behind him.*)

HAKON (*in strong but repressed excitement*).   Earl Skule, who is king in this land?

EARL SKULE.   Who is king?

HAKON.   That was my question.   I bear the kingly title, but who holds the kingly might?

EARL SKULE.   The kingly might should dwell with him who has the kingly right.

HAKON.   So should it be; but is it so?

EARL SKULE.   Do you summon me to judgment?

HAKON.   That do I; for that right I have towards every man in the land.

EARL SKULE.   I fear not to answer for my dealings.

HAKON.   Well for us all if you can.   (*Mounts one of the steps of throne-daïs, and leans upon one arm of the throne.*)   Here stand I as your King, and ask: Know you that Jon, Earl of Orkney, has risen against me?

EARL SKULE. Yes.

HAKON. That he denies to pay me tribute?

EARL SKULE. Yes.

HAKON. And is it true that you, Sir Earl, have this day sent him a letter?

EARL SKULE. Who says so?

IVAR BODDE. That do I.

DAGFINN. Jostein Tamb dared not deny to carry it, since it bore the King's seal.

HAKON. You write to the King's foes under the King's seal, although the King knows nought of what is written?

EARL SKULE. So have I done for many a year, with your good will.

HAKON. Ay, in the days of your regency.

EARL SKULE. Never have you had aught but good thereby. Earl Jon wrote to me praying that I would mediate on his behalf; he offered peace, but on terms dishonourable to the King. The war in Vermeland has weighed much upon your mind; had this matter been left to you, Earl Jon had come too lightly off—I can deal better with him.

HAKON. We choose rather to deal with him ourselves.—And what have you answered?

EARL SKULE. Read my letter.

HAKON. Give it me!

EARL SKULE. I deemed you had it.

DAGFINN. You well know we have it not. Gregorius Jonsson was too swift of foot; when we came on board, the letter was gone.

EARL SKULE (turns to GREGORIUS JONSSON). Sir Baron, give the King the letter.

GREGORIUS JONSSON (*coming close to him, uneasily*). Hearken, Earl——!

EARL SKULE.   What now?

GREGORIUS JONSSON (*softly*).   Bethink you, there were sharp words in it concerning the King.

EARL SKULE.   My words I shall answer for.   The letter!

GREGORIUS JONSSON.   I have it not!

EARL SKULE.   You have it not?

GREGORIUS JONSSON.   Dagfinn the Peasant was at our heels.   I snatched the letter from Jostein Tamb, tied a stone to it——

EARL SKULE.   Well?

GREGORIUS JONSSON.   It lies at the bottom of the fiord.

EARL SKULE.   You have done ill—ill.

HAKON.   I await the letter, Sir Earl.

EARL SKULE.   I cannot give it you.

HAKON.   You *cannot*!

EARL SKULE (*advancing a step towards the* KING). My pride brooks not to be put to shifts, as you and your men would call them——

HAKON (*controlling his rising wrath*).   And so ——?

EARL SKULE.   In one word—I *will* not give it you!

HAKON.   Then you defy me!

EARL SKULE.   Since so it must be—Yes, I defy you.

IVAR BODDE (*forcibly*).   Now, my lord King, now I scarce think you or any man can need more proof!

DAGFINN.   Ay, now I think we know the Earl's mind.

HAKON (*coldly, to the* EARL). You will give the Great Seal to Ivar Bodde.

MARGRETE (*rushes with clasped hands towards the daïs, where the* KING *is standing*). Hakon, be a kind and gracious husband to me!

(HAKON *makes an imperative gesture towards her ; she hides her face in her veil, and goes up towards her mother again.*)

EARL SKULE (*to* IVAR BODDE). Here is the Great Seal.

IVAR BODDE. This was to be the last evening of the feast. It has ended in a heavy sorrow for the King ; but sooner or later it needs must come, and methinks every true man must rejoice that it *has* come.

EARL SKULE. And I think every true man must feel bitter wrath to see a priest thus make mischief between us Birchlegs ;—ay, Birchlegs, I say ; for I am every whit as good a Birchleg as the King or any of his men. I am of the same stock, the stock of Sverre, the kingly stock—but you, Priest, you have built up a wall of distrust around the King, and shut me out from him ; that has been your task this many a year.

PAUL FLIDA (*enraged, to the bystanders*). Earl's men ! Shall we abide this longer ?

GREGORIUS JONSSON. No, we cannot and will not abide it any more. 'Tis time to say it plainly—none of the Earl's men can serve the King in full trust and love, so long as Ivar Bodde comes and goes in the palace, and makes bad blood between us.

PAUL FLIDA. Priest ! I bid you look to life and

limb, wheresoever I meet you—in the field, on shipboard, or in any unconsecrated house.

MANY EARL'S-MEN.   I too! I too! You are an
outlaw to us!

IVAR BODDE.   God forbid I should stand between
the King and so many mighty chieftains.—Hakon, my
gracious lord, my soul bears me witness that I have
served you in all faithfulness.   True, I have warned
you against the Earl; but if I have ever done him
wrong, I pray God forgive me.   Now have I no
more to do in the palace; here is your Seal; take it
into your own hands; there it should have rested
long ago.

HAKON (*who has come down from the daïs*).   You
shall remain!

IVAR BODDE.   I cannot.   If I did, my conscience
would gnaw and rend me night and day.   Greater
evil can no man do in these times than to hold the
King and the Earl asunder.

HAKON.   Ivar Bodde, I command you to remain!

IVAR BODDE.   If the sainted King Olaf should
arise from his silver shrine to bid me stay, still I
needs must go.   (*Places the Seal in the* KING'S *hand.*)
Farewell, my noble master!   God bless and prosper
you in all your life-work!

   (*Goes out through the crowd, to the right.*)

HAKON (*gloomily, to the* EARL *and his Men*).
There have I lost a trusty friend for your sakes;
what requital can you offer great enough to make
good that loss?

EARL SKULE.   I offer myself and all my friends.

HAKON.   I almost fear 'twill not suffice. Now

must I gather round me all the men I can fully trust. Dagfinn the Peasant, let a messenger set out forthwith for Halogaland ; Vegard Væradal must be recalled.

DAGFINN (*who has been standing somewhat towards the back, in conversation with a Man in travelling dress who has entered the hall, approaches and says with emotion :*) Vegard cannot come, my lord.

HAKON. How know you that ?

DAGFINN. I have **even now** received tidings of him.

HAKON. What tidings ?

DAGFINN. That Vegard Væradal **is slain.**

MANY VOICES. Slain !

HAKON. Who slew him ?

DAGFINN. Andres Skialdarband, the Earl's friend.
    (*A short pause; uneasy whispers pass among the men.*)

HAKON. **Where** is the messenger ?

DAGFINN (*leading the man forward*). Here, my lord King.

HAKON. What was the cause of slaying ?

THE MESSENGER. That no man knows. The talk fell upon the Finnish tribute, and on a sudden Andres sprang up and gave him his death-wound.

HAKON. Had there been quarrels between them before ?

THE MESSENGER. Ever and anon. Andres was oft heard to say that a wise councillor here in the south had written to him that he should be as rock and flint towards Vegard Væradal.

DAGFINN. Strange ! Ere Vegard set forth he

told me that a wise councillor had said he should be as rock and flint towards Andres Skialdarband.

Bishop Nicholas (*spitting*).   Shame upon such councillors!

Hakon.   We will not question more closely from what root this wrong has grown.   Two faithful souls have I lost this day.   I could weep for Vegard; but 'tis no time for weeping; it must be life for life.   Sir Earl, Andres Skialdarband is your sworn retainer; you offered me all service in requital for Ivar Bodde. I take you at your word, and look to you to see that this misdeed be avenged.

Earl Skule.   Of a truth, bad angels are at work between us to-day.   On any other of my men, I would have suffered you to avenge the murder——

Hakon (*expectantly*).   Well?

Earl Skule.   But not on Andres Skialdarband.

Hakon (*flaring up*).   Will you shield the murderer?

Earl Skule.   *This* murderer I *must* shield.

Hakon.   And the reason?

Earl Skule.   That none but God in heaven may know.

Bishop Nicholas (*softly, to* Dagfinn).   I know it.

Dagfinn.   And I suspect it.

Bishop Nicholas.   Say nought, good Dagfinn.

Hakon.   Earl, I will believe as long as I may, that you mean not in earnest what you have said to me——

Earl Skule.   Were it my own father Andres Skialdarband had slain, he should still go free.   Ask no more.

HAKON.   Good.   Then we ourselves must see to the matter!

EARL SKULE (*with an expression of alarm*).   There will be bloodshed on both sides, my lord King!

HAKON.   So be it; none the less shall vengeance be taken.

EARL SKULE.   It shall *not* be taken!—It *cannot* be taken!

BISHOP NICHOLAS.   Nay, there the Earl is right.

HAKON.   Say you so, my honoured lord?

BISHOP NICHOLAS.   Andres Skialdarband has taken the Cross.

HAKON AND EARL SKULE.   Taken the Cross!

BISHOP NICHOLAS.   And has already sailed from the land.

EARL SKULE.   'Tis well for all of us!

HAKON.   The day wanes; the bridal-feast must now be at an end.   I thank you, Sir Earl, for all the honour that has been shown me in these days.—You are bound for Nidaros, as I think?

EARL SKULE.   That is my intent.

HAKON.   And I for Viken.—If you, Margrete, choose rather to abide in Bergen, then do so.

MARGRETE.   Whither you go, I go too, until you forbid.

HAKON.   Good; then come with me.

SIGRID.   Now is our kindred spread far abroad. (*Kneels to* HAKON.)   Grant me a grace, my lord King!

HAKON.   Rise, Lady Sigrid; whatever you crave shall be granted.

SIGRID.   I cannot go with the Earl to Nidaros.

The nunnery at Rein will soon be consecrated ; write to the Archbishop—take order that I be made Abbess.

EARL SKULE.   You, my sister ?

HAKON.   You will enter a nunnery!

SIGRID (*rising*).   Since my bloody wedding-night at Nidaros, when the Baglers came and hewed down my bridegroom, and many hundreds with him, and fired the town at all its corners—since then, it has been as though the blood and fire had dulled and deadened my sight for the world around me.   But I learned to catch glimpses of that which other eyes see not—and one thing I now see : that a time of great dread hangs over this land !

EARL SKULE (*vehemently*).   She is sick! Heed her not !

SIGRID.   A plenteous harvest is ripening for him that reaps in the darkness.   Every woman in Norway will have but one task now—to kneel in church and cloister, and pray and pray both day and night.

HAKON (*shaken*).   Is it prophecy or soul-sickness that speaks thus ?

SIGRID.   Farewell, my brother—we shall meet once more.

EARL SKULE (*involuntarily*).   When ?

SIGRID (*softly*).   When you have taken the crown ; in the hour of danger,—when you are fain of me in your direst need.

(*Goes out to the right, with* MARGRETE, LADY RAGNHILD, *and the women.*)

HAKON (*after a short pause, draws his sword, and*

says with quiet determination). All the Earl's men shall take the oath of fealty.

EARL SKULE (*vehemently*). Is this your settled purpose? (*Almost imploringly.*) King Hakon, do not so!

HAKON. No Earl's-man shall leave Bergen ere he has sworn fealty to the King.

> (*Goes out with his Guard. All except the* EARL *and the* BISHOP *follow him.*)

BISHOP NICHOLAS. He has dealt hardly with you to-day!

> (EARL SKULE *is silent, and looks out after the* KING, *as though struck dumb.*)

BISHOP NICHOLAS (*more loudly*). And mayhap not king-born after all.

EARL SKULE (*turns suddenly, in strong excitement, and seizes the* BISHOP *by the arm*). Trond the Priest's confession—where is it?

BISHOP NICHOLAS. He sent it to me from England ere he died ; I know not by whom—and it never reached me.

EARL SKULE. But it must be to be found!

BISHOP NICHOLAS. I doubt not but it may.

EARL SKULE. And if you find it, you will give it into my hands?

BISHOP NICHOLAS. That I promise.

EARL SKULE. You swear it by your soul's salvation?

BISHOP NICHOLAS. I swear it by my soul's salvation!

EARL SKULE. Good ; till that time I will work against Hakon, wherever it can be done secretly and unnoted.   He must be hindered from growing mightier than I, ere the struggle begins.

BISHOP NICHOLAS.   But should it prove that he is in truth king-born—what then?

EARL SKULE.   Then must I try to pray—to pray for humbleness, that I may serve him with all my might, as a faithful chieftain.

BISHOP NICHOLAS.   And if he be not king-born?

EARL SKULE.   Then shall he give place to me! The kingly title and the kingly throne, host and guard, fleet and tribute, towns and castles, all shall be mine!

BISHOP NICHOLAS.   He will betake him to Viken——

EARL SKULE.   I will drive him out of Viken!

BISHOP NICHOLAS.   He will ensconce him in Nidaros.

EARL SKULE.   I will storm Nidaros!

BISHOP NICHOLAS.   He will shut himself up in Olaf's holy church——

EARL SKULE.   I will force the sanctuary——

BISHOP NICHOLAS.   He will fly to the high altar, and cling to Olaf's shrine——

EARL SKULE.   I will drag him down from the altar, though I drag the shrine along with him——

BISHOP NICHOLAS.   But the crown will still be on his head, Earl!

EARL SKULE.   I will strike off the crown with my sword!

BISHOP NICHOLAS.   But if it sits too tight——?

EARL SKULE. Then, in God's name or Satan's—I will strike off the head along with it!

(*Goes out to the right.*)

BISHOP NICHOLAS (*looks out after him, nods slowly, and says:*) Ay—ay—in that mood I like the Earl!

THE CURTAIN FALLS.

Act Third.

(*A room in the Bishop's Palace at Oslo.[1]   On the right is the entrance door.   In the back, a small **door**, standing open, leads into the Chapel, which is lighted up.   A curtained door in the left wall leads **into** the Bishop's sleeping-room.   In front, on the same side, **stands** a cushioned couch.   Opposite, on the right, is a writing-table, with letters, documents, and a lighted lamp.*)

(*At first the room is empty; behind the curtain on the left, the singing of monks is heard.   Presently* PAUL FLIDA, *in travelling dress, enters from the right, stops by the door, waits, looks around, and then knocks three times with his staff upon the floor.*)

SIRA VILIAM (*comes out from the left, and exclaims in a hushed voice*).   Paul Flida!   God be praised;— then the Earl is not far off.

PAUL FLIDA.   The ships are already at Hoved-isle; I came on ahead.   And how goes it with the Bishop?

SIRA VILIAM.   He is now receiving the Extreme Unction.

PAUL FLIDA.   Then there is great danger?

SIRA VILIAM.   Master Sigard of Brabant has said that he cannot outlive the night.

PAUL FLIDA.   Meseems he has summoned us too late.

SIRA VILIAM.   Nay, nay,—he has his full senses

---

[1] An ancient city close to the present Christiania.

and some strength to boot,—every moment he asks if the Earl comes not soon.

PAUL FLIDA. You still call him Earl; know you not that the King has given him the title of Duke?

SIRA VILIAM. Ay ay, we know it well; 'tis but old custom. Hist!

> (*He and* PAUL FLIDA *cross themselves and bow their heads. From the* BISHOP'S *door issue two acolytes with candles, then two more with censers; then priests bearing chalice, paten and crucifix, and a church banner; behind them a file of priests and monks; acolytes with candles and censers close the procession, which passes slowly into the chapel. The door is shut behind them.*)

PAUL FLIDA. Now has the old lord made up his account with this world.

SIRA VILIAM. I can tell him that Duke Skule comes so soon as may be?

PAUL FLIDA. He comes straight from the wharf up here to the Palace. Farewell! (*Goes.*)

> (*Several priests, amongst them* PETER, *with some of the* BISHOP'S *servants, come out from the left with furs, cushions, and a large brazier.*)

SIRA VILIAM. Why do you this?

A PRIEST (*arranging the couch*). The Bishop wills to lie out here.

SIRA VILIAM. Is that prudent?

THE PRIEST. Master Sigard thinks we may humour him. Here he is.

> (BISHOP NICHOLAS *enters, supported by* MASTER

SIGARD *and a Priest. He is in his canonicals, but without crozier and mitre.*)

BISHOP NICHOLAS. Light more candles. (*He is led to a seat upon the couch, near the brazier, and is covered with furs.*) Viliam! Now have I obtained forgiveness for all my sins! They took them all away with them ;—meseems I am so light now.

SIRA VILIAM. The Duke sends you greeting, my lord ; he has already passed Hoved-isle!

BISHOP NICHOLAS. 'Tis well, very well. Belike the King, too, will soon be here. I have been a sinful hound in my day, Viliam ; I have grievously trespassed against the King. The priests in there averred that all my sins should be forgiven me ;—well well, it may be so ; but 'tis easy for them to promise ; 'tis not against them that I have trespassed. No no; it is safest to have it from the King's own mouth. (*Exclaims impatiently.*) Light, I say! 'tis so dark in here.

SIRA VILIAM. The candles are lighted——

MASTER SIGARD (*stops him by a sign, and approaches the* BISHOP). How goes it with you, my lord ?

BISHOP NICHOLAS. So-so—so-so ; my hands and feet are cold.

MASTER SIGARD (*half aloud, as he moves the brazier nearer*). Hm—'tis the beginning of the end.

BISHOP NICHOLAS (*apprehensively, to* VILIAM). I have commanded that eight monks shall chant and pray for me in the chapel to-night. Have an eye to them ; there are idle fellows amongst them.

(SIRA VILIAM *points silently towards the chapel, whence singing is heard, which continues during what follows.*)

BISHOP NICHOLAS.   So much still undone, and to go and leave it all!   So much undone, Viliam!

SIRA VILIAM.   My lord, think of heavenly things!

BISHOP NICHOLAS.   I have time before me;—till well on in the morning, Master Sigard thinks——

SIRA VILIAM.   My lord, my lord!

BISHOP NICHOLAS.   Give me mitre and crozier!— You say well that I should think—— (*A Priest brings them.*)   So, set the cap there, 'tis too heavy for me; give me the crozier in my hand; there, now am I equipped.   A bishop!—— The Evil One dare not grapple with me now!

SIRA VILIAM.   Desire you aught beside?

BISHOP NICHOLAS. No.   Stay—tell me;—Peter, Andres Skialdarband's son,—all speak well of him——

SIRA VILIAM.   In truth, his is a blameless soul.

BISHOP NICHOLAS.   Peter, you shall watch beside me until the King or the Duke shall come.   Leave us, meanwhile, you others, but be at hand.

(*All except* PETER *go out on the right.*)

BISHOP NICHOLAS (*after a short pause*).   Peter!

PETER (*approaches*).   My lord?

BISHOP NICHOLAS.   Have you ever seen old men die?

PETER.   No.

BISHOP NICHOLAS.   They are all afeard; that I dare swear.   There on the table lies a large letter with seals to it; give it to me. (PETER *brings the letter.*)   It is to your mother.

PETER.   To my mother?

BISHOP NICHOLAS.   You must get you northward to Halogaland with it.   I have written to her touching a great and weighty matter; tidings have come from your father.

PETER.   He is fighting as a soldier of God in the Holy Land.   Should he fall there, he falls on hallowed ground ; for there every foot's-breadth of earth is sacred.   I commend him to God in all my prayers.

BISHOP NICHOLAS.   Is Andres Skialdarband dear to you ?

PETER.   He is an honourable man ; but there lives another man whose greatness my mother, as it were, fostered and nourished me withal.

BISHOP NICHOLAS (*hurriedly and eagerly*).   Is that Duke Skule ?

PETER.   Ay, the Duke—Skule Bårdsson.   My mother knew him in younger days.   The Duke must sure be the greatest man in the land !

BISHOP NICHOLAS.   There is the letter; get you northward with it forthwith !   Are they singing in there ?

PETER.   Yes, my lord !

BISHOP NICHOLAS.   Eight lusty fellows with throats like trumpets, they must surely help some-what, methinks ?

PETER.   My lord, my lord !   I would pray myself !

BISHOP NICHOLAS.   I have too much still undone, Peter.   Life is all too short;—besides, the King will surely forgive me when he comes——

(*Gives a start, in pain.*)

PETER.   My lord suffers ?

BISHOP NICHOLAS.   I suffer not; but there is a ringing in mine ears; and lights keep twinkling before mine eyes——

PETER. 'Tis the heavenly bells ringing you home, and the twinkling **of the** altar-lights God's angels have kindled for you.

BISHOP NICHOLAS. Ay, sure 'tis so;—there is no danger if only they lag not with their prayers in **there**. Farewell; set forth at once with the letter.

PETER. Shall I not first—— ?

BISHOP NICHOLAS. Nay, go; I fear **not** to be alone.

PETER. Well **met** again, then, what time the heavenly bells shall sound **for me too**.

(Goes out on the right.)

BISHOP NICHOLAS. The heavenly bells,—ay, 'tis easy talking when you still **have two** stout legs to stand upon.—So much undone! But much will live after me, notwithstanding. I promised the Duke **by my** soul's salvation to **give** him Trond the Priest's confession if it came into my hand;—'tis well I have **not** got **it**. Had he certainty, he would conquer or fall; and **then** one of **them** would **be** the mightiest man that ever lived in Norway. **No** no,—what I could not reach none other shall reach. Uncertainty serves best; **so long as the** Duke is burdened **with** that, they two **will** waste each other's strength wheresoever they may; towns will be burnt, dales will be harried,—neither will gain by the other's loss—— (*Terrified.*) Mercy, pity! **It** is I who bear the guilt—I, who set it all agoing! (*Calming himself.*) Well, **well**, well! but now the King is coming—'tis he that suffers most—he will forgive me—prayers and masses shall be said; there is no danger;—I am a bishop, and I have never slain any man with mine own hand.—'Tis well that Trond the Priest's confession came not; the saints are with me, they will not tempt me to break my promise.—Who knocks at the door? It must be the Duke! (*Rubs his hands with glee.*) He will implore me for proofs as to the kingship,—and I have no proofs to give him!

(INGA OF VARTEIG *enters; she is dressed in black, with a cloak and hood.*)

BISHOP NICHOLAS (*starts*).   Who is that?

INGA.   A woman from Varteig in Borgasyssel, my honoured lord.

BISHOP NICHOLAS.   The King's mother!

INGA.   So was I called once.

BISHOP NICHOLAS.   Go, go! 'Twas not I counselled Hakon to send you away.

INGA.   What the King does is well done; 'tis not therefore I come.

BISHOP NICHOLAS.   Wherefore then?

INGA.   Gunnulf, my brother, is come home from England——

BISHOP NICHOLAS.   From England——!

INGA.   He has been away these many years, as you know, and has roamed far and wide; now has he brought home a letter——

BISHOP NICHOLAS (*breathlessly*).   A letter——?

INGA.   From Trond the Priest. 'Tis for you, my lord.

(*Hands it to him.*)

BISHOP NICHOLAS.   Ah, truly;—and *you* bring it?

INGA.   It was Trond's wish. I owe him great thanks since the time he fostered Hakon. It was told me that you were sick ; therefore I set forth at once ; I have come hither on foot——

BISHOP NICHOLAS. It hasted not so much, Inga !

(DAGFINN THE PEASANT *enters from the right.*)

DAGFINN. God's peace, my honoured lord !

BISHOP NICHOLAS. Comes the King ?

DAGFINN. He is now riding down the Ryen hills, with the Queen and the King-child and a great following.

INGA (*rushes up to* DAGFINN). The King,—the King ! Comes he hither ?

DAGFINN. Inga ! You here, much-suffering woman !

INGA. She is not much-suffering who has so great a son.

DAGFINN. Now will his hard heart be melted.

INGA. Not a word to the King of me. Oh, but I must see him ;—tell me,—comes he hither ?

DAGFINN. Ay, presently.

INGA. And it is dark evening. The King will be lighted on his way with torches ?

DAGFINN. Yes.

INGA. Then will I hide me in a gateway as he goes by ;—and then home to Varteig. But first will I into Hallvard's church ; the lights are burning there to-night ; there will I call down blessings on the King, on my fair son.

(*Goes out to the right.*)

DAGFINN. I have fulfilled mine errand ; I go to meet the King.

BISHOP NICHOLAS. Bear him most loving greeting, good Dagfinn !

DAGFINN (*as he goes out to the right*).   I would not be Bishop Nicholas to-morrow.

BISHOP NICHOLAS.   Trond the Priest's confession ——!   So it has come after all—here I hold it in my hand.   (*Muses and stares before him.*)   A man should never promise aught by his soul's salvation, when he is as old as I.   Had I years before me, I could always wriggle free from such a promise; but this evening, this last evening—no, that were imprudent.—But can I keep it?   Is it not to endanger all that I have worked for, my whole life through?—(*Whispering.*) Oh, could I but cheat the Evil One, only this once more! (*Listens.*)   What was that? (*Calls.*)   Viliam, Viliam!

(SIRA VILIAM *enters from the right.*)

BISHOP NICHOLAS.   What is it that whistles and howls so grimly?

SIRA VILIAM.   'Tis the storm; it grows fiercer.

BISHOP NICHOLAS.   The storm grows fiercer!   Ay truly, I will keep my promise!   The storm, say you——?   Are they singing in there?

SIRA VILIAM. Yes, my lord.

BISHOP NICHOLAS.   Bid them bestir themselves, and chiefly brother Aslak; he always makes such scant prayers; he shirks when he can; he skips, the hound! (*Strikes the floor with his crozier.*)   Go in and say to him 'tis the last night I have left; he shall bestir himself, else will I haunt him from the dead!

SIRA VILIAM.   My lord, shall I not fetch Master Sigard?

BISHOP NICHOLAS.   Go in, I say! (VILIAM *goes into the chapel.*)   It must doubtless be heaven's will

18

that I should reconcile the King and the Duke, since it sends me Trond's letter now. This is a hard thing, Nicholas ; to tear down at one single wrench what you have spent your life in building up. But there is no other way; I must e'en do the will of heaven this time.—If I could only read what is written in the letter ; but I cannot see a word ! Mists drive before my eyes ; they sparkle and flicker ; and I dare let none other read it for me——! Is human cunning, then, so poor a thing that it cannot govern the outcome of its contrivances in the second and third degree? I spoke so long and so earnestly to Vegard Væradal about making the King send Inga from him, that at length it came to pass. That was wise in the first degree ; but had I not counselled thus, then Inga had not now been at Varteig, the letter had not come into my hands in time, and I had not had any promise to keep—therefore was it unwise in the second degree. Had I yet time before me——! but only the space of one night, and scarce even that. I must, I will live longer ! (*Knocks with his crozier ; a Priest enters from the right.*) Bid Master Sigard come ! (*The Priest goes ; the* BISHOP *crushes the letter in his hands.*) Here, under this thin seal, lies Norway's saga for a hundred years! It lies and dreams, like the birdling in the egg ! Oh, that I had more souls than *one*—or else *none! (Presses the letter wildly to his breast.*) Oh, were not the end so close upon me,— and judgment and punishment—I would hatch you out into a hawk that should cast the deadful shadow of his wings over all the land, and strike his sharp talons into every heart ! (*With a sudden shudder.*)

But the last hour is at hand! (*Shrieking.*) No, no! You shall become a swan, a white swan! (*Throws the letter far from him, onto the floor, and calls:*) Master Sigard, Master Sigard!

MASTER SIGARD (*from the right*). How goes it, honoured lord?

BISHOP NICHOLAS. Master Sigard—sell me three days' life!

MASTER SIGARD. I have told you——

BISHOP NICHOLAS. Yes, yes; but that was in jest; 'twas a little revenge on me. I have been a tedious master to you; therefore you thought to scare me. Fie, that was evil,—nay, nay—'twas but just! But, now be good and kind! I will pay you well;—three days' life, Master Sigard, only three days' life!

MASTER SIGARD. Though I myself were to die in the same hour as you, yet could I not add three days to your span.

BISHOP NICHOLAS. *One* day, then, only *one* day! Let it be light, let the sun shine when my soul sets forth! Listen, Sigard! (*Beckons him over, and drags him down upon the couch.*) I have given well-nigh all my gold and silver to the Church, to have high masses said for me. I will take it back again; you shall have it all! How now, Sigard, shall we two fool them in there? He-he-he! You will be rich, Sigard, and can depart the country; I shall·have time to cast about me a little, and make shift with fewer prayers. Come, Sigard, shall we——! (SIGARD *feels his pulse; the* BISHOP *exclaims anxiously:*) How now, why answer you not?

MASTER SIGARD (*rising*). I have no time, my lord. I must prepare you a draught that may ease you somewhat at the last.

BISHOP NICHOLAS. Nay, wait with that! Wait, —and answer me!

MASTER SIGARD. I have no time; the draught must be ready within an hour.

(*Goes out to the right.*)

BISHOP NICHOLAS. Within an hour! (*Knocks wildly.*) Viliam! Viliam!

(SIRA VILIAM *comes out from the chapel.*)

BISHOP NICHOLAS. Call more to help in there! The eight are not enough!

SIRA VILIAM. My lord——?

BISHOP NICHOLAS. More to help, I say! Brother Kolbein has lain sick these five weeks,—he cannot have sinned much in that time——

SIRA VILIAM. He confessed yesterday.

BISHOP NICHOLAS (*eagerly*). Ay, *he* must be good ; call him! (VILIAM *goes into the chapel again.*) Within an hour! (*Dries the sweat off his brow.*) Pah—how warm it is here !—The miserable hound— what boots all his learning, when he cannot add an hour to my life? There sits he in his closet day by day, piecing together his cunning wheels and weights and levers ; he thinks to fashion a machine that shall go and go and never stop—*perpetuum mobile* he calls it. Why not rather turn his art and his skill to making man such a *perpetuum mobile*? (*Stops and thinks; his eyes brighten.*) *Perpetuum mobile*,—I am not strong in Latin——but it means somewhat that has power to work eternally, throughout all ages. If I myself, now, could but——?   *That* were a deed to end my life withal!   That were to do my greatest deed in my latest hour!   To set wheel and weight and lever at work in the King's soul and the Duke's; to set them going so that no power on earth can stop them; if I can but do that, then shall I live indeed, live in my work—and, when I think of it, mayhap 'tis that which is called immortality.—Comfortable, soothing thoughts, how ye do the old man good!   (*Draws a deep breath, and stretches himself comfortably upon the couch.*)   Diabolus has pressed me hard to-night. That comes of lying idle; *otium est pulvis—pulveris—* pooh, no matter for the Latin——   Diabolus shall no longer have power over me; I will be busy to the last; I will——; how they bellow in yonder—— (*Knocks;* VILIAM *comes out.*)   Tell them to hold their peace; they disturb me.   The King and the Duke will soon be here; I have weighty matters to ponder.

SIRA VILIAM.   My lord, shall I then——?

BISHOP NICHOLAS.   Bid them hold awhile, that I may think in peace.   Look you, take up yonder letter that lies upon the floor.—Good.   Reach me the papers here——

SIRA VILIAM (*goes to the writing-table*).   Which, my lord?

BISHOP NICHOLAS.   It matters not——; the sealed ones; those that lie uppermost —So; go now in and bid them be silent.   (VILIAM *goes.*)   To die, and yet rule in Norway!   To die, and yet contrive things so that no man may come to raise his head above the rest.   A thousand ways may lead towards that goal; yet is there but one that will reach it;—and now to find that one—to find it and follow it.—— ——Ha! The way lies so close, so close at hand! Ay, so it must be. I will keep my promise; the Duke shall have the letter in his hands;—but the King—hm, he shall have the thorn of doubt in his heart. Hakon is upright, as they call it; many things will go to wreck in his soul along with the faith in himself and in his right. Both of them shall doubt and believe by turns, still swaying to and fro, and finding no firm ground beneath their feet—*perpetuum mobile!*—But will Hakon believe what I say? Ay, that will he; am I not a dying man?—And I will begin by cramming him with truths.—My strength fails, but fresh life fills my soul;—I no longer lie on a sick-bed, I sit in my work-room; I will work the last night through, work—till the light goes out——

DUKE SKULE (*enters from the right and advances towards the* BISHOP). Peace and greeting, my honoured lord! I hear it goes ill with you.

BISHOP NICHOLAS. I am a corpse in the bud, good Duke; this night shall I blossom; to-morrow you may scent my perfume.

DUKE SKULE. Already to-night, say you?

BISHOP NICHOLAS. Master Sigard says: within an hour.

DUKE SKULE. And Trond the Priest's letter—— ?

BISHOP NICHOLAS. Think you still upon that?

DUKE SKULE. 'Tis never out of my thoughts.

BISHOP NICHOLAS. The King has made you Duke; before you, no man in Norway has borne that title.

DUKE SKULE. 'Tis not enough. If Hakon be not the rightful king, then must I have all!

BISHOP NICHOLAS. Ha, 'tis cold in here; the blood runs icy through my limbs.

DUKE SKULE. Trond the Priest's letter, my lord! For Almighty God's sake,—have you it?

BISHOP NICHOLAS. At least, I know where it can be found.

DUKE SKULE. Tell me then, tell me!

BISHOP NICHOLAS. Wait——

DUKE SKULE. Nay, nay—lose not your time; I see it draws to an end;—and they tell me the King comes hither.

BISHOP NICHOLAS. Ay, the King comes; thereby you may best see that I am mindful of your cause, even *now.*

DUKE SKULE. What is your purpose?

BISHOP NICHOLAS. Mind you, at the King's bridal—you said that Hakon's strength lay in his steadfast faith in himself?

DUKE SKULE. Well?

BISHOP NICHOLAS. If I confess, and raise a doubt in his mind, then his faith will fall, and his strength with it.

DUKE SKULE. My lord, this is sinful, sinful, if he be the rightful king.

BISHOP NICHOLAS. It will lie with you to restore his faith. Ere I depart hence, I will tell you where Trond the Priest's letter may be found.

SIRA VILIAM (*from the right*). The King is now coming up the street, with torch-bearers and attendants.

BISHOP NICHOLAS. He shall be welcome. (VILIAM *goes.*) Duke, I beg of you one last service. Do you carry on my feuds against mine enemies. (*Takes out a letter.*) I have written them down here. Those whose names stand first I would fain have hanged, if so it could be ordered.

DUKE SKULE. Think not upon vengeance now; you have but little time left——

BISHOP NICHOLAS. Not upon vengeance, but upon punishment. Promise me to wield the sword of punishment over all mine enemies when I am gone. They are your foemen no less than mine; when you are King you must chastise them; do you promise me that?

DUKE SKULE. I promise and swear it; but Trond's letter——!

BISHOP NICHOLAS. You shall learn where it is;— but see — the King comes; hide the list of our foemen!

> (*The* DUKE *hides the paper; at the same moment*
>   HAKON *enters from the right.*)

BISHOP NICHOLAS. Well met at the grave-feast, my lord King.

HAKON. You have ever withstood me stubbornly; but that shall be forgiven and forgotten now; death wipes out even the heaviest reckoning.

BISHOP NICHOLAS. That lightened my soul! Oh how marvellous is the King's clemency! My lord, what you have done for an old sinner this night shall be tenfold——

HAKON. No more of that; but I must tell you that I greatly marvel you should summon me hither to obtain my forgiveness, and yet prepare for me such a meeting as this.

BISHOP NICHOLAS.   Meeting, my lord?

DUKE SKULE.   'Tis of me the King speaks.   Will you, my lord Bishop, assure King Hakon, by my faith and honour, that I knew nought of his coming, ere I landed at Oslo wharf?

BISHOP NICHOLAS.   Alas, alas!   The blame is all mine!   I have been sickly and bedridden all the last year; I have learnt little or nought of the affairs of the kingdom; I thought all was now well between the noble kinsmen!

HAKON.   I have marked that the friendship between the Duke and myself thrives best when we hold aloof from one another; therefore farewell, Bishop Nicholas, and God be with you where you are going.

(Goes towards the door.)

DUKE SKULE *(softly and uneasily)*.   Bishop, Bishop, he is going!

BISHOP NICHOLAS *(suddenly, and with wild energy)*.   Stay, King Hakon!

HAKON *(stops)*.   What now?

BISHOP NICHOLAS.   You shall not leave this room until old Bishop Nicholas has spoken his last word!

HAKON *(involuntarily lays his hand upon his sword)*. Mayhap you have come well-attended to Viken, Duke.

DUKE SKULE.   I have no part in this.

BISHOP NICHOLAS.   'Tis by force of words that I will hold you.   Where there is a burial in the house, the dead man ever rules the roost; he can do and let alone as he will—so far as his power reaches.   Therefore will I now speak my own funeral-speech; in

days gone by, I was ever sore afraid lest King Sverre
should come to speak it——

HAKON.   Talk not so wildly, my lord!

DUKE SKULE.   You shorten the precious hour still
left to you!

HAKON.   Your eyes are already dim!

BISHOP NICHOLAS.   Ay, my sight is dim; I scarce
can see you where you stand; but before my inward
eye, my whole life is moving past in shining light.
There I see sights——; hear and learn, oh King!—
My race was the mightiest in the land; many
great chieftains had sprung from it; I longed to be
the greatest of them all.   I was yet but a boy when I
began to thirst after great deeds; meseemed I could
by no means wait till I were grown.   Kings arose
who had less right than I,—Magnus Erlingsson, Sverre
the Priest——; I also would be king; but I must
needs be a chieftain first.   Then came the battle at
Ilevoldene; 'twas the first time I went out to war.
The sun went up, and gleaming lightnings flashed from
a thousand burnished blades.   Magnus and all his men
advanced as to a game; I alone felt a tightness at my
heart.   Bravely our troop dashed forward; but I
could not follow—I was afraid!   All Magnus's other
chieftains fought manfully, and many fell in the fight;
but I fled up over the mountain, and ran and ran, and
stayed not until I came down to the fiord again, far
away.   Many a man had to wash his bloody clothes
in Trondhiem fiord that night;—I had to wash mine
too, but not from blood.   Ay, King, I was afraid;—
born to be a chieftain—and afraid!   It fell upon me
as a thunderbolt; from that hour I hated all men.   I

prayed secretly in the churches, I wept and knelt before the altars, I gave rich gifts, made sacred promises ; I tried and tried in battle after battle, at Saltösund, at Jonsvoldene that summer the Baglers lay in Bergen,—but ever in vain. Sverre it was who first noted it ; he proclaimed it loudly and with mockery, and from that day forth, not a man in the host but laughed when Nicholas Arnesson was seen in war-weed. A coward, a coward—and yet was I filled with longing to be a chief, to be a king ; nay, I felt I was born to be King. I could have furthered God's kingdom upon earth ; but 'twas the saints themselves that barred the way for me.

HAKON. Accuse not heaven, Bishop Nicholas! You have hated much.

BISHOP NICHOLAS. Ay, I have hated much; hated every head in this land that raised itself above the crowd. But I hated because I could not love. Fair women,—oh, I could devour them even now with glistening eyes! I have lived eighty years, and yet do I yearn to kill men and kiss women ;—but my lot in love was as my lot in war : naught but an itching will, my strength sapped from my birth ; dowered with seething desire—and yet a weakling ! So I became a priest : king or priest must that man be who would have all might in his hands. (*Laughs.*) I a priest ! I a churchman ! Yes, for *one* clerkly office Heaven had notably fitted me—for taking the high notes—for singing with a woman's voice at the great church-festivals. And yet they up yonder claim of me—the half-man—what they have a right to claim only of those they have fully equipped for their life-work.

There have been times when I fancied such a claim
might be just; I have lain on my sick-bed crushed
by the dread of doom and punishment. Now it is
over; my soul has fresh marrow in its bones! *I* have
not sinned; it is *I* that have suffered wrong; *I* am
the accuser!

DUKE SKULE (*softly*). My lord—the letter! You
have little time left!

HAKON. Think of your soul, and humble you!

BISHOP NICHOLAS. A man's life-work is his soul,
and my life-work will live on upon the earth. But
you, King Hakon, you should beware; for as Heaven
has stood against *me*, and got harm for its reward, so
are you standing against the man who holds the
country's welfare in his hand——

HAKON. Ha—Duke, Duke! Now I see the bent
of this meeting!

DUKE SKULE (*angrily, to the* BISHOP). Not a
word more of this!

BISHOP NICHOLAS (*to* HAKON). He will stand
against you so long as his head sits fast on his
shoulders. Share with him! I will have no peace
in my coffin, I will rise again, if you two share not
the kingdom! Neither of you shall add the other's
height to his own stature. If that befell, there would
be a giant in the land, and here shall no giant be; for
I was never a giant!

(*Sinks back exhausted on the couch.*)

DUKE SKULE (*falls on his knees beside the couch
and cries to* HAKON). Summon help! For God's
pity's sake, the Bishop must not die yet!

BISHOP NICHOLAS. How it waxes dusk before

my eyes!—King, for the last time—will you share with the Duke?

HAKON. Not a shred will I let slip of that which God gave me.

BISHOP NICHOLAS. Well and good. (*Softly.*) Your faith, at least, you shall let slip. (*Calls.*) Viliam!

DUKE SKULE (*softly*). The letter! The letter!

BISHOP NICHOLAS (*not listening to him*). Viliam! (VILIAM *enters; the* BISHOP *draws him close down to him and whispers.*) When I received Extreme Unction, all my sins were forgiven me?

SIRA VILIAM. All your sins from your birth, till the moment you received the Unction.

BISHOP NICHOLAS. No longer? Not until the very end?

SIRA VILIAM. You will not sin to-night, my lord!

BISHOP NICHOLAS. Hm, who knows——? Take the golden goblet Bishop Absalon left me—give it to the Church—and say seven high masses more.

SIRA VILIAM. God will be gracious to you, my lord!

BISHOP NICHOLAS. Seven more masses, I say— for sins I may commit to-night! Go, go! (VILIAM *goes; the* BISHOP *turns to* SKULE.) Duke, if you should come to read Trond the Priest's letter, and it should mayhap prove that Hakon is the rightful king—what would you do then?

DUKE SKULE. In God's name—king he should remain.

BISHOP NICHOLAS. Bethink you; much is at stake. Search every fold of your heart; answer as though you stood before your Judge! What will you do, if he be the rightful king?

DUKE SKULE. Bow my head and serve him.

BISHOP NICHOLAS (*mumbles*). Then bide the issue. (*To* SKULE.) Duke, I am weak and weary; a mild and **charitable** mood comes over me——

DUKE SKULE. It is death! Trond the Priest's letter! Where is it?

BISHOP NICHOLAS. First another matter;—I gave you the list of my enemies——

DUKE SKULE (*impatiently*). Yes, yes; I will take full revenge upon them——

BISHOP NICHOLAS. No, my soul is filled with mildness; I will forgive, **as the** scripture commands. As you would renounce might, I will renounce revenge. **Burn the list!**

DUKE SKULE. Ay, ay; as you will.

BISHOP NICHOLAS. Here, in the brazier, so that I may see it——

DUKE SKULE (*throws the paper into the fire*). There now; see, it burns. And now, speak, speak! You risk thousands of lives if you speak not now!

BISHOP NICHOLAS (*with sparkling eyes*). Thousands of lives! (*Shrieks.*) Light! Air!

HAKON (*rushes to the door and cries*). Help! The Bishop is dying!

 (SIRA VILIAM *and several of the* BISHOP'S *men*
  · *enter.*)

DUKE SKULE (*shakes the* BISHOP'S *arm*). You risk Norway's happiness through hundreds of years, mayhap its greatness to all eternity!

BISHOP NICHOLAS.   To all eternity! (*Trium-phantly.*)   *Perpetuum mobile!*

DUKE SKULE.   By our souls' salvation,—where is Trond the Priest's letter?

BISHOP NICHOLAS (*calls*).   Seven more masses, Viliam!

DUKE SKULE (*beside himself*).   The letter!   The letter!

BISHOP NICHOLAS (*smiling in his death-agony*). 'Twas it you burned, good Duke!   (*Falls back on the couch and dies.*)

DUKE SKULE (*with an involuntary scream, starts backwards and covers his face with his hands*). Almighty God!

THE MONKS (*rushing in flight from the chapel*). Save you, all who can!

SOME VOICES.   The powers of evil have broken loose!

OTHER VOICES.   There rang a loud laugh from the corner!—A voice cried: "We have him!" All the lights went out!

HAKON.   Bishop Nicholas is even now dead.

THE MONKS (*fleeing to the right.*)   *Pater noster—pater noster!*

HAKON (*approaches* SKULE, *and says in a low voice*). Duke, I will not question what secret plots you were hatching with the Bishop ere he died;—but from to-morrow must you give up your powers and dignities into my hands; I see clearly now that we two cannot go forward together.

DUKE SKULE (*looks at him absently*).   Go forward together——?

HAKON. To-morrow I hold an Assembly in the Palace; then must all things come to settlement between us.

(*Goes **out** to the right.*)

DUKE SKULE. The Bishop dead and the letter burnt! A life full of doubt and strife and dread! Oh, could I but pray!—No—I must act; this evening must the stride be taken, once for all! (*To* VILIAM.) Whither went the King?

SIRA VILIAM. Christ save me,—what would you with him?

DUKE SKULE. Think you I would slay him to-night?

(*Goes out **to** the right.*)

SIRA VILIAM (*looks after him, shaking his head, while the house-folk bear the body out to the left*). Seven more masses, the Bishop said; I think 'twere safest we should say fourteen.

(*Follows the others.*)

(*A room **in** the Palace. **In the back** is the entrance-door; in each of the **side** walls a smaller door; in front, **on** the right, **a** window. Hung from the roof, a lamp **is** burning. **Close to** the door on the left stands **a bench**, and further **back** a cradle, in which **the** King-child is sleeping;* MARGRETE *is kneeling beside the child.*)

MARGRETE (*rocks the cradle and sings*).
    Now roof and rafters blend with
    the starry vault on high;
    now flieth little Hakon
    on dream-wings through the sky.

    There mounts a mighty stairway
    from earth to God's own land;
    there Hakon with the angels
    goes climbing, hand in hand.

    God's angel-babes are watching
    thy cot, the still night through;
    God bless thee, little Hakon,
    thy mother watcheth too.

(*A short pause.* DUKE SKULE *enters from the back.*)

MARGRETE (*starts up with a cry of joy and rushes to meet him*). My father!—Oh, how I have sighed and yearned for this meeting!

DUKE SKULE. God's peace be with you, Margrete! Where is the King?

MARGRETE. With Bishop Nicholas.

DUKE SKULE. Hm,—then must he soon be here.

MARGRETE. And you will talk together and be at one, be friends again, as in the old days?

DUKE SKULE. That would I gladly.

MARGRETE. 'Twould make Hakon, too, so glad; and I pray to God every day that so it may be. Oh, but come hither and see——

(*Takes his hand and leads him to the cradle.*)

DUKE SKULE. Your child!

MARGRETE. Ay, that lovely babe is mine;—is it not marvellous? He is called Hakon, like the King! See, his eyes—nay, you cannot see them now he is sleeping—but he has great blue eyes; and he can laugh, and stretch out his hands to grasp me,—and he knows me already.

(Smoothes out the bed-clothes tenderly.)

DUKE SKULE. Hakon will have sons, the Bishop foretold.

MARGRETE. To me this little child is a thousand times dearer than all Norway's land—and to Hakon too. Meseems I cannot rightly believe my happiness; I have the cradle standing by my bedside; every night, as often as I waken, I look to see if it be there—I am fearful lest it should all prove a dream——

DUKE SKULE *(listens and goes to the window).* Is not that the King?

MARGRETE. Ay; he is going up the other stair; I will bring him! *(Takes her father's hand and leads him playfully up to the cradle.)* Duke Skule! Keep watch over the King-child the while—for he is a King-child — though I can never remember it! Should he wake, then bow deeply before him, and hail him as men hail kings! Now will I bring Hakon. Oh, God, God! now at last come light and peace over our house!

(Goes out to the right.)

DUKE SKULE *(after a short and gloomy silence).* Hakon has a son. His race shall live after him. If he dies, he leaves an heir who stands nearer the throne than all others. All things thrive with Hakon.

Mayhap he is not the rightful king; but his trust in himself stands firm as ever; the Bishop would have shaken it, but Death gave him not time, God gave him not leave.   God watches over Hakon, and suffers him to keep the girdle of strength.   Were I to tell him now?   Were I to make oath to what the Bishop told me?   What would it avail?   None would believe me, neither Hakon nor the others.   He would have believed the Bishop in the hour of death; the doubt would have rankled poisonously in him; but it was not to be.   And deep-rooted as is Hakon's confidence, so deep-rooted is my doubt; what man on earth can weed it out?   None, none.   The ordeal has been performed, God has spoken, and still Hakon may not be the rightful king, while my life goes to waste. (*Seats himself broodingly beside a table on the right.*) And if, now, I won the kingdom, would not the doubt dwell with me none the less, gnawing and wearing and wasting me away with its endless icy drip, drip?—True, true; but 'tis better to sit doubting on the throne than to stand down in the crowd, doubting of him who sits there in your stead.—There must be an end between me and Hakon!   An end? But how?   (*Rises.*)   Almighty, thou who hast thus bestead me, thou must bear the guilt of the issue! (*Goes to and fro, stops and reflects.*)   I must break down all bridges, hold only one and conquer or fall there—as the Bishop said at the bridal-feast at Bergen.   That is now nigh upon three years since, and through all that time have I spilt and wasted my strength in trying to guard all the bridges.   (*Quickly.*) Now must I follow the Bishop's counsel; now or never!

Here are we both in Oslo; this time I have more men
than Hakon, why not seize the advantage—'tis so
seldom on my side. (*Vacillating.*) But to-night——?
At once——? No, no! Not to-night!—Ha-ha-ha—
there again!—pondering, wavering! Hakon knows not
what that means; he goes straight forward, and so he
conquers! (*Going up the room, stops suddenly beside
the cradle.*) The King-child!—How fair a brow! He
is dreaming. (*Smoothes out the bed-clothes, and looks
long at the child.*) Such an one as thou can save many
things in a man's soul. I have no son. (*Bends
over the cradle.*) He is like Hakon—— (*Shrinks
suddenly backwards.*) The King-child, said the Queen!
Bow low before him and hail him as men hail kings!
Should Hakon die before me this child will be raised
to the throne; and I—I shall stand before him, and
bow low and hail him as king! (*In rising agitation.*)
This child, Hakon's son, shall sit on high, on the seat
that I, mayhap, have a truer right to—and I shall
stand before his footstool, white-haired and bowed
with age, and see my whole life-work lying undone—
die without having been king!—I have more men
than Hakon—there blows a storm to-night, and the
wind sweeps down the fiord—! If I took the King-
child? I am safe with the Trönders.[1] What would
Hakon dare attempt, if his child were in my power?
My men will follow me, fight for me and conquer.
They know I will reward them in kingly wise.—So be
it! I will take the stride; I will leap the abyss, for
the first time! Could I but see if thou hadst Sverre's

---

[1] Men of the Trondhiem district.

eyes—or Hakon Sverresson's——! He sleeps. I cannot see them. (*A pause.*) Sleep is as a shield. Sleep
in peace, thou little Pretender! (*Goes over to the
table.*) Hakon shall decide; once again will I speak
with him.

MARGRETE (*enters, with the* KING, *from the room
on the right*). The Bishop dead! Oh, trust me, all
strife dies with him.

HAKON. To bed, Margrete! You must be tired
after the journey.

MARGRETE. Yes, yes. (*To the* DUKE.) Father,
be kind and yielding—Hakon has promised to be the
like! A thousand good-nights, to both of you!

> (*Makes a gesture of farewell at the door on the
> left, and goes out; two women carry out the
> cradle.*)

DUKE SKULE. King Hakon, this time we must
not part as foes. All evil will follow; there will fall
a time of dread upon the land.

HAKON. The land has been wont to nought else
through many generations; but, see you, God is with
me; every foeman falls that would stand against me.
There are no more Baglers, no Slittungs, no Ribbungs; Earl Jon is slain, Guthorm Ingesson is dead,
Sigurd Ribbung likewise—all claims that were put
forth at the folkmote at Bergen have fallen power-
less—from whom, then, should the time of dread now
come?

DUKE SKULE. Hakon, I fear it might come from
me!

HAKON. When I came to the throne, I gave you
the third part of the kingdom——

DUKE SKULE. But kept two-thirds!

HAKON. You ever thirsted after more; I eked out your share until now you hold half the kingdom.

DUKE SKULE. There lack ten ship-wards.[1]

HAKON. I made you Duke; that has no man been in Norway ere you.

DUKE SKULE. But you are king! I must have no king over me! I was not born to serve you; I must rule in my own right!

HAKON (*looks at him for a moment, and says coldly:*) Heaven guard your understanding, my lord. Good night.

(*Going.*)

DUKE SKULE (*blocking the way*). You shall not go from me thus! Beware, or I will forswear all faith with you; you can no longer be my overlord; we two must share!

HAKON. You dare to say this to me!

DUKE SKULE. I have more men than you in Oslo, Hakon Hakonsson.

HAKON. Mayhap you think to——

DUKE SKULE. Hearken to me! Think of the Bishop's words! Let us share; give me the ten ship-wards; let me hold my share as a free kingdom, without tax or tribute. Norway has ere this been parted into two kingdoms;—we will hold firmly together——

HAKON. Duke, you must be soul-sick, that you can crave such a thing.

DUKE SKULE. Ay, I am soul-sick, and there is no other healing for me. We two must be equals; there must be no man over me!

---

[1] *Skibreder*, districts each of which furnished a ship to the fleet.

Hakon. Every treeless holm is a stone in the edifice which Harald Hårfager and the sainted King Olaf reared ; would you have me break in twain what they have mortised together ?   Never !

Duke Skule.   Well, then let us reign by turns ; let each bear sway for three years !   You have reigned long ; now my turn has come.   Depart from the land for three years ;—I will be king the while ; I will even out your paths for you against your home-coming ; I will guide everything for the best ;—it wears and blunts the senses to sit ever on the watch. Hakon, hear me—three years each ; let us wear the crown by turns !

Hakon.   Think you my crown would sit well on your temples ?

Duke Skule.   For me is no crown too wide.

Hakon. It needs a God-sent right and a God-sent calling to wear the crown.

Duke Skule. And know you so surely that you have a God-sent right ?

Hakon.   I have God's own word for that.

Duke Skule. Rest not too surely on it. Had the Bishop said all he might—but that were bootless now ; you would not believe me.   Ay, truly you have mighty allies on high ; but I defy you none the less ! You will not reign by turns with me ?   Well—then must we try the last resort ;—Hakon, let us two fight for it, man to man, with heavy weapons, for life or death !

Hakon.   Speak you in jest, my lord ?

Duke Skule.   I plead for my life-work and for my soul's salvation !

HAKON. Then is there small hope for the saving of your soul.

DUKE SKULE. You will not fight with me? you shall, you shall!

HAKON. Oh blinded man! I cannot but pity you. You think 'tis the Lord's calling that draws you towards the throne; you see not that 'tis nought but arrogance. What is it that allures you? The royal circlet, the purple-bordered mantle, the right to be seated three steps above the floor;—pitiful, pitiful! Were *that* kingship, I would cast it into your hat, as I cast a groat to a beggar.

DUKE SKULE. You have known me since your childhood, and you judge me thus!

HAKON. You have wisdom and courage and all noble gifts of the mind; you are born to stand nearest a king, but not to be a king yourself.

DUKE SKULE. That will we now assay.

HAKON. Name me a single king's-task you achieved in all the years you were regent for me! Were the Baglers or the Ribbungs ever mightier than then? You were a full-grown man, yet the land was harried by rebellious factions; did you quell a single one of them? I was young and untried when I came to the helm—look at me—all fell before me when I became king; there are no Baglers, no Ribbungs left!

DUKE SKULE. That should you least boast of; for there lies the greatest danger. Party must stand against party, claim against claim, region against region, if the king is to have the might. Every village, every family must either need him or fear him. If you kill dissension, you kill your power at the same stroke.

HAKON. And you would be king—you, who think thus! You had been well fitted for a chieftain's part in Erling Skakke's days ; but the time has grown away from you, and you know it not. See you not, then, that Norway's realm, as Harald and Olaf built it up, may be likened to a church that stands as yet unconsecrate ? The walls soar aloft with mighty buttresses, the vaultings have a noble span, the spire points upwards, like a fir-tree in the forest ; but the life, the throbbing heart, the fresh blood-stream, is lacking to the work ; God's living spirit is not breathed into it ; it stands unconsecrate.—*I* will bring consecration ! Norway has been a *kingdom*, it shall become a *people*. The Trönder has stood against the man of Viken, the Agdeman against the Hordalander, the Halogalander against the Sogndalesman ; all shall be one hereafter, and all shall feel and know that they are one ! That is the task which God has laid on my shoulders ; that is the life-work which now lies before the King of Norway. That life-work, Duke, I think you were best to leave untried, for truly it is beyond you !

DUKE SKULE (*impressed*). To unite——? To unite the Trönders and the men of Viken,—all Norway——? (*Sceptically.*) 'Tis impossible ! Norway's saga tells of no such thing !

HAKON. For you 'tis impossible, for you can but work out the old saga afresh; for me, 'tis as easy as for the falcon to cleave the clouds.

DUKE SKULE (*in uneasy agitation*). To unite the

whole people—to awaken it so that it shall know itself one! Whence got you so strange a thought? It runs like ice and fire through me. (*Vehemently.*) It comes from the devil, Hakon; it shall never be carried through while I have strength to buckle on my helm!

HAKON. I have the thought from God, and shall never let it slip while I bear Saint Olaf's circlet on my brow!

DUKE SKULE. Then must Saint Olaf's circlet fall from your brow!

HAKON. Who will make it fall?

DUKE SKULE. I, if none other.

HAKON. You, Skule, will be harmless after the to-morrow's Assembly.

DUKE SKULE. Hakon! Tempt not God! Drive me not out upon the verge of the precipice!

HAKON (*points to the door*). Go, my lord—and be it forgotten that we have spoken with sharp tongues this night.

DUKE SKULE (*looks hard at him for a moment, and says:*) Next time, we will speak with sharper tongues.

(*Goes out by the back.*)

HAKON (*after a short pause*). He threatens!—No, no, it cannot come to that. He must, he shall yield and fall at my feet; I have need of that strong arm, that cunning brain.—Whatsoever courage and wisdom and strength there may be in this land, all gifts that God has endowed men withal, are but granted them to my uses. 'Tis for my service that Duke Skule received all his noble gifts; to defy me is to defy

Heaven; 'tis my duty to punish whosoever shall set himself up against Heaven's will; for Heaven has done so much for me.

Dagfinn the Peasant (*enters from the back*). Be on your guard to-night, my lord; the Duke has surely evil in his mind.

Hakon.   What say you?

Dagfinn.   What he is devising, I know not; but sure am I that something is brewing.

Hakon.   Can he think to fall upon us?   Impossible, impossible!

Dagfinn.   No, 'tis something else.   His ships lie clear for sailing; he has summoned an Assembly on board them.

Hakon.   You must mistake——!   Go, Dagfinn, and bring me sure tidings.

Dagfinn.   Ay ay; trust to me.   (*Goes.*)

Hakon.   No,—'tis not to be thought of!   The Duke dare not rise against me.   God will not suffer it—God, who has hitherto guided my course so marvellously.   I must have peace now, I must set about my work!—I have done so little yet; but I hear the infallible voice of the Lord calling to me: Thou shalt achieve a great king's-task in Norway!

Gregorius Jonsson (*enters from the back*).   My lord and King!

Hakon.   Gregorius Jonsson!   Come you hither?

Gregorius Jonsson.   I offer myself for your service.   Thus far have I followed the Duke; but now I dare follow him no further.

Hakon.   What has befallen?

GREGORIUS JONSSON. That which no man will believe, when 'tis rumoured through the land.

HAKON. Speak, speak!

GREGORIUS JONSSON. I tremble to hear the sound of my own words; know then——

(He seizes the KING'S *arm and whispers.)*

HAKON (*starts backwards with a cry*). Ha, are you distraught?

GREGORIUS JONSSON. Would to God I were.

HAKON. Unheard of! No, it cannot be true!

GREGORIUS JONSSON. By Christ's dear blood, so is it!

HAKON. Go, go; sound the trumpet-call for my guard; get all my men under arms.

(GREGORIUS JONSSON *goes.*)

HAKON (*paces the room once or twice, then goes quickly up to the door of* MARGRETE'S *chamber, knocks at it, continues to pace the room once or twice, then goes again to the door, knocks, and calls*). Margrete! (*Goes on pacing up and down.*)

MARGRETE (*in the doorway, attired for the night, with her hair down; she has a red cloak round her shoulders, holding it close together over her breast*). Hakon, is it you?

HAKON. Yes, yes; come hither.

MARGRETE. Oh, but you must not look at me; I was in bed already.

HAKON. I have other things to think of.

MARGRETE. What has befallen?

HAKON. Give me a good counsel! I have even now received the worst of tidings.

MARGRETE (*alarmed*). What tidings, Hakon?

HAKON. That there are now two kings in Norway.

MARGRETE. Two kings in Norway!—Hakon, where is my father?

HAKON. He has proclaimed himself king on board his ship; now is he sailing to Nidaros to be crowned.

MARGRETE. Oh God, thou almighty——!
  (*Sinks down on the bench, covers her face with her hands and weeps.*)

HAKON. Two kings in the land!

MARGRETE. My husband the one—my father the other!

HAKON (*goes restlessly up and down*). Give me a good counsel, Margrete! Should I hasten across by the Uplands, come first to Nidaros, and prevent the crowning? No, it may not be done; I have too few men with me; there in the north he is more powerful than I.—Give me counsel; how can I have the Duke slain, ere he come to Nidaros?

MARGRETE (*imploringly, with folded hands*). Hakon, Hakon!

HAKON. Can you not hit upon a good device, I say, to have the Duke slain?

MARGRETE (*sinks down from the bench in agony and remains kneeling*). Oh, can you so utterly forget that he is my father!

HAKON. Your father——; ay, ay, it is true; I had forgotten. (*Raises her up.*) Sit, sit, Margrete; comfort you; do not weep; you have no fault in this. (*Goes over to the window.*) Duke Skule will be worse for me than all other foemen! God, God,—why hast thou stricken me so sorely, me, who have not sinned!

(*A knock at the door in the back; he starts, listens, and cries:*)   Who knocks so late?

INGA'S VOICE (*outside*).   One who is a-cold, Hakon!

HAKON (*with a cry*).   My mother!

MARGRETE (*springs up*).   Inga!

HAKON (*rushes to the door and opens it;* INGA *is sitting on the doorstep*).   My mother!   Sitting like a dog outside her son's door!   And I ask why God has stricken me!

INGA (*stretches out her arms towards him*).   Hakon, my child!   Blessings upon you!

HAKON (*raising her up*).   Come—come in; here are light and warmth!

INGA.   *May* I come in to you?

HAKON.   Never shall we part again.

INGA.   My son — my King — oh, but you are good and loving!   I stood in a corner and saw you, as you came from the Bishop's Palace; you looked so sorrowful; I *could* not part from you thus.

HAKON.   God be thanked for that!   No one, truly, could have come to me more welcome than you!   Margrete—my mother—I have greatly sinned; I have barred my heart against you two, who are so rich in love.

MARGRETE (*falls on his neck*).   Oh, Hakon, my beloved husband; do I stand near you now?

HAKON.   Ay, near me, near me; not to give me cunning counsels, but to shed light over my path.   Come what will, I feel the Lord's strength within me!

DAGFINN THE PEASANT (*enters hastily from the back*).   My lord, my lord!   The worst has befallen!

HAKON (*smiles confidently, while he holds* MAR-
GRETE *and* INGA *closely to him*). I know it; but be
not cast down, good Dagfinn! If there be two kings
in Norway, there is but one in Heaven—and He will
guide all things aright!

THE CURTAIN FALLS.

Act Fourth.

(*The great hall in Oslo Palace. KING SKULE is feasting with his Guard and his Chiefs. In front, on the left, stands the throne, where SKULE sits, richly attired, with a purple mantle and the royal circlet on his head. The supper-table, by which the guests are seated, stretches from the throne towards the background. Opposite to SKULE sit PAUL FLIDA and BÅRD BRATTE. Some of the humbler guests are standing, to the right. It is late evening; the hall is brightly lighted. The banquet is drawing to a close; the men are very merry, and partly drunk; they drink to each other, laugh, and all talk together.*)

PAUL FLIDA (*rises and strikes the table*).   Silence in the hall; Jatgeir Skald will say forth his song in honour of King Skule.

JATGEIR (*stands out in the middle of the floor*).[1]
  Duke Skule he summoned the Örething [2]
  when 'twas mass-time in Nidaros town;
  and the bells rang and swords upon bucklers
      clashed bravely
  when Duke Skule he donned the crown.

  King Skule marched over the Dovrefjeld,
  his host upon snow-shoes sped;
  the Gudbranddalesman he grovelled for grace,
  but his hoard must e'en ransom his head.

---

[1] The metre of this song is very rugged in the original, and the wording purposely uncouth.   See Appendix.

[2] See note, p. 217.

King Skule south over Miösen fared,—
the Uplander cursed at his banner;
King Skule hasted through Raumarike
to Låka in Nannestad manor.

'Twas all in the holy Shrove-tide week
we met with the Birchleg horde;
Earl Knut was their captain—the swords with
        loud tongue
in the suit for the throne made award.

They say of a truth that since Sverre's days
was never so hot a fight ;
red-sprent, like warriors' winding-sheets,
grew the upland that erst lay white.

They took to their heels did the Birchenlegs,
flinging from them both buckler and bill there;
many hundreds, though, took to their heels
        nevermore,
for they lay and were icily chill there.

No man knows where King Hakon hideth;—
King Skule stands safe at the helm.
All hail and long life to thee, lord, in thy state
as monarch of Norway's realm !

Skule's Men (*spring up with loud jubilation, hold
goblets and beakers aloft, clash their weapons, and
repeat :*)
        All hail and long life to thee, lord, in thy state
        as monarch of Norway's realm !

KING SKULE. Thanks for the song, Jatgeir Skald! 'Tis as I best like it; for it praises my men to the full as much as myself.

JATGEIR. 'Tis to the King's honour that his men should be praised.

KING SKULE. Take as guerdon this arm-ring, stay with me, and be of my household; I will have many skalds about me.

JATGEIR. 'Twill need many, my lord, if all your achievements are to be sung.

KING SKULE. I will be threefold more bountiful than Hakon; the skald's song shall be honoured and rewarded like all other noble deeds, so long as I am king. Be seated; now you belong to my household; all you have need of shall be freely given you.

JATGEIR (seats himself). What I most need, I shall soon lack utterly, my lord.

KING SKULE. What mean you?

JATGEIR. Foes to King Skule, whose flight and fall I can sing.

MANY OF THE MEN (amid laughter and applause). Well said, Icelander!

PAUL FLIDA (to JATGEIR). The song was good; but 'tis known there goes a spice of lying to every skald-work, and yours was not without it.

JATGEIR. Lying, Sir Marshal?

PAUL FLIDA. Ay; you say no man knows where King Hakon is hiding; that is not true; we have certain tidings that Hakon is at Nidaros.

KING SKULE (smiling). He has claimed homage for the King-child, and given it the kingly title.

JATGEIR. That have I heard; but I knew not that

any man could give away that which he himself does not possess.

King Skule.   'Tis easiest to give what you yourself do not possess.

Bård Bratte.   But it can scarce be easy to beg your way in midwinter from Bergen to Nidaros.

Jatgeir.   The fortunes of the Birchlegs move in a ring; they began hungry and frozen, and now they end in like case.

Paul Flida.   'Tis rumoured in Bergen that Hakon has forsworn the Church and all that is holy; he heard not mass on New Year's day.

Bård Bratte.   He could plead lawful hindrance, Paul; he stood all day cutting his silver goblets and dishes to pieces—he had naught else wherewith to pay his household.

(*Laughter and loud talk among the Guests.*)

King Skule (*raises his goblet*).   I drink to you, Bård Bratte, and thank you and all my new men. You fought manfully for me at Låka, and bore a great part in the victory.

Bård Bratte.   It was the first time I fought under you, my lord; but I soon felt that 'tis easy to conquer when such a chieftain as you rides at the head of the host.   But I would we had not slain so many and chased them so far; for now I fear 'twill be long ere they dare face us again.

King Skule.   Wait till the spring comes, and we shall meet them again, never fear.   Earl Knut lies with the remnant at Tunsberg rock, and Arnbiörn Jonsson is gathering a force eastward in Viken; when they deem themselves strong enough, they will soon let us hear from them.

BÅRD BRATTE.   They will never dare to, after the great slaughter at Låka.

KING SKULE.   Then will we lure them forth with cunning.

MANY VOICES.   Ay, ay—do so, lord King!

BÅRD BRATTE.   You have good store of cunning, King Skule.   Your foemen have never warning ere you fall upon them, and you are ever there where they least await you.

PAUL FLIDA.   'Tis therefore that the Birchlegs call us Vårbælgs.[1]

KING SKULE.   Others say Vargbælgs ; but this I swear, that when next we meet, the Birchlegs shall learn how hard it is to turn such Wolf-skins inside out.

BÅRD BRATTE.   With their good will shall we never meet—'twill be a chase the whole country round.

KING SKULE.   Ay, that it shall be.   First we must purge Viken, and make sure of all these east-ward parts; then will we get our ships together, and sail round the Naze and up the coast to Nidaros.

---

[1] The derivation of this word is doubtful.   In the form *Vargbælg* it means Wolf-skin, from Icelandic *Vargr* = a wolf, and *Belgr* = the skin of an animal taken off whole.   The more common form, however, is *Varbelg*, which, as P. A. Munch suggests (*Det Norske Folks Historie*, iii. 219), may possibly come from *var* (our word " ware "), a covering, and may be an allusion to the falsity and cunning of the faction.   What Ibsen understands by the form *Vårbælg* I cannot discover.   *Vår* (Icelandic *Vár*) means the springtide.   The nick-name had been applied to a political faction as early as 1190, and was merely revived as a designation for Skule's adherents.

BÅRD BRATTE.   And when you come in that wise
to Nidaros, I scarce think the monks will deny to
move Saint Olaf's shrine out to the mote-stead, as
they did in the autumn, when we swore allegiance.

KING SKULE.   The shrine *must* out; I will bear
my kingship in all ways lawfully.

JATGEIR.   And I promise you to sing a great
death-song, when you have slain the Sleeper.

   (*An outburst of laughter among the men.*)

KING SKULE.   The Sleeper?

JATGEIR.   Know you not, my lord, that King
Hakon is called "Hakon the Sleeper," because he sits
as though benumbed ever since you came to the
throne?

BÅRD BRATTE.   They say he lies ever with his
eyes closed. Doubtless he dreams that he is still king.

KING SKULE.   ·Let him dream; he shall never
dream himself back into the kingship.

JATGEIR.   Let his sleep be long and dreamless,
then shall I have stuff for songs.

THE MEN.   Yes, yes, do as the skald says!

KING SKULE.   When so many good men counsel
as one, the counsel must be good; yet will we not
talk now of that matter. But one promise I will
make:—each of my men shall inherit the weapons
and harness, and gold and silver, of whichever one of
the enemy he slays; and each man shall succeed to
the dignities of him he lays low. He who slays a
baron shall himself be a baron; he who slays a thane,
shall receive his thaneship; and all they who already
hold such dignities and offices, shall be rewarded after
other kingly sort.

THE MEN (*spring up in wild delight*).   Hail, hail, King Skule!   Lead us against the Birchlegs!

BÅRD BRATTE.   Now are you sure to conquer in all battles.

PAUL FLIDA.   I claim Dagfinn the Peasant for myself; he owns a good sword that I have long hankered after.

BÅRD BRATTE.   I will have Bård Torsteinsson's hauberk; it saved his life at Låka, for it withstands both stroke and thrust.

JATGEIR.   Nay, but let me have it; 'twill fit me better; you shall have five golden marks in exchange.

BÅRD BRATTE.   Where will you find five golden marks, Skald?

JATGEIR.   I will take them from Gregorius Jonsson when we come northwards.

THE MEN (*all talking together*).   And I will have —I will have—— (*The rest becomes indistinct in the hubbub.*)

PAUL FLIDA.   Away!   Every man to his quarters; bethink you that you are in the King's hall.

THE MEN.   Ay, ay,—hail to the King, hail to King Skule!

KING SKULE.   To bed now, good fellows!   We have sat long over the drinking-table to-night.

A MAN-AT-ARMS (*as the crowd are about to go*). To-morrow we will cast lots for the Birchlegs' goods.

ANOTHER.   Rather leave it to luck!

SEVERAL.   Nay, nay!

OTHERS.   Ay, ay!

BÅRD BRATTE.   Now the Wolf-skins are fighting for the bear-fell.

PAUL FLIDA.   And they have yet to fell the bear.

(*All go out by the back.*)

KING SKULE (*waits till the men are gone; the tension of his features relaxes; he sinks upon a bench*). How weary I am, weary to death. To live in the midst of that swarm day out and day in, to look smilingly ahead as though I were so immovably assured of right and victory and fortune. To have no creature with whom I may speak of all that gnaws me so sorely. (*Rises, with a look of terror.*) And the battle at Låka! That I should have conquered there! Hakon sent his host against me; God was to judge and award between the two kings—and I conquered, conquered, as never any before has conquered the Birchlegs! Their shields stood upright in the snow, but there was none behind them—the Birchlegs took to the woods, and fled over upland and moor and lea as far as their legs would carry them. The unthinkable came to pass; Hakon lost and I won. There is a secret horror in that victory. Thou great God of Heaven! there rules, then, no certain law on high, that all things must obey? The right carries with it no conquering might? (*With a wild outburst.*) I am sick, I am sick!—Wherefore should not the right be on my side? May I not deem that God himself would assure me of it, since he let me conquer? (*Broodingly.*) The possibilities are even;—not a feather-weight more on the one side than on the other; and yet—(*shakes his head*)—yet the scale dips on Hakon's part. When the thought of the kingly right comes over me unawares, 'tis ever he, not I, that is the true king. When I would see myself as the true king, I must do it with forethought, I must build up a whole fabric of subtleties, a work of cunning; I must hold memories aloof, and take faith by storm. It was not so before. What has befallen to fill me so full of doubt? The burning of the letter? No—that made the uncertainty eternal, but not greater. Has Hakon done any great and kingly deed in these later days? No, he achieved his greatest deeds while I least believed in him. (*Seats himself on the right.*) What *is* it? Ha, strange! It comes and goes like a marsh-fire; it dances at the tip of my tongue, as when one has lost a word and cannot find it. (*Springs up.*) Ha! Now I know it! No——! Yes, yes! Now I know it!— "Norway has been a *kingdom*, it shall become a *people;* all shall be one, and all shall feel and know that they are one!" Since Hakon spoke these madman's words, he stands ever before me as the rightful king. (*Whispers, with fixed and anxious gaze.*) What if God's calling glimmered through these strange words? If God had garnered up the thought till now, and would now strew it forth—and had chosen Hakon for his sower?

PAUL FLIDA (*enters from the back*). My lord King, I have tidings for you.

KING SKULE. Tidings?

PAUL FLIDA. A man who comes from down the fiord brings news that the Birchlegs in Tunsberg have launched their ships, and that many men have gathered in the town in these last days.

King Skule. Good, we will go forth to meet them—to-morrow.

Paul Flida. It might chance, my lord King, that the Birchlegs would come to meet us first.

King Skule. They have not ships enough for that, nor men.

Paul Flida. But Arnbiörn Jonsson is gathering both men and ships, all round in Viken.

King Skule. The better for us; we will crush them at one blow, as we did at Låka.

Paul Flida. My lord, 'tis not so easy to crush the Birchlegs twice following.

King Skule. And wherefore not?

Paul Flida. Because Norway's saga tells not that the like has ever befallen.—Shall I send spies out to Hoved-isle?

King Skule. 'Tis needless; the night is dark, and there is a sea-fog to boot.

Paul Flida. Well well, my lord knows best; but bethink you that all men are against you here in Viken. The townsfolk of Oslo hate you, and should the Birchlegs come they will make common cause with them.

King Skule (*with animation*). Paul Flida, were it not possible that I could win over the men of Viken to my side?

Paul Flida (*looks at him in astonishment, and shakes his head*). No, my lord, it is not possible.

King Skule. And wherefore not?

Paul Flida. Why, for that you have the Trönders on your side.

KING SKULE. I will have both the Trönders and the men of Viken!

PAUL FLIDA. Nay, my lord, that cannot be!

KING SKULE. Not possible! cannot be! And wherefore—wherefore not?

PAUL FLIDA. Because the man of Viken is the man of Viken, the Trönder is the Trönder; because so it has always been, and no saga tells of a time when it was otherwise.

KING SKULE. Ay, ay—you are right. Go.

PAUL FLIDA. And send forth no spies?

KING SKULE. Wait till daybreak. (PAUL FLIDA goes.) Norway's saga tells of no such thing; it has never been so yet; Paul Flida answers me as I answered Hakon. Are there then upward as well as downward steps? Stands Hakon as high over me as I over Paul Flida? Has Hakon an eye for unborn thoughts, that is lacking in me? Who stood so high as Harald Hårfager in the days when every headland had its king, and he said: Now they must fall—hereafter shall there be but one? He threw the old saga to the winds, and made a new saga. (*A pause; he paces up and down lost in thought; then he stops.*) Can one man take God's calling from another, as he takes weapons and gold from his fallen foe? Can a Pretender clothe himself in a king's life-task, as he can put on the kingly mantle? The oak that is felled to be a ship's timber, can it say: Nay, I will be the mast, I will take on me the task of the fir-tree, point upwards, tall and shining, bear the golden vane at my top, spread bellying white sails to the sunshine, and meet the eyes of all men, from afar!—No, no, thou heavy gnarled oak-trunk, thy place is beneath the keel; there shalt thou lie, and do thy work, unheard of and unseen by those aloft in the daylight; it is thou that shalt hinder the ship from being whelmed in the storm; while the mast with the golden vane and the bellying sail shall bear it forward toward the new, toward the unknown, toward alien strands and the saga of the future! (*Vehemently.*) Since Hakon uttered his great king-thought, I can see no other thought in the world but that only. If I cannot take it and make substance of it, I see no other thought to fight for. (*Broodingly.*) And can I not make it mine? If I cannot, whence comes my great love for Hakon's thought?

JATGEIR (*enters from the back*). Forgive my coming, lord King——

KING SKULE. You come to my wish, Skald!

JATGEIR. I overheard some townsfolk at my lodging talking darkly of——

KING SKULE. Let that wait. Tell me, Skald: you who have fared far abroad in strange lands, have you ever seen a woman love another's child? Not only be kind to it—'tis not that I mean; but *love* it, love it with the warmest passion of her soul.

JATGEIR. That can only those women do who have no child of their own to love.

KING SKULE. Only those women——?

JATGEIR. And chiefly women who are barren.

KING SKULE. Chiefly the barren——? They love the children of others with all their warmest passion?

JATGEIR. That will oftentimes befall.

KING SKULE. And does it not sometimes befall that such a barren woman will slay another's child, because she herself has none?

JATGEIR. Ay, ay; but in that she does unwisely.

KING SKULE. Unwisely?

JATGEIR. Ay, for she gives the gift of sorrow to her whose child she slays.

KING SKULE. Think you the gift of sorrow is a great good?

JATGEIR. Yes, lord.

KING SKULE (*looks fixedly at him*). Methinks there are two men in you, Icelander. When you sit amid the household at the merry feast, you draw cloak and hood over all your thoughts; when one is alone with you, sometimes you seem to be of those among whom one were fain to choose his friend. How comes it?

JATGEIR. When you go to swim in the river, my lord, you would scarce strip you where the people pass by to church; you seek a sheltered privacy.

KING SKULE. True, true.

JATGEIR. My soul has the like shyness; therefore I do not strip me when there are many in the hall.

KING SKULE. Hm. (*A short pause.*) Tell me, Jatgeir, how came you to be a skald? Who taught you skaldcraft?

JATGEIR. Skaldcraft cannot be taught, my lord.

KING SKULE. Cannot be taught? How came it then?

JATGEIR. I got the gift of sorrow, and I was a skald.

KING SKULE. Then 'tis the gift of sorrow the skald has need of?

Jatgeir.   I needed sorrow; others there may be who need faith, or joy—or doubt——

King Skule.   Doubt as well?

Jatgeir.   Ay; but then must the doubter be strong and sound.

King Skule.   And whom call you the unsound doubter?

Jatgeir.   He who doubts of his own doubt.

King Skule (*slowly*).   That, methinks, were death.

Jatgeir.   'Tis worse; 'tis neither day nor night.

King Skule (*quickly, as if shaking off his thoughts*).   Where are my weapons? I will fight and act—not think. What was it you would have told me when you came?

Jatgeir.   'Twas what I noted in my lodgings. The townsmen whisper together secretly, and laugh mockingly and ask if we be well assured that King Hakon is in the westland; there is somewhat they are in glee over.

King Skule.   They are men of Viken and therefore against me.

Jatgeir.   They scoff because King Olaf's shrine could not be brought out to the mote-stead when we did you homage; they say it boded ill.

King Skule.   When next I come to Nidaros, the shrine *shall* out! It shall stand under the open sky, though I should have to tear down St. Olaf's church and widen out the mote-stead over the spot where it stood.

Jatgeir.   That were a strong deed; but I shall make a song of it, as strong as the deed itself.

KING SKULE.   Have you many unmade songs within you, Jatgeir?

JATGEIR.   Nay, but many unborn; they are conceived one after the other, come to life, and are brought forth.

KING SKULE.   And if I, who am King and have the might, if I were to have you slain, would all the unborn skald-thoughts you bear within you die along with you?

JATGEIR.   My lord, it is a great sin to slay a fair thought.

KING SKULE.   I ask not if it be a *sin;* I ask if it be *possible!*

JATGEIR.   I know not.

KING SKULE.   Have you never had another skald for your friend, and has he never unfolded to you a great and noble song he thought to make?

JATGEIR.   Yes, lord.

KING SKULE.   Did you not then wish that you could slay him, to take his thought and make the song yourself?

JATGEIR.   My lord, I am not barren; I have children of my own; I need not to love those of other men.   (*Goes.*)

KING SKULE (*after a pause*).   The Icelander is in very deed a skald.   He speaks God's deepest truth and knows it not.   *I* am as a barren woman.   Therefore I love Hakon's kingly thought-child, love it with the warmest passion of my soul.   Oh, that I could but adopt[1] it!   It would die in my hands.   Which were best, that it should die in my hands, or wax

_____
[1] *Knæsætte;* see note, p. 138.

great in his? Should I ever have peace of soul if that came to pass? Can I forego all? Can I stand by and see Hakon make himself famous for all time! How dead and empty is all within me—and around me. No friend—ah, the Icelander! (*Goes to the door and calls:*) Has the skald gone from the palace?

A GUARD (*outside*). No, my lord; he stands in the outer hall talking with the watch.

KING SKULE. Bid him come hither. (*Goes forward to the table; presently* JATGEIR *enters.*) I cannot sleep, Jatgeir; 'tis all my great kingly thoughts that keep me awake, you see.

JATGEIR. 'Tis with the king's thoughts as with the skald's, I doubt not. They fly highest and grow quickest when there is night and stillness around.

KING SKULE. Is it so with the skald's thoughts too?

JATGEIR. Ay, lord; no song is born by daylight; it may be written down in the sunshine; but it makes itself in the silent night.

KING SKULE. Who gave you the gift of sorrow, Jatgeir?

JATGEIR. She whom I loved.

KING SKULE. She died, then?

JATGEIR. No, she deceived me.

KING SKULE. And then you became a skald?

JATGEIR. Ay, then I became a skald.

KING SKULE (*seizes him by the arm*). What gift do I need to become a king?

JATGEIR. Not the gift of doubt; else would you not question so.

KING SKULE. What gift do I need?

JATGEIR.   My lord, you *are* a king.

KING SKULE.   Have you at all times full faith that you are a skald?

JATGEIR (*looks silently at him for a while, and asks*). Have you never loved?

KING SKULE.   Yes, once—burningly, blissfully, and in sin.

JATGEIR.   You have a wife.

KING SKULE.   Her I took to bear me sons.

JATGEIR.   But you have a daughter, my lord—a gracious and noble daughter.

KING SKULE.   Were my daughter a son, I would not ask you what gift I need. (*Vehemently.*) I must have some one by me who sinks his own will utterly in mine—who believes in me unflinchingly, who will cling close to me in good hap and ill, who lives only to shed light and warmth over my life, and must die if I fall.   Give me counsel, Jatgeir Skald!

JATGEIR.   Buy yourself a dog, my lord.

KING SKULE.   Would no man suffice?

JATGEIR.   You would have to search long for such a man.

KING SKULE (*suddenly*).   Will *you* be that man to me, Jatgeir?   Will *you* be a son to me?   You shall have Norway's crown to your heritage— the whole land shall be yours, if you will be a son to me, and live for my life-work, and believe in me.

JATGEIR.   And what should be my warranty that I did not feign——?

KING SKULE.   Give up your calling in life; sing no more songs, and then will I believe you!

JATGEIR.　No, lord—that were to buy the crown too dear.

KING SKULE.　Bethink you well—'tis greater to be a king than a skald.

JATGEIR.　Not always.

KING SKULE.　'Tis but your unsung songs you must sacrifice!

JATGEIR.　Songs unsung are ever the fairest.

KING SKULE.　But I must—I *must* have one who can trust in me! Only one. I feel it—had I that one, I were saved!

JATGEIR.　Trust in yourself and you will be saved!

PAUL FLIDA (*enters hastily*).　King Skule, look to yourself! Hakon Hakonsson lies off Elgjarness with all his fleet!

KING SKULE.　Off Elgjarness——! Then he is close at hand.

JATGEIR.　Get we to arms then! If there be bloodshed to-night, I will gladly be the first to die for you!

KING SKULE.　You, who would not live for me!

JATGEIR.　A man can die for another's life-work; but if he go on living, he must live for his own.
　　(*Goes.*)

PAUL FLIDA (*impatiently*).　Your commands, my lord! The Birchlegs may be in Oslo this very hour.

KING SKULE.　'Twere best if we could fare to Saint Thomas Beckett's grave; he has helped so many a sorrowful and penitent soul.

PAUL FLIDA (*more forcibly*).　My lord, speak not so wildly now; I tell you, the Birchlegs are upon us!

KING SKULE.   Let all the churches be opened, that we may betake us thither and find grace.

PAUL FLIDA.   You can crush all your foemen at one stroke, and yet would betake you to the churches!

KING SKULE.   Yes, yes, keep all the churches open!

PAUL FLIDA.   Be sure Hakon will break sanctuary, when 'tis Vårbælgs he pursues.

KING SKULE.   That will he not; God will shield him from such a sin;—God always shields Hakon.

PAUL FLIDA (*in deep and sorrowful wrath*).   Hearing you speak thus, men could not but ask: Who is king in this land?

KING SKULE (*smiling mournfully*).   Ay, Paul Flida, that is the great question: *who* is king in this land?

PAUL FLIDA (*imploringly*).   You are soul-sick to-night, my lord; let me act for you.

KING SKULE.   Ay, ay, do so.

PAUL FLIDA (*going*).   First will I break down all the bridges.

KING SKULE.   Madman! Stay!—Break down all the bridges!   Know you what that means?   I have assayed it;—beware of that!

PAUL FLIDA.   What would you then, my lord?

KING SKULE.   I will talk with Hakon.

PAUL FLIDA.   He will answer you with a tongue of steel.

KING SKULE.   Go, go;—you shall learn my will later.

PAUL FLIDA.   Every moment is precious!   (*Seizes*

his hand.)   King Skule, let us break down all the bridges, fight like Wolves,[1] and trust in Heaven!

KING SKULE (*softly*).   Heaven trusts not in me; I dare not trust in Heaven.

PAUL FLIDA.   Short has been the saga of Varg-bælgs.   (*Goes out by the back.*)

KING SKULE.   A hundred cunning heads, a thousand mighty arms, are at my beck; but not a single loving, trusting heart.   That is kingly beggary; no more, no less.

BÅRD BRATTE (*from the back*).   Two wayfarers from afar stand without, praying to have speech with you, my lord.

KING SKULE.   Who are they?

BÅRD BRATTE.   A woman and a priest.

KING SKULE.   Let the woman and the priest approach.

(BÅRD *goes;* KING SKULE *seats himself, musing, on the right; presently there enters a black-robed Woman; she wears a long cloak, a hood, and a thick veil, which conceals her face; a Priest follows her, and remains standing by the door.*)

KING SKULE.   Who are you?

THE WOMAN.   One you have loved.

KING SKULE (*shaking his head*).   There lives no one who remembers that I have loved.   Who are you, I ask?

THE WOMAN.   One who loves you.

KING SKULE.   Then are you surely one of the dead.

---

[1] *Varger*, the first part of the word *Vargbælg.*

THE WOMAN (*comes close to him and says softly and passionately*).   Skule Bårdsson!

KING SKULE (*rises with a cry*).   Ingeborg!

INGEBORG.   Do you know me now, Skule?

KING SKULE.   Ingeborg,—Ingeborg!

INGEBORG.   Oh, let me look at you—look long at you, so long! (*Seizes his hand; a pause.*) You fair, you deeply-loved, you faithless man!

KING SKULE.   Take off that veil; look at me with the eyes that once were as clear and blue as the sky.

INGEBORG.   These eyes have been but as rain-clouds for twenty years; you would not know them again, and you shall never see them more.

KING SKULE.   But your voice is fresh and soft and young as ever!

INGEBORG.   I have used it only to whisper *your* name, to imprint your greatness in a young heart, and to pray to the sinners' God for grace towards us twain, who have loved in sin.

KING SKULE.   You have done that?

INGEBORG.   I have been silent save to speak loving words of you;—therefore has my voice remained fresh and young.

KING SKULE.   There lies a life-time between. Every fair memory from those days have I wasted and let slip——

INGEBORG.   It was your right.

KING SKULE.   And meantime *you*, Ingeborg, loving, faithful woman, have sat there in the north, guarding and treasuring your memories, in ice-cold loneliness!

INGEBORG.   It was my happiness.

King Skule. And I could give you up to win might and riches! With you at my side, as my wife, I had found it easier to be a king.

Ingeborg. God has been good to me in willing it otherwise. A soul like mine had need of a great sin, to arouse it to remorse and expiation.

King Skule. And now you come——?

Ingeborg. As Andres Skialdarband's widow.

King Skule. Your husband is dead!

Ingeborg. On the way from Jerusalem.

King Skule. Then has he atoned for the slaying of Vegard.

Ingeborg. 'Twas not therefore that my noble husband took the Cross.

King Skule. Not therefore?

Ingeborg. No; it was my sin he took upon his strong, loving shoulders; 'twas that he went to wash away in Jordan stream; 'twas for that he bled.

King Skule (*softly*). Then he knew all?

Ingeborg. From the first. And Bishop Nicholas knew it, for to him I confessed. And there was one other man that came to know it, though how I cannot guess.

King Skule. Who?

Ingeborg. Vegard Væradal.

King Skule. Vegard!

Ingeborg. He whispered a mocking word of me into my husband's ear, and thereupon Andres Skialdarband drew his sword, and slew him on the spot.

King Skule. *He* kept ward over her whom I betrayed and forgot.—And wherefore seek you me now?

INGEBORG.   To bring you the last sacrifice.

KING SKULE.   What mean you?

INGEBORG (*points to the Priest who stands by the door*).   Look at him!—Peter, my son, come hither!

KING SKULE.   Your son——!

INGEBORG.   And *yours*, King Skule!

KING SKULE (*half bewildered*).   Ingeborg!

(PETER *approaches in silent emotion, and throws himself before* KING SKULE.)

INGEBORG.   Take him!   For twenty years has he been the light and comfort of my life;—now are you King of Norway; the King's-son must enter on his heritage; I have no longer any right to him.

KING SKULE (*raises him up, in a storm of joy*). Here, to my heart, you whom I have yearned for so burningly! (*Presses him in his arms, lets him go, looks at him, and embraces him again.*) My son! My son! I have a son! Ha-ha-ha! who can stand against me now? (*Goes over to* INGEBORG *and seizes her hand.*) And you, you give him to me, Ingeborg! You take not back your word? You give him to me indeed?

INGEBORG.   Heavy is the sacrifice, and scarce had I had strength to make it, but that Bishop Nicholas sent him to me, bearing a letter with tidings of Andres Skialdarband's death.   'Twas the Bishop that laid on me the heavy sacrifice, as atonement for all my sin.

KING SKULE.   Then is the sin blotted out, and henceforth he is mine alone; is it not so, mine alone?

INGEBORG.   Yes; but one promise I crave of you.

KING SKULE.   Heaven and earth, crave all you will!

INGEBORG.   He is pure as a lamb of God, as I now give him into your hands.   'Tis a perilous path that leads up to the throne; let him not take hurt to his soul.   Hear you, King Skule, let not my child take hurt to his soul!

KING SKULE.   That I promise and swear to you!

INGEBORG (*seizes his arm*).   From the moment you mark that his soul suffers harm, let him rather die!

KING SKULE.   Rather die!   I promise and swear it!

INGEBORG.   Then shall I be of good cheer as I go back to Halogaland.

KING SKULE.   Ay, you may be of good cheer.

INGEBORG.   There will I repent and pray, till the Lord calls me.   And when we meet before God, he shall come back to me pure and blameless.

KING SKULE.   Pure and blameless!   (*Turning to* PETER.)   Let me look at you!   Ay, your mother's features and mine; you are he for whom I have longed so sorely.

PETER.   My father, my great, noble father!   Let me live and fight for you!   Let your cause be mine; and be your cause what it may—I know that I am fighting for the right.

KING SKULE (*with a cry of joy*).   You trust in me!   You trust in me!

PETER.   Immovably!

KING SKULE.   Then all is well; then am I surely saved!   Listen: you shall cast off the monkish hood; the Archbishop shall loose you from your vows; the King's-son shall wield the sword, shall go forward unwavering to might and honour.

PETER. Together with **you, my** noble father! We will go together!

KING SKULE (*drawing the youth close up to himself*). Ay, together, we two alone!

INGEBORG (*to herself*). To love, to sacrifice all and be forgotten, that is my saga. (*Goes quietly out by the back.*)

KING SKULE. Now shall a great king's-work be done in Norway! Listen, Peter, my son! We will awaken the whole people, and gather it into one; the man of Viken and the Trönder, the Halogalander and the Agdeman, the Uplander and the Sogndaleman, all shall be one great family! Then shall you see how the land will come to flourish!

PETER. **What a** great and dizzy thought——!

KING SKULE. Do you grasp it?

PETER. Yes—yes!—Clearly——!

KING SKULE. And **have** you faith in it?

PETER. **Yes, yes;** for I have faith in you!

KING **SKULE** (*wildly*). Hakon Hakonsson must die!

PETER. **If you will it,** then it is right that he die.

KING SKULE. 'Twill cost blood; **but** that we cannot heed!

PETER. The **blood is not** wasted that flows in your cause.

KING SKULE. All the might shall be yours when I have built **up** the kingdom. You shall sit on the throne with the circlet on your brow, with the purple mantle flowing wide over your shoulders; all men in the land shall bow before you—— (*The sounds of*

distant horns[1] *are heard.*) Ha! what was that?
(*With a cry.*) The Birchleg host! What was it Paul
Flida said——? (*Rushes towards the back.*)

PAUL FLIDA (*enters and cries*). The hour is upon
us, King Skule!

KING SKULE (*bewildered*). The Birchlegs! King
Hakon's host! Where are they?

PAUL FLIDA. They are swarming in thousands
down over the Ekeberg.

KING SKULE. Sound the call to arms! Sound,
sound! Give counsel; where shall we meet them?

PAUL FLIDA. All the churches stand open for us.

KING SKULE. 'Tis of the Birchlegs I ask——?

PAUL FLIDA. For them all the bridges stand open.

KING SKULE. Unhappy man, what have you done!

PAUL FLIDA. Obeyed my King!

KING SKULE. My son! My son! Woe is me; I
have lost your kingdom!

PETER. No, you will conquer! So great a king's-
thought cannot die!

KING SKULE. Peace, peace! (*Horns and shouts
are heard, nearer at hand.*) To horse! To arms!
More is at stake here than the life and death of men!
  (*Rushes out by the back; the others follow him.*)

———

(*A street in Oslo. On each side, low wooden houses,
  with porches. At the back, Saint Hallvard's churchyard, enclosed by a high wall with a gate. On the*

———

[1] *Lur*, the long wooden horn still used among the mountains in
Norway.

left, at the end of the wall, is seen the church, the chief portal of which stands open. It is still night; after a little, the day begins to dawn. The alarm-bell is ringing; far away on the right are heard battle-shouts and confused noises.)

KING SKULE'S HORNBLOWER (*enters from the right, blows his horn, and shouts*). To arms! To arms, all King Skule's men! (*Blows his horn again, and proceeds on his way; presently he is heard blowing and shouting in the next street.*)

A WOMAN (*appears at a house-door on the right*). Merciful God, what is astir?

A TOWNSMAN (*who has come out, half-dressed, from a house on the other side of the street*). The Birchlegs are in the town! Now will Skule have his reward for all his misdeeds.

ONE OF SKULE'S MEN (*enters with some others, bearing their cloaks and weapons on their arms, from a side street on the left*). Where are the Birchlegs?

ANOTHER OF SKULE'S MEN (*coming from a house on the right*). I know not!

THE FIRST. Hist! Listen!—They must be down at the Geite-bridge.

THE SECOND. Off to the Geite-bridge then!
   (*They all rush out to the right; a Townsman comes running in from the same side.*)

THE FIRST TOWNSMAN. Hey, neighbour, whence come you?

THE SECOND TOWNSMAN. From down at the Lo-river; there's ugly work there.

THE WOMAN. Saint Olaf and Saint Hallvard! Is it the Birchlegs, or who is it?

THE SECOND TOWNSMAN. Who else but the Birchlegs! King Hakon is with them; the whole fleet is laying in to the wharves; but he himself landed with his best men out at Ekeberg.

THE FIRST TOWNSMAN. Then will he take revenge for the slaughter at Låka!

THE SECOND TOWNSMAN. Ay, be sure of that.

THE FIRST TOWNSMAN. See, see! The Vårbælgs are flying already!

(*A troop of* SKULE's *men enter in full flight, from the right.*)

ONE OF THEM. Into the church! None can stand against the Birchlegs as they lay about them to-night.

(*The troop rushes into the church and bars the door on the inside.*)

THE SECOND TOWNSMAN (*looking out to the right*). I see a standard far down the street; it must be King Hakon's.

THE FIRST TOWNSMAN. See, see, how the Vårbælgs are running!

(*A second troop enters from the right.*)

ONE OF THE FUGITIVES. Let us betake us to the church and pray for grace. (*They rush at the door.*)

SEVERAL VÅRBÆLGS. 'Tis barred! 'tis barred!

THE FIRST. Up over Martestokke then!

ANOTHER. Where is King Skule?

THE FIRST. I know nót. Away! yonder I see the Birchlegs' standard!

(*They flee past the church, out to the left.* HAKON *enters from the right with his Standard-bearer,*

Gregorius Jonsson, Dagfinn the Peasant,
   and several other men.)

Dagfinn.   Hark to the war-cry! Skule is gathering his men behind the churchyard.

An Old Townsman (*calls from his porch, to*
Hakon).   Take heed for yourself, dear my lord ; the
Vargbælgs are fierce, now they are fighting for
life.

Hakon.   Is it you, old Guthorm Erlendsson?
You have fought both for my father and for my grandfather.

The Townsman.   Would to God I could fight for
you as well.

Hakon.   For that you are too old, and there is no
need ; men pour in upon me from all sides.

Dagfinn (*pointing off over the wall to the right*).
There comes the Duke's standard !

Gregorius Jonsson.   The Duke himself ! He
rides his white war-horse.

Dagfinn.   We must hinder his passage through
the gate here!

Hakon.   Wind the horn, wind the horn ! (*The
Hornblower does so.*) You blew better, whelp, when
you blew for money on Bergen wharf.

   (*The Hornblower winds another blast, louder than
       the first ; many men come rushing in.*)

A Vårbælg (*from the right, fleeing towards the
church, pursued by a Birchleg*). Spare my life ! Spare
my life !

The Birchleg. Not though you sat on the
altar ! (*Cuts him down.*) Methinks you wear a
costly cloak; 'twill fit me well. (*Is about to take the*

cloak, but utters a cry and casts away his sword.)   My lord King! I strike not another stroke for you!

DAGFINN.   You say that in such an hour as this?

THE BIRCHLEG.   Not another stroke!

DAGFINN (*cuts him down*).   Then shall you have reason to refrain!

THE BIRCHLEG (*pointing to the dead Vårbælg*). Methought I had done enough when I slew my own brother.   (*Dies.*)

HAKON.   His brother!

DAGFINN.   What!

(*Goes up to the Vårbælg's body.*)

HAKON.   Is it true?

DAGFINN.   I fear me it is.

HAKON (*shaken*).   Here see we what a war we are waging.   Brother against brother, father against son; —by God Almighty, this must have an end!

GREGORIUS JONSSON.   There comes the Duke, in full fight with Earl Knut's troop!

DAGFINN.   Bar the gate against him, king's-men!

> (*On the other side of the wall, the combatants come in sight.   The Vårbælgs are forcing their way towards the left, driving the Birchlegs back, foot by foot.   KING SKULE rides his white war-horse, with his sword drawn.   PETER walks at his side, holding the horse's bridle, and with his left hand uplifting a crucifix.   PAUL FLIDA bears SKULE'S standard, which is blue, with a golden lion rampant, without the axe.*)[1]

KING SKULE.   Cut them down!   Spare no man!

---

[1] The arms of Norway consist of a lion rampant, holding an axe.

There is come a new heir[1] to the throne of
Norway!

THE BIRCHLEGS.   A new heir, said he?

HAKON. Skule Bårdsson, let us share the kingdom!

KING SKULE.   All or naught!

HAKON.   Think of the Queen, your daughter!

KING SKULE. I have a son, I have a son! I think
of none but him!

HAKON.   I too have a son;—if I fall the kingdom
will be his!

KING SKULE.   Slay the King-child, wherever you
find it! Slay it on the throne; slay it at the altar;
slay it in the Queen's arms!

HAKON.   There did you utter your own doom!

KING SKULE (*slashing about him*).   Slay, slay
without mercy! King Skule has a son! Slay, slay!

(*The fight gradually passes away to the left.*)

GREGORIUS JONSSON.   The Vargbælgs are hewing
their way through!

DAGFINN.   Ay, but only to flee.

GREGORIUS JONSSON. Yes, by Heaven,—the other
gate stands open; they are fleeing already!

DAGFINN.   Up towards Martestokke. (*Calls out.*)
After them, after them, Earl Knut! Take vengeance,
for the slaughter at Låka!

HAKON.   You heard it: he proclaimed my child
an outlaw—my innocent child, Norway's chosen king
after me!

THE KING'S MEN.   Ay, ay, we heard it!

HAKON.   And what is the punishment for such a
crime?

---

[1] *Et nyt kongs-emne.*

THE MEN. Death!

HAKON. Then must he die! (*Raises his hand to make oath.*) Here I swear it: Skule Bårdsson shall die, wherever he be met on unconsecrated ground!

DAGFINN. 'Tis every true man's duty to slay him.

A BIRCHLEG (*from the left*). Duke Skule has taken to flight!

THE TOWNSFOLK. The Birchlegs have conquered!

HAKON. What way?

THE BIRCHLEG. Past Martestokke, up towards Eidsvold; most of them had horses waiting up in the streets, else had not one escaped with his life.

HAKON. Thanks be to God that helped us this time too! Now may the Queen safely come ashore from the fleet.

GREGORIUS JONSSON (*points off to the right*). She has already landed, my lord; there she comes!

HAKON (*to those nearest him*). The heaviest task is yet before me; she is a loving daughter;—listen— no word to her of the danger that threatens her child. Swear to me, one and all, to keep ward over your King's son; but let her know nothing.

THE MEN (*softly*). We swear it.

MARGRETE (*enters, with ladies and attendants, from the right*). Hakon, my husband! Heaven has shielded you; you have conquered and are unhurt!

HAKON. Yes, I have conquered. Where is the child?

MARGRETE. On board the King's-ship, in the hands of trusty men.

HAKON. Go more of you thither. (*Some of the men go.*)

MARGRETE.   Hakon, where is—Duke Skule?

HAKON.   He has made for the Uplands.

MARGRETE.   He lives, then!—My husband, may I thank God that he lives?

HAKON (*in painful agitation*).   Hear me, Margrete: you have been a faithful wife to me, you have followed me through good and evil, you have been unspeakably rich in love ;—now must I cause you a heavy sorrow ; I am loath to do it ; but I am King, therefore must I——

MARGRETE (*in suspense*).   Has it to do with—the Duke ?

HAKON.   Yes.   No bitterer lot could befall me than to live my life far from you ; but if you think it must be so after what I now tell you—if you feel that you can no longer sit by my side, no longer look at me without turning pale—well, we must even part—live each alone—and I shall not blame you for it.

MARGRETE.   To part from you !   How can you think such a thought ?   Give me your hand——!

HAKON.   Touch it not !—It has even now been lifted in oath——

MARGRETE.   In oath ?

HAKON.   An oath that was as the inviolable seal upon a death-warrant.

MARGRETE (*with a shriek*).   My father !   Oh, my father !   (*Totters ; two women rush forward to support her.*)

HAKON.   Yes, Margrete—his King has doomed your father to death.

MARGRETE.   Then well I know he has committed a greater crime than when he took the kingly title.

HAKON. That has he ;—and now, if you feel that we must part, so let it be.

MARGRETE (*coming close to him, firmly*). We can never part! I am your wife, naught in the world but your wife!

HAKON. Are you strong enough ? Did you hear and understand all ? I have doomed your father.

MARGRETE. I heard and understood. You have doomed my father.

HAKON. And you ask not to know what was his crime ?

MARGRETE. 'Tis enough that *you* know it.

HAKON. But it was to death that I doomed him !

MARGRETE (*kneels before the* KING, *and kisses his hand*). My husband and noble lord, your doom is righteous !

THE CURTAIN FALLS.

Act Fifth.

A MAN-AT-ARMS.   How fiercely it glows!

A SECOND.   It stretches over half the sky, like a flaming sword.

BÅRD BRATTE.   Holy King Olaf, what bodes such a sign of dread ?

AN OLD VÅRBÆLG.   Assuredly it bodes a great chief's death.

PAUL FLIDA.   Hakon's death, my good Vårbælgs. He is lying out in the fiord with his fleet ; we may look for him in the town to-night.   This time, 'tis our turn to conquer!

BÅRD BRATTE.   Trust not to that ; there is little heart in the host now.

THE OLD VÅRBÆLG.   And reason enough, in sooth ; ever since the flight from Oslo has King Skule shut himself in, and will neither see nor speak with his men.

THE FIRST MAN-AT-ARMS.   There are those in the town who know not whether to believe him alive or dead.

PAUL FLIDA.   The King must out, however sick

he may be.   Speak to him, Bård Bratte—the safety of all is at stake.

BÅRD BRATTE.   It avails not ; I have spoken to him already.

PAUL FLIDA.   Then must I try what I can do. (*Goes to the door on the left, and knocks.*) My lord King, you must take the helm in your own hands ; things cannot go on in this fashion.

KING SKULE (*within*).   I am sick, Paul Flida.

PAUL FLIDA.   What else can you look for?   You have eaten nought these two days ; you must nourish and strengthen you——

KING SKULE.   I am sick.

PAUL FLIDA.   By the Almighty, 'tis no time for sickness.   King Hakon lies out in the fiord, and may be upon us here in Nidaros at any moment.

KING SKULE.   Strike him down for me! Slay him and the King-child!

PAUL FLIDA.   You must come with us, my lord!

KING SKULE.   No, no, no,—you are surest of fortune and victory when I am not there.

PETER (*enters from the right ; he is in armour*). The townsfolk are ill at ease ; they flock together in great masses before the palace.

BÅRD BRATTE.   Unless the King speak to them, they will desert him in the hour of need.

PETER.   Then must he speak to them. (*At the door on the left.*) Father! The Trönders, your trustiest subjects, will fall away from you if you do not give them courage.

KING SKULE.   What said the skald?

PETER.   The skald!

KING SKULE.   The skald who died for my sake at Oslo.   A man cannot give what he himself does not possess, he said.

PETER.   Then neither can you give away the kingdom; for it is mine after you!

KING SKULE.   Now I come!

PAUL FLIDA.   God be praised!

KING SKULE (*comes forward in the door-way; he is pale and haggard; his hair has grown very grey*). You shall not look at me!   I will not have you look at me when I am sick!   (*Goes up to* PETER.)   Take the kingdom from you, did you say?   Great God in heaven, what was I about to do!

PETER.   Oh, forgive me;—I know that what you do is ever the right.

KING SKULE.   No, no, not hitherto; but I will be strong and sound now—I will act!

LOUD SHOUTS (*without, on the right*).   King Skule! King Skule!

KING SKULE.   What is that?

BÅRD BRATTE (*at the window*).   The townsmen are flocking together; the whole courtyard is full of people;—you must speak to them.

KING SKULE.   Do I look like a king?   Can I speak now?

PETER.   You must, my noble father!

KING SKULE. Well, be it so.   (*Goes to the window and draws the curtain aside, but lets it go quickly and starts back in terror.*)   There stands the flaming sword over me again!

PAUL FLIDA.   It bodes that the sword of victory is drawn for you.

KING SKULE. Ah, were it but so! (*Goes to the window and speaks out.*) Trönders, what would you? Here stands your King.

A TOWNSMAN (*without*). Leave the town! The Birchlegs will burn and slay if they find you here.

KING SKULE. We must all hold together. I have been a gracious king to you; I have craved but small war-tax——

A MAN'S VOICE (*down in the crowd*). What call you all the blood, then, that flowed at Låka and Oslo?

A WOMAN. Give me my betrothed again!

A BOY. Give me my father and my brother!

ANOTHER WOMAN. Give me my three sons, King Skule!

A MAN. He is no king; he has not been homaged on St. Olaf's shrine!

MANY VOICES. No, no, he has not been homaged on St. Olaf's shrine! He is no king!

KING SKULE (*shrinks behind the curtain*). Not homaged——! No king!

PAUL FLIDA. 'Twas a dire mischance that the shrine was not brought forth when you were chosen.

BÅRD BRATTE. Should the townsfolk desert us, we cannot hold Nidaros when the Birchlegs come.

KING SKULE. And they *will* desert us so long as I am not homaged on the Saint's shrine.

PETER. Then let the shrine be brought forth, and take our homage now!

PAUL FLIDA (*shaking his head*). How should that be possible?

PETER. Is aught impossible, where he is concerned?

Sound the call for the folkmote, and bring forth the shrine!

SEVERAL OF THE MEN (*shrinking back*). Sacrilege!

PETER. No sacrilege!—Come, come! The monks are well disposed towards King Skule; they will grant us——

PAUL FLIDA. That will they not; they dare not, for the Archbishop.

PETER. Are you king's-men, and will not lend your aid when so great a cause is at stake! Good, there are others below of better will. My father and King, the monks shall give way; I will pray, I will beseech; sound the summons for the folkmote; you shall bear your kingship rightfully. (*Rushes out to the right.*)

KING SKULE (*beaming with joy*). Saw you him! Saw you my gallant son! How his eyes shone! Yes, we will all fight and conquer. How strong are the Birchlegs?

PAUL FLIDA. Not stronger than that we may master them, if but the townsfolk hold to us!

KING SKULE. They *shall* hold to us. We must all be at one now and put an end to this time of dread. See you not that 'tis Heaven's command that we should end it? Heaven is wroth with all Norway for the deeds that have so long been doing. A flaming sword glows night by night in the sky; women swoon and bear children in the churches; a frenzy creeps abroad among priests and monks, causing them to run through the streets and proclaim that the last day is come. Ay, by the Almighty, this shall be ended at one stroke!

PAUL FLIDA.   What are your commands?

KING SKULE.   All the bridges shall be broken down!

PAUL FLIDA.   Go, and let all the bridges be broken down.   (*One of the Men-at-arms goes out to the right.*)

KING SKULE.   Gather all our men upon the fore-shore; not one Birchleg shall set foot in Nidaros.

PAUL FLIDA.   Well spoken, King.

KING SKULE.   When the shrine is borne forth, a folkmote shall be summoned.   The host and the townsfolk shall be called together.

PAUL FLIDA (*to one of the men*).   Go forth and bid the hornblower wind his horn in all the streets.

(*The man goes.*)

KING SKULE (*addresses the people from the window*). Hold fast to me, all my sorrowing people.   There shall come peace and light over the land once more, as in Hakon's first glad days, when the fields yielded two harvests every summer.   Hold fast to me; believe in me and trust to me; 'tis that I need so unspeakably. I will watch over you and fight for you; I will bleed and fall for you, if need be; but fail me not, and doubt not——! (*Loud cries, as though of terror, are heard among the people.*)   What is that?

A WILD VOICE.   Atone!   Atone!

BÅRD BRATTE (*looks out*).   'Tis a priest possessed of the devil!

PAUL FLIDA.   He is tearing his cowl to shreds and scourging himself with a whip.

THE VOICE.   Atone, atone!   The last day is come.

MANY VOICES. Flee, flee! Woe upon Nidaros! A deed of sin!

KING SKULE. What has befallen?

BÅRD BRATTE. All flee, all shrink away as though a wild beast were in their midst.

KING SKULE. Yes, all flee. (*With a cry of joy.*) Ha! it matters not. We are saved! See, see—King Olaf's shrine stands in the middle of the court-yard.

PAUL FLIDA. King Olaf's shrine!

BÅRD BRATTE. Ay, by Heaven—there it stands!

KING SKULE. The monks are true to me; so good a deed have they never done before!

PAUL FLIDA. Hark! the call to the folkmote!

KING SKULE. Now shall I be lawfully homaged.

PETER (*enters from the right*). Take on you the kingly mantle; now stands the shrine out yonder.

KING SKULE. Then have you saved the kingdom for me and for yourself; and tenfold will we thank the pious monks for yielding.

PETER. The monks, father—you have nought to thank them for.

KING SKULE. 'Twas not they that helped you?

PETER. They laid the ban of the Church on whoever should dare to touch the holy thing.

KING SKULE. The Archbishop then! At last he gives way.

PETER. The Archbishop hurled forth direr curses than the monks.

KING SKULE. Ah, then I see that I still have trusty men. You here, who should have been the first to serve me, stood terrified and shrank back—but down

in the crowd have I friends who for my sake fear not
to take a sin upon their souls.

PETER.   You have not one trusty man who dared
to take the sin upon him.

KING SKULE.   Almighty God! has then a miracle
come to pass?   Who bore out the holy thing?

PETER.   I, my father!

KING SKULE (*shrieks*).   You!

THE MEN (*shrink back appalled*).   Church-robber!

(PAUL FLIDA, BÅRD BRATTE, *and one or two
others go out.*)

PETER.   The deed had to be done.   No man's
faith is assured ere you be lawfully homaged.   I
begged, I besought the monks; it availed not.   Then
I broke open the church door; none dared to follow
me.   I sprang up to the high altar, gripped the
handle, and pressed hard with my knees; 'twas as
though an unseen power gave me more than human
strength.   The shrine came loose, I dragged it after
me down the nave, while the ban moaned like a
storm high up under the vaultings.   I dragged it out
of the church; all fled and shrank from me.   When I
came to the middle of the courtyard the handle broke;
here it is!   (*Holds it aloft.*)

KING SKULE (*quietly, appalled*).   Church-robber!

PETER.   For your sake; for the sake of your
great king's-thought!   You will wipe out the sin; all
that is evil you will wipe away.   Light and peace
will follow you; a glorious day will dawn over the
land—what matter, then, if there were a storm-night
before it?

KING SKULE.   There was as 'twere a halo round

your head when your mother brought you to me;—
now I see in its stead the lightnings of the ban.

PETER. Father, father, think not of me; be not
afraid for my woe or weal. Is it not your will I have
fulfilled?—how can it be accounted to me for a
crime?

KING SKULE. I hungered for your faith in me,
and your faith has turned to sin.

PETER (*wildly*). For your sake, for your sake!
Therefore God dare not deny to blot it out!

KING SKULE. "Pure and blameless," I swore to
Ingeborg—and he scoffs at heaven!

PAUL FLIDA (*entering*). All is in uproar! The
impious deed has struck terror to your men; they
flee into the churches.

KING SKULE. They *shall* out; they *must* out!

BÅRD BRATTE (*entering*). The townsfolk have
risen against you; they are slaying the Vårbælgs
wherever they find them, on the streets or in the
houses!

A MAN-AT-ARMS (*entering*). The Birchlegs are
sailing up the river!

KING SKULE. Summon all my men together!
None must fail me here!

PAUL FLIDA. They will not come; they are
benumbed with dread.

KING SKULE (*despairingly*). But I cannot fall
now! My son must not die with a deadly sin upon
his soul!

PETER. Think not of me; 'tis you alone that are
to be thought of. Let us make for Indherred; there
all men are true to you!

King Skule.   Ay, to flight!   Follow me, whoso would save his life!

Bård Bratte.   What way?

King Skule.   Over the bridge!

Paul Flida.   All the bridges are broken down, my lord.

King Skule.   Broken down——!   All the bridges broken down, say you?

Paul Flida.   Had you broken them down at Oslo, you might have let them stand at Nidaros.

King Skule.   We must over the river none the less;—we have our lives and our souls to save!   To flight!   To flight!

(*He and* Peter *rush out to the left.*)

Bård Bratte.   Ay, better so than to fall at the hands of the townsfolk and the Birchlegs.

Paul Flida.   In God's name, then, to flight!

(*All follow* Skule).

(*The room stands empty for a short time; a distant and confused noise is heard from the streets; then a troop of armed Townsmen rushes in by the door on the right.*)

A Townsman.   Here!   He must be here!

Another.   Slay him!

Many.   Slay the church-robber too!

A Single One.   Go carefully!   They may yet bite!

The First Townsman.   No need; the Birchlegs are already coming up the street.

A Townsman (*entering*).   Too late—King Skule has fled!

Many.   Whither?   Whither?

THE NEW-COMER.   Into one of the churches, methinks; they are full of Vargbælgs.

THE FIRST TOWNSMAN.   Then let us seek for him; great thanks and reward will King Hakon give to the man who slays Skule.

ANOTHER.   Here come the Birchlegs.

A THIRD.   King Hakon himself!

MANY OF THE CROWD (*shout*).   Hail to King Hakon Hakonsson!

HAKON (*enters from the right, followed by* GRE-GORIUS JONSSON, DAGFINN THE PEASANT, *and many others*).   Ay, now are you humble, you Trönders; you have stood against me long enough.

THE FIRST TOWNSMAN (*kneeling*).   Mercy, my lord!   Skule Bårdsson bore so hardly on us!

ANOTHER (*also kneeling*).   He compelled us, else had we never followed him.

THE FIRST.   He seized our goods and forced us to fight for his unrighteous cause.

THE SECOND.   Alas, noble lord, he has been a scourge to his friends no less than to his foes.

MANY VOICES.   Ay, ay,—Skule Bårdsson has been a scourge to the whole land.

DAGFINN.   That, at least, is true enough.

HAKON.   Good; with you townsfolk I will speak later; 'tis my purpose to punish sternly all transgres-sions; but first there are other matters to be thought of.   Knows any man where Skule Bårdsson is?

MANY.   In one of the churches, lord!

HAKON.   Do you know it certainly?

THE TOWNSMEN.   Ay, there are all the Varg-bælgs.

HAKON (*softly, to* DAGFINN).   He must be found ; set a watch on all the churches in the town.

DAGFINN.   And when he is found, he must be slain without delay.

HAKON (*softly*).   Slain !   Dagfinn, Dagfinn, how hard it seems !

DAGFINN.   My lord, you swore it solemnly at Oslo.

HAKON.   And all men in the land will call for his death.   (*Turns to* GREGORIUS JONSSON *and says, unheard by the others.*)   Go ; you were once his friend ; seek him out and prevail on him to fly the land.

GREGORIUS (*joyfully*).   You will suffer it, my lord !

HAKON.   For my gentle, well-beloved wife's sake.

GREGORIUS JONSSON.   But should he not flee ?   If he will not or cannot ?

HAKON.   Then, in God's name, I cannot spare him ; then must my kingly word be fulfilled.   Go !

GREGORIUS JONSSON.   I go, and shall do my utmost.   Heaven grant I may succeed.

(*Goes out by the right.*)

HAKON.   You, Dagfinn, go with trusty men down to the King's-ship ; you shall conduct the Queen and her child up to Elgesæter[1] convent.

DAGFINN.   My lord, think you she will be safe there ?

HAKON.   Nowhere safer.   The Vargbælgs have shut themselves up in the churches, and she has besought to be sent thither ; her mother is at Elgesæter.

DAGFINN.   Ay, ay, that I know.

---

[1] *Elgesæter* = Elk-châlet.

HAKON.   Greet the Queen most lovingly from me ; and greet Lady Ragnhild also.   You may tell them that so soon as the Vargbælgs shall have made submission and received pardon, all the bells in Nidaros shall be rung, for a sign that there has come peace in the land once more.—You townsfolk shall reckon with me to-morrow, and punishment shall be meted to each according to his misdeeds.

(Goes with his men.)

THE FIRST TOWNSMAN.   Woe upon us to-morrow!

THE SECOND.   We will have a long reckoning to pay.

THE FIRST.   We, who have stood against Hakon so long—who took part in acclaiming Skule when he took the kingly title.

THE SECOND.   Who gave Skule both ships and war-tribute—who bought all the goods he seized from Hakon's thanes.

THE FIRST.   Ay, woe upon us to-morrow !

A TOWNSMAN (*rushes in from the left*).   Where is Hakon ?   Where is the King ?

THE FIRST.   What would you with him ?

THE NEW-COMER.   Bring him great and weighty tidings.

MANY.   What tidings ?

THE NEW-COMER.   I tell them not to others than to the King himself.

MANY.   Ay, tell us, tell us !

THE NEW-COMER.   Skule Bårdsson is fleeing up towards Elgesæter.

THE FIRST.   It cannot be !   He is in one of the churches.

The New-comer. No, no; he and his son put over the river in a skiff.

The First. Ha, then we can save us from Hakon's wrath!

The Second. Ay, let us forthwith give him to know where Skule is.

The First. Nay, better than that; we will say nought, but ourselves go up to Elgesæter and slay Skule.

The Second. Ay, ay—that will we!

A Third. But did not many Vargbælgs go over the river with him?

The New-comer. No, there were but few men in the boat.

The First. We will arm us as best we can. Oh, now are we townsfolk safe enough! Let no man know what we are about; we are enough for the task! —And now, away to Elgesæter.

All (*softly*). Ay, away to Elgesæter!

(*They go out to the left, rapidly but cautiously.*)

———

(*A fir-wood on the hills above Nidaros. It is moon-light, but the night is misty, so that the background is seen indistinctly, and sometimes scarcely at all. Tree-stumps and great stones lie round about.* King Skule, Peter, Paul Flida, Bård Bratte, *and other* Vårbælgs *come through the wood from the left.*)

Peter. Come hither and rest you, my father.

KING SKULE.   Ay, let me rest, rest.   (*Sinks down beside a stone.*)

PETER.   How goes it with you?

KING SKULE.   I am hungry!   I am sick, sick!   I see dead men's shadows!

PETER (*springing up*).   Help here—bread for the King!

BÅRD BRATTE.   Here is every man king; for life is at stake.   Stand up, Skule Bårdsson, if you be king!   Lie not there to rule the land.

PETER.   If you scoff at my father, I will kill you!

BÅRD BRATTE.   I shall be killed whatever betides; for me King Hakon will have no grace; for I was his thane, and I deserted him for Skule's sake.   Think of somewhat that may save us.   No deed so desperate but I will risk it now.

A VÅRBÆLG.   Could we but get over to the convent at Holm?

PAUL FLIDA.   Better to Elgesæter.

BÅRD BRATTE (*with a sudden outburst*).   Best of all to go down to Hakon's ship and bear away the King-child.

PAUL FLIDA.   Are you distraught?

BÅRD BRATTE.   No, no; 'tis our one hope, and easy enough to do.   The Birchlegs are searching every house, and keeping watch on all the churches; they think none of us can have taken flight, since all the bridges are broken.   There can be but few men on board the ships; when once we have his heir in our power, Hakon must grant us peace, else will his child die with us.   Who will go with me to save our lives?

Paul Flida. Not I, if they are to be saved in such wise.

Several. Not I! Not I!

Peter. Ha, but if it were to save my father——!

Bård Bratte. If you will go with me, come. First I go down to Hladehammer; there lies the troop we met at the bottom of the hill; they are the wildest dare-devils of all the Vargbælgs; they had swam the river, knowing that they would find no grace in the churches. They are the lads for a raid on the King's-ship! Which of you will follow me?

Some. I! I!

Peter. Mayhap I too; but first must I see my father into safe shelter.

Bård Bratte. Ere daybreak will we make speed up the river. Come, here goes a short way downwards towards Hlade. (*He and some others go out to the right.*)

Peter (*to* Paul Flida). Speak not to my father of aught of this; he is soul-sick to-night, we must act for him. There *is* safety in Bård Bratte's work; ere daybreak shall the King-child be in our hands.

Paul Flida. To be slain, most like. See you not that it is a sin——

Peter. Nay, 'tis no sin; for my father doomed the child in Oslo. Sooner or later it must die, for it blocks my father's path;—my father has a great king's-thought to carry through; it matters not who or how many fall for its sake.

Paul Flida. Baleful for you was the day you came to know that you were King Skule's son.

(*Listening.*)   Hist!—cast you flat to the ground; people are coming.

> (*All throw themselves down behind stumps; a troop of people, some riding, some on foot, can be seen indistinctly through the mist and between the trees; they come from the left, and pass on to the right.*)

PETER.   'Tis the Queen!

PAUL FLIDA.   Ay; she is talking with Dagfinn the Peasant.   Hush!

PETER.   They are making for Elgesæter.   The King-child is with them!

PAUL FLIDA.   And the Queen's ladies.

PETER.   But only four men!   Up, up, King Skule —now is your kingdom saved!

KING SKULE.   My kingdom?   'Tis dark, my kingdom—like the angel's that rose against God.

> (*A party of* MONKS *comes from the right.*)

A MONK.   Who speaks there?   Is it King Skule's men.

PAUL FLIDA.   King Skule himself.

THE MONK (*to* SKULE).   God be praised that we met you, dear lord!   Some townsmen gave us to know that you had taken the upward path, and we are no less unsafe than you in Nidaros.

PETER.   You have deserved death, you who denied to give forth Saint Olaf's shrine.

THE MONK.   The Archbishop forbade it; but none the less we would fain serve King Skule; we have ever held to him.   See, we have brought with us robes for you and your men; put them on, and then can you easily make your way into one convent or another, and can seek to gain grace of Hakon.

King Skule. Ay, let me put on the robe; my son and I must stand on consecrated ground. I will to Elgesæter.

Peter (*softly, to* Paul Flida). See that my father comes safely thither.

Paul Flida. Bethink you that there are Birchlegs at Elgesæter.

Peter. But four men ; you may easily deal with them, and once inside the convent walls they will not dare to touch you. I will seek Bård Bratte.

Paul Flida. Nay, do not so !

Peter. 'Tis not on the King's-ship, but at Elgesæter, that the outlaws shall save the kingdom for my father.

(*Goes quickly out to the right.*)

A Vårbælg (*whispering to another*). Go you to Elgesæter with Skule ?

The Other. Hist; no ; there are Birchlegs there !

The First. Neither do I go; but say naught to the rest.

The Monk. And now away, two and two,—one spearman and one monk.

Another Monk (*sitting on a stump behind the rest*). I will take King Skule.

King Skule. Know you the way ?

The Monk. The broad way.

The First Monk. Haste you ; let us spread over different paths and meet outside the convent gate.

(*They go out among the trees, to the right ; the*

fog lifts and the comet shows itself, red and glowing, through the hazy air.)

KING SKULE. Peter, my son——! (*Starts backwards.*) Ha, there is the flaming sword in heaven!

THE MONK (*sitting behind him on the stump*). And here am I!

KING SKULE. Who are you?

THE MONK. An old acquaintance.

KING SKULE. Paler man have I never seen.

THE MONK. But you know me not?

KING SKULE. 'Tis you who are to lead me to Elgesæter.

THE MONK. 'Tis I that will lead you to the throne.

KING SKULE. Can you do that?

THE MONK. I can, if it be your will.

KING SKULE. And by what means?

THE MONK. By the means I have used before; —I will take you up into a high mountain and show you all the glory of the world.

KING SKULE. All the glory of the world have I seen ere now, in dreams of temptation.

THE MONK. 'Twas I that gave you those dreams.

KING SKULE. Who are you?

THE MONK. An ambassador from the oldest Pretender in the world.

KING SKULE. From the oldest Pretender in the world?

THE MONK. From the first Earl, who rose against the greatest kingdom, and himself founded a kingdom that shall endure beyond doomsday!

King Skule (*shrieks*).   Bishop Nicholas!
The Monk (*rising*).
Do you know me now?   We were friends of yore,
and 'tis you that have brought me back;
once the self-same galley our fortunes bore,
and we sailed on the self-same tack.
At our parting I quailed; how the tempest did roll!
and a hawk had his talons deep sunk in my soul;
I besought them to chant and to ply the bell,
and I bought me masses and prayers as well,—
they read fourteen though I'd paid but for seven;
yet they brought me no nearer the gates of heaven.
King Skule.   And   you   come   from   down
yonder——?
The Monk.   Yes, from the kingdom down yonder
    I'm faring;
the kingdom men always so much miscall.
I vow 'tis in nowise so bad after all,
and the heat, to my thinking, is never past bearing.
King Skule.   And I hear you have learnt skald-
craft, old Bagler-chieftain!
The Monk.   Not only skald-craft, but stores of
    Latinity!
Once my Latin was not over strong, you know;
now few can beat it for ease and flow.
To take any station in yonder vicinity,
ay, even to pass at the gate, for credential
a knowledge of Latin is well-nigh essential.
You can't but make progress with so many able
and learned companions each day at the table,—
full fifty ex-popes by my side carouse, and
five hundred cardinals, skalds seven thousand.

KING SKULE.   Greet your Master and give him my thanks for his friendship.   Tell him he is the only king who sends help to Skule the First of Norway.

THE MONK.   Hear now, King Skule, what brings
     me to you—
my Master's henchmen down there are legion,
and each up here is allotted a region;
they gave Norway to me, as the place I best knew.
Hakon Hakonsson serves not my Master's will;
we hate him, for he is our foeman still—
so he must fall, leaving you at the helm,
the sole possessor of crown and realm.

KING SKULE.   Ay, give me the crown!   When once I have that, I will rule so as to buy myself free again.

THE MONK.   Ay, that we can always talk of later——
we must seize the time if we'd win the fight.
King Hakon's child sleeps at Elgesæter;
could you once wrap him in the web of night,
then like storm-swept motes will your foes fly routed,
then your victory's sure and your kingship undoubted!

KING SKULE.   Think you surely that the victory were mine?

THE MONK.   All men in Norway are sighing for
     rest;
the king with an heir[1] is the king they love best—
a son to succeed to the throne without wrangling;
for the people are tired of this hundred-years'
     jangling.
Rouse you, King Skule! one great endeavour!

---

[1] *Et kongs-emne.*

the foe must perish to-night or never !
See to the northward how light it has grown,
see how the fog lifts o'er fiord and o'er valley—
there gather noiselessly galley on galley—
hark ! men are marching with rumble and drone !
One word of promise, and all is your own—
hundreds of glittering sails on the water,
thousands of warriors hurtling to slaughter.

KING SKULE.   What word would you have ?

THE MONK.   For raising you highest, my one
condition
is just that you follow your heart's ambition ;
all Norway is yours, to the kingship I'll speed you,
if only you vow that your son shall succeed you !

KING SKULE (*raising his hand as if for an oath*).
My son shall—— (*Stops suddenly, and breaks forth in
terror.*)   The church-robber !   All the might to him !
Ha ! now I understand ;—you seek for his soul's
perdition !   Get thee behind me, get thee behind me !
(*Stretches out his arms to heaven.*)   Oh have mercy
on me, thou to whom I now call for help in my
sorest need !

(*He falls prone to the earth.*)

THE MONK.   Accursëd !   He's slipped through
my fingers at last—
and I thought of a surety I held him so fast !
But the Light, it seems, had a trick in store
that I knew not of—and the game is o'er.
Well, well ; what matters a little delay ?
Perpetuum mobile's well under way ;
my might is assured through the years and the ages,
the haters of light shall be still in my wages ;

in Norway my empire for ever is founded,
though it be to my subjects a riddle unsounded.
　　(*Coming forward.*)
While to their life-work Norsemen set out
will-lessly wavering, daunted with doubt,
while hearts are shrunken, minds helplessly shivering,
weak **as a** willow-wand wind-swept and quivering,—
while **about** one thing alone they're united,
namely, that greatness be stoned and despited,—
when they seek honour in fleeing and falling
under the banner of baseness unfurled,—
then Bishop Nicholas 'tends to his calling,
the Bagler-Bishop's at work in the world !
　　(*He disappears in the fog among the trees.*)

　KING SKULE (*after a short pause, half rises and looks around*).   Where is he, my black comrade ? (*Springs up.*) My guide, my guide, where are you ? Gone !—No matter ; now I myself know the way, both to Elgesæter and further.
　　(*Goes out to the right.*)

———

(*The Courtyard of Elgesæter Convent. To the left lies the chapel, with an entrance from the courtyard ; the windows are lighted up. Along the opposite side of the space stretch some lower buildings ; in the back, the convent wall with a strong gate, which is locked. It is a clear moonlight night. Three* BIRCHLEG CHIEFS *stand by the gate ;* MARGRETE, LADY RAGNHILD, **and** DAGFINN THE PEASANT *come out from the chapel.*)

Lady Ragnhild (*half to herself*). King Skule had to flee into the church, you say! He, he, a fugitive! begging at the altar for peace—begging for his life mayhap—oh no, no, that cannot be; but God will punish you who dared to let it come to this!

Margrete. My dear, dear mother, curb yourself; you know not what you say; 'tis your grief that speaks.

Lady Ragnhild. Hear me, ye Birchlegs! 'Tis Hakon Hakonsson that should lie before the altar, and beseech King Skule for life and peace.

A Birchleg. It ill beseems faithful men to listen to such words.

Margrete. Uncover before a wife's sorrow!

Lady Ragnhild. King Skule doomed! Woe upon you, woe upon you all, when he recovers his power!

Dagfinn. That will never be, Lady Ragnhild.

Margrete. Hush, hush!

Lady Ragnhild. Think you Hakon Hakonsson dare let his doom be fulfilled if the King should fall into his hands?

Dagfinn. King Hakon himself best knows whether a king's oath can be broken.

Lady Ragnhild (*to* Margrete). And this man of blood have you followed in faith and love! Are you your father's child? May the wrath of heaven——! Go from me, go from me!

Margrete. Blessed be your lips, although they curse me now.

Lady Ragnhild. I must down to Nidaros and into the church to find King Skule. He sent me from him when he sat victorious on the throne ; then, truly, he had no need of me—now will he not **be** wroth if I come to him. Open the gate for me ; let me go to Nidaros !

MARGRETE.   My mother, for God's pity's sake——!

(*A loud knocking at the convent gate.*)

DAGFINN.   Who knocks ?

KING SKULE (*without*).   A king.

DAGFINN.   Skule Bårdsson.

LADY RAGNHILD.   King Skule !

MARGRETE.   My father !

KING SKULE.   Open, open !

DAGFINN.   We open not here to outlaws.

KING SKULE.   'Tis a king who knocks, I tell you ; a king who has no roof over his head ; a king whose **life is** forfeit if he reach not consecrated ground.

MARGRETE.   Dagfinn, Dagfinn, 'tis my father !

DAGFINN (*goes to the gate and opens a small shutter*). Come you with many men to the convent ?

KING **SKULE**.   With all the men that remained true to me in my need.

DAGFINN.   And how many be they ?

KING SKULE.   Fewer than one.

MARGRETE.   He is alone, Dagfinn.

LADY RAGNHILD.   Heaven's wrath will fall upon you if you deny him consecrated ground !

DAGFINN.   In God's name, then !

(*He opens the gate ; the Birchlegs respectfully uncover their heads.* KING SKULE *enters the courtyard.*)

MARGRETE (*throwing herself on his neck*).   My father ! My dear, unhappy father !

LADY RAGNHILD (*interposing wildly between him and the Birchlegs*). Ye who feign reverence for him, ye will betray him, like Judas. Dare not to come near him ! Ye shall not lay a finger on him while I live !

DAGFINN. He is safe, for he is on consecrated ground.

MARGRETE. And not one of all your men had the heart to follow you this night !

KING SKULE. Both monks and spearmen brought me on the way ; but they slipped from me one by one, for they knew there were Birchlegs at Elgesæter. Paul Flida was the last to leave me ; he came with me to the convent gate ; there he gave me his last hand-grip, in memory of the time when there were Vargbælgs in Norway.

DAGFINN (*to the Birchlegs*). Get you in, chieftains, and set you as guards about the King-child ; I must to Nidaros to acquaint the King that Skule Bårdsson is at Elgesæter ; in so weighty a matter 'tis for him to act.

MARGRETE. Oh, Dagfinn, Dagfinn, have you the heart for that?

DAGFINN. Else should I ill serve King and land. (*To the men.*) Lock the gates after me, watch over the child, and open to none until the King be come. (*Softly, to* SKULE.) Farewell, Skule Bårdsson—and God grant you a blessed end.

> (*Goes out by the gate ; the Birchlegs close it after him, and go into the chapel.*)

LADY RAGNHILD. Ay, let Hakon come ; I will not loose you ; I will hold you straitly and tenderly in my arms, as I have never held you before.

MARGRETE. Oh, how pale you are—and aged; you are cold.

KING SKULE. I am not cold—but I am weary, weary.

MARGRETE. Come in then, and rest you——

KING SKULE. Yes, yes; 'twill soon be time to rest.

SIGRID (*from the chapel*). You come at last, my brother!

KING SKULE. Sigrid! you here?

SIGRID. I promised that we should meet when you were fain of me in your sorest need.

KING SKULE. Where is your child, Margrete?

MARGRETE. He sleeps, in the sacristy.

KING SKULE. Then is our whole house gathered at Elgesæter to-night.

SIGRID. Ay, gathered after straying long and far.

KING SKULE. Hakon Hakonsson alone is wanting.

MARGRETE AND LADY RAGNHILD (*cling about him, exclaiming sorrowfully*). My father!—My husband!

KING SKULE (*looking at them, much moved*). Have you loved me so deeply, you two? I sought after happiness abroad, and noted not that I had a home wherein I might have found it. I pursued after love through sin and guilt, little dreaming that 'twas mine already, in right of God's law and man's.—And you, Ragnhild, my wife, you, against whom I have sinned so deeply, you cling to me warmly and softly in the hour of my sorest need; you can tremble and be afraid for the life of the man who has never cast a ray of sunshine upon your path.

LADY RAGNHILD. Have *you* sinned! Oh, Skule,

speak not so; think you I should ever dare accuse you! From the first I was too mean a mate for you, my noble husband; there can rest no guilt on any deed of yours.

King Skule. Have you believed in me so surely, Ragnhild?

Lady Ragnhild. From the first day I saw you.

King Skule (*with animation*). When Hakon comes, I will beg grace of him! You gentle, loving women,—oh, but it is fair to live!

Sigrid (*with an expression of terror*). Skule, my brother! Woe to you if you stray from the path this night!

(*A loud noise without; immediately afterwards, a knocking at the gate.*)

Margrete. Listen, listen! Who is rushing hitherward?

Lady Ragnhild. Who knocks at the gate?

Voices (*without*). Townsfolk from Nidaros! Open! We know that Skule Bårdsson is within!

King Skule. Ay, he is within; what would you with him?

Noisy Voices (*without*). Come out, come out! Death to the evil man!

Margrete. You townsfolk dare to threaten that?

A Single Voice. King Hakon doomed him at Oslo.

Another. 'Tis every man's duty to slay him.

Margrete. I am the Queen; I command you to depart!

A Voice. 'Tis Skule Bårdsson's daughter, and not the Queen, that speaks thus.

ANOTHER. You have no power over life and death; the King has doomed him!

LADY RAGNHILD. Into the church, Skule! For the merciful God's sake, let not the bloodthirsty caitiffs approach you!

KING SKULE. Ay, into the church; I would not fall at the hands of such as these. My wife, my daughter; meseems I have found peace and light; oh, I cannot lose them again so soon! (*Moves towards the chapel.*)

PETER (*without, on the right*). My father, my king! Now will you soon have the victory!

KING SKULE (*with a shriek*). He! He! (*Sinks upon the church steps.*)

LADY RAGNHILD. Who is that?

A TOWNSMAN (*without*). See, see! the church-robber climbs over the convent-roof!

OTHERS. Stone him! Stone him!

PETER (*appears on a roof to the right, and jumps down into the yard*). Well met again, my father!

KING SKULE (*looks at him aghast*). You—I had forgotten you——! Whence come you?

PETER (*wildly*). Where is the King-child?

MARGRETE. The King-child!

KING SKULE (*starts up*). Whence come you, I ask?

PETER. From Hladehammer; I have given Bård Bratte and the Vargbælgs to know that the King-child lies at Elgesæter to-night.

MARGRETE. Oh God!

KING SKULE. You have done that! And now——?

PETER. He is gathering together his men, and

they are hasting up to the convent.—Where is the King-child, woman?

Margrete (*who has placed herself before the church-door*).   He sleeps in the sacristy!

Peter.   'Twere the same if he slept on the altar! I have dragged out St. Olaf's shrine—I fear not to drag out the King-child as well.

Lady Ragnhild (*calls to* Skule).   He it is you have loved so deeply!

Margrete.   Father, father!   How could you forget us all for his sake?

King Skule.   He was pure as a lamb of God when the penitent woman gave him to me;—'tis his faith in me has made him what he now is.

Peter (*without heeding him*).   The child must out! Slay it, slay it in the Queen's arms,—that was King Skule's word in Oslo!

Margrete.   Oh shame, oh shame!

Peter.   A saint might do it unsinning, at my father's command!   My father is King; for the great king's-thought is his!

Townsmen (*knocking at the gate*).   Open!   Come out, you and the church-robber, else will we burn the convent down!

King Skule (*as if seized by a strong resolution*). The great king's-thought!   'Tis that has poisoned your young loving soul!   Pure and blameless I was to give you back; 'tis faith in me that drives you thus wildly from crime to crime, from deadly sin to deadly sin!   Oh, but I can save you yet: I can save us all!   (*Calls towards the background.*)   Wait, wait, ye townsmen without there: I come!

MARGRETE (*seizing his hand in terror*). My father! what would you do?

LADY RAGNHILD (*clinging to him with a shriek*). Skule!

SIGRID (*tears them away from him, and calls with wild, radiant joy*). Loose him, loose him, women;— now his thought puts forth wings!

KING SKULE (*firmly and forcibly, to* PETER). **You saw in me the** heaven-chosen one,—him who should **do the** great king's-work in **the land.** Look **at me** better, bewildered boy! The rags of kingship I have decked myself withal, they were borrowed and stolen —now I put them off me, one by one.

PETER (*in dread*). My great, **noble** father, speak **not thus!**

KING SKULE. **The** king's-thought is Hakon's, not mine ; to him alone has the Lord granted the power **that can make** substance of it. You have believed in a lie ; turn from me, and save your soul.

PETER (*in a broken voice*). The king's-thought is Hakon's!

KING SKULE. I yearned to be the greatest in the land. **My God!** my **God!** behold, I abase myself before thee, and stand as the least of **all men.**

PETER. **Take** me from the earth, O Lord! Punish me for all my sin ; but **take** me from the earth ; for here am I homeless now! (*Sinks upon the church-steps.*)

KING SKULE. I had **a** friend who bled for me at Oslo. He **said :** A man **can** die for another's life-work ; but if he is to go on living, he must live for his own. I have no life-work **to** live for, neither can I live for Hakon's,—but I can die for it.

MARGRETE. Nay, nay, that shall you never do!

KING SKULE (*takes her hand, and looks at her tenderly*). Do you love your husband, Margrete?

MARGRETE. Better than the whole world.

KING SKULE. You could endure that he should doom me; but could you also endure that he should cause the doom to be fulfilled?

MARGRETE. Lord of heaven, give me strength!

KING SKULE. Could you, Margrete?

MARGRETE (*softly and shuddering*). No, no—we should have to part,—I could never see him more!

KING SKULE. You would darken the fairest light of his life and yours;—be at peace, Margrete,—it shall not be needful.

LADY RAGNHILD. Flee from the land, Skule; I will follow you whithersoever you will.

KING SKULE (*shaking his head*). With a mocking shade between us?—To-night have I found you for the first time; there must fall no shade between me and you, my silent, faithful wife;—therefore must we not seek to unite our lives on this earth.

SIGRID. My kingly brother! I see you need me not;—I see you know what path to take.

KING SKULE. There are men born to live, and men born to die. My desire was ever thitherward where God's finger pointed not the way for me; therefore I never saw my path clear, till now. My peaceful home-life have I wrecked — that I can never restore. My sins against Hakon I can atone by freeing him from a kingly duty which must have parted him from his dearest possession. The townsfolk stand without; I will not wait for King

Hakon! The Vargbælgs **are** near; **so** long **as** I live they will not swerve from their purpose; if they find me here, I cannot save your child, Margrete. —See, look upwards! See how it wanes and pales, the flaming sword that has hung over my head! Yes, yes,—God has spoken and I have understood him, and his wrath is appeased. Not in the sanctuary of Elgesæter will I cast me down and beg for grace of an earthly king;—I must into the mighty church **roofed** with the vault of stars, **and** 'tis the King of Kings I must implore for grace and salvation over all my life-work.

SIGRID. Withstand him not! Withstand not the call of God! The day dawns; **it dawns** in Norway **and it** dawns in his restless soul! Have not we trembling women stood long enough in our closets, terror-stricken and hidden in the darkest corners, listening to all the horror that was doing without, listening to the bloody pageant that stalked over the land from end to end? Have we not lain pale and stone-like in the churches, not daring to look forth, even as Christ's disciples lay in Jerusalem on the Great Good Friday when the Lord was led by to Golgotha! Use thy wings, and woe to them who would **bind** thee now!

LADY RAGNHILD. Fare forth in peace, my husband; fare thither, where no mocking shade shall stand between us, when we meet.

(*Hastens into the chapel.*)

MARGRETE. My father, farewell, farewell, — a thousand times farewell!

(*Follows* LADY RAGNHILD.)

SIGRID (*opens the church door and calls in*).   Forth, forth, all ye women!   Assemble yourselves in prayer; send up a message in song to the Lord, proclaiming to him that now Skule Bårdsson comes penitent home from his rebellious race on earth.

KING SKULE.   Sigrid, my faithful sister, greet King Hakon from me; tell him that even in my last hour I know not whether he be king-born ; but this I know of a surety : he it is whom God has chosen.

SIGRID.   I will bring him your greeting.

KING SKULE.   And yet another greeting must you bear.   There sits a penitent woman in the north, in Halogaland ; tell her that her son has gone before; he followed with me when there was great danger for his soul.

SIGRID.   That will I.

KING SKULE.   Tell her, it was not with the heart he sinned ; pure and blameless shall she surely meet him again.

SIGRID.   That will I. (*Points towards the background.*)   Hark ! they are breaking the lock !

KING SKULE (*points towards the chapel*).   Hark ! they are singing loud to God of salvation and peace !

SIGRID.   Hark again !   All the bells in Nidaros are ringing——!

KING SKULE (*sorrowfully*).   They are ringing a king to his grave.

SIGRID.   Nay, nay, they ring for your true crowning !   Farewell, my brother, let the purple robe of His blood flow wide over your shoulders ; under it may all sin be hidden !   Go forth, go into the great church and take the crown of life. (*Hastens into the chapel.*)

(*Chanting and bell-ringing continue during what follows.*)

VOICES (*outside the gate*). The lock has burst! Force us not to break the peace of the church!

KING SKULE. I come.

THE TOWNSMEN. And the church-robber must come too!

KING SKULE. Ay, the church-robber shall also come. (*Goes over to* PETER.) My son, are you ready?

PETER. Ay, father, I am ready.

KING SKULE (*looks upwards*). O God, I am a poor man, I have but my life to give; but take that, and keep watch over Hakon's great king's-thought. See now, reach me your hand.

PETER. Here is my hand, father.

KING SKULE. And fear not for that which is now to come.

PETER. Nay, father, I fear not, when I go with you.

KING SKULE. A safer way have we two never gone together. (*He opens the gate; the* TOWNSMEN *stand without with upraised weapons.*) Here are we; we come willingly;—but strike him not in the face.

(*They go out, hand in hand; the gate glides to.*)

A VOICE. Aim not, spare not;—strike them where ye can!

KING SKULE'S VOICE. 'Tis base to deal thus with chieftains!

(*A short noise of weapons; then a heavy fall is heard; all is still for a moment.*)

A VOICE. They are dead, both!

(*The* KING'S *horn sounds.*)

ANOTHER VOICE. There comes King Hakon with all his guard!

THE CROWD. Hail Hakon Hakonsson; now have you no longer any foemen.

GREGORIUS JONSSON (*stops a little before the corpses*). So I have come too late!

(*Enters the convent yard.*)

DAGFINN. It had been ill for Norway had you come sooner. (*Calls out.*) In here, King Hakon!

HAKON (*stopping*). The body lies in my way!

DAGFINN. If Hakon Hakonsson would go forward, he must pass over Skule Bårdsson's body!

HAKON. In God's name then!

(*Steps over the corpse and comes in.*)

DAGFINN. At last you can set about your king's-work with free hands. In there are those you love; in Nidaros they are ringing in peace in the land ; and yonder he lies who was your direst foe.

HAKON. All men misjudged him; there was a mystery over him.

DAGFINN. A mystery?

HAKON (*seizes him by the arm, and says softly*). Skule Bårdsson was God's step-child on earth ; that was the mystery.

> (*The song of the women is heard more loudly from the chapel; all bells are still ringing in Nidaros.*)

THE CURTAIN FALLS.

APPENDIX.

ÖRNULFS DRAPA.

(Page 196.)

Sind, som svær-mod stinger,
savner Brages glæde ;
sorgfuld skald så såre
kvides ved at kvæde.

Skaldeguden skænked
evne mig at sjunge ;—
klinge lad min klage
for mit tab, det tunge!

Harmfuld norne hærged
hårdt mig verdens veje,
listed lykken fra mig,
ödte Örnulfs eje.

Sönner syv til Örnulf
blev af guder givet ;—
nu går gubben ensom,
sönnelös i livet.

Sönner syv, så fagre,
fostret mellem sværde,
værned vikings hvide
hår, som gævest **gærde.**

Nu er gærdet jævnet,
mine sonner döde ;
glædelös står gubben,
og hans hus står **öde.**

Torolf,—du, min yngste !
Boldest blandt de bolde !
Lidet gad jeg klage,
fik jeg dig beholde.

Vén du var, som våren,
mod din fader kærlig,
arted dig **at** ældes
til en helt sa herlig.

Ulivs-sår, usaligt,
værste ve mon volde,
har min gamle bringe
klemt, som mellem skjolde.

Nidsyg norne nödig
nægted mig sit eje,—

dryssed smertens rigdom
over Örnulfs veje.

Vegt er visst mit værge.
Fik jeg guders evne,
en da blev min idræt:
nornens færd at hævne.

En da blev min gerning:
nornens fald at friste,—
hun, som har mig rövet
alt—og nu det sidste!

Har hun alt mig rövet?
Nej, det har hun ikke;
tidligt fik jo Örnulf
Suttungs mjöd at drikke.

Minne sönner tog hun;
men hun gav min tunge
evnen til i kvæder
ud min sorg at sjunge.

På min mund hun lagde
sangens fagre gave;—
lydt da lad den klinge,
selv ved sönners grave!

Hil jer, sönner gæve!
Hil jer, der I rider!
Gudegaven læger
verdens ve og kvider!

MARGRETES VUGGEVISE.

(Page 289.)

Nu löftes laft og lofte
til stjernehvælven blå ;
nu flyver lille Håkon
med drömmevinger på.

Der er en stige stillet
fra jord til himlen op ;
nu stiger lille Håkon
med englene tiltop.

Guds engle små, de våger
for vuggebarnets fred ;
Gud sign' dig, lille Håkon,
din moder våger med.

JATGEIRS KVAD.

(Page 304.)

Hertug Skule blæste til Örething
under messen i Nidaros by;
hertug Skule tog kongsnavn, mens klokkerne
    ringed,
og sværdslag på skjold gav gny.

Kong Skule skred over Dovreskard
med tusende svende på ski ;
Gudbrandsdölerne græd for grid
og köbte for sölv sig fri.

Kong Skule sörover Mjösen foer,—
Oplændingen svor og snærred;
kong Skule foer gennem Raumarike
til Låka i Nannestad herred.

Det var den hellige faste-uge ;
Birkebejnerhæren kom ;
Knut jarl var hövding,—sværdene talte
og fældte i kongstrætten dom.

Det siges forvisst : siden Sverres dage
stod aldrig så hed en strid ;
blommet, som blodige kæmpers lagen,
blev vidden, der för var hvid.

De satte på sprang, de Birkebejner,—
slang fra sig både biler og skjolde ;
mange hundrede satte dog ikke på sprang,
for de lå og var isende kolde.—

Ingen ved hvor kong Håkon færdes ;—
kong Skule har byer og borge.
Hil dig, herre !   Længe sidde du stor,
som konge for hele Norge !

Printed by WALTER SCOTT, Felling, Newcastle-on-Tyne.

www.ingramcontent.com/pod-product-compliance
Lightning Source LLC
Chambersburg PA
CBHW032137110726
47902CB00003B/605